7/19

DATE DUE FOR RETURN

2 4 SEP 2019

SURGEON PRINCE, CINDERELLA BRIDE

ANN McINTOSH

ROYAL DOC'S SECRET HEIR

AMY RUTTAN

MILLS & BOON

First Published in Great Britain 2019
by Mills & Boon, an imprint of HarperCollins*Publishers*
1 London Bridge Street, London, SE1 9GF

Surgeon Prince, Cinderella Bride © 2019 by Ann McIntosh

Royal Doc's Secret Heir © 2019 by Amy Ruttan

ISBN: 978-0-263-26986-4

MIX
Paper from
responsible sources
FSC™ C007454

This book is produced from independently certified FSC™ paper
to ensure responsible forest management.
For more information visit www.harpercollins.co.uk/green.

Printed and bound in Spain
by CPI, Barcelona

SURGEON PRINCE, CINDERELLA BRIDE

ANN McINTOSH

MILLS & BOON

To my friend, critique partner, and inspiration, Amy Ruttan.
Through thick and thin!

PROLOGUE

1988

IT WAS AS though Yasmine floated just ever so slightly outside her skin, so the sounds and smells of the maternity ward were muffled by the disconnect between flesh and spirit. Even the sensations of her body, the gritty pain each time she blinked her closed lids, the movement of the baby, the interminable heat, were distant things.

The observation ward wasn't full. Just her and one other lady, who was also alone. Neither of them spoke, although the curtain between their beds had been left open.

She let herself drift, leaving the agonizing present to go back in time to the night she'd lain in her husband's arms, and joy had been their only companion.

The night she'd told him she was finally, miraculously, pregnant.

Brian had been ecstatic, had shifted down in the bed so his face rested next to her belly.

"My child," he'd said. "My son or daughter. Prince or princess."

Her heart had leapt at his words.

For thirty years he'd held fast to the rule: no one must

ever know who they were. What he was. Not one lax moment was to be tolerated. Yet here he was, saying it out loud. It had given her a chill, and involuntarily her gaze shifted to the closed door of their room, as though expecting people to burst through to tear them apart.

She'd had to stop herself from asking him not to say such things again, reassured herself he was using it in the North American way, as an endearment toward a child so longed for, it would be treated like royalty.

And Brian *had* longed for this child. His disappointment as the years passed and Yasmine didn't conceive was as acute as her own. Yet he never placed blame. Never suggested he should seek another woman who could give him an heir. Indeed, this baby would be heir to very little. Their need to keep a low profile had taken them to Fort McMurray, Alberta, Canada, where they'd remained.

When asked where they were from, Brian always said, "Just outside Bombay," because it was a city he'd once known well, and could make intelligent conversation about. They both had diverse ethnic backgrounds, including Indian ancestors, but in her opinion neither really looked as though they came from India. However, the Canadians they came in contact with didn't seem to notice.

Sometimes, as ethnic diversity stretched north, they got skeptical looks, but although Brian had thrown off all the trappings of royalty, he'd lost none of the confidence seemingly bred into his bones.

No one really pressed him about it.

Yasmine had simply kept her mouth shut most of the time, not completely trusting herself to maintain the fiction, should she get too close to anyone. She'd been homesick and heartsick for a lot of those years, secretly regretting not being able to go to university, having to work low-paying jobs, but having Brian made up for it all.

Now he was gone, and Yasmine couldn't find a way back into her body to mourn, or even to be angry.

Four months before, his strange symptoms had started—arm pain, moments of disorientation and lack of balance, among others. He'd made light of it all, so Yasmine had never realized the seriousness of it until he'd collapsed with a seizure at the rail yard and had been taken to the hospital. After tests and scans he'd been transferred to Edmonton, where he'd had more of both. Then the oncologist had been glaringly blunt, although Yasmine thought the sympathetic glint in his eyes somewhat negated his directness.

"It's stage four colon cancer, which has already metastasized to your liver, lungs and brain. I'm afraid there's nothing we can do, other than arrange pain management and hospice care for you going forward."

For the first time in their marriage, Yasmine had been the one to fight, to raise her voice, to insist there must be—*must be*—something they could do.

Brian had sat there, as still as the statue of his ancestor in the center of Huban, which commemorated not just the first King but also repelling the French from their shores.

The doctor had given him six months. He'd only lived three and a half. And every moment of the time he'd had left had been devoted to thinking about their child.

"Take our child home, Yasmine," he'd said.

"To Fort McMurray? Of course." Where else had he thought she would go? At least there she knew her way around, had a job, a few friends.

"No, no," he'd whispered, squeezing her fingers. "Home, to take his or her rightful place."

She wouldn't say either yes or no. Her habitual fear may have been rendered distant and weak by the pain of watching him slip away, but it still held sway.

Finally, wanting to understand, she'd asked, "Why would you put such a burden on our child, when you didn't want it yourself?"

He'd shaken his head. "I would have carried the burden, but my need for you was far stronger than the need to fulfill my responsibilities to the country."

He had been dying by then, so she hadn't let loose the words gathering beneath her tongue, threatening to choke her if she didn't spit them out.

He'd hated it all. His unpredictable, forbidding, controlling and manipulative mother. The constant rounds of royal protocol and living in a fishbowl. When he'd told her he was taking off, it hadn't been couched as, *I can't live without you: run away with me.* No, he told her he was leaving and asked if she wished to go.

Of course, she'd said yes.

At sixteen, she would have done anything for him.

Now he was trying to push her to take their child, her baby, back to a place where, if they believed Yasmine's story, they'd take him or her away; probably imprison Yasmine too. Her father had some influence, but not enough to save her from the repercussions of that long-ago decision.

Perhaps it had been the cancer that had made Brian misremember, but Yasmine didn't have the same problem. The palace had been a frightening place; Queen Nargis a despot. She was long dead now, but Yasmine knew nothing of the family who had ascended to the throne. Father had intimated things were better, both in governance and for the people, but she wouldn't take the chance.

After all, her child would threaten their right to rule. Who knew what they might be willing to do to hold onto power?

And when it came out that her father had known where they were, his life might be endangered too.

No. Her child would have a normal existence. As good as she and Brian…

Mind stumbling over the thought, she cupped her belly, the stab of grief like a sword inserted, twisted.

It was just her. Brian was gone.

Now her pain underwent a metamorphosis, took her to a place of clarity.

Nothing was sure. Nothing was a given.

She abruptly sat up, opening eyes closed so long the sudden light was blinding.

"Nurse." Her voice was wispy, a ribbon in a windstorm, but somehow it carried, as one of the nurses came bustling in.

"Are you in pain, Mrs. Haskell?" She immediately began checking the monitors.

"No. No. I need to see a social worker, right away."

The nurse paused, and the sympathy in her eyes was obvious. Yasmine had vaguely heard them talking through the fog of her disconnect.

"Husband died yesterday…"

"She collapsed…"

"High-risk pregnancy to begin with…"

"First child, although she's in her late forties…"

"Says there's no next of kin…"

The nurses knew she was in a bad place, and this one made no effort to offer comforting platitudes or dissuade her.

"I'll put the call in right away for you." She eased Yasmine back against the pillows, and pulled the unnecessary blanket back up over her distended stomach. "You just relax. We'll take good care of you."

Was it a premonition, or just the aftereffects of watching Brian slide away from this world to the next? Yasmine didn't know. All she could see was her baby, alone, with no one to care for him or her.

She wouldn't let that happen.

And she wouldn't let them take the baby back to Kalyana either.

CHAPTER ONE

BEYOND THE WINDOW of the hotel suite a flurry of mixed rain and ice pellets swirled, but although Dr. Farhan Alaoui gazed out through the glass, he wasn't really paying attention to the weather.

This was a fool's errand, and he the fool his father had chosen to go on it.

In years past, knowing how little regard his father had for him, Farhan would have simply refused to come to Canada, telling King Uttam to find another way to deal with the matter. It wouldn't have been the first time, or even the hundredth time, they would have butted heads. The pattern had started from when Farhan was a child, and had only stopped ten years ago, when he'd left Kalyana for Australia, cutting off contact with his father, determined not to return until absolutely necessary.

Had his conscience bitten at him over the decision? Of course it had. He'd still been mourning Ali, trying to reconcile himself to being Crown Prince in his beloved brother's place. The loss, along with his mother's unassailable grief, which had made her pull even further away from her other two sons, had been excruciating. He hadn't needed his father to intimate he was ill equipped to take on the role Ali had excelled at. Certainly hadn't needed to be left with the feeling he would never do as well, so he may as well go back to school, finish his medical studies.

There was to be a referendum, the King said, looking down his nose at his son. If they were lucky, the people would decide to make Kalyana a republic, abolishing the monarchy.

Farhan had understood what his father hadn't said outright.

If that were to happen, the island kingdom would be spared the inept and unprepared King that Farhan clearly would be.

Unfortunately for them all, the people had decided to keep the monarchy, and Farhan remained next in line to the throne. That was something he'd done his best to ignore, living in Australia as a normal person, working as a surgeon in a large hospital, until the night his younger brother Maazin had called to say their father had had a stroke.

Of course, he'd had to return then.

And he was a different person. More assured, ready to take on the responsibility he'd avoided for so long. A little less inclined to argue, or dig in his heels in the way he used to.

What he hadn't been prepared for was his father's tacit refusal to assist him in learning his new role.

Or being sent to Canada to track down the woman who should, by birthright, be the true monarch of Kalyana.

When Farhan had reported finding her, he hadn't been sure what his father's reaction would be.

Uttam's fingers had curled into a fist on his desk, and Farhan had interpreted the motion as signifying anger. Or perhaps, considering the King's unusual pallor, some other, stronger emotion. It made the physician in Farhan watch the older man closely, looking for any signs of cardio-pulmonary distress. After his father's diagnosis of atrial fibrillation the entire family worried about his health.

No one more so than Farhan.

King Uttam tapped the folder in front of him, his dark gaze boring into Farhan's. Despite the King's macular degeneration, he still had the ability to fix a person in place with just one look.

"Are you positive this woman is Bhaskar's descendant?"

Suppressing a sigh, Farhan shook his head. "I don't have Bhaskar's DNA to make the comparison. However, I can say she is a direct descendant of Queen Nargis, and since the records show Bhaskar as Nargis's only child…"

The slam of Uttam's fist on the desk was so unexpected everyone else in the office—Farhan, Maazin, and the King's aide-de-camp, Joseph Malliot—started.

"All these years our family has been blamed, accused of doing away with Bhaskar to gain the throne, while he has been out there, somewhere, living his life as he wished—"

Breaking off his unusually impassioned speech and rising abruptly, Uttam paced across the room. Stopping at the large birdcage housing his pet macaw, Uttam kept his back to his aide and two sons, reaching in to stroke a finger down Sophie's cherry-red poll.

No one spoke. Like acrid smoke, the King's words hung in the office, thickening the already tense atmosphere. Farhan sent a quick glance at Maazin. He seemed relaxed, although his eyelids were lowered, hiding his true expression.

After a moment, Uttam asked, "What do you know of her—this child of Bhaskar?"

All the information was in the file on his father's desk, but Farhan had made sure to bring his own copy.

He'd gone through it fully, of course, and memorized most of it. The private investigator had been thorough, and Farhan was of the opinion the shy and quiet doctor was not, and never would be, a threat to the kingdom.

Even her pictures gave the impression of harmlessness. She was no beauty, being a little plain, with a serious yet pleasant expression in all the photographs.

But his father wasn't interested in Farhan's opinion on things, so, opening the folder on his lap, he read out the salient facts.

"Dr. Sara Greer, general practitioner, thirty-one years old, resident of London, Ontario, Canada. She was adopted at approximately three weeks old by Karen and Everton Greer, who subsequently had two more daughters. Dr. Greer graduated summa cum laude from Eastern University, and now works at an urgent care clinic."

Uttam's free hand sliced through the air, cutting off Farhan's recitation. "Does she know she could be the rightful heir to the throne of Kalyana?"

"It would be impossible for her to know." Being on the receiving end of a quick, skeptical glare, Farhan explained, "When, as you requested, DNA was collected from Nargis's remains the results were posted privately on a number of genealogical websites. That means any matches would be reported to me, as the administrator of that DNA sample, but not to the other parties. No matter what other familial matches Dr. Greer may make, the match with Nargis is the only one that could alert her to the royal bloodline, and she can't see it."

His father's back seemed to relax fractionally, but

Uttam still didn't turn around; just stood stroking the macaw's head through the bars, making Sophie chuckle and coo with pleasure.

Farhan exchanged a look with his brother, now seeing the same impatience he felt in Maazin's expression. None of this was germane to the running of the country.

Farhan was compelled to say, "Father, this is all ancient history, and since Dr. Greer will never know who she is, she's no threat. On top of that, our constitution is clear: without documentation showing the direct lineage between her and Crown Prince Bhaskar, her claim, should she make one, would be denied.

"Adoption records retrieved by the PI show Dr. Greer's birth parents as Brian and Yasmine Haskell, residents of Fort McMurray, Canada, both deceased. Immigration records show the Haskells entering Canada in 1958 as citizens of Great Britain, although there are no records of either of their names in the British archives. Clearly Bhaskar must have had help creating a new identity, but unraveling that, at this stage, would be nigh on impossible."

He should have known better. His father was unmovable on the subject. The near rebellion caused when Uttam's father had taken the throne had, it seemed, made him paranoid. He was absolutely sure one day some supporters of the missing Bhaskar would rise up to try to end his reign, and endanger them all.

With a final scratch of Sophie's head, Uttam turned to walk back to his desk.

"We will not take the chance," he said, as he settled into his chair. "This is a matter that must be dealt with, immediately."

Despite the return of his father's usual stoic demeanor, Farhan was aware of an undercurrent beneath the cool declaration. Maazin shifted, as though suddenly uncomfortable, but before Farhan had a chance to react, Uttam continued.

"Farhan, you will travel to Canada and marry this Dr. Greer; produce an heir to unite the two lines."

Once again he felt the icy fingers of disbelief run down his spine, just as they had then.

The one thing he'd decided when Ali died was never to become a parent. His father had made it clear: the throne—the country—took precedence over everything. Farhan had no interest in producing a child only to have to sacrifice it on the altar of duty. He would do what he could to carry out the first part of his father's order, if he could, but the second part wouldn't happen.

Ever.

The door to the suite opened, rousing Farhan from his memories, and Kavan—his bodyguard, chauffeur, and friend—came in, rubbing his hands together.

"How do people live in this weather all the time?" he grumbled. "It's just gone four o'clock, and it's already dark outside. Not to mention colder than normal people can bear, and the ice and slush is everywhere."

Only then did Farhan realize the murky sunlight had faded, and the street lights had come on. It was time to find and speak to Dr. Sara Greer.

His heart stuttered, but he refused to let his trepidation show. Instead he stood and walked to the hall closet to pull out his wool coat, a warm silk scarf looped under the lapels.

"There are benefits to living everywhere," he replied, as he pulled on his winter wear. "This wouldn't be my first choice, but it certainly is a beautiful country."

"In summer, perhaps," Kavan said, pulling open the room door and holding it for Farhan to precede him out. "But ice should be in a glass, with Scotch on it, not under my feet."

And Farhan found himself chuckling, despite the apprehension gnawing at his insides.

I have to get my life together.

The thought ran on a loop in Dr. Sara Greer's head as she limped from the bus stop through slush and snow toward her home.

It had been one of those days, starting from when she'd got up to find her roommate's dog, Diefenbaker, had torn the insoles out of her shoes. The right one was salvageable. The left one, not at all. And who knew there was a metal bar just above the soles? She hadn't until she'd seen it for herself. With no time to stop and buy an insole, she'd put two socks on that foot and, planning to run out at lunchtime and buy new shoes, hoped for the best.

That idea went out the window when her sister, Mariah, turned up before the clinic even opened.

"I need your car," she said, making it a demand, rather than a request. "I have an appointment at ten on the other side of town."

"Use Mom's, or Dad's." Yet, even as Sara tried to be firm, she knew it was probably a losing battle. "I have stuff I have to do at lunchtime."

"Dad's gone to Clinton to work, and Mom has some errands to run, so I need your car."

Sara's heart sank. Although her dad was a semi-retired farrier, "going to Clinton" usually meant more drinking beer than actual work, especially on a Friday during the London harness racing season. Not to mention the fact that Dad was notoriously horrible about getting people to settle their accounts. Even if he did work, he'd probably never see a dime.

And despite their perennial need for money, Mom didn't have the heart to nag him about his lack of financial acumen.

Mariah turned from demanding to wheedling. "I'll get it back to you before lunchtime. This is really important. A job interview."

"You could take the bus, you know. There's plenty of time."

"Not when I have to go home and change first. I'd need to take two buses, and it looks like it's going to rain. I'd be a mess when I get there, and it might cost me the job."

The thought of one of her sisters being gainfully employed was a heady one, given their propensity for drifting along, doing as little as possible to get by.

"Okay." Even as she capitulated, Sara knew she shouldn't. "But, seriously, I need it back before lunch. I have to get new shoes, and I promised to check in on Nonni too."

Mariah wrinkled her nose, one corner of her lip curling.

"I don't know why you bother. Aunt Jackie is there all the time with her, and she was always so mean to you. You shouldn't waste your time on her."

Sara hadn't argued the point. Mariah was right about how cruel their maternal grandmother had been to her adopted grandchild, but whatever Sara did for the now senile old woman had nothing to do with Nonni. She was helping her aunt and mother, who had given her nothing but love and acceptance her entire life.

"I promised I'd go, so make sure you bring the car back on time, okay?"

"Sure, sure," was her sister's response but, up until the time Sara's shift ended at four, she still hadn't returned it.

Then Cyndi, their younger sister, had started calling and texting at about eleven, as usual wanting Sara to intervene in one of her interminable arguments with their mother.

"She won't listen to me, Sissie." Sara knew there was nothing but trouble ahead when Cyndi used that particular nickname. "I can't get into the culinary course on time if Mom and Dad won't pay for it now."

"I'm not getting involved, Cyndi. Sorry."

"But if you tell Mom it's a good idea, she'll listen."

Sara actually *didn't* think it a good idea for Cyndi to sign up for yet another course, when she'd failed to finish either of the other two she'd started over the last three years. Yet her saying so would only make Cyndi dig in her heels.

"Listen, why don't you save up some money and take the course the next time it's offered? That way you don't have to depend on Mom and Dad to be able to do it."

Cyndi didn't even dignify that suggestion with an answer, just moved on to the next plan of attack.

"Couldn't you lend me the money? It's only two thousand dollars."

Only? What world was Cyndi living in that two thousand dollars wasn't a lot of money?

"Firstly, I just made my student loan payment," Sara told her. "I don't have any cash to spare. Secondly, saying you want to borrow it really doesn't fly, since I don't see how you'd pay it back." Not wanting a protracted argument, she finished up with, "I have to go back to work. Talk to you later."

Undeterred, Cyndi sent so many texts, the tone increasingly desperate, that Sara had ended up turning off the ringer on her phone.

To make it all worse, the freezing cold January rain and ice mix Mariah had predicted had waited to start until Sara was standing at the bus stop. With the exception of her jacket, all the rest of her winter gear—boots, gloves and toque—was in her car. After all, she hadn't expected to have to take the bus or walk to get home.

Really, though, she shouldn't be surprised. Her family, sisters in particular, seemed to feel it was Sara's responsibility to do whatever was necessary to make their lives more comfortable, and Sara let herself be a pushover.

She remembered when Mariah had been born. Sara had already been seven when her mother had got pregnant, despite the doctors saying it would never happen, and she'd been so excited to go from lonely only to big sister. When the baby had come home, she'd eagerly helped her mother and father, and somehow it seemed she'd never stopped.

It often felt there was no time for herself, to work toward her own dreams and goals. Being viewed as an easy mark was one thing, but when you added being caught in a tug of love between Cyndi and her mom, and looking after Nonni, it often felt like too much. The emotional strain and financial pressure had stressed her to the point of a functional gastrointestinal disorder. Sometimes just seeing one of her family members' numbers pop up on her phone made her stomach roil and burn, her teeth clench.

That wasn't something she shared with her family, though. Since childhood everyone had commented on how independent and reliable she was, and, as she finally opened her front door, Sara reflected that there were far worse ways her family could think of her.

Her relief at finally getting home evaporated when, calling out to the French bulldog jumping up and down in the kitchen, she saw the note from her roommate.

Sara, going to be late. Walk Dief for me.

Not even a "please" or a "thank you."

But it wouldn't be fair to take out her bad mood on the dog by refusing to walk him when he'd been locked up by himself all day.

"Well, Dief, since I'm already wet, we might as well go for that walk now."

And she had to giggle when, hearing her say "walk," the dog danced on his hind legs, turning in circles.

After changing into a pair of dry sneakers, Sara let him out of the kitchen and hooked his leash to his collar.

"Walkies," she sang, loving the way he pirouetted on the way back to the front door. "Walkies," she sang again, as she pulled the door open...

And walked straight into the man standing on her doorstep.

The air left her chest in a *whoosh*, and when she gasped to inflate her lungs again her head filled with the most delectable male scent she'd ever encountered. Firm fingers gripped her upper arms, steadying her as she wobbled.

Quickly stepping back and pulling a now barking Diefenbaker with her, Sara looked up.

And lost her breath all over again.

Dark yet somehow cool eyes stared down at her from a face too pretty to be traditionally handsome and yet too roughly hewn to be beautiful. Toffee-toned skin stretched over an undeniably masculine bone structure. Midnight-black hair waved back from a wide forehead, which was balanced by a strong jawline and ever so slightly hooked nose. And his unsmiling but deliciously shaped lips made her legs suddenly weak.

Her heart started racing, not in fright but with the intense sensation of recognition firing through her body, making her head spin. Although she could swear she'd never seen him before, something in his inscrutable gaze, the set of his head, the scent still lingering in her nostrils called to her primal, feminine core.

Then common sense returned.

Snapping her gaping mouth shut, she tugged Dief close to her side. Looking down at the dancing, yapping Frenchie gave her welcome respite from staring at the man before her.

"Diefenbaker, enough. Sit."

Giving her a doleful glare, the little dog did as she commanded, his barking replaced by little rumbles in his throat.

Steeling herself, Sara looked back up and stuttered, "C-can I help you?"

Great. Not only was she a bedraggled mess, but she couldn't even speak to the most gorgeous man she'd ever seen without sounding like a dork.

"Dr. Sara Greer?"

It was only nominally a question. His deep, accented tones made it more of a haughty statement, and Sara just stopped herself from shyly dipping her chin. Instead, she forced herself to look directly into his eyes.

"Yes?"

"My name is Dr. Farhan Alaoui." He paused almost expectantly, his gaze watchful. "Crown Prince of Kalyana."

For a long moment the words sounded like gibberish. Of course she'd heard them loud and clear, but they made no sense to her on an intellectual level.

Had she fallen on the way home, hit her head and lapsed into some kind of concussed dream? That seemed more likely than a man claiming to be a crown prince standing on her doorstep.

"Wh-who?"

Obviously sensing her rising anxiety, Dief stood up and growled. Sara bent to scoop him up. The little dog was trembling—or was it her shaking that way?

"Dr. Farhan Alaoui. Crown Prince of Kalyana," he repeated, tipping his head back so he was looking down that impressive nose at her, and enunciating every syllable as though speaking to a child.

"D-don't b-be ridiculous." She could hardly catch her breath, between the pounding of her heart and rising nausea. "Is this some kind of joke? Who put you up to this?"

Her mind was spinning as she tried to figure out what was going on. There were only three people she'd shared her DNA results with, all trusted family members. Would any of them play such a cruel hoax on her?

"No joke, Dr. Greer." The corners of his lips twitched downward, reminding her of her least favorite lecturer at university. The one for whom she could do no right. "I've come to offer you a job."

"A job?" she repeated, still trying to sort through the chaos in her head. She peeked around his broadshouldered frame, expecting to see Cyndi or maybe Mariah behind him, holding a camera and giggling. "A-as what?"

His lips tightened, and she actually heard him inhale before he said, "My wife."

CHAPTER TWO

OF COURSE SHE thought he was crazy, although she was intrigued enough to put aside her skepticism and at least listen to what he had to say.

If even two months earlier someone had said her roots lay in the small kingdom of Kalyana, she wouldn't have had a clue where they were talking about. After getting her DNA results she'd had to look it up online.

Lying on her bed, computer on her lap, she'd fallen in love with the pictures of the country and the faces of the people. A chain of thirty-plus small islands in the Indian Ocean, it was a melting pot, she'd learned from her research. A mixture of Indian, Arab, African and European, which lent her DNA breakdown credence.

The need to understand where her ancestors came from had been growing inside her for a long time, and had become a compulsion. It wasn't anything she could discuss with her adoptive parents or younger sisters. How could she explain, although they were her family, the yearning to have a biological connection to other people, to an ancestral home, was overwhelming? Although they knew she'd looked up her birth parents' names and had done the DNA test, it wasn't something they'd talked about much, as though it wasn't that important.

Her parents had a commendable, egalitarian outlook on life.

"Everyone's the same, under their skin," was one of her mom's favorite sayings, but knowing that hadn't helped Sara when she'd been a kid, going to school, trying to field questions about her origins.

With her burnt-caramel skin tone, thick, kinky black hair, dark brown eyes and plump build, she'd stood out, especially when compared to her tall, thin, fair-skinned, blonde sisters. There had been a few other children of color in the schools she'd gone to, but the difference had been that they had all known what their roots were. Sara never had.

It had left a hole inside; empty spots in her soul.

Crown Prince Farhan seemed able to fill in some of those blanks, although she found it difficult to comprehend what he was saying.

"Explain it to me again," she said.

Sitting in a slightly seedy coffee shop down the road from her house, she was supremely aware of the man across the table, and the avid stares of the other early evening customers. Who could blame them for being curious?

With his beautifully fitting coat, even in jeans and with a silk scarf looped informally around his throat, there was nothing casual about the overall effect Crown Prince Farhan projected.

Everything about him, from his aura of wealth to the bodyguard, who he'd introduced as Kavan, sitting at an adjacent table, was beyond Sara's, and no doubt the other patrons', ken.

It made her aware of the slightly rundown aura of her blue-collar neighborhood. Heightened her discomfort and confusion.

With exaggerated patience he replied, "In a nutshell, you're part of the Kalyanese royal family. A part that was thought to have died off."

"But I looked at my adoption records. My father was Brian Haskell, not this…"

"Bhaskar Ahuja," he helpfully supplied.

"Right. Him. So I can't be who you think I am."

"According to the DNA results, you're definitely the granddaughter of Queen Nargis, and Bhaskar was her only child. *Ergo…*"

She shook her poor befuddled head.

"This is crazy. And how does any of this relate to your proposition that we marry?"

Just saying the words made her blood pressure sky-rocket, bringing a slow-building headache.

"Through your father, you could, if you wish to exercise it, have a claim to the throne. Should certain factions find that out, you may be used as a rallying point for a revolution."

"I—I don't *want* the throne," she'd said, quite sure it would be the end of the conversation. The craziness.

But Crown Prince Farhan had simply shaken his head.

Apparently, in the worlds of royalty and politics, nothing was that simple. She wouldn't even have to participate in the rebellion, could denounce it, and that still wouldn't be enough.

Farhan wrapped long, nimble fingers around the disposable cup half-filled with coffee and leaned closer across the small table. At that distance, in the garish light, she realized his eyes weren't as dark as she'd thought.

Or as cold.

In the rich brown tones there was, she thought, a hint

of sympathy, although what she interpreted as determination took precedence.

"Even though there is no way to connect Brian Haskell with Bhaskar, except through your DNA, some might consider you the true Queen of Kalyana. My father hopes that, should your lineage become public knowledge, uniting the bloodlines through our marriage would appease those inclined to overthrow his reign."

At least some semblance of her logical brain was still functioning. Not that she knew much about royalty and rights of inheritance, but she did know enough to ask, "But don't thrones pass from father to son? And if my father ran off rather than take the throne, shouldn't he be considered to have abdicated?"

He surprised her with the briefest hint of a smile. Just enough to chase the solemn, arrogant expression from his face and create deep, slashing laugh lines in his cheeks. With just that small change his face, already gorgeous, became shockingly beautiful.

Tingles of awareness shot through her veins, and heat settled low in her belly.

"Not in Kalyana. It's always been the oldest child, irrespective of gender. And there are people who might say Bhaskar was forced to run away by my family, rather than him leaving of his own accord."

A little chill ran up her spine at his words, and she had to ask, "Could there possibly be any truth to that? And if we're both part of the royal family, aren't we related?"

His face tightened, became forbidding, yet he replied, "No, we're not related and I think it doubtful my grandfather even knew he was next in line, since we'd cut off all contact with the kingdom by that point. My branch of the family had left Kalyana about a century before, and was living prosperously in Australia. By all accounts, my grandfather, his wife and children underwent great upheaval when he agreed to take the throne. And their transition was difficult, because of the suspicion surrounding your father's disappearance."

Her mind was going a million miles an hour, and she latched onto a subject that felt distant enough to be tenable. "How old was your father when they moved there?"

His eyebrows rose slightly, as though the question caught him off-guard. "About nine or so, I think."

"Poor soul," she murmured, imagining herself at that age moving halfway across the world into a new and hostile environment. She'd had life changes happen at about the same age, and the effects still lingered, even after so many years. "That must have been rough on him."

Prince Farhan's eyes widened slightly, then he dropped his gaze to his cup, not replying.

There were too many threads to unravel, but one thing was foremost in her mind.

"Why can't I just sign a document saying I promise not to try to take over the country? Wouldn't that work as well?"

He looked up at her again, but it felt as though he'd pulled his mind back to their conversation from somewhere far away.

"The vast majority of the Kalyanese people have no problem with the monarchy. However, even after more than fifty years, the suspicions about my family have lingered, so having you aligned with our side of the family would…*should*…put all that to rest, once and for all."

It was too much to take in, and she struggled to

contain her anxiety, the panic making her pre-ulcerous stomach burn and her hands shake.

Sara wasn't impulsive. She'd had neither the luxury nor the inclination to be. In life, and particularly in her job, she was cautious and deliberate, to the point where the manager of the walk-in clinic often asked her speed up diagnosing and treating patients.

And yet here she was, seriously considering his proposition.

It wasn't just the money, although the lump sum he'd offered, along with an amount he'd called a monthly stipend but had sounded like a yearly salary to her, would definitely be a godsend. More than that, though, the gorgeous man sitting across from her seemed to embody adventure, and offer her a chance to see her ancestral home. He was also dangling a chance to play a fairy-tale role in front of her like the ultimate carrot.

Her. Plain, unremarkable, sensible and reliable Sara Greer, contemplating running off into the sunset with a real life prince to become a princess in her own right?

She must be losing her mind.

As though to distract her, her brain went off at a tangent and she heard herself say, "You sound Australian, but Kalyana is in the Indian Ocean. Have your family kept their accents after all this time?"

Farhan shook his head. "I don't sound like the rest of my family because I went to medical school and practiced in Australia up until a year or so ago."

In the midst of all the nonsense, she'd forgotten he was a doctor too. Somehow knowing that made her relax fractionally.

"What is your specialty?"

"I'm a general surgeon. My brother, Maazin, is one as well, although, having trained with the Royal

Guard, his experiences have been far more interesting than mine."

"Do you have a practice in Kalyana now?"

His expression was rueful as he replied, "I keep my hand in, but it feels as though I do more administrative work than actually practicing medicine. I've been trying to upgrade the medical systems, which has turned out to be more difficult than I'd imagined."

"I'd need to work, if I agree to come with you."

The words fell between them, were followed by a thick silence. Farhan's eyes narrowed, and Sara knew why.

Despite the ambivalence of the statement, it sounded like capitulation.

Hadn't she recently been thinking how much she wanted to see the place her ancestors came from? Wasn't she longing for adventure, for a chance to advance, to make things better?

I'm going to do this.

And it was, as the old saying goes, all over bar the shouting at that point.

Somehow, before going to Canada to find her, when reading the PI's report and looking at the photographs accompanying it, Farhan had felt he knew who Sara Greer was. Quiet and serious. Competent medically, but socially withdrawn. Nothing fun or fancy about her.

Yet when she'd tugged open her door before he could knock, and he'd seen her in the flesh for the first time, shock had fired through his system.

Damp and flushed, laughing down at the dog capering around her ankles, the sight had almost made him smile despite the stress he'd been under. But when their bodies had collided and she'd looked up, her gleaming brown eyes widening in shock, all his amusement had fled, replaced with a jolt of desire.

It still simmered beneath his skin, and he found himself taking in her every expression, every gesture, trying to parse them, wanting to understand what each one meant.

Not the most auspicious start to what was supposed to be strictly a business arrangement. This sudden surge of attraction was unwanted, as was the tug of sympathy he felt toward Sara Greer. Even as a child, he'd recognized the subtle danger of allowing himself to feel too much for others. Ali had been the golden son, Maazin the baby. Farhan had felt lost in the shuffle, ignored until he did something wrong. He'd craved his mother's love, his father's approval, but their attention had rarely strayed his way. Withdrawing into himself and avoiding emotional involvement had served him well.

A marriage of convenience, especially of a short duration, would suit him perfectly. With his need to serve his country foremost in his mind, he had no time for complications and messy relationships.

And it was time he made that aspect of it absolutely clear.

"What I propose is that we marry, and agree to stay together for at least a year." Something in the way her cheeks pinked up made his pulse escalate, but he kept his face expressionless, and his voice level. "Obviously, this won't be a union based on emotion and, while I'm content with that, I doubt you'd want to be locked into such an arrangement long term."

"How would a short-term marriage help the situation, though?"

"If within the year no one finds out about your lineage, I'd think it would be safe to part ways, and the chances of anyone finding out who your father was are nil. I'm sure if anyone knew Bhaskar was alive all those years, they would have said something."

The skeptical look she gave him made him impatient. She'd seemed set to agree to his terms, and now he felt victory slipping away.

"Look," he said, leaning closer over the table, trying to ignore the way the lights made her eyes seem speckled with gold dust, "I'm doing this because my father ordered me to. He's not been well, and I think he's trying to wrap up loose ends as best he can, although I suspect he'll live for many years to come. In his mind, a marriage of convenience is perfectly acceptable and you should be happy to become a part of a wealthy, royal family. He entered into such a marriage, and I knew eventually I would also, but trying to explain to him that modern women, like you, would find it strange and potentially insulting did no good.

"So I'm following his orders in the best way I know how, trying to be fair to you in the process. As Bhaskar's daughter you would probably have inherited a bankrupt country, as my grandfather did, but I believe you're still due compensation as his heir, so think of the lump sum in that light, even though it comes with strings. The monthly stipend will be for the sheer upheaval moving and playing your part will bring."

He wouldn't tell her the deal he offered wasn't sanctioned by his father, who believed theirs would be a true, lasting union, not the limited one Farhan envisioned.

Sara still looked unsure, however, so he continued, "If after a time we part ways, my father won't be happy, but that wouldn't be his decision to make. He can order me to marry, but he can't order you to stay in the marriage if you don't want to."

"That makes sense," she said, shifting her empty cup back and forth between her hands. Then she cleared her throat, the blush now suffusing her entire face, but she bravely held his gaze as she said, "Before I agree, I have to ask: would you be expecting me to fulfill *all* the usual roles as your wife?"

He knew what she was asking; would have found her delicacy amusing if it weren't for the ramifications of even thinking that way, coupled with the rush of heat up his spine at the thought of having her in his bed.

"No," he said, quickly enough that her blush deepened. "Us being intimate isn't part of the bargain."

If his father had his way it would have been written into the contract. Uttam had gone so far as to say he would give Sara a million dollars to produce an heir within the first year, saying it might, "smooth the way to compliance." Farhan found his father's suggestion offensive in every way, and had no intention of telling her about it. Ever.

She looked back down at her cup, and he held his breath. He'd thought it would take weeks, perhaps even months to convince her to marry him, but beyond the shyness and anxiety in her gaze there was also curiosity and something akin to excitement. Farhan hoped it would be enough to get her to agree to his terms.

"Okay, but I'll need time to get everything sorted out."

Outwardly calm, but inside doing fist pumps and cartwheels, he said mildly, "That's good. You won't regret it."

Then, with ruthless efficiency, he steamrollered over every objection that would delay their return to Kalyana, or make her change her mind as the reality of her agreement set in.

No, she didn't need time to give notice or to pack. He was royalty, and rich. They'd hire people to deal with those pesky details.

"You can leave all that to me, and we'll be on our way in two weeks."

Eyes wide, she'd gasped. "Wait. You're kidding, right?" Waving her hands, she continued, "I don't know anything about being royalty; what to do or say. It'll be a disaster, and an embarrassment. I can't do it."

"I'll arrange for you to learn whatever you need to know, as well as make sure you're completely kitted out for the part. If we get everything squared away here over the next week or so we'll go to Toronto, get married there, and then head to Paris or Milan to get you a new wardrobe."

The mingled horror and shock on her face was obvious, yet she didn't object again. Instead she muttered, "And what the heck do I tell my family?"

"The truth?" he ventured, only to be met with a scathing glance.

"Oh, heck, no. All this princess business would blow their minds."

"They'll find out sooner or later that you're marrying a prince, albeit one from a tiny kingdom."

She nibbled at the corner of her lip, and then replied, "And we're going to have to come up with a realistic backstory about how we met, and why we're marrying in such a rush."

He shrugged, and gave her a smile. "I came to Canada on business. We met and I fell head over heels for you. I refused to go home without you, and you finally gave in."

Her scathing glance and answer made him smile.

"You're going to have to come up with a better

story than that. No one would believe *you'd* fall for *me* like that."

"We'll see," was all he said, rising to get another coffee, which he found to be surprisingly good. "Want another drink?"

CHAPTER THREE

FOR THE LAST month and a half Sara had lived in a fog of unreality, waiting for—no, expecting—someone to jump out of the bushes, or a doorway, or her closet, and yell, "Surprise! Got you good, didn't we?"

Even now, thousands of feet in the air aboard a luxurious private jet, and more than seven thousand miles from her home in Canada, she was quite sure it was all a crazy dream.

But the huge ruby winking from the third finger on her left hand seemed to slyly assure her it wasn't. And the still unaccustomed feeling of a horrendously expensive silk dress and amazingly comfortable, not to mention incredibly beautiful, leather shoes also hinted that what was happening wasn't an elaborate—and totally impractical—practical joke.

"We should be landing in thirty minutes, Your Highness. Can I get you anything more?"

And then there was *that*.

The title still made her want to look around to see who the other person was speaking to.

Oh, yeah. It's me.

"No, thank you, Juana," she murmured, giving the other woman a little smile.

Anything more than that tiny upward tilt of her lips was beyond her just now.

Farhan was seated at a table on the other side of the cabin with his PA, Seth Lee, official documents spread out before them. Looking over at him only made her already collywobble-infested stomach give another twist.

On the rare occasion Sara had thought of a possible husband, she'd pictured someone as ordinary looking as herself, not a man so handsome it almost made her eyes hurt just to look at him.

Even standing in front of the justice of the peace in Toronto and saying, "I do," felt like part of a dream. Farhan had tried to make it less clinical than it was in reality. The ceremony had taken place in their suite at the opulent hotel where they'd been staying, the entire living area beautifully decorated. Her cream crêpe de Chine dress had been simple but elegant, and she'd held a bouquet of vanilla orchids, their delicate petals almost the same shade as her dress but with a slightly more yellow tone. She'd learned afterwards they were the national flower of Kalyana, and Farhan, resplendent in a dark blue suit that fit his muscular form to perfection, had worn one as well, as a boutonnière.

He'd even asked if she wanted her family in attendance, but she'd declined his offer. They were already in too much of a tailspin as it was.

As though sensing her gaze, Farhan met it with his own. Cool, dark, and unfathomable, his autocratic expression only intensified her anxiety and fear. After a second, the corner of his mouth lifted in a half-smile. No doubt supposed to be reassuring, instead it washed her with heat and upped her stress quotient.

When he looked away, Sara drew in a shaky breath

and turned her head, as though looking out at the clouds below.

Had it really only been just over a month since he'd entered her life, turning it upside down? It felt like much longer since her orderly, if stressful life had come crashing to a halt.

"Are you sure he isn't a sex trafficker? This is all so very sudden."

Her mother's question had made her want to laugh, but the worry lines on the older woman's face kept Sara from doing so.

"I'm sure, Mom. You can look him up online, if you don't believe me."

She'd originally planned to wait a few days after meeting Farhan to tell her parents what was happening. That decision had gone out the window when, just as they'd got back to her house, Mariah had turned up to return her car. Finally.

"And who's this?" Mariah drawled, flipping her wheat-blonde hair back over her shoulder.

"Oh, um, Mariah, meet Dr. Farhan Alaoui," Sara replied, not knowing what else to say.

"Sara's fiancé," he'd added, making Mariah's mouth drop open and her eyebrows all but disappear into her hairline.

No doubt it would have turned into a three-ring circus if Mariah's friends, waiting in another car, hadn't started calling for her to hurry up, they were going to be late.

Still speechless, Mariah had rushed off, leaving Sara to glare at Farhan.

"Wow. Thanks a lot. I better call my mom before Mariah gets to her." The weight of her decision suddenly made her shoulders drop. "I wasn't planning to tell them just yet."

His chin had tipped up in that autocratic way, and he'd replied, "I don't plan to stretch this out, Sara. So do what you have to do, as quickly as possible. We're leaving for Toronto in two weeks, at the most."

Her parents' suspicions were allayed by meeting Farhan, whom they'd invited over to dinner. Sara hadn't known what to expect. Her parents were salt-of-the-earth types, while Farhan was clearly from a whole different world.

To her surprise he'd charmed them both.

Sara had sat back, as she usually did, watching everyone interacting. Aunt Jackie had come over too and brought Nonni with her, so Sara helped the elderly lady eat her dinner, while her sisters flirted shamelessly with Farhan, until her mother put a stop to it.

"Behave yourselves, both of you," she said, in that mild voice they all knew to take heed of. "That's Sara's fiancé you're talking to."

Only somewhat abashed, Cyndi said, "Well, do you have any brothers?"

But Farhan had just chuckled, and Dad had engaged him in conversation about horses, which had taken them through the rest of the meal.

By the time she'd left Canada, they'd had her parents' blessing, which made Sara just shake her head in disbelief. They'd totally bought her story of having met Farhan through her search for more information about her birth father, without stopping to wonder why a prince would be getting involved in something so mundane. It gave her a warm feeling, however, that none of them, not even her sisters, had seemed surprised that Farhan would want to marry her. She'd been expecting a lot more questions than any of them had seemed inclined to ask!

As though in sync with her thoughts, her phone vibrated, and she picked it up to see a message from her mother, who couldn't seem to grasp just how far away her daughter actually was.

Nonni hates the nurse you hired. Can we get someone else?

Just what she needed to have to deal with within minutes of landing in her new country. She was so nervous it took all her concentration to tap out a reply.

Sure, Mom. Just call the agency and have them send a replacement, But although Nonni has dementia she still probably realizes there's been a change and doesn't like it. You might want to give her a chance to get used to the nurse before you get someone new and start the cycle all over again.

The captain requested they prepare for landing, and Sara's racing heart dropped down into her belly as she switched off her phone before fastening her seatbelt.

Despite the coaching, the lessons in etiquette she'd diligently applied herself to over the last month, the beautiful wardrobe and jewelry, she knew she wasn't ready for this.

Was nowhere near ready to be introduced to the Kalyanese people as their new Crown Princess.

The jet taxied toward the terminal in Huban, Kalyana's capital city as the flight crew prepared for their passengers to disembark.

As he shrugged into his suit jacket, Farhan saw a sea of blue, green, and gold beyond the plane windows, as children and adults alike waved Kalyanese flags. Interspersed among them were a number of red and white Canadian flags, in honor of their new Crown Princess's country of origin.

Even from the other side of the aisle, Farhan could see Sara trembling. He felt for her, knowing how big a step she was about to take. Although she'd frequently baulked, he hadn't intended to allow her to back out, and so, with uncharacteristic arrogance, he'd simply reminded her that she'd already agreed to his terms.

Not to mention the "little" matter of their marriage, already three weeks old.

It still felt strange to think of her as his wife, although since getting to know her better he thought the arrangement, albeit not permanent, a good one. Over the time they'd spent together they'd both been busy during the day, he with official business, she with her lessons and fittings, but they'd spent their evenings together.

"It's important that we know a certain amount about each other, to make our marriage seem believable," he'd said, and although she'd muttered something about there not being much to know about her, he'd learned a lot from their talks.

Like how much her family depended on her, emotionally and otherwise.

And how much she longed to have a practice of her own, somewhere where she could build relationships with her patients, rather than have them coming in and out as if through a revolving door.

"I was born in the wrong time," she'd said one night over dinner. "Having patients I've seen from they were young, maybe even several generations of the same family, is my dream. We don't practice medicine like that much anymore."

Beneath her quiet exterior lay a compassionate heart, seemingly born to serve others. Perfect for the role of Crown Princess.

As the plane door was opened, the steps already in place outside, Farhan actually hoped he was right in that assessment, and her time in Kalyana would be a success.

He'd been aware of his interest in her growing, rather than abating, and was sure it wasn't a good thing. So he'd maintained as polite a distance as possible, and now, as he held out his hand to her, Farhan promised himself to keep that remoteness as best he could. He had no intention of making things more difficult for her, or for himself, by allowing either of them to become attached.

Sara's fingers were freezing, and trembling, and as if to negate the very decision he'd just made, Farhan rubbed them briskly between his palms.

"You'll be fine," he said. "And you look beautiful."

She cast him a grateful glance, smoothing her free hand over the skirt of her royal blue dress. Chosen by the stylist in Paris, it appeared to flow around her body, highlighting her full breasts and emphasizing her small waist in elegant, haute couture style.

Farhan found himself wondering how long it would take to unbutton all those tiny fastenings to reveal the soft skin beneath...

"Fine feathers, and all that," she muttered, yanking him out of his little fantasy. "I'll admit I'm glad your parents won't be on the tarmac. That would be truly terrifying."

Not the time to tell her Uttam terrified everyone, no matter the setting, was it?

No!

"It'll just be my brother, Maazin, representing the family, along with the parliamentarians, plus some cultural displays."

"I remember. I studied the program as though there'd be an exam on it and my medical degree was at stake."

And, to his surprise, her answer made him smile, just as they stepped to the open doorway, and cheers erupted from the crowd.

Her fingers tightened on his arm and for one moment he thought she was going to bolt back into the plane. There were foreign reporters among the local news crews, including a couple he was sure were Canadian. An official decree had gone out the week before regarding their marriage, and Maazin had told him the palace had been inundated with requests for more information. He wondered if her parents were watching back in Canada, and what they'd make of seeing their daughter this way.

Bending, he put his lips close to her ear, so as to be heard above the military band. "I think they like you already."

And, although her smile was a little wobbly, she held her head up as they descended the staircase.

Maazin waited at the bottom of the steps, a smile on his face. When Farhan had discussed with his brother their father's directive to marry Sara, Maazin had simply said, "I just hope this works out better for you than it did for me, brother."

The resignation in Maazin's voice had reminded Farhan that an arranged marriage was always on the cards, since that was his family's tradition, and three years ago, Maazin's engagement to Lady Meleena had been announced. However, only close family knew that

Lady Meleena had recently left Maazin for someone else. Farhan knew he was lucky that he and Sara had entered their marriage on their own terms. There was much to be said for that.

At the foot of the stairs, Maazin smiled at Sara. Farhan introduced them formally, and his brother bent to kiss Sara's cheeks, saying, "Welcome, sister."

"Thank you, Prince Maazin," she murmured in reply, the tremor in her voice making Maazin's smile soften in sympathy.

"Just Maazin, to you, and you're already doing wonderfully," he soothed. "Ready to run the gauntlet?"

"Wow. I was, until you called it that," she rebutted, making both Farhan and Maazin chuckle.

Sara bent to accept a bunch of flowers from a pair of children, taking a few moments to ask their names and ages, and compliment them on their clothing. The little boy and girl basked in her attention, until someone hustled them away again.

The aide charged with keeping the welcome ceremony on time started making discreet little clucking noises, and Farhan knew she wanted them to move on to the receiving line. Ignoring her, he took a moment to tuck Sara's free hand back into the crook of his arm and give her a lift of his brows.

"Shall we?"

"Yes," she replied, her voice carrying a hint of steel that made him unaccountably proud.

And his admiration for her grew as they went down the line of dignitaries. She'd obviously memorized the pronunciation of all their names and the positions they held, and, with her soft voice and obvious interest in each person, turned a formal affair into something almost intimate.

Just as they came to the end of the line, screams rang out from behind the barriers holding the spectators at bay. Farhan swung around in time to see part of the crowd surge forward, confusion threatening to turn to chaos in an instant. Police officers stationed around the runway, along with military personnel, moved to do crowd control. Seeing people falling, perhaps being trampled, caused Farhan to rush to assist, shouldering his way through the ring of palace guards that immediately surrounded them.

It was only once at the barrier he realized Sara was right behind him. Before he could stop her, she slipped beneath the arm of a soldier trying to hold back the panicked crowd and disappeared into the swirling mass of humanity.

"Sara!"

Heart thundering, he shoved past a police officer to plunge in after her, just as the small stampede petered out.

Sara was kneeling, hunched over a woman who was lying on the ground curled into a ball. She had her arms curved protectively around the woman's head and, as Farhan strode toward them, he heard the distinctive screams of a young child.

A member of the Royal Guard got to them first and bent to say something to Sara, who looked up and waved him away.

"I need to examine them, see what their injuries are," Farhan heard her say, as he got to her side. "No, I won't leave you to take care of them."

"Stand down, Major," he said.

"Yes, Your Highness." The soldier saluted and stepped back, and if Farhan hadn't been so angry at the fright she'd given him, he might have found the sympathetic glance the soldier gave him amusing.

Before he could say anything, Sara snapped, "Get an ambulance. She has a laceration on her arm, and I don't know if she or the baby have other injuries."

His training took over, and as the major spoke into his headset, summoning medics, Farhan shifted to the opposite side of the woman.

"Lie still," Sara said to the young woman, who, after starting to roll over, froze, then stared up at Sara and Farhan, her mouth agape in shock. "Let me take a look at your baby."

With a bit more coaxing, the woman let Sara take the baby and set him across her lap, where she could inspect him more carefully, while Farhan began his visual examination of the woman.

"Where hurts?" he asked, but the woman only blinked, making no attempt to answer.

He took her pulse, found it strong and only slightly elevated. But when she tugged her wrist free, he made no attempt to do anything further. Some of the women from more traditional backgrounds were uncomfortable with having a male doctor and, realizing she may be one, he decided to wait for the medics.

One of his first acts since coming back to Kalyana had been to revamp the emergency system, recruiting more women paramedics for just such a situation. It had been a fight, but he'd got it done.

"It's okay, little man," Sara was cooing to the little boy, her nimble, sure hands examining the squirming infant.

As though hypnotized by her attention, the baby quieted, and by the time the medics ran up he was smiling up at her, arms and legs waving freely.

Something shifted in Farhan's chest to see Sara cradling the baby in her arms, warmth flowing out to settle in his belly and climb his spine. It was a picture of tenderness, as close to motherly love as it could be without it being her own child.

Why that had him staring, his insides churning with a sensation he didn't recognize and didn't wish to put a name to, he didn't know.

She looked up then, their gazes colliding. Her eyes gleamed softly, and her lips were curved into a sweet, gentle smile.

Then the smile faded from her face and a touch of color stained her cheeks as she quickly looked away, turning her attention to the medics and relinquishing her hold on the infant.

As two female paramedics fitted the mother with a cervical collar, Farhan rose to get out of their way and held out his hand to help Sara to her feet. Her previously neat coif was a little disheveled and, along with her rosy blush, brought to mind that first startling moment he'd seen her, realized her quiet beauty.

"Your Highnesses." The protocol aide, followed by Sara's new assistant, Mara, came rushing over, and were let through the cordon of soldiers surrounding them. Farhan tore his gaze away from Sara to give the aide his attention. "You're behind schedule now, and Princess Sara will have to freshen up before the audience at the palace."

"Oh, but the children haven't had a chance to sing for us yet. They'll be terribly disappointed, having waited in the sun for so long." Sara turned questioning eyes to Farhan. "Can't we at least let them do one song before we leave?"

No, they couldn't. They were due at the palace at a specific time, and it wouldn't do to keep his father waiting.

Yet he wavered, unaccountably wanting to make her happy.

Maazin came over, brushing off his uniform, having also jumped into the fray.

"It was a bench that collapsed under the weight of people standing on it. The injured are being taken to the hospital. We should be going. Is there a hold-up?"

And Farhan heard himself say stiffly, "My wife would like to hear the children sing." He turned to the aide and said, "Please advise the palace there will be a small delay."

He turned away to offer Sara his arm, but not quickly enough to miss Maazin's raised eyebrows and grin.

Dammit, it was her first day in Kalyana, and if she wanted to hear the children sing, then let her hear them sing!

CHAPTER FOUR

EVEN WITH THE DELAY, they got to the palace on time, and with Sara buffed and polished. With ruthless efficiency Farhan arranged for Mara to travel with them in the limousine, and her personal assistant efficiently brushed a smear of dust from Sara's dress, as well as fixing her hair and make-up.

Not that Sara made the job easy for her.

"Please, Your Highness, if you could turn your head this way…"

But Sara could hardly take her eyes off the people lining the streets, the scenery visible beyond the colorful buildings.

Kalyana was gorgeous, and seeing it, and its people, made her heart sing.

She'd never felt more excited in her life.

It truly felt like coming home.

Perhaps not the smartest way to feel, since she was only here for a relatively short time, but it was impossible to ignore the way her heart pounded with joy.

The royal palace was on a hill, and her first glimpse of it made Sara gasp. It was like something out of a fairy-tale. Not a European tale, though, something more Eastern.

She'd seen pictures of Moorish castles, and Huban Palace seemed closer in design to those.

The walls of warm-hued stone gave a sense of solidity, but the ranks of arched windows lightened the fortress-like façade. Ringed by lush vegetation and bright flowers, it was a picture-perfect scene.

And the interior of the palace was so gorgeous she stood for a moment, gaping like the country bumpkin she knew herself to be.

They walked through huge, wonderfully carved doors into a majestic entranceway of creamy stone walls, with two curved staircases sweeping upward on either side. Intricate carving adorned the arches around doorways and gave life to the stone balustrades, while the marble floor gleamed beneath their feet, reflecting the colors of massive floral arrangements.

Her awe only intensified when she was presented to her new father-in-law.

At first Farhan's resemblance to his father made her want to smile, but King Uttam's steely scrutiny made her nape prickle with discomfort.

"Princess Sara." His voice matched his cool gaze, increasing her nerves.

"Your Majesty," she murmured, as she curtsied the way Mara had taught her, feeling slightly silly as she did so. Sara secretly thought all the pomp rather pointless. Nevertheless, despite the transient nature of her involvement, she wouldn't embarrass Farhan by not following protocol.

Well, unless it involved watching the school children, dressed in tropical colors, faces bright with pride and excitement, sing a traditional folk song. Then protocol and schedules could go hang.

The Queen gave Sara a small smile, but had little to

say beyond welcoming her, and Sara noticed the sadness in her eyes. It was so very similar to what she'd noticed in Maazin's and she wondered if it had anything to do with the death of Crown Prince Ali and his wife, ten years before. When she'd read about the tragedy in the book she'd been given to familiarize herself with the country's history, there'd been little detail. She'd wanted to ask Farhan what exactly had happened, but it seemed too intimate a subject to bring up.

Now, even more than before, her curiosity was piqued.

Thankfully, the King and Queen didn't seem inclined to get to know her better, and they only exchanged small talk regarding their trip and the welcome ceremony. There was to be a family dinner later, but she breathed a sigh of relief when Farhan escorted her from the throne room after less than an hour.

With the long flight from Dubai and the excitement of the day her neck muscles were aching and her body felt heavier than usual.

Yet, when Farhan suggested she might want to rest for a couple of hours before she had to dress for dinner, she found herself saying, "Actually, I'd like to go to the hospital and check up on the people who were hurt this afternoon."

"That isn't necessary, you know. There are perfectly competent doctors to look after them."

She shrugged lightly. "I'm sure there are, but I feel somewhat responsible. I just want to know how everyone is doing."

The glance he gave her made butterflies start fluttering in her stomach, and she was reminded of the moment they'd shared at the airport, when he'd looked at her in a way he never had before. When her heart had leapt, heat creeping through her veins to warm her through and through.

Thankfully, this time his gaze didn't linger on hers. Instead he turned back to look where he was walking.

"We can certainly do that, if you wish, but it might cause a bit of a commotion. You are, after all, royalty now, not just a doctor popping in to check on her patients."

"Don't remind me," she muttered.

He chuckled. "It gets easier, believe me."

As he summoned a car for them, and after she'd refused his offer for her to change, since he wasn't going to, Sara went back over the events of the day.

Farhan had been angry with her for running to help the young woman earlier. She'd seen it in his eyes. But there was something else bothering her, and she was in two minds about whether to tax him with it or not.

Then she got distracted by the fact it was an SUV that was brought to a side door for them, and that Farhan, rather than a chauffeur, was going to drive it.

"No Kavan to drive you?" she asked, since the other man had hardly seemed to leave Farhan's side while they'd been in Canada and Paris.

"When I'm here in Huban I usually drive myself, and don't feel as though I need a bodyguard. I sometimes take him with me when I visit the other islands, but more for convenience than out of necessity. He has a pilot's license, so he can fly if I want him to, and if I'm tired after a long day at a clinic, it's often nice not to have to think about navigating narrow, winding roads."

There was something reassuringly normal about getting into the passenger seat, having him get behind the wheel.

And that sense of normality made her relax for the

first time that day, and gave her the courage to ask, "Earlier, I noticed you didn't try to examine the baby's mother. Was there a reason for that?"

She was almost fearful of what he might say, since she couldn't think of any good reason why he wouldn't have done so, but there were a number of what she would consider bad ones.

"Some of our more conservative residents don't look kindly at their female family members being touched by males outside their family, even a prince. When I took her pulse, she pulled her arm away, so I didn't want to make it uncomfortable for her, and didn't try to do anything further."

Her relief was sharp, and a bit ridiculous. Why should she care whether he was a snob or not? She already knew he was arrogant, didn't she? His being elitist shouldn't make any difference, but it would have.

"Ah, that makes sense, and explains the two female paramedics." Rolling her head against the headrest so as to look at his profile, she asked, "Have you set up a women's clinic yet? Somewhere the women can go, knowing for sure they will see a female doctor?"

As they were saluted through a gate, Farhan brought the SUV to a stop to check for oncoming traffic, then made the turn before he replied.

"It's on my list of recommendations, which I suspect is gathering dust on the Minister of Health's desk, or perhaps has already found its way into the dustbin."

That surprised her. "But you're the Crown Prince. Shouldn't they be doing what you say?"

Farhan chuckled, but there was little amusement in the sound. "I was gone for a long time and, since coming back, have been made completely aware of how little influence I really have. It was a fight just to get more female paramedics trained. Perhaps if I'd been here over the last ten years it might be different but, as it is, I have to pick my battles."

Sympathy wasn't something she'd ever expected to feel for her arrogant husband, but it moved through her now.

"That must be incredibly frustrating for you. And, now that I think about it, would you have to set up a series of such clinics, for the various islands? I didn't really consider the logistics of it."

He nodded. "For administrative purposes the islands are clustered into eight districts, each district having as few as one island or as many as five. My recommendation was to start with two clinics, one here in Huban and the other in the Southeast District, which is the next most populous, to serve as many women as possible."

"That makes sense," she replied, distracted by the various sights they were passing.

Beyond the windows was a combination of newer buildings and older, some colonial in style and others simple wooden structures. The city glowed like a jewel in the bright afternoon sun and, with the cerulean sea visible in the distance, it all made Sara's heart lift and soar with pleasure.

In Canada the winter winds were howling still, snow or slush and ice on the ground, everyone bundled up against the cold. Here in the southern hemisphere it was summer, and she knew from her research that the temperature wouldn't get much lower even in the winter season.

It felt so right. She'd always disliked winter. Oh, she was used to it, and fully equipped to get through it, but she'd had to monitor her moods to ensure she didn't fall into depression, and use a daylight lamp to get the Vitamin D her body demanded.

"It's so beautiful," she murmured.

"Some of the other islands are even more so," he replied, as they turned into the hospital grounds. "We'll have to make arrangements for you to see some, if not all of them."

There was no more time to talk as they drew up beneath a portico, and she saw two women in somewhat old-fashioned nurses' uniforms and a man in scrubs standing outside turn to stare.

"Don't be surprised at the fuss that's about to ensue," he warned, as he opened his door, but there was a teasing tone to the remark, so Sara didn't pay him too much mind.

She should have though, as their arrival created excitement far beyond what she'd expected.

"Y-Your Highnesses," the young man outside the front door stammered. "I don't think anyone told the director you'd be coming, or he'd be here to greet you."

"That's fine, since he didn't know. The Crown Princess wanted to check on the people hurt this afternoon," Farhan replied.

He looked as stern as usual, and both the doctor and nurses looked terrified, so Sara tried to defuse the situation by smiling at them and saying, "This isn't an official visit, just a spur-of-the-moment thing. There's no need to disturb the director."

"He'd be very displeased, Your Highness, if no one informed him. May I suggest coming with me to his office, or giving me the opportunity to call up and let him know you're here?"

Silently sighing to herself at the proposed delay, which would no doubt mean *not* seeing what she wanted to, Sara replied, "Of course you must tell him if you think that's best."

Farhan interjected, "Dr…?"

"Patel, Your Highness. Imran Patel."

"It's a pleasure to meet you, Dr. Patel. You must have been exceptionally busy whenever I've been here in the past for us not to have crossed paths before."

The young doctor's eyes blinked rapidly a few times before he replied, "I'm still very new here, sir. Doing a residency under Dr. Anwar."

"Ah, one of our finest internists." He turned to Sara, and she couldn't help noticing the twinkle in his eyes. He was up to something. "My dear, we should find Dr. Andrade, the director, so we don't get Dr. Patel into trouble. While he and I do that, I'm sure these ladies will be happy to show you to the wards where the patients are."

She couldn't help smiling back at him in appreciation. Their time was limited, and he knew she didn't want to waste it with nonsense.

"That's a wonderful idea." When she turned to the nurses, she only just stopped her smile turning into a grin at their expressions of mingled amazement and pride. "As long as it won't be any trouble. I know how busy you nurses always are."

"Oh, no, Your Highness. No trouble at all," the older of the two replied, while the younger one's face glowed with a blush.

Before any of them could change their minds, Sara headed into the hospital, the nurses a step behind.

But, even with Farhan's warning, she found it difficult to understand the upheaval that took place wherever she went in the hospital. People bowed, often with palms together, fingers pointing upward, some of the women curtsied, and work stopped as people stared at her going past. Many of the staff and patients seemed too tongue-tied to answer her questions, so she checked charts and said encouraging things to the injured, letting them know she hoped they recovered soon.

It was tiring, and made the quick check-in she'd wanted take far longer than she'd expected. She'd been glad, but also disappointed, to hear the young mother and baby she'd helped at the airport had already been discharged. While she was happy neither had been seriously hurt, she'd also hoped to get one more chance to hold the baby.

She also noted that while the hospital wasn't as modern as those she was used to, with some of the wards open to the outer air and the layouts somewhat inefficient, it was scrupulously clean, and the equipment was up to date.

As they were leaving the last patient on the women's ward, she heard a low moan from behind a curtained bed, and stopped, arrested by the utter agony of it.

"That's not one of the patients from the airport, Your Highness," Kadiah, her nurse and guide, said quickly.

Too quickly, Sara thought.

Ignoring Kadiah's apparent hope she wouldn't investigate, Sara stepped across and slipped between the curtains.

There was a woman lying on the bed, curled into a ball, holding her abdomen. Perspiration dotted her face, and her lips were dry and cracked, but it was the low, rhythmic groaning that made the hair on the back of Sara's neck stand up.

Touching the patient's face told Sara her temperature was elevated, as was her pulse when she checked it. Stepping to the foot of the bed, she picked up the chart stored there and quickly scanned the information. What she read made her blood boil.

She turned to the younger nurse.

"Deena, please go and find Prince Farhan. Ask him to come here, immediately."

CHAPTER FIVE

THE TWO NURSES froze for a moment, but before Sara could reiterate her command, Kadiah nodded at Deena, and the younger woman took off, speed-walking out of the ward.

"Why hasn't this woman been taken to surgery already?" Sara could hardly contain the anger in her voice. "It shows here that Dr. Patel diagnosed her with a ruptured appendix and abscess over three hours ago, and she's been ill for over a week. If she's not operated on as soon as possible she could develop sepsis, if she hasn't already."

Kadiah explained, "Dr. Patel has been trying to contact the surgeon on call, Your Highness, but hasn't had a response."

"But Prince Farhan is here now. Dr. Patel should have informed him of the problem and asked for his help."

"Yes, Your Highness, but we were specifically told not to bother the Crown Prince while he was on his honeymoon."

Taking a deep breath, Sara tamped down her emotions, consciously relaxing her grip on the clipboard in her hand. It was no use arguing about it now. The patient was all-important.

"He'll need an operating room, surgical nurses, and

an anesthesiologist. Can you arrange that, please? As quickly as possible."

"Yes, Ma'am."

She too rushed from the room, leaving Sara with the patient, whose name, according to the chart, was Eshaal Saleem. Anger still shimmered under her skin, but she acknowledged the unfairness of blaming either Dr. Patel or the nurses. They had been doing as they were told.

Blowing out a calming breath, she slotted the chart back into its holder and looked around for something positive to do while she waited.

There was a bowl of water beside the bed, a washcloth submerged in it. Fishing out the cloth, she wrung it out and leaned over to wipe the woman's face.

"You'll be all right, Eshaal," she murmured, hoping she was pronouncing her name correctly. "We'll take good care of you."

The woman's eyelids fluttered then lifted for a moment, before wearily closing again.

As she ministered as best she could to the patient, Sara was suddenly struck with a disturbing thought.

She had no way to know how Farhan would react to being volunteered to operate. It wasn't something she'd given a moment's thought to. In her eyes, it was the right thing to do.

But would he feel the same way?

Dread swamped her, making her hands tremble as she wrung out the cloth again. Despite earlier reveling in the heat, now the sultry air suddenly seemed so oppressive she could hardly catch her breath. When brisk footsteps heralded Farhan's arrival, nausea threatened, and Sara swallowed thickly against it, afraid of revealing her weakness in front of strangers.

In front of him.

"Sara, you wanted to see me?"

Why did he have to sound so grim, so terrifying, most of the time?

Gathering all her courage, she turned to face him and, hoping he wouldn't notice the sheen of perspiration on her forehead, lifted her chin.

"Yes. I think you should examine this patient."

Farhan's expression didn't change, but his gaze sharpened. Without taking his eyes off Sara, he stepped farther into the cubicle to pick up Eshaal's chart.

"Oh?"

He looked down to read the notations and Sara almost gasped with the relief of being released from the hold of those deep, inscrutable eyes. Taking a deep breath, she decided to go all in.

"I've asked for an anesthesiologist to be called and an operating room be prepared for you, since they've been unable to contact the surgeon on call."

"Oh, that won't be necessary." Sara had been so focused on Farhan she hadn't paid any attention to the other man, who she now assumed was the director, Dr. Andrade. "I'm sure the on-call surgeon will be found soon enough, Your Highness."

"Will he?" Farhan asked, his deep voice quiet but with what sounded like a dangerous tone to Sara. "It says here that Dr. Patel made these notes three hours ago. Is that accurate, Dr. Patel?"

Poor Dr. Patel looked from Farhan to Dr. Andrade and back again, his Adam's apple bobbing convulsively a few times, before he answered, "Yes, Your Highness."

"And there's been no response from the surgeon?"

Farhan had replaced the chart and moved to Eshaal's bedside, beginning his examination.

"No, sir."

Kadiah slipped back into the cubicle and Sara raised her eyebrows, sending her a questioning look. The nurse nodded in reply.

Farhan spoke gently to the pain-racked woman as he palpated her stomach. Then he straightened.

"Has Mrs. Saleem signed the consent form?"

"Yes, sir," Dr. Patel replied. "And her husband is waiting outside to hear from the surgeon too."

"As soon as the anesthesiologist arrives and is ready, I'll operate. Does anyone know when he or she'll be here?"

Kadiah spoke up. "Dr. Tam is on call, sir, and Dr. Patel had already put her on notice that she'd be needed, so she'll be here in about ten minutes."

"Thank you. I just need to make a phone call and speak to my wife, then I'll go and scrub in."

Sara's heart raced, her anxiety ratcheting up a notch. All she could hope was that he wasn't too upset, and wouldn't tear a strip off her where anyone could hear. She didn't think he would. More likely he'd be cold and cutting, but that would be just as bad.

"You can use my office, Sir."

Dr. Andrade made the offer but Farhan, who had already taken out his cellphone, just shook his head.

"Thank you, but I think the verandah will be fine. Sara?"

She preceded him back through the ward to the open doors leading to the wraparound balcony. There was one corner, near a set of stairs, that seemed to offer a bit of privacy, so she made a beeline there.

If she was going to get a talking-to, she wanted as few people as possible to overhear.

Farhan was saying into the phone, "Kavan, sorry to bother you so soon after you got home, but could you pick up Princess Sara at the hospital and take her back to the palace? Thank you… I'll let her know."

As he touched the screen to hang up, he said in a distant tone, "Kavan will be here to pick you up in about twenty minutes."

"Okay," she muttered, braced for whatever would come next.

Farhan's eyebrows dipped together. "What's wrong?"

Might as well get it out in the open, and take whatever he had to say on the chin.

"I'm sorry for putting you on the spot like that. I didn't think it through. It's just that she's going to die if nothing gets done soon."

The words were rushed, and little more than a strained whisper through a throat tight with stress. Farhan's frown deepened, and her heart sank. Putting her hands behind her back, she clasped her fingers together and squeezed, hard, using the pain to center herself.

Farhan's expression lightened, and he shook his head. "I was angry with you earlier when you rushed into the stampede, and I'm upset with the surgeon who's missing in action. I'm even annoyed that no one told me about this patient sooner, but I'm definitely not angry with you. You did the right thing."

Relief arced through her, making her scalp tingle and her legs wobbly. Why it was so strong, she didn't know, but she was forced to turn away so he couldn't see the moisture gathering in her eyes.

She heard his footsteps approaching, but wasn't prepared for the weight of his arm across her shoulders, or the safety and contentment the gesture immediately brought. When he bent his head and placed his lips close to her ear, Sara stiffened, not with surprise but in an effort to suppress the shiver creeping up her spine.

"I know we don't know each other as well as we could, but never doubt that my first responsibility is to the people of Kalyana. It is my duty to do all I can for them, and that includes using my medical training."

His arm tightened around her shoulders for an instant, and goosebumps fired along her arms and up her torso.

"If anything," he continued softly, "I should apologize to you."

"Wh-what for?"

"For leaving you to face my family alone this evening. There's no way I'll get finished in Theatre in time for dinner, but thank goodness it's not formal, just my parents, Maazin, and some close family friends."

It was daunting, just the type of situation that should send her anxiety levels through the roof and have her ulcer burning, and yet...

"Your parents are a little scary, especially your father, but somehow I'm not too worried."

"Really?"

The touch of humor in his voice made her smile.

"Maybe because of our arrangement, I know it doesn't really matter whether your parents like or approve of me or not," she replied, recognizing the truth in that statement.

And wondering why, then, *Farhan's* approval meant so much!

King Uttam had a favorite phrase.

Punctuality is imperative.

He was also known to elaborate on this philosophy.

"If you are five minutes early, you are already ten minutes late."

The King didn't make those statements lightly. In

fact, each of his sons had, at one time or another, been on the receiving end of a lecture, or gone without supper, for being tardy.

In the palace the standing rule was: if you are not going to be on time, do not turn up at all, as you will not be welcome.

Normally Farhan adhered to that rule, because although he was no longer the young, awestruck boy who feared his father, it was just simpler. As an adult he recognized his mother's discomfiture when his father made cutting remarks and the atmosphere turned cold, and tried to spare her when he could.

So on the few occasions he had to miss a family gathering because he was in the operating room, Farhan stayed away.

Tonight, however, was different.

Sara deserved his attendance, even though she'd assured him she'd be fine.

Even if his late arrival had the potential to make King Uttam apoplectic.

Having showered and changed into dinner clothes, Farhan strode into the dining room, a determined smile on his face.

The assembled group was already having dessert, and silence fell, as though no one could believe his temerity. Cheerfully he greeted his parents, their friends, and Maazin, before walking directly to Sara. He bent and kissed her cheek, and she stiffened slightly, although she didn't pull away. Probably he should've made the salutation brief, but he instead let his mouth linger for a moment longer than necessary, enjoying the soft warmth beneath his lips.

"How did the operation go?" she murmured.

"It went well. She has a long road ahead, but I'm assured she'll recover fully."

The smile she gave him more than made up for his father's glower.

"I'm afraid you're too late for dinner, Farhan." There was no doubt about the annoyance and command in his father's voice.

"That's fine, Father. They kindly fed me at the hospital. I would, however, love some of that trifle."

For a second he thought his father was going to tell him it would not be allowed, but when the King merely frowned before taking another bite of his own dessert, the butler hurried to bring a serving of trifle for Farhan.

"Are you sure you've had enough to eat? There must be some lamb left, if you're still hungry," said Sara.

Not a surprised silence now, but one of shock at her egregious breach of protocol—although Farhan doubted Sara noticed. She was completely focused on *him*, the concern in her dark eyes filling him with joy and the kind of tenderness he'd never thought himself capable of. There was a spluttering sound from Maazin's direction—probably a stifled laugh—but Farhan couldn't tear his gaze from Sara's. Tingling warmth spread through his belly and up his spine.

"Anyone who is late to my table does not get fed."

His father's cold words thankfully broke the spell. Sara blinked, then turned her attention to the King. Farhan expected her to blush, or stammer, the way she did when he spoke to her, but, instead, she just smiled faintly.

"And no doubt that discipline was instrumental in your sons becoming the men they are now. I wish my parents had been stricter with us, for just that reason."

Farhan snapped his head around so fast to see his father's reaction it was surprising he didn't get whiplash. Yet what was truly shocking was watching Uttam's lips twitch at the corners.

"Perhaps the first time I've ever heard a child say such a thing about their parents." Looking down at his trifle, the King continued. "Farhan, Maazin, I suggest that you listen carefully to everything Sara says from now on. She's obviously extremely intelligent and may even be a good influence on you."

They all stared at him, Farhan wondering who this man smiling down into his pudding was, and where his father had disappeared to.

Then his mother giggled, the sound so unexpected, so sweet Farhan found himself joining in. Sara lost it next, with Maazin and his parents' guests following right after, until the entire dining room rang with laughter.

It was like being in a dream, surreal. Especially when he looked at his father and found him still smiling into his beard.

Uttam had never been particularly congenial, and what vestige of humor he'd once possessed had seemed to have died with Ali.

To see him like this was a revelation...

And a relief.

Somehow the woman sitting across from him, her face glowing with humor, had already made a huge change in all their lives.

Especially his.

Now all he had to figure out was why she exerted such a pull on him, and how he could resist.

CHAPTER SIX

DINNER WAS A lot less stressful than she'd expected, but Sara knew part of that was her own attitude toward the entire royalty issue.

Frankly she couldn't give a hoot about whether they could trace their lineage back a thousand years, or that they ruled an entire—albeit small—country. If her parents had successfully taught her anything, it was that everyone deserved the same respect.

That attitude was coming in mighty handy just about now. But although she was fine with treating King Uttam as though he were her elderly next-door neighbor, and Maazin like a brother, she couldn't get over her hyper-awareness of Farhan.

From the moment he'd walked in her calm had all but deserted her, leaving instead a tingle dancing just under her skin. Knowing he was putting on a show for the others when he kissed her cheek didn't stop her heart from jumping, or her traitorous body from wanting to melt at his feet.

Telling herself it was just because he was so incredibly handsome didn't help, or even ring true. While they were different in appearance, some people would say Maazin was even more attractive than Farhan, but Sara's pulse didn't race when she saw him. Electricity didn't spark through her system, neither did sexual tension tighten her nerves.

No, Maazin did nothing for her in that regard, whereas Farhan made her think thoughts so naughty she was sure her cheeks were constantly aflame whenever he was around.

She'd never had anyone affect her that way before, and she wasn't sure how to handle it. Ignoring it would probably be the best thing, but there was no way to stop her visceral reaction to his scent, his nearness, his dark, often mysterious gaze.

Even now, hours later, she could easily recall the sensation of those gorgeous lips on her cheek and the memory made her nipples tighten, warmth filling her belly.

Thankfully, when they cited their long day and said goodnight to the older couples, leaving them to their after-dinner cocktails, Maazin excused himself too.

"I'll walk with you," he said, as they exited the sitting room, not into the corridor but onto the verandah outside.

"Going out this evening?" Farhan asked.

Maazin gave him a strange look, one that Sara couldn't decipher.

"No, I have some paperwork to finish up. I thought I'd go back to my office and get it done."

"All work and no play..."

Maazin just shook his head and bent to kiss Sara's cheeks.

"Goodnight, little sister, and most annoying older brother."

"What was that all about?" Sara asked, as Maazin strode off toward the east wing, where she supposed his office was located.

Farhan didn't answer immediately, just took her hand

and tucked it into the crook of his arm, to lead her along the softly lit walkway.

Thinking he wasn't going to answer, she tried to ignore the heat of arousal building in her body by looking out over the extensive parklands stretching away from the palace. Beautifully landscaped, they sloped down into a small valley and gleamed softly in the light of the waxing, gibbous moon rising beyond the distant hills. A lovely floral aroma wafted on the warm breeze, but it wasn't enough to mask Farhan's masculine scent, which went straight to Sara's head like a shot of rum.

"Maazin has no social life, hasn't had one for years. He's a workaholic, getting old before his time, trying to make up for something I, personally, believe he should forgive himself for."

"What did he do?" Perhaps now she'd learn what that sadness was she saw in Maazin's gaze when he thought no one was looking.

Farhan moved her hand from his elbow and, instead, entwined his fingers with hers, linking them in a way that intensified the intimacy of their conversation.

"He was a hell raiser when he was young, and fell in with a bad crowd. One night he went to a party out in the countryside, got drunk and fell asleep. When he woke up, his friends had left him. He walked far enough to get cell signal and called our brother, Ali, asking him to come and get him. I think he knew if he called one of the guards, or anyone else, they'd tell Father what had happened, but Ali always looked out for us."

She knew what was coming, wished she didn't have to hear it.

"They got into an accident on the way home. Ali and his wife, Chandni, who'd gone with him, were killed instantly, while Maazin only had a badly dislocated shoulder."

"I'm so sorry, Farhan."

He squeezed her fingers. "Don't feel badly. It was a long time ago, and it's time Maazin got past it."

Yet, even with his factual recitation and acknowledgement of Maazin's pain, she knew his brother wasn't the only one still adversely affected. She'd only just met them, but she was sure it explained so much she'd already noticed. The way the family interacted, as though each inhabited a bubble the others could see through but never penetrate.

"Easier said than done, I should think. The same for the rest of you too. You were away when it happened?"

Now he stopped to rest his back against the balustrade, turning her so she stood in front of him, their fingers still linked. Though he made no move to urge her closer, Sara wanted to lean into him, the magnetic pull she always felt suddenly overwhelmingly strong.

His face was partially shadowed, but his gaze still easily snagged and held hers.

"I was in med school, in Sydney. I came back as soon as I could, expecting to have to stay and take up where Ali left off, even though I was already working toward my fellowship."

There was a sense of having to tread gently, but he had brought it up, so she asked the obvious.

"Why didn't you stay?"

His lips thinned for an instant, then he replied, "My father said it wasn't necessary; told me to go and complete my surgical training."

It had hurt him. She didn't know how she knew, but she was sure of it.

"You all must have been grieving so horribly then.

Shock and pain make people say things, make decisions they might not have otherwise." Here in the moonlight, it was easy to open up to him. "When my grandpa died, my mother's family pretty much imploded for a while."

His gaze was searching.

"What happened? Was your *nonni* heartbroken?"

The sound she instinctively made was derisive, and she regretted it as soon as it came out. She'd tried to make peace with her feelings for Nonni, but obviously she hadn't succeeded.

"No, although she was the source of the rifts that opened up. You see, she'd run off and left Grandpa and her three children something like twenty years before. No one knew where she was in all that time, until she turned up one day at Aunt Jackie's, asking if she could stay with her to recover from a bad motorcycle accident. Aunt Jackie didn't know what to do. She didn't want to be disloyal to Grandpa but, being the youngest— she was only six when Nonni took off—she wasn't as angry, I guess, as Mom or my Uncle Ed.

"Plus, Aunt Jackie's marriage had just ended. It was a bad time for her, and she ended up taking Nonni in, after getting Grandpa's blessing. About six months later, Grandpa had a massive heart attack, a widow-maker, and that's when things fell apart."

She could still remember it, as though it had happened the day before. Uncle Ed shouting that Aunt Jackie had broken Grandpa's heart by taking Nonni in; Nonni making things worse by not staying out of it.

"What happened?"

Sara shook her head, trying to push the memories back.

"My uncle blamed Nonni and Aunt Jackie for

Grandpa's death, and said he was done with the family. Never wanted to see any of us again."

Farhan squeezed her fingers.

"How old were you?"

"Eight, almost nine." She inhaled, then let the air out in a rush. "It was pretty traumatic, to be honest. There was a lot of dirty laundry aired, and a lot of mean things said. For about a year Mom didn't speak to Nonni or Aunt Jackie either, and it took Uncle Ed five, maybe six years to speak to either of his siblings again."

"Did your grandmother at least try to smooth things over?"

"That isn't her way, or wasn't before she developed dementia. She was the type of person who said whatever she wanted, and damn the consequences. I think she enjoyed making people angry. At least I'm sure that wasn't your father's intention when he said what he said to you."

Farhan's lips firmed into a hard line, but then they relaxed again into a sad smile.

"Ali was...special. The perfect son. The best of brothers. I think, when Father told me to go back, I used it as an excuse to not try to fill Ali's shoes, because I knew I couldn't. Not in a million years. Staying away was easy after that."

But why hadn't his father asked him to come back or, as she suspected would be more King Uttam's way, commanded him? Sara suspected Farhan thought it was because, in King Uttam's eyes too, he wasn't worthy to take his brother's place.

"I'm sure Ali was special, but you have so much to offer Kalyana too. Maybe what you bring to the table is different, but don't sell yourself short."

Farhan didn't reply, just stared at her for a long

moment. The air between them seemed infused with electricity, so the fine hairs on Sara's arms lifted, and, although she felt suddenly shy, she couldn't look away.

Then he turned his head, as though looking out over the gardens, and when he looked back at her, her breath hitched in her throat, although she didn't know why.

Swinging her hand back and forth, he asked, "I meant to ask you earlier: are you comfortable with our suite? There are many others we could move to, if you aren't."

She shook her head, surprised at the sudden change in topic. "You're kidding, right? It's beautiful."

And it was, although to call it a suite was damning it with faint praise. It was like a house within the palace, complete with a central courtyard where a fountain played the soothing sounds of splashing water. Huge rooms, decorated in keeping with the rest of the palace, had creamy marble floors offset by lush carpets and intricate decorative painting on the walls. Touches of turquoise, gold, and red turned the living area into a feast for the eyes, and her bedroom had literally taken her breath away when she'd first seen it.

All white and gold, with fuchsia accents, it was the most feminine yet restful room she'd ever seen. The bed was a huge four-poster, draped with sheer panels, while gold-framed mirrors lined one wall.

She still hadn't gotten over the bathroom, with its mosaic tiles and sunken tub either.

Farhan lifted one shoulder, in an abbreviated shrug.

"That one is old-fashioned. It hasn't been updated in decades. There are others more modern, if you'd prefer."

"No. Seriously, I love it. Please, can we stay there?"

He chuckled, reaching out to smooth a little curl of hair off her cheek, and replied, "Of course."

When had she moved so close to him? The thought had hardly entered her mind when he gently tugged her closer yet. Near enough that the heat of his body touched her like a caressing hand, and his mouthwatering scent completely filled her head.

Part of her wanted to step forward and experience the thrill of his muscular body against hers, but the saner part of her had her stiffening, stepping back. She could only go so far, however, since he was still holding her hand.

"You have to get used to my touching you."

There was no amusement in his voice, just a deep, velvety tone that made her legs tremble and heat flow out from her core.

"I—I don't see w-why."

Good grief. She hadn't stammered since she'd been in fourth grade, but whenever Farhan got too close her tongue refused to co-operate.

"We're married, Sara. If we're to make people believe it's true, you can't pull away every time I touch you."

"I—I d-don't!"

His free hand came up to skim her arm, a gentle, evocative brush of fingers, his thumb finding the ultra-sensitive inner flesh. An intense flash of yearning raked her, and she jerked.

"See?"

"You startled me."

How absurd to be proud of not stammering, of holding up her head when she wanted to duck and hide.

"Come here. Let me startle you a little more."

She should resist, not let herself be drawn in, physically and figuratively. Her experience with men was limited.

Okay, pretty much non-existent. One abbreviated

love affair in med school, which had ended when the guy decided she spent too much time and energy on her family, hadn't prepared her for Farhan Alaoui.

There was no way she could tangle with him and not get severely emotionally injured, especially knowing this was all a ruse to him. A joke played on his father, and the world.

Yet, when he gently tugged, she went to him, the motion as natural as breathing, swallowing.

Living.

His arms went around her, not too tightly, just enough to bring their bodies into soft alignment, and she forgot how to breath or swallow.

But, oh, she was instantly, completely, fully alive for the first time.

His hard frame shouldn't be so comfortable or his grip evoke such safety, even as arousal swirled through her, tangling up her common sense, blurring her reasoning capabilities. How had she never known a hug could be so glorious, leave her desire-struck, melting inside, even as every sense sharpened almost painfully, so she could soak in his every nuance?

"Did I tell you how beautiful you look tonight?"

That had her stiffening again, need draining away, leaving her bereft and damp-eyed, wanting to step back but not wanting him to see her silly tears.

"Don't, please."

But he wasn't so easily dissuaded.

"Don't, what? Tell you how lovely you look? Why not?"

There were no easy answers to his questions, only prevarications or self-pitying proclamations about long ago having accepted her own plainness. If she was honest, she would stay right where she was for as long as possible, and listen to him lie about her beauty as much as he wanted.

Yet she was a pragmatist. There had never been a time when she'd been able to avoid or evade reality, and this wasn't a good time to start. But she stayed where she was, taking the crumbs of intimacy he offered, too weak to pull away.

Hiding as best she could, even as she stated the brutal truth.

"I don't need you to tell me things like that, Farhan. I know I'm no beauty, and even these gorgeous clothes can't turn a sow's ear into a silk purse."

The sound he made was one she didn't recognize, and she didn't expect his arms to pull her closer yet, bringing her flush against him, from their hips to their torsos.

"Oh!"

"Yes," he murmured, bending so the word whispered over her ear, making her shiver, a little moan rising in her throat. "Does that reassure you I'm not lying?"

Did it?

Sara had no brain power left to work it out, not with his erection resting against her belly, his breath rushing hard against her cheek, one hand sliding over her back, the other coming up to cup the back of her head.

He kissed her cheek, but there was nothing casual or cursory about the movement. It was, instead, as though he tasted her, explored each millimeter as he went, his lips seemingly learning things about her she somehow divined on a cellular level.

Like how to arouse her, to fill her with mindless lust, so that when his mouth reached hers, she was ready to accept whatever he had to offer.

Fingers thrust into her hair, he tilted her head back and paused, their lips only a breath apart.

"Sara." There was a question in her name, and she wasn't sure what he was asking, her cognitive abilities impaired by his nearness. Her need. "Sara, may I kiss you?"

How could those words make her want him even more than she already did?

"Yes."

It whispered from her lips onto his, acceptance and surrender all in one.

He kissed her slowly, gently, his lips brushing hers, coaxing, playing. She lost track of time, forgot her fears about her inexperience, instinct guiding her to open to him, to taste him as he tasted her.

Farhan groaned, deepening the kiss. They were fused together, her fingers clutching the back of his jacket, desperately seeking an anchor in a world gone haywire beneath her feet. Those same fingers longed to know what his sleek, hot skin felt like, just as the rest of her body yearned to find out too.

When his lips left hers to travel down to her throat, she could hardly stand, her entire body trembling, aching for him.

"You're delicious."

The words rumbled into her flesh, and a rushed sound of assent rose in her throat, blocking it, rendering her unable to reply.

Her head dipped of its own accord, giving him complete access, and he took full advantage of her compliance. With lips and tongue and teeth, he brought every nerve ending to sparking, shivering life.

A sound came from below, the echo of footsteps, the quiet drone of conversation. Sara hardly registered it, but Farhan slowly raised his head, a sigh whispering between them.

The sudden distance between their bodies came as a surprise, and it was only Farhan's hands on her shoulders that stopped her from swaying, perhaps even falling.

"That went further than I planned." His voice was cool, and she wondered how he went from the heat of passion to his usual icy self so swiftly, when she could still hardly catch her breath. "But don't worry. It won't happen again."

How to respond to that, when everything inside her wanted more of his kisses?

Luckily, she didn't have to reply as he continued, "I like you, and now you know I'm physically attracted to you, but our situation could get…messy if we aren't careful."

Not sure what he meant, she repeated, "Messy?"

His chin tilted up in that way it so often did. "Yes, as all relationships do when there is emotion involved."

Ah. He was afraid she'd fall for him and get silly. Knowing that steadied her, and gave her a jolt of moxie too. She replied in as light a tone as she could manage, "I wouldn't worry too much about that. I can't speak for you, but I've no interest in getting emotionally entangled. With all I go through with my family, I have enough of that in my life as it is."

Farhan nodded slowly, and offered her his arm as he turned toward their suite. "I should have known you were too sensible not to understand."

All Sara could do was walk alongside him, willing her still trembling legs not to let her down and wondering why hearing herself described that way annoyed her the way it did.

CHAPTER SEVEN

THE FOLLOWING FEW days were a whirlwind of activity, and Farhan watched Sara manage it all with commendable aplomb.

The day after their dinner with his parents, he'd gone to the hospital to check on his patient first thing in the morning, and then there was an official reception in the palace gardens, followed far too swiftly by a state dinner.

"Your wife is making quite an impression on everyone," Maazin commented to him at the garden party. "She's very charming, in her quiet, easy way. Just as you are, when you aren't playing Crown Prince."

Ignoring his brother's jab, Farhan replied, "She's a born giver. I'll have to make sure no one takes advantage of her."

"Well," Maazin said, laughter in his voice, "Glaring at the people she's speaking to will definitely do the trick."

Realizing he probably did look rather fierce, Farhan forced himself to adopt a neutral expression just as Sara glanced back and gave him a smile. Something inside him softened, and he couldn't help smiling back.

The night before she'd taken his statement about not wanting to get tangled up in emotion well, yet now he wondered if he weren't the one who needed the warning. The taste and feel of her were indelibly locked into his memory, and he wanted more of both. But the danger of forging emotional ties with her wasn't something he wanted to contemplate.

Yet later, seeing Sara in the soft pink sari-inspired ball gown she'd donned for the dinner, which hugged her luscious curves in all the right ways, was another revelation. It made him want to turn her around and take her somewhere private, not share her with the world.

It was, he reassured himself, just physical attraction. All his energy had to be channeled into his position, the work he was trying to do for his country. Sara would be gone in a short time, but Kalyana would continue on, and he had to be prepared to lead her into the future.

On Sunday, they were expected to attend church in the cathedral and afterwards had another round of official visits and introductions. As he explained to Sara, it was better to get it all over with as soon as possible, rather than stretch it out over a couple of weeks.

"If we did that, I'd get no work done at all."

"That makes complete sense, especially since I'm looking forward to going back to the hospital and seeing what I can do to help out."

She'd seemed understanding, but he'd also seen the fatigue in her eyes, and the way she locked her fingers together when she thought no one was watching. Hopefully being back in a medical setting would alleviate some of her stress.

He knew he should be as aloof as possible with her, yet her warmth and genuine personality made him also not want to hurt her in any way. There was no mistaking how she fractionally withdrew each time he forced himself to be cool with her and, strangely, it hurt him too.

Yet it also reinforced the knowledge of his own short-comings, the part of his character so reminiscent of his father. The ability to pull away from people, to lock away his emotions, become cold and clinical. She deserved better, even in a pretend husband, but Farhan wasn't prepared to open himself up to the danger of caring too much for her, only to have to send her away.

On the other hand, Sara was, in some ways, irresistible. Okay, in many ways. If they were separated during official functions, he found himself in her orbit, keeping an eye on her, moving closer and closer, until he was back by her side.

And when she smiled at him in seeming relief, the sensation of being her champion filled him with warmth.

And desire.

Desire she seemed to share.

Walking back to their apartments, she said, "It's so interesting meeting all these people, hearing their stories. Everyone I've spoken to seems very happy to have you back in the country and so engaged."

Her words shouldn't please him so much, but they did. However, he was cautious in his reply. "I doubt anyone would tell you otherwise, Sara. After all, you're my wife."

Her hand on his arm stopped him in mid-step, and when he turned to face her, the earnest expression on her face was arresting.

"Farhan, as a doctor, don't you know when your patients are skirting the truth? Like when you ask how much they drink, or smoke, and they give you an answer, but just from their demeanor you know it's probably more?"

"Yes." It was indeed something he'd learned to watch for.

"Well, it's something I'm very good at, and I can usually tell when someone's telling the truth or just schmoozing. You have nothing to worry about when it comes to whether you're appreciated here or not."

There was such sincerity in her voice, her soft gaze, he found himself stepping closer, his heart unusually light. Lighter than it had been in a very long time. Perhaps since the night he'd heard of his brother's death.

"Your Highness," he murmured, teasing in his tone. "If you're not careful, you'll turn my head, saying things like that."

And his heart raced when she blushed.

Irresistible, in all ways.

Leaning against the wall, so she knew she could step away if she wanted to, he eased her warm body into his arms.

She didn't pull away but wrapped her arms around his neck, although she murmured, "Farhan, someone might see."

Sliding his lips close to her ear, he whispered, "See me kissing my wife? I think that's acceptable."

"In the hallway?" Her question came out in a rush, her voice breathy, hopefully from the sensation of his teeth gently playing with her earlobe.

He searched for her lips, halted with his a millimeter away from her sweet, seductive mouth.

"We're the Crown Prince and Princess. We can kiss wherever we like."

Then he put action to his words, tasting and sipping until she opened for him, their kisses getting deeper and deeper, until he knew he had to stop, lest he drown. Seeing her flushed, her eyes gleaming, lips damp, was almost his undoing. It took him close to forgetting his finer instincts, his need close to pain.

Drawing away, putting a stop to it, was far more difficult than he liked, and turning the conversation back to safe, boring topics took everything he had. But it had to be done, for his own safety and sanity.

On Monday, he came out of his bedroom after another restless night where his dreams were bedeviled with images of Sara, to find her already up, dressed and ready to go.

"You're going to the hospital this morning, right?"

"Yes," he replied, sitting at the breakfast table and smiling his thanks to the young woman pouring his coffee.

"Good. I'm coming with you. There's no way I'm sitting around here all day with nothing to do."

Even if he wanted to gainsay her, the smile lighting her face when he nodded would have changed his mind.

As soon as she entered the hospital there was a flurry of excitement, which she quelled with a few calm, well-chosen words.

"I'm here to work, not disrupt anything. Take me up to the director's office and let's figure out where best I can help."

That was the last he saw of her, except for glimpses of her hurrying off down corridors, totally unaware of him staring after her, wondering why the hospital, which had been a refuge for him, now felt like a jail.

Then his father called, catching Farhan in his office just before he went in to operate on a young man with a diaphragmatic hernia, and demanded their presence at dinner.

Clearly Farhan wasn't the only person fascinated

with Sara. In the year since he'd been home, they'd established a routine of family dinners once every two weeks. Of course, he saw his parents at other times, and his brother almost every day, but to be summoned again so soon made Farhan wonder what his father was up to.

Ali's wife had been the child of a wealthy Indian businessman who was one of Uttam's oldest friends, and the match had been conceived between the fathers and dutifully carried out by the children. She'd been used to a far grander, more cosmopolitan life than Kalyana could offer, but Ali had been devoted to his position, determined to assure his father the throne would be in safe hands after his death. Chandni had accepted that, and had set out to make a place for herself in Kalyana, although she had never been as hands-on as Sara seemed determined to be.

Queen Aruna had loved Chandni, and she and her daughter-in-law had taken trips together to Dubai, Milan, Paris, and London to shop and enjoy the bright lights. His mother had been devastated by the loss of Ali and Chandni. She'd never been the same. An air of sadness enveloped her even ten years later, and she'd become reclusive, the world outside the palace seemingly holding no interest for her anymore.

Sara wasn't like Ali's wife, who'd been worldly and supremely elegant, and Farhan hoped she didn't suffer by any comparisons.

As he'd suffered from being compared to Ali.

Before going to surgery, he went looking for Sara to tell her about his father's invitation, or command, depending on how one chose to look at it. He found her in the clinical area, where non-emergency patients came for treatment.

"You're lucky this wasn't worse, but because of how

it happened, I'll be prescribing antibiotics. Are you allergic to any medications?"

Even over the hubbub of the clinic, his ears picked up her soft, calm voice immediately, and he drifted toward the cubicle it was coming from.

"No, Your Highness."

The curtains weren't pulled closed, so he peeped in, glimpsing Sara stitching a gash on an elderly woman's leg. Then he stepped back so as not to be noticed, leaning on the wall across from the cubicle to wait for her to finish.

"Will your son or daughter-in-law be able to help you for a few days? You should stay off this leg as much as possible to give it a chance to heal. And I want you to come back and get the bandages changed for at least three days, so we can make sure it's healing properly and there's no infection."

As he listened to her instruct the patient, interjecting little comments that made the elderly lady laugh, he was struck by the way she connected so easily with the other woman. It was apparent she'd learned a lot about the patient's situation in their time together, not just a medical history and information about her immediate ailment. Farhan liked to think he had a pleasant bedside manner, but now he wondered if it was as sorely lacking as he was beginning to think.

Realizing Sara was finishing up with her patient, he moved over to the nurses' desk, so neither of the women exiting the cubicle would realize he'd been eavesdropping.

They both saw him as Sara helped the limping lady toward the waiting area, and the elderly patient whispered something to Sara that had her blushing and saying, "Hush, you!"

Her patient laughed, and paused to greet Farhan in traditional Kalyanese fashion, her palms together, head bowed.

Before he could offer his assistance, a younger woman came hurrying over and, with much bowing and thanks, the patient was helped on her way.

Sara stripped off her gloves and tossed them into the nearest medical waste receptacle.

"Took a fishhook to the thigh, poor soul. And she's diabetic, too."

It seemed she'd been avoiding looking at him, but suddenly faced him head on, a frown between her brows. "I gave her a prescription for antibiotics. Do you think she'll be able to fill it? I can see she's not terribly wealthy. Is there another way I should have handled that?"

Totally unprofessional to want to hug her in the middle of the clinic, but that's exactly the urge Farhan had to fight.

"No," he replied, shoving his hands into his pockets so they wouldn't embarrass him and grab her. "It should be fine. The government has a subsidy program in place for medications and if she can't pay the rest, there are other programs for that too. I think you'll find the patients who can't afford it will say so, because often they can get the drugs free here in the hospital dispensary before they go, and they want the voucher immediately."

The palpable relief on her face made a flash of warmth fire along his spine, and he quickly told her about his father's invitation, and hightailed it back to his office.

Putting thoughts of anything other than his patient out of his mind was imperative before going into the operating theatre, but it wasn't as easy as usual. His wife had a very unsettling effect on him. One he knew had to be curbed, for both their sakes.

Scrubbing in, he went over the upcoming surgery in his head. The patient lived on a small island forty-five minutes away from the capital, accessible by private boat or public ferry. Unfortunately he'd ignored his symptoms for a while, thinking he had a gastrointestinal ailment, but after four days of vomiting and beginning to have trouble breathing, he'd gone to the local clinic. X-rays had shown an anomaly in the left thoracic cavity, and the doctor had told him to make the crossing to the hospital in Huban.

Subsequent tests had revealed the presence of a Bochdalek hernia, strange in that those were usually congenital and the patient couldn't recall any trauma he'd suffered to explain its sudden development.

Farhan was glad, however, that it appeared, at this point, repairable by laparoscopic surgery. Of course, if once he got a look inside there was a sign that any of the displaced organs were gangrenous, they would have to open the patient up. Then what was normally a ninety-minute operation would be much longer.

As the nurse put on his gloves, Farhan found his mind drifting once more to Sara. The blush that had bloomed in her cheeks when the patient had whispered to her had him wondering what had been said.

"Your Highness, they're ready for you in the OR."

The nurse's quizzical tone brought him back to the moment, forced him to put it all from his mind as he shouldered his way through the swinging doors.

Perhaps his fascination would fade if they spent even more time together? Farhan couldn't decide if that would be the best or worst thing ever.

* * *

"Your Highnesses will make beautiful babies."

While busy in the clinic, Sara tried to put her patient's words out of her head but they lingered.

Farhan had made it clear there would be no intimacy between them, yet twice now he'd kissed her senseless. Mind you, immediately afterward, while she'd been trying to figure out up from down, he'd reverted to his usual autocratic self as though nothing had happened.

His blowing hot and cold was so confusing.

And Mrs. Ramakesh's comment had made her wonder something she'd not given any thought to before.

Wasn't one of Farhan's duties to produce an heir? Thinking about it, there was no doubt in her mind that Uttam was demanding one.

Was that why Farhan kept initiating intimate moments between them? Was the entire population of Kalyana watching and speculating about when she'd become pregnant?

His assertion about them having to be comfortable with each other to make their marriage seem real had made sense at the time, but now she questioned his motives.

And his kisses hadn't made her more comfortable. If anything, her awareness of him, already intense, had been heightened. She'd tossed and turned for the last few nights, reliving each moment, every touch of his hands, lips, tongue. Just thinking of it now made her temperature rise and tingling, needy warmth trail through her body.

As a doctor, she knew her physiological reactions were normal. After all, there was nothing wrong with her libido; no trauma in her past to give her a psychological fear of sex. Yet it had never been terribly important to her either. She'd been too darned busy studying, working, and trying to keep her family afloat to give it much headspace. The one relationship she'd thought might lead to intimacy had died on the vine, a casualty of her complicated life, and she'd put that aspect of life on hold.

And it might have stayed that way until she'd opened her front door and seen Farhan standing on the other side.

Now desire infiltrated any brain cell not otherwise occupied, which seemed to be far too many of them. Work usually completely consumed her, but although she was fully engaged in the jobs at hand, doing whatever came her way with customary care, Farhan was constantly on her mind.

And what had been the expression on his face earlier, when he'd told her about his father's invitation to dinner? One moment he'd seemed pleasant, approachable, the next closed off, looking down that arrogant nose at her. It was horribly confusing, and just one more reason not to trust that his kisses stemmed only from attraction.

Confrontation wasn't in her comfort zone when it came to personal matters, but by the end of the day she realized that speaking to Farhan about the matter of an heir was imperative. For her own peace of mind, if nothing else.

So, on the drive home, while they were alone, she took a deep breath and said, "I get the feeling we're under scrutiny, everyone watching to see if I get pregnant. I hope that wasn't part of your plan in marrying me."

The look he slanted her from the driver's seat was so autocratic it almost made her courage flee.

"It was not." There was no mistaking the steel in his voice. "I have no plans to procreate with you, or anyone else."

Shocked, she turned in the seat so as to better see his face. "Why not? Well, I know why not with me, but why not with anyone else, after our marriage is over?"

"Being ruler of Kalyana is a full-time, twenty-four-seven job. Fatherhood would have to take a backseat, and I don't think that's fair to a child."

His cool, controlled tone didn't fool her. Behind it was a shadow of pain, of rejection, and her heart ached for him. For the little boy, the young man she could somehow picture. The one who'd needed his father in a way the older man had been unable to fulfill.

She'd come to know Farhan, at least a little, over the time they'd spent together and couldn't, somehow, bear the thought of him going through life depriving himself of something she was positive he would excel at.

Carefully, trying to tread lightly, she replied, "Perhaps your reign will be different, because you're different from your father. I think you could be both an excellent father and King at the same time."

Farhan shrugged slightly, his eyes firmly on the road ahead. "My father is a good ruler, well respected and effective. I'd like to be the same."

"I have no doubt you will be, when the time comes, but what happens if you fall in love and the woman wants children?"

"Love doesn't come into the equation. I'm not even sure I'm capable of it, since I've never felt it, or sought it out. It's never been a part of my plan, since arranged marriages are traditional in my family. Once Ali died, I knew one day I'd enter into one, and since

I couldn't offer a real relationship, I made sure not to lead women on."

He'd shielded his heart, she thought, rather than risk having it broken by falling for someone and then having to let them go. Still intent on his profile, she contemplated the loneliness he must have felt, both as a youngster who'd just wanted his father, and as a man who didn't dare to love. She'd often felt an outsider, alone because of not knowing where, exactly, she came from. Now she realized that having the deepest of roots didn't make everything magically better. In fact, it could isolate you from the world even more.

She ached for him, wished she knew the right words to make him see how amazing he was, and make him believe it.

His eyes met hers, caught her staring. Trapped, she froze, her heart suddenly hammering. Then he looked back at the road, and she gazed down at her fingers, knotted in her lap, able to catch her breath again, although the air in the SUV felt thick.

Then Farhan broke the silence. "I've decided to push really hard on the idea of women's clinics across the kingdom, but I'm going to need your help."

Surprised, she glanced back up at him. "My help? In what way?"

He made the turn into the palace grounds, raising his hand to the soldier at the gate before he replied.

"I'm going to arrange a tour of the islands for us. We, you in particular, can speak to the women and get their input on what's actually needed. What they say will hopefully make it harder for the minister to keep putting it on the back burner."

That sounded innocuous enough. "You know I'll help however I can."

"Good," he replied, in that stern way he had of speaking.

Why, then, did her heart jump and her body tingle in anticipation?

CHAPTER EIGHT

THEIR PLAN, ACCORDING to Farhan, was to take three weeks or so, going from island to island, working their way from north to south. What she hadn't really considered was that they would be going alone, since usually they were constantly surrounded by people.

Yet here they were, just the two of them in an amphibious plane, heading to the northernmost island, Agung.

No Kavan.

Or Maazin.

Or even assistants Mara and Seth.

Just her and the man whose mere presence made her want to jump out of her skin. Whose large, capable hands were controlling the plane with ease and assurance, reminding her of how masterfully they'd held her.

It was still so confusing, though. He'd kissed her so passionately, yet otherwise kept a respectable distance, keeping her on edge, waiting, wanting to be intimate that way with him again. The memories of his kisses kept her awake at night, need a constant tingle in her veins, shaken to her soul with desire.

Worse was imagining what else they could do together, how it would feel to be skin to skin with Farhan, having her every need met.

"We'll be there in just under an hour."

His voice came through the headset she was wearing, the warm, rich tone raising goosebumps along her arms.

"Okay."

He seemed different once they got to the airport. More relaxed. Perhaps it was just being able to get out of the capital for a while, or out of his father's sphere.

King Uttam had commanded their appearance at dinner twice more during the preceding couple of weeks, and there was no mistaking the chill between the two men. Father and son had a distant way of interacting and Sara now had an idea of why, even as she realized where Farhan had inherited his arrogance.

Yet seeing him in that light didn't ring true to her anymore. What she'd ascribed to bone-deep haughtiness was overshadowed now by what she'd seen since they'd come to Kalyana. The way he spoke to his patients and the staff at the hospital, his interactions while doing his royal duties all spoke of a man deeply connected to and concerned about others.

If anything, seeing him that way made her want him more. How many times had she caught herself staring at his mouth, entranced and aroused? Thinking about it now had heat gathering in her belly, rising up to her cheeks, and she turned to look out over the azure water below so he wouldn't see her blush.

Over the last few days she'd found herself wondering if Farhan might not be the perfect man to gain some sexual experience with. After all, their temporary marriage was without all of the emotional baggage that could make a physical relationship messy, and at least now she knew he wasn't trying to seduce her in hopes of producing an heir.

On top of which, she had no intention of falling for

him, and after their talk had no fear he'd fall for her either. If he truly was interested in sleeping with her, why not give in to her own desire?

Her brain shied away from the thought, too exhausted to process it properly. Besides not sleeping well, it felt as though they were constantly on the go. Not that she minded working at the hospital. That, at least, brought some normality to her life. Practicing medicine was what she was born to do, and it made her happy to help people. But all the other stuff? Trying to remember the correct protocols, watching every word coming out of her mouth, every gesture she made? All that did was tire her out and give her tension headaches.

Not to mention the constant barrage of texts from Canada, none asking how she was doing but all wanting her to help or advise in some way. There was no let-up.

Farhan had told her she was doing well, but she knew she'd made some missteps. Caught between wanting to be herself and not embarrass Farhan, the strain was immense.

"Look over there," he said, pointing to the east, the motion of his hand wafting his compelling scent her way. "That's Patang, or Kite Island. It's not much more than a sand bar, but because of the reef on the western side it's a great place to swim, and on the east, if the conditions are right, you can surf."

"Why's it called Kite Island?" she asked, twisting slightly in her seat to get a better view. The water surrounding the part of the island she could see was a shade of aqua so intense it looked as though it had been enhanced digitally.

"It's roughly diamond-shaped, with the reef coming off one end like the tail of a kite. When we come back

I'll fly closer, so you can see. Actually, since we're not really on a tight agenda, we could go there."

"If you like," she replied, too tired to really care.

"It was one of our favorite places to go as children. Ali loved it, especially when the waves were high and he could surf. Believe it or not, my father was a good surfer too, and even my mother enjoyed a day at the beach."

Her ears pricked up. Here was a memory that seemed to belie his sense of his father having no time for his family. It was the first time he'd spoken of him in such a fond, reminiscent way.

"I can't imagine your father surfing."

He chuckled, then replied, "I'm not surprised, but remember, he grew up in Australia and was already surfing by the time he moved here."

She still couldn't picture it. "I can't even think of your father ever being a child, much less a surfer dude."

Farhan laughed. Not a chuckle but a full-on laugh. It was such a rare thing she wanted to watch him at it, but forced herself not to look. Except she could still see his reflection in the glass beside her, and realized she was already fixated on that.

"So he was more approachable when you were young?"

Amusement dropped from his face, and she regretted its fading as he replied, "Approachable isn't a word I'd ever use to describe my father, but he was a bit more… mellow…before my grandfather died and he took the throne."

"Perhaps he was patterning what he'd seen as a child. From what you said and I've read, your grandfather inherited a mess when Nargis died. He was probably consumed with trying to put the country to rights, without a lot of time to spare."

For a few moments the hum of the engines was the only sound in the cockpit, as Farhan fiddled with the controls.

Finally, he said, "That much is true. The country's finances were in a shambles, mostly because Nargis wouldn't stop spending money. She was a compulsive collector. Not to mention what she spent trying to find out what had happened to Bhaskar. My grandfather had to rebuild the economy in the face of staunch opposition from those who'd benefited from Nargis's rule. They didn't like it that he was trying to create a more egalitarian society."

"Were you close to your grandfather?" From her calculations, Farhan would have been about ten when his grandfather had died.

"Not really. He loved horses and playing polo, and I didn't, so we didn't have much in common. Ali was the one who was into those things."

Another male figure who'd shown Farhan little interest. No wonder he thought taking the throne would mean giving his children short shrift. She wasn't going to point that out, though, but maybe she could give him something to think about. Plant a seed in the hope it would flower into something good after she was gone.

Why did the thought of leaving make such a wave of sadness flood her?

Pushing her own feelings aside, she said, "Well, your grandfather and father had the worst of it, I think. Barring disaster, you're inheriting a far more stable country, in pretty good financial shape, thanks to them."

"That is true." Farhan sounded distant, almost disinterested. "And sound economic management isn't a trait many of the rulers before them had."

He seemed to want to turn the conversation away from the personal, and she followed his lead.

"Oh, but the royal family has had some hard knocks too, haven't they, over the years? Like the plane crash that killed five members. That must have been a horrible blow."

The look he gave her warmed her from head to toes, and all points in between, although she wasn't sure why.

"That's right. That happened just after the start of World War II. You really dove into the history of Kalyana, didn't you?"

"I—I have almost perfect recall of things I read." Why was she stuttering? God, she was so silly sometimes. "And it was interesting, trying to figure out how your family ended up inheriting the throne."

"Yes. The plane crash in 1940, then the war. The tradition of younger sons going into the army took its toll, with three Princes being killed between the two World Wars. Then there were a couple of Kings who didn't or couldn't procreate. By the time it got down to Nargis, the line of succession went to Bhaskar, and then to her sole surviving uncle. When Bhaskar disappeared, the uncle was already on his death bed, and the next in line, as crazy as it sounds, was my grandfather."

Sara sighed, thinking about what he'd said, that ache she'd carried in her heart all her life intensifying. "It must be nice to know your history that way, know exactly where you come from and how you ended up where you are."

The touch of his fingers on hers was a warm surprise and, unthinking, she turned her hand, linking them together.

"It's your history too, beautiful. You've found your place, your family's past to add to your own."

Something opened inside her, pain cracked wide by his words. She looked over at him. Farhan was smiling at her, his eyes warm and understanding.

Welcoming.

What he'd said was real and true, something she'd never thought, even after the DNA test, finding out about her biological father, or reading the history of the Kalyanese royal family. Until he'd said those words she'd been the perpetual outsider looking in. But now...

"Thank you," she whispered.

His eyes darkened, his smile faded. Sara's heart lurched, then raced, as his fingers tightened on hers, and dangerous sparks seemed to fill the air between them.

Then he turned back to the controls, letting go of her hand.

Trying to catch her breath, she looked down at her lap and her empty hand.

"Was it difficult for you, growing up as an adopted child?"

He asked it casually, as though giving her a chance to tell him to mind his own business. Funnily enough, she had no qualms about answering, even though it was a subject she usually avoided.

"For the most part, no," she replied. "You met my parents. They're great people and even when Mom had Mariah and Cyndi, they never treated me as anything other than their child. Most of the rest of the family was the same."

"Most?"

The sharpness of his tone made her look his way, but his expression was bland, and now she hesitated to answer. It was a subject she never spoke about, even with her family.

Then she reminded herself it was a long time ago,

ancient history, and she should be over it by now. Besides, for some unknown reason, she wanted to tell him.

"When Nonni came back into our lives, it wasn't easy. She said some pretty hurtful things about me, and they mostly kept me away from her after that. It was scary, at that age, to feel as though someone hated me that much."

"What kinds of things did she say?"

There was no mistaking the dangerous tone in his voice, and somehow it lightened Sara's heart, taking the sting out of the well-remembered words.

"Oh, that my parents had no idea where I came from, and I could be the child of a murderer. And that no doubt I'd turn out to be a thief and, once I'd taken everything I could from them, would run off, leaving them destitute."

"Good God. And you were how old?" The horror in his voice was like a balm to her soul.

"Eight, almost nine. I think that's why, when you mentioned the age your father was when they moved here, surrounded by suspicion and tension, I could relate."

Farhan was silent for a moment, his face tight, and the look he sent her was filled with a mixture of anger and sympathy.

"That explains a lot," he said, rather cryptically. Then, before she could ask what he meant, he added, "We'll be landing soon."

Usually, talking about her family would make her stomach ache, but somehow it hadn't happened. In fact, it hadn't happened much since she'd got to Kalyana, despite the stress she'd been under. But she was glad he didn't pursue the conversation about her family further.

But then he said, "Sara, thank you for trusting me enough to tell me that story. I think..." He hesitated, just for a moment, then said, "We've become friends, haven't we, over these weeks?"

Her eyes got misty, and she turned her face toward the side window so he wouldn't see. "Yes. I think we have too."

And acknowledging that fact once more made her consider taking him as her lover, and she kept her face turned away from him to hide the blush that rushed to her cheeks.

CHAPTER NINE

THE ANGER IN his chest burned like lit coals.

How could someone be that unkind to a child? Their own granddaughter, albeit an adopted one? Bless her mother for not standing for it, for protecting Sara as best she could.

Yet Farhan could see, clearly, what those words had done to Sara. They explained her almost compulsive need to be of service to her family and, by extension, everyone else. Perhaps without that horrible experience she might not be the person she was today, but he wished with all his heart she hadn't had to go through it anyway.

What she'd said about his father was something he'd have to think about later. It felt strange to be forced to see his father in a different light, think of him as a young, frightened boy who had probably lost his father to the throne and needs of Kalyana. But, again, if what she said was true, it too would explain much.

Right now, though, Farhan was solely focused on Sara, and the surprise he'd planned for her. Watching her these last couple of weeks, he'd seen her exhaustion. She'd been thrown into a life unlike any she'd known and it had taken its toll. Little bags had formed under those wide, expressive eyes, and while she'd treated everyone with her usual calm demeanor, Farhan had been aware of her knotted fingers and forced smiles.

And he doubted that being under constant scrutiny, especially now that she'd realized everyone was waiting for her to get pregnant, was helping her stress levels. So he'd arranged for them to have a couple of days away from it all at the royal villa on Agung before they started on their official tour. Set in fifty acres of woodland, right on the water, it was Farhan's favorite royal residence.

He wasn't sure why he'd kept it secret, and hopefully she wouldn't take it the wrong way. All he wanted was to give her a chance to relax, to be herself, in one of the most beautiful places he knew. There was no ulterior motive on his part, and he hoped she'd realize that.

As Agung came into view in the distance, he said, "There it is."

And he turned to watch her expression as she saw the island for the first time, wasn't disappointed when her eyes widened and her lips formed an "O" of surprise.

She gasped, leaning forward to see the island better, an emerald set in a sea shaded from cobalt through to aquamarine. "How gorgeous."

Her reaction warmed him.

"It's a beautiful island. Originally, it was a marine trading outpost for goods moving back and forth between Africa and Asia, and it's one of the most culturally diverse of the Kalyanese islands. When the marine trade dried up, the population declined, but now it's a popular tourist destination, and it's thriving again."

They were close enough to see the main town, and he banked the plane to give her a good view. It was built on a natural harbor, the colorful buildings flowing down off the surrounding hills toward the sea. Around a headland was a three-mile-long beach, dotted with low hotels and guest houses, mature trees keeping the landscape lush and green and contrasting with the huge granite boulders pushing up from the sea.

Sara turned to look out the side window as he passed over the town and tourist areas, continuing north.

"Wasn't that the airport back there?"

"Yes, but we're not landing there. The locals have planned an official welcome for us in a couple of days at Government House."

He could feel her gaze on him, even though he didn't take his eyes off the controls.

"So where are we going?"

The muscles in the back of his neck tightened. "There is a royal compound on the northwest side of the island. I thought you might enjoy a couple of days with absolutely nothing to do but laze around and relax, and there's nowhere better to do that than there."

She was silent for a moment and then, just when curiosity was about to make him turn to look at her, she exhaled.

"Thank goodness. I think that's exactly what I need."

And he quietly exhaled too, feeling as relieved as she sounded.

As the villa came into sight, he banked the plane and did a fly over, to let Okello know they were there. Sara was leaning toward the window, craning her neck to see everything at once.

"Is that it? It's beautiful. What are those plants all along the hillside around the house?"

"Frangipani, and they give the villa its name."

"Gorgeous!"

Farhan found himself looking at the villa, which was a place he'd known his entire life, with new eyes.

Through her enthusiasm, he felt his love for the land expand, grow along with his pride.

Villa Frangipani nestled among large flame trees on a promontory jutting out into the sea. The long slope of lawn from mansion to water was beautifully landscaped with swirls of the eponymous shrubs, now covered in waxy flowers. From above the house glowed like a pearl in the sun, and although it and the pool were clearly visible Farhan knew that once inside, veiled by the trees, there was an air of peaceful seclusion.

On the other side of the headland from their approach lay a smooth strip of pearl-pink sandy beach, sheltered from the rougher ocean waves by a reef and a dock. As he circled to come in for a landing on the smooth water, he saw Okello heading to the dock on the golf cart.

Touching down on the water and employing the flaps to slow the plane, he heard Sara give a little sigh of relief.

"Were you nervous?" he asked, smiling and sliding her a glance.

"Of course I was. I've never been on a seaplane; didn't even know you were a pilot."

"Good thing I knew what I was doing, then, huh?"

Her laughter filled the cockpit and, for some weird reason, his heart did as well.

More than ever before, he was looking forward to the next two days, telling himself it was strictly because they'd both have a chance to relax.

After all, why else would he be anticipating being practically alone with Sara?

Sara had never known her soul could sing, or that a place could make her feel so incredibly happy. The entire island of Agung had appeared lovely from the air but Villa Frangipani and its surroundings were perhaps the most glorious sight she'd ever seen, even in pictures. As Farhan helped her out of the plane onto the dock, the mingled scents of sea and flowers went to her head, and she had to fight the urge to laugh out loud in joy.

"Are you okay?"

Farhan was still holding her hand from when she'd taken his to step from the rocking plane, and she squeezed his fingers.

"More than okay," she replied, grinning up at him.

The quiet chug of an approaching vehicle attracted her attention and she turned to look, a little sorry when Farhan had to release her hand to close the plane door. A golf cart came down the gravel path from the house, then stopped at the end of the dock. A large, muscular man unfolded himself from it, rising to an impressive height before striding toward them.

Dressed in a brightly colored shirt and white cotton pants, his grin made his teeth appear dazzling white against his mahogany skin. He had strong features and kind, twinkling eyes.

"Your Highnesses."

He bowed over his hands, his voice surprisingly soft for such a huge man. Farhan stepped forward to shake the other man's hand, and then pulled him in for one of those male, back-slapping hugs.

"Okello. It's so good to see you."

"Farhan, yes, it's been too long, yeah? I thought you were avoiding me. Back a year and only just making it to Villa Frangipani."

Farhan gave a snort of laughter.

"You know how it is, my friend. Father keeps me on my toes."

"No doubt. No doubt."

Okello's gaze shifted to Sara, and she found herself being given a comprehensive once-over. Not that it made her feel uncomfortable. She thought she saw more curiosity than anything else in his dark, intelligent eyes.

"My wife, Sara. Sara, this is one of my oldest, dearest friends, Okello. He lives here and looks after the villa, while he's writing his novels."

"Nice to meet you, Okello." She held out her hand, and found it totally enveloped by his. "And, please, call me Sara."

His smile widened. "Thank you, Sara. I've been hearing about you on the news, and it's a pleasure to meet the woman who's willing to put up with Farhan."

She chuckled, not bothering to reply. She couldn't think of a single woman who'd toss Farhan out for eating crackers in bed, so she knew he was poking fun.

"Okay, that's enough." Farhan didn't sound particularly amused, even though he was still smiling. "Let's get the Princess up to the house."

While the men took the bags out of the plane and loaded them into the golf cart, Sara looked around, entranced by the scenery, deeply inhaling the fragrant air. This, more so than anything she'd experienced to that point, felt dreamlike, her heart seeming to beat in sync with the rush of the waves, every birdsong a symphony.

Was this what love at first sight felt like?

When Farhan put his hand on the small of her back to guide her toward the cart, it felt right in tune with her emotions. Looking up at him to smile, her heart skipped a beat when he smiled back, dipping his head as though about to kiss her, and her disappointment when he didn't was the only thing to mar her crazy happiness.

The ride up to the house passed quickly, Sara still taking in everything around her, captivated by the sight of the carefully pruned frangipani, with their blooms of cream or pink with yellow centers. The flowers looked like waxed satin, set against the deep green of the leaves. Filling in between the frangipani plants were lower bushes with small, light purple blooms, the entire effect one of tropical splendor.

The path led around the side of one wing of the two-story villa to the front door.

Farhan commented to her, "Normally when we're here we use the garden door to go in and out, especially when heading for the beach. Since this is your first time here, it'll be nice for you to see the house from the front and give you the official welcome."

It was only as they rounded the final corner that she realized the house was U-shaped, the two wings creating a central courtyard in front of the villa. A circular drive-way looped around a fountain bearing the Kalyanese coat of arms with two dolphins leaping above. The entire effect was astoundingly beautiful.

Yet, although the outside of the villa was stately, the inside, while grand, was surprisingly soothing and comfortable. Instead of the gilded and elaborate orna-mentation she'd grown used to at the palace, the Villa Frangipani was decorated in beige, white, and aqua, with pops of hot tropical colors as accents.

"My mother redecorated the house years ago, when we used to travel around as a family. Since my grand-father died it's hardly ever used for entertaining. Be-fore then, he'd host polo parties here. Now if there's an official function, we use the Governor's residence. The villa is strictly for relaxing."

He led her up the curved staircase from the high-ceilinged entrance hall, into a huge, bright sitting room. Sara looked around, and then instinctively moved straight out through the open French doors onto the wide verandah beyond. From that vantage point she could see the pool below through the boughs of the flame trees and, in the distance, the glistening water of the ocean. A warm breeze tickled her playfully, working a few strands of hair loose from her bun to blow across her face, and birds called back and forth from the trees.

Spreading her arms wide, as though to embrace it all, she said, "This is paradise. I could live here forever and be absolutely happy."

"Me too," Farhan replied, a strange note in his voice. Strange enough to make Sara spin to look at him.

His expression made her legs weak in an instant. Intent, his gaze, which was revealed by his having taken off his dark glasses, was the same as just before they'd kissed.

CHAPTER TEN

"MISHA WILL BE up to serve you lunch at one o'clock, so you have time to go swimming or snorkeling if you want."

Sara had been so focused on Farhan she hadn't noticed Okello coming up behind him, and from the way Farhan started, he hadn't noticed the other man either.

"Thank you," Farhan replied, not taking his eyes off Sara, leaving her shaken and suddenly completely aroused.

How could he do that with just a look?

"And Trinka was asking if you'll be coming by while you're here."

Who the heck was Trinka, and why did she expect a visit from him?

As Sara spun around to put her back to him, Farhan said, "Tell her I said hello, but I doubt I'll have time this visit. We'll be back soon, though."

Was it her imagination or did Farhan sound a little curt? It wasn't like him, so Sara risked a glance over her shoulder and caught him giving his friend a glare.

"Okay. Give me a shout if you need anything."

Okello grinned before melting away as quietly as he'd appeared, and Sara quickly went back to staring at the scenery. The thrilling cord of awareness that had stretched between Farhan and her had been severed by the other man's arrival, and she wasn't sure whether to be happy about it or not.

"Hey, do you want to change into something cooler, or go for a swim?"

Ugh. She'd been dreading this moment from when it had first crossed her mind; Farhan seeing her in a swimsuit. Knowing he'd spent most of his adult life in Australia, she'd pictured him dating tall, willowy blondes like her sisters, and knew she couldn't compete in the body department. Yet what did it matter, in the grand scheme of things? Theirs wasn't a real marriage, so she shouldn't be silly about it.

Besides, the four swimsuits Mara had insisted she buy were all custom made and gorgeous. When she'd tried them on, even she'd thought she looked pretty good. She'd been dying to wear the emerald one. Whatever Farhan thought of her in it, he could go fly a kite.

But her internal pep talk didn't really help.

"A swim in the pool would be nice," she replied, trying for a distant tone, so as not to reveal her nervousness.

"We have snorkels and scuba gear if you'd rather go down to the beach. Do you scuba dive?"

The little snort broke from her lips before she could stop it. "I'd never even seen the ocean before coming on this trip, much less learned how to scuba dive. I think I'd like to go down to the sea, though, as long as it won't be boring for you."

"Of course not," he replied. "I love the sea. Let's get changed and head down."

They shared a suite in the northwest wing, consisting of a sitting room and two bedrooms, each with an en suite bathroom. Because of where the villa was built, all the bedrooms had wonderful sea views. On their shared balcony was a double-bed-sized swing, hung with sheer mosquito netting, suspended from the ceiling, and it called to her.

"There isn't one spot in this place that isn't perfect," she said, going over and trying it out immediately.

He came and stood beside the swing, a little smile playing around his lips.

"This place was a refuge for me, especially after Ali died, when I had to decide whether to follow what my father said, or give up my training and stay, the way I thought I should. But even before that, I'd spend most of my summers here, while my brothers traveled or stayed in Huban. There's something about the air here that makes all the colors brighter, and gives me so much peace of spirit."

On top of being gorgeous and a fine surgeon, he also had the soul of a poet.

How could she resist that combination?

Right then she wished he would come and lie on the swing with her, pull her close, kiss her again. Never before had kissing seemed so important to her, but with Farhan it took on a whole new importance. And never before had she wished she was more experienced when it came to men and how to seduce them.

Get a grip, Sara!

Jumping up off the swing, she said briskly, "Let's get going, so we aren't late for lunch."

They changed into swimsuits, packed the golf cart with all they'd need and drove it down to the beach. Once there, Sara fussed over which of the lounge chairs she'd use, putting her bottled water and towel on it before, in a little flurry of action, tugging off her cover-up and dashing into the sea. Running in until the water was deep enough, she plunged in up to her neck, amazed at how warm it was, in comparison to the lake water she was used to in Canada. There, even in summer, most of the lakes were cold.

Turning to say as much to Farhan, she was just in time to see him pull off his shirt.

The warm sea suddenly felt like it was boiling, or perhaps she was spontaneously combusting?

His back and arms rippled with muscles, and since he was wearing just his swim trunks she was also treated to the delectable sight of his strong legs and truly luscious butt. When he turned to walk toward the surf's edge, Sara's temperature rose another five degrees.

That chest!

Those abs!

The entire package should damn well be illegal.

Needing to cool off, she dipped her head under the water, uncaring that it would undo all the careful pampering Mara had been doing to her hair on an almost daily basis.

And came up spluttering.

"You okay?"

Farhan's voice was so close, Sara tried to open her eyes even before she'd properly wiped her face, and got another horrid surprise.

"Ugh, I didn't realize just how salty it would be. And it stings the eyes."

As she pushed back her hair, which was flopping in her face, gentle fingers wiped her eyes, and she opened them again to blink up at him, her breath catching in her throat at his nearness.

"You weren't kidding when you said you'd never been in the sea, were you?"

"N-no." She cleared her throat as best she could before continuing, "My parents would take us camping sometimes at the lakes, but never had money for vacations out of province."

"Hmm," Farhan said, reaching behind her head with one hand, the motion bringing him even closer. The action of the waves rocked their bodies together briefly, and Sara's insides melted. If he wasn't careful she was going to throw caution to the wind, reach up and grab him.

"You're about to start shedding hairpins."

Disappointment sliced through her arousal as she reached to take the errant pin from his hand, not knowing what she'd do with it.

Farhan held onto it, the brush of their fingers sending a zing of current through her skin.

"Let me," he said, sliding the pin onto the front of her suit, just above her right breast. "It should stay there."

She couldn't reply, trying as she was to keep her breathing level when his scent was filling her head and the innocent sensation of his fingers on her chest was giving her anything but innocent thoughts.

Then he reached both hands back behind her head, and started pulling the rest of the pins out of her hair.

No use trying to regulate her breath now, not with his chest lightly rubbing back and forth across her breasts, those gorgeous arms bracketing her head. And his lips, slightly pursed in concentration, were just within her eyesight, stealing her concentration for themselves.

"I've never seen you with your hair down, or in a bathing suit. It's a day for firsts."

His fingers were searching for any stray pins, and her entire scalp was tight and tingling from the attention, and it wasn't alone. Even through the padded swimsuit top, her breasts grew ever more taut with each brush of his chest, and delicious, unwanted lust heated her entire body even more. Sara bit the inside of her lip to stop the moan rising in her throat from escaping. If Farhan wasn't careful, she'd melt away to nothing, get washed out past the reef, and disappear.

Apparently satisfied that he'd removed all the pins, he gently untwisted her bun and fluffed her hair until it fell free.

Then, just when she thought her torture was through, he started putting the other pins with the first, warm fingers lightly running over her skin with each placement. Shivering despite the fire rampaging through her veins, she closed her eyes and felt as though she was floating away.

"I like this color on you. It suits you so well. But, then, I've yet to see you look bad in anything you've worn."

That made her snicker, despite the arousal careening through her body. At least having a laugh would take her mind off his proximity, right?

"Nobody looks good in scrubs," she countered, proud that she didn't stutter, although there was a decided hitch in her voice.

"You do."

He really needed to stop saying those types of things, or she'd just have to jump him.

"How about my ratty winter coat when we first met?"

He didn't answer immediately, not until he'd placed the final pin. Then he cupped her cheeks and lifted her face so she was forced to meet his gaze.

"Sara, the day you opened that door and I saw you there, laughing at the dog, I thought you beautiful. And I'm not saying that for any reason other than it's true."

Again he stole her breath, and with it her voice. His

eyes were darker than usual, his face stern, wreathed in what she'd always thought of as arrogance but now wondered if it masked something else.

Farhan inhaled deeply, his lips firming briefly before he spoke again.

"I like you, think you're beautiful, smart, an amazing person. When my father instructed me to find you and marry you, I did it out of duty, but I couldn't be happier with the person I found when you opened that door."

Sara drew in a shaky breath, gob-smacked by his words, not knowing how to answer. But Farhan wasn't finished.

"I'm also very attracted to you, physically. Being around you all the time is difficult, because I want to touch you, kiss you, make love with you, but I don't know whether any of that is what you want."

He took another deep breath, and, if anything, his face got sterner.

"So I'm leaving it up to you to decide. If you want things to stay the way they are, with us as friends, then that's how they'll stay. Just let me know."

Her heart was pounding so fast her head spun, but she forced herself to breathe, slowly. Once. Twice.

His honesty was more effective than any soft words or calculated seduction could be. Knowing he wanted her, hearing him say it so plainly, made her want him even more in return.

Yet was it enough? Would she be able to share that kind of intimacy with him and walk away unscathed?

She wasn't sure, and until she could be, it would be wise to wait. But she owed him the same honesty he'd offered her, no matter how embarrassing it might be to admit.

Gathering her courage, and with a cold ball of fear

gathering in her stomach, she said, "I'm not sure what I want, Farhan. The truth is, I've never slept with anyone before."

His eyes widened slightly, but he didn't pull away, just smoothed his thumbs over her still overheated cheeks.

"I didn't realize," he said. "But I'm glad you told me." Then his brow creased slightly. "Is there a reason for that? Religious, or—?"

"No," she replied quickly. "I just always thought of sex, and marriage too, to be honest, as something that would happen one day, sometime in a nebulous future I didn't give much thought to."

He nodded slowly, then bent and kissed her lightly on the cheek.

"Then I was doubly right to say you have to make the choice, especially since I suspect beneath it all, the real reason you waited is probably far more romantic in nature."

She considered that, searching within herself, then said, "If you mean I wanted to be in love before sleeping with someone, I hadn't given it much thought. I wanted a connection, to be attracted, of course, but really I was simply too busy with school, and then work, and my family to put in the effort relationships need. As for marriage, yes, I always thought I'd fall in love before taking that step, but here we are."

Farhan's lips tilted at the edges. Not a smile but something gentler. Almost tender.

"Yes, here we are." For a moment she thought he wouldn't say any more but, with that characteristic lift of his chin, he continued. "But if you decide to take this further, you know what to expect. I can't promise you something I don't have to give."

He meant love. She didn't want his love anyway, so it was moot.

Or was it?

She pushed that thought away and gently disengaged from his hold. Then she stepped back, needing some distance so she could start processing all he'd said.

Farhan's arms dropped to his sides and he smiled, but she thought there was a hint of sadness in his eyes.

"I'll think about what you've said, Farhan. And…"

He waited patiently while she sorted out exactly what she wanted to say. Everything they'd spoken about swirled in her head, but there were a couple of things that stood out.

They were, indeed, friends, despite the strange way they'd met, their sham of a marriage, and having him acknowledge that filled her with happiness.

Secondly, he was allowing, no, insisting she take the lead in whatever happened next between them. The relief she felt was heady.

Finally, she found the words she needed, the most important, which she'd almost forgot to say.

"Thank you."

CHAPTER ELEVEN

FARHAN MADE A concerted effort to put aside the seriousness of their talk in the water and, after a short time, Sara seemed to do so too. It felt amazing to be away from the official business of state, the life and death stress of their medical practices, and just enjoy the sun and surf.

Just before one o'clock they packed up the cart and went back up to the villa, where they found Okello's daughter, Misha, had the table set and lunch ready.

"Your Highnesses," she said, when they walked into the dining area, but then she grinned and gave Farhan a huge hug. "Uncle Farhan, it's been too long."

Farhan held her by the shoulders, giving her a searching look. "When did you receive royal permission to get so grown up, Misha? Didn't I specifically tell you to stay five years old forever?"

The young woman just laughed, and set about serving their meal—a simple one of deliciously prepared fish, vegetables, and tomato rice—all the while answering Farhan's questions about school and her plans for the future.

Then she slipped away, telling them to ring for her if they needed anything.

It was just the way he'd requested, since he'd wanted

a completely relaxing couple of days, without people hovering over them all the time. It was a rare enough occurrence to be refreshing.

Just as they finished lunch, there was the slam of a door downstairs and then pounding footsteps. Okello came through the door like a torpedo.

"Farhan, Trinka just called. A retaining wall collapsed on one of the workers and she's asking if you'd come. It'll take the ambulance at least twenty minutes to get there."

He was on his feet in an instant, tossing his napkin onto the table.

"Do you know how badly hurt he is?"

"No. They were still digging him out when she called." Okello was already heading to the staircase as he spoke. "I'm going to get the car. Pick you up at the side door."

"Sara, I'll be right back," Farhan said, turning and realizing she was already on her feet too, and halfway to their suite.

"I'll come with, since you don't know how severe his wounds are, and an extra pair of trained hands might come in handy."

It was said over her shoulder, as she went through the door into the hallway beyond.

"Five minutes," he called out after her, hurrying to catch up and go change, glad she was going with him, hoping she'd be ready by the time Okello got back.

She was, with two minutes to spare, although she had her sneakers in one hand, medical bag in the other, and her hair was twisted into a rather precarious knot.

Hopping on first one foot and then the other, she got her shoes on just as Okello's SUV came barreling down the drive.

They scrambled in, and the vehicle was in motion again almost before the doors closed.

"Where did it happen?" Farhan asked.

"Back behind the grooming shed. Trinka noticed the other day that a tree up on the hillside was pushing out some of the rocks, so she decided to cut it down and repair the wall. I'm not sure what happened after that."

They rocketed through the gates, which Okello must have called ahead to have open, and turned onto the park, not toward the main road but north on a gravel side road. Farhan glanced back to see Sara trying to better secure her hair, now unruly after her swim.

The memory of taking down her hair and clipping the pins to her swimsuit tried to insinuate itself into his head, and Farhan had to make a concerted effort to push it away.

"Sara, seatbelt," he said, earning himself a mischievous glance from beneath her long, dark lashes.

"Yes, Dad," she muttered, even as she reached for the strap.

And somehow the frown he tried to send her for her teasing turned into a grin.

Sara appreciated the seatbelt when Okello took a corner on what she was sure was two wheels. She had no idea where they were going, but it didn't matter. What was important was that they get to the trapped worker as quickly as possible. Know that made the sticky feeling of her scrubs rubbing on salty skin bearable.

She'd debated whether to bring scrubs on their trip. After all, she wasn't just Dr. Greer anymore but Crown Princess, and people expected her to dress the part. However, since she'd be talking to women in clinics, it seemed less threatening to present herself the way they expected a doctor to dress, rather than all dolled up.

Now she was glad she'd decided to bring a few pairs, since it definitely sounded as though they were in for a dirty job.

The land they were driving through seemed untouched, large trees close together, covered in vines, with thick undergrowth. Wondering whether they were still on Villa Frangipani land, Sara stuck the last of the pins into her hair, hoping they would hold it up. Mara had a way of taming Sara's hair that Sara herself envied. She'd fought her hair all her life, only growing it out after she'd found a West Indian hairdresser in Toronto who'd helped her learn how to control it. But that was Canada, and this was Kalyana, where the humidity, no matter how light, made every strand want to do its own thing.

And now she knew seawater wasn't her friend either.

Thank goodness Farhan had stuck her hairpins onto the front of her suit, where she was able to grab them when she needed them.

Remembering him doing it, his face focused and intent, his fingers brushing her skin, made her heat through and through all over again.

Everything he'd said played in her mind.

He liked and was attracted to her.

Wanted her.

But wasn't in love with her.

The latter was fine. Like him, she'd never been in love, but she was pretty sure what she was feeling was lust, nothing more. He was gorgeous and a nice man, not the arrogant ass she'd thought him to be at first. Was that enough to make her sleep with him? It certainly was tempting. A chance like this might never come again.

They got to the top of a hill, went around another bend and there, in a little valley, was what she assumed to be their destination. The compound was encircled by a stone wall with a wooden gate, there were about six or so buildings and, in an area encircled with chain-link fencing…

"Dogs!"

She leaned forward to get a better look, noting the solid buildings, all clean and brightly painted.

"It's an animal sanctuary," Okello explained, as he pressed the accelerator hard, pushing the vehicle to go as fast as possible down the hill.

There was no time to ask any more questions as they roared through the gate to follow the drive around the buildings to the far corner of the compound, where a group of people had gathered.

Jumping out of the now stopped SUV, Sara reached in to grab her medical bag and ran after Farhan and Okello, who had a head start on her.

The crowd parted, and Sara's stomach dropped when she saw the pile of stones men were frantically pulling away from the still body barely visible beneath them.

Farhan got to the man's head first, with Sara right behind him.

To her shock, when she knelt down beside him, she saw the man's eyes were open, aware, although shadowed with pain. Farhan was already doing his assessment, so Sara decided to be his back-up, listening and taking note of all the man said in response to questions. Opening her bag, she took out and put on a pair of gloves, and then, using antiseptic solution and soft gauze, started cleaning up the young man's face. From her visual inspection, she suspected his nose was broken, and there was a gash above his right eye, which she wanted to check the severity of. While there was a flap of skin hanging down over his eyebrow, and copious bleeding, as was usual with head wounds, her opinion was that it was minor, although there could be concussion.

Farhan was examining the young man, who said his name was Nolan, asking him how the accident had happened while gently inspecting his head and neck. His pupils looked normal, his color surprisingly good for someone stuck under a pile of rocks. Sara looked to see the progress of the other men, still heaving stones away, and was glad to see Nolan's chest was almost free.

"I was below the wall, sir, marking where it needed to be repaired, when I heard the stones creaking. I tried to run, but tripped and fell."

"There's a drainage ditch just about here, isn't there? Did you fall into that?"

"I'm not sure, sir."

At least he was lucid and, although having to breathe through his mouth because of his broken nose, didn't seem to be in major distress.

Farhan looked up at her. "Do you have a neck brace in your kit?"

"No," she replied.

"Then unless it's absolutely necessary to move him, I think we should leave him here until the ambulance arrives."

Sara nodded and as the last of the stones over Nolan's chest and abdomen were removed, she shifted so Farhan could take his examination lower.

It was almost miraculous. Nolan professed to feel no pain in his back, chest, or abdomen, but as they pulled the last of the stones away, Sara's heart sank. His leg was twisted under him at an abnormal angle, obviously either broken or badly dislocated at the knee.

The sound of a siren in the distance was a huge relief. There really wasn't much either Farhan or she could do under the circumstances, and without the right equipment.

She made a mental note to get a larger medical bag and stock it with a neck brace for any future emergencies. Not that she was hoping for any more excitement like this. The whole situation made her painfully aware of how sheltered her medical experience really had been to that point. Working in the field, without the amenities she was used to having at her fingertips, was nerve-racking.

Farhan turned to a woman standing on the sidelines, her arms wrapped around her waist, a worried expression on her weathered face.

"Is there an orthopedic surgeon at the hospital? His leg is going to need surgery."

"Yes. Dr. Ronan. I hear he's good."

The ambulance arrived, and Farhan brought the supervisor up to speed on all he'd seen. Then he fitted Nolan's neck and back braces himself, and made sure no one tried to straighten the young man's leg.

"It's definitely dislocated, and it needs to be dealt with at the hospital."

"Yes, sir."

Poor Nolan tried to be brave, but the pain from his leg had him groaning and swearing as they transferred him to a gurney.

Stripping off her gloves, Sara watched the ambulance pull away. Farhan was standing with the woman he'd asked about the surgeon, deep in conversation, and she didn't want to interrupt. Then they walked over to her, and the woman held out her hand.

"Your Highness, I'm Trinka Daniels, and I'm in charge of this crazy place. Thank you for coming to help Nolan."

"It's nice to meet you, Trinka," she said politely, taking the outstretched hand and getting a firm handshake.

"Well, since you're here, Farhan, do you want to nose around and see what we've been up to since you last visited? It's been a while, and although I keep you updated, it's different when you can see it all for yourself. Take the Princess with you, while I supervise feeding time."

They ended up spending most of the rest of the afternoon at the sanctuary, which Sara learned Farhan had set up himself.

Something else she hadn't known about him; another facet in his complex personality.

She couldn't resist wading into the pack of dogs in the field, greeting all those that wanted attention, trying to coax a few of the shyer ones to come to her. Farhan had retreated into a businesslike demeanor, speaking mostly to Trinka and Okello, all but ignoring Sara. Yet, although he didn't speak to her directly more than two or three times, there were a great deal more times that she looked at him and found his gaze focused entirely on her.

And she couldn't help noticing how gentle and involved he was with the dogs who came to him, wanting affection.

"I'm glad to see the adoption numbers have been going up," he remarked to Trinka, who nodded.

"We've made quite a bit of headway in that regard, especially when it comes to the puppies. But I want to increase the number of older dogs we rehome, and get more people to foster dogs, to give them a bit of basic training, increase their socialization and chance of finding a forever home. A few of us have been talking about setting up a support animal training program too, but that's later on. None of us have the time or expertise right now."

Sara looked up from where she was sitting cross-legged on a low wooden platform, three dogs draped over her lap, all wanting rubs at the same time.

"I know someone in Ottawa who's involved in the training of medical and emotional support animals. Whenever you're ready, let me know and I'll put you in touch with him."

"Him?" Farhan asked. His tone was mild, but the question made her want to blush for some reason.

"Yes. It's my Uncle Stanton, my dad's brother. Most of that side of the family is involved with animals in some way."

Thankfully, the conversation shifted to other topics, and Sara could concentrate on the little dog who'd won pride of place on her lap. Of indeterminate breed, he was a shaggy little fellow with big brown eyes peering from behind a floppy fringe.

"That's Coco, short for Coconut, and he normally doesn't go to people," Trinka remarked. "You obviously have the touch."

Stroking his wiry fur, Sara wished she had the wherewithal to take Coco when she left, but didn't say anything. Maybe before she went back to Canada, she'd come back and liberate him. Hopefully he wouldn't have to be quarantined back home. She'd look into it when it got closer to the time for her to leave.

Suppressing a sigh, she cuddled the dog a little closer, looking around at the verdant hills, tuning out the human conversation to focus on the birds, the whisper of breeze through the foliage. Canada seemed so very far away despite the constant contact with her family. It was a different life, and one that she didn't miss as much as she'd thought she would. Kalyana had a completely different rhythm, the country's heart beating at a slower rate, the people moving at a pace most Canadians would find unbearably leisurely.

Sara, however, was growing to love it all. Sitting here under a sky so blue it could make you cry, the sun warm on her head, there was nowhere she would rather be, and the thought of leaving it behind one day made her unbearably sad.

Coco sat up abruptly, whined under his breath, then reached up to lick her chin.

"Are you okay?"

She didn't notice Farhan moving until he stooped down next to where she was sitting. The expression on his face was one she didn't remember ever seeing before. Was that concern tightening the skin around his eyes?

"Of course. Why?"

He shook his head. "You just looked...a little off."

She smiled at him, wanting so badly to smooth away the wrinkles between his brows, curling her fingers into Coco's fur to stop herself doing it.

"I'm fine. Really."

But leaving the little dog behind all but broke her heart, and on the way back to Villa Frangipani, she stared out the side window of the SUV, wondering when her life had gone from simple to so darned complicated.

CHAPTER TWELVE

SHE WAS STILL pondering that question while she showered and changed once they got back.

It was, of course, all about Farhan. He'd turned her life upside down, and not just because of his proposition. No, it was *him*. Him and the life he'd shown her here in Kalyana, a place that called to her heart just as he did.

The thought brought her up short, made a shiver run down her spine.

She couldn't fall for him. She just wouldn't.

Putting aside all his wonderful attributes, his stated attraction to her and the pleasure it gave her to know he wanted her, that would be the stupidest thing she'd ever done in her life. The year would fly by. And, when it was over, if she allowed herself to care for him in any way more than as a friend, the heartbreak would be immense.

She still wasn't sure she could sleep with him and not get emotionally involved. Even Farhan's warnings didn't quell the intensity of her desire.

He'd told her the choice was hers, and he'd go along with whatever she decided.

She'd just have to make sure she didn't make the wrong choice.

No matter how hard that ultimately might be.

But Sara almost had to eat her own words when she stepped out onto the verandah and saw Farhan standing in the final glow of the setting sun. He was wearing a plain white kurta over pants of the same fabric, the soft linen doing nothing to conceal his wonderful physique. His hair was damp, and from where she stood, frozen, behind him, she could see his strong, wide-palmed hands gripping the balustrade.

Memories of those hands holding and caressing her crashed through her system, trailing fire in their wake. Her determination not to give in to her own lust had been made in the vacuum of solitude, somehow not taking into consideration the bone-deep effect that being in his presence had on her.

He turned then, as though sensing her standing there, and the look he gave her almost melted her on the spot.

It wasn't the sultry air making it impossible to breathe. It was the darkness of his gaze, the slight softening of his stern lips, the sensation of being pulled toward each other, although neither of them moved.

"Dinner is ready, Uncle Farhan."

Misha's voice from farther down the verandah broke the silent, heat-saturated moment between them, allowing Sara to take a breath into her oxygen-starved lungs.

"Come, beautiful." He gestured for her to precede him to the table set on the verandah, decorated with frangipani blossoms and candles sending flickering light over the crisp white cloth.

She couldn't reply, her voice still lost in the timeless, thrilling instant just gone.

He pulled out her chair, as he always did, and Sara braced herself for the proximity when slipping by him.

But even so his subtle, delicious scent still went straight to her head.

The man was a walking intoxicant.

"I'm glad we had time to visit the animal shelter," Farhan said, during dinner. "There's another main one in the south, not as big as this one but with a wider variety of animals. Some horses, donkeys, goats, as well as dogs and cats. If we have time, we'll go."

It was the first time he'd mentioned the sanctuaries, and Sara now felt comfortable asking, "Trinka mentioned you'd set them up yourself, when you were in your teens. How did it all happen?"

He lifted one shoulder; a self-effacing gesture she'd come to recognize.

"I never got used to seeing all the stray dogs wandering the street. I used to bring some of them home to the palace, but my parents weren't too happy about that."

Sara chuckled, picturing the King and Queen realizing the palace was being overrun with strays.

"One day I picked up a stray, intending to take it home, but I found out it wasn't a stray at all. It actually belonged to someone who loved it very much but didn't have the wherewithal to properly care for it. The dog hadn't been neutered, so it was constantly in fights. It was riddled with worms, and showed signs of mange."

He wasn't looking at her as he spoke, but out into the moonlit gardens.

"I started paying for people to spay and neuter their animals, and told my father the government should do something about all the strays. He told me people come first, and if I wanted something done about it, then it was up to me. So I did, using some of my inheritance from my grandfather. But it's really the people running the sanctuaries and shelters who are doing all the work."

He said it so matter-of-factly, as though it were no big deal. His humbleness moved her in a soul-deep way.

"But you don't have any animals of your own?"

A fond smile, tinged with sadness, tipped the edges of his lips.

"I had two dogs in Australia, but they both died a couple of years ago. I haven't had the heart to get any more since. When I need a dog fix, I go and volunteer at the shelter in Huban."

"I love dogs too," she said, scooping up a bit of her crème brûlée, which was so delicious that each bite was like a symphony on her taste buds. "In fact, I'd like to take that little dog Coconut back with me when I return to Canada. I'm not sure how that works, though. I'd hate for him to have to spend a long time in quarantine or anything."

The look he gave her was unfathomable, but he nodded. "We're rabies free, and have good contact with the Canadian government. I'm sure it can be arranged."

"Oh, thank you," she said, smiling across at him, happy in a way she couldn't remember being before.

Their gazes met, held, and the now-familiar heat flooded her system, until it felt as though warm honey flowed in her veins.

It was then, at that moment, she decided.

She wanted him, and she wanted him here, at Villa Frangipani, the most beautiful place in the world.

Now, if she could just figure out how to let him know without embarrassing herself in the process.

Why did he hate hearing her speak about returning to Canada? It wasn't as though he didn't know she was eventually going and, in fact, he was glad it was still foremost in her mind. In some ways he felt they were getting too close, speaking about subjects close to their hearts, while the way he really wanted to get intimate with her seemed unlikely to happen.

He wanted her in his bed, not his head. And definitely not in his heart.

Sara went quiet, not looking at him, and in the soft candlelight and moonlight it was impossible to read her expression.

Instead of trying to engage her, Farhan let his mind wander.

What she'd said about his father still nagged at him.

She'd been able to imagine the turmoil the child, suddenly second in line to an unwanted throne, must have felt. How the enmity of those around him, along with how busy his father had been while putting the country to rights, must have affected him, scarred him in a fundamental way.

It certainly explained his distance and sternness, and the obsession with the missing Bhaskar, which had set Farhan and Sara on this strange path together. What else about his father, who Farhan had often thought of as a cypher, could that explain?

Recalling the conversation that had led to her comment just made his blood boil all over again. Her grandmother had treated her abominably, yet Sara had held no grudge. Indeed, she was actively involved in the old woman's care, and he remembered her even feeding her at dinner while the rest of the family did nothing to help.

Sara was so giving. Too giving. Was she still trying to prove her worth to her family, and now to the people of Kalyana? She'd been distressed by people requesting her patronage for various charities and causes, asking his advice.

"Anyone who approaches you directly, tell them to

send an official request, in writing, outlining the work the charity does, and the role they envision you playing, along with last year's financial statement. I'll get Seth to collate it all, as well as doing due diligence to make sure they're above board, then you can decide."

"But I won't be here very long, Farhan. I don't want to accept a role I won't be able to fulfill in the future."

"Then don't accept any of them," he'd said, in what he'd thought was a reasonable response, but Sara had just looked more distressed.

"But I want to help," she'd said softly.

They'd talked about it some more, without being able to come to a firm decision, but it was so clear to him: Sara would give everything to everyone around her, perhaps to her own detriment.

Dinner finished, he suggested a walk on the beach, but she declined.

"I—I think I'd prefer to stay u-up here," she stammered, and he saw a blush rise to her cheeks. It sharpened his focus, had him drawing closer to her so as to see the expression in her eyes.

And when she twined her arms around his neck and tilted her face up to his, his body reacted with a surge of arousal so strong he was instantly hard.

"May I kiss you?" she asked, her voice breathless, a little unsure.

CHAPTER THIRTEEN

FARHAN'S EXPRESSION CYCLED from surprise to desire in a tick of a heartbeat.

Then his mouth was on hers, the kiss urgent, compelling her lips to open instinctively, a moan rising in her throat as her insides melted, lust flashing out like a wildfire.

With the last of her functioning brain she gave thanks that he hadn't asked for an explanation, hadn't made her tell him why she'd had this abrupt change of heart.

From the moment they'd met the attraction she felt was more intense than she'd ever imagined possible, and it had only grown stronger with each passing day.

He was only hers for a little while. So much time had already gone by. This was her opportunity to do exactly what she'd secretly hoped all her adult life.

Share herself, on the most intimate level, with someone she cared about. It didn't matter if he didn't care as much.

This was for her.

Farhan pulled her closer, and she let her hands roam his back, the thin linen of his kurta doing nothing to stop her from tracing the muscles but annoying her nonetheless.

She wanted to feel his bare skin, learn, once and for all, if it was as smooth as it looked.

Pressed against his chest, she wallowed in the exquisite sensations turning her insides to lava, burning for him in a way she'd never thought herself capable of. This level of want, of sheer unadulterated need, was beyond her wildest imaginings, but it didn't frighten her at all. If anything, it only made her more determined to take this moment to the ultimate conclusion.

How could she live with herself after she left Kalyana if all she took with her were regrets rather than beautiful memories?

Memories of making love with Farhan.

Farhan lifted his head and she stood on tiptoes, trying to re-establish the kiss.

"Wait." It was a growl, the strain in his voice so obvious she shivered with the knowledge she affected him that way. "Sara, you have to tell me when to stop. I want you so badly, you'll have to tell me if I go too far."

Her heart, already racing, seemed to trip over itself, and she swallowed to clear her throat before she could reply.

"I'll tell you, Farhan."

But she had no intention of telling him to stop. She wanted to experience everything he could give.

Leading him upstairs to her bedroom didn't seem too daunting; knowing what to do when they got there was another thing altogether.

Thankfully, Farhan took over, pulling her back into his arms as soon as the door closed behind them.

"Sara." Her name sounded like a benediction when he said it. "Beautiful."

Her knees weakened, her body tightening in anticipation as he found her lips once more.

Then they were on the bed, still fully clothed, and she lost herself in the wonder of his kisses again.

Yet eventually she realized he wasn't taking it any further. Not that kissing him wasn't thrilling, but she wanted more.

And realized she was going to have to ask for it.

She didn't know the words. Didn't know how people navigated situations like this. But if she wanted to make love with Farhan, she was going to have to put her shyness and fear aside, and let him know.

They were lying side by side, one of his hands on her ribcage, the other lost somewhere among the pillows. Would it be enough to simply shift his hand up to cover her breast?

That would be a small step, and she wasn't in the mood for those.

Before he realized what she was about to do, she rolled away from him and sat up.

She heard his indrawn breath, felt him run a finger gently down her back.

No doubt he thought she was putting a halt to their lovemaking and, for a moment, she froze, terrified by what she was planning to do.

She got up off the mattress, and turned to face him, and the sight of him stole her breath, had shivers of lust coursing down her spine. His hair was mussed from her fingers running through the strands, his eyes still dark with passion, his lips soft from her kisses. It felt so right to see him in her bed, one leg bent so the foot was flat on the mattress, the other canted to one side, his erection clearly delineated beneath his clothing.

She reached for the side zipper of her dress and it was then she realized her fingers were shaking, but she willed them to get the simple chore done.

His gaze followed the motion of her hand as she tugged the zipper down to her hip, then snapped up to her face as she slid her arms out of the dress, letting it fall to the carpet.

Her toes curled at his expression, her temperature skyrocketing at the mingled shock and need on his face.

"Sara..."

It was a warning and an invitation, all in one, but she ignored the former, knowing it was the latter that was important.

You can do this, Sara.

But her fingers weren't just shaking, they were also ice cold as she reached back to unclip her bra. When her breasts swung free, she gasped, heat suffusing her chest and face at exposing her body to him so boldly.

Suddenly she realized she didn't know what to do next. Just the thought of taking off her panties froze her in place, and she only just stopped herself from crossing her arms over her chest.

And there was nowhere to run. This was, after all, her room.

Farhan sat up. Then he pulled off his shirt, and Sara's breath caught deep in her chest at how gorgeous he was.

Holding out his hand, he said, "Come here, beautiful."

And all her fear and trepidation disappeared as she went to him.

There was something dreamlike in how Farhan touched her; the slow drag of his fingers over her skin, the play of his mouth on hers. Although she'd clearly shown him she was ready, no, eager for his possession, he was in no rush to get there.

"Beautiful," he murmured into her flesh, and she didn't know whether he was using it as a proper noun—

his nickname for her—or an adjective, and didn't care. She was too lost in these new, entrancing sensations to worry about it.

His fingers stroked over her breasts, bringing her nipples to tight oversensitive peaks, his lips dipped from her mouth to her throat. Her body bowed, arousal pulling it tighter and tighter.

"Beautiful."

When the tip of his tongue swirled around her nipple, Sara whimpered, her fingers finding the back of his head to hold him in position, loath to let him stop the sweet torture.

But he had just begun to introduce her to the world of passion, and each touch and lick and kiss ushered her into new realms of desire.

His lips on the inside of her elbow, his mouth on her stomach. Neither of these were actions she would have associated with the act of sex, or with foreplay. In life outside these four walls, she never would've considered they could make her body twist with wanton need.

Yet when Farhan kissed from her shoulder to her wrist, her rushed breathing hitched, and she pressed her thighs together, the ache between them building toward unbearable.

The heat of his mouth on her breast, the sweet drag of his palm on its mate brought her back off the mattress, little cries of sweet, agonizing craving breaking, unfettered, from her lips.

Then he moved lower, and she trembled at the slow, concentrated flicking of his tongue, as it traced back and forth over her abdomen.

"Farhan…" she whispered, her throat too dry to allow anything louder.

He lifted his head, and in the darkness of his gleaming eyes she saw a hint of the pleasure to come.

"Is this enough, beautiful? Do you want me to stop?"

If he stopped now, she might lose her sanity.

"No. No."

His face tightened, became almost feral, and her heart rejoiced to see it.

"How much further do you want me to go, Sara? I need to know."

She understood. He was asking how much restraint he needed to build up. It made her adore him even more, knowing he would go as far as she said and no further, regardless of his own needs.

It gave her the courage to say what she truly wanted, out loud, making it clear to them both.

"I want to make love with you," she said.

And there wasn't even a hint of a stutter in her voice.

He gazed at her for a long moment, the air between them heavy with passion, and then he said, "I want to make love with you too, but my initial promise still stands. If you want to stop, at any point, tell me."

Unable to resist, she reached down and cupped his face, curling down so as to kiss him, long and deep.

"I won't change my mind," she murmured against his lips. "I want you so badly, I'm burning up inside."

His lips curled into a smile as she lay back down, and he replied, "I'm glad, for I feel the same way. I'll be right back. Don't move."

Rising quickly, he strode to the connecting door between their rooms, but was gone only for a minute. When he returned, it was to toss a small, foil-wrapped package onto the nightstand, and Sara mentally kicked herself for not thinking of protection first. Thank goodness one of them had the presence of mind to do so.

Lying back down in the same position he'd been in before, Farhan dipped his head to kiss a slow trail down her belly and then around her navel, Sara's entire body trembled with delightful anticipation. Rising to his knees, he traced a finger across the top of her panties.

"May I?"

She lifted her hips in reply, although a fresh wave of trepidation washed over her skin.

Farhan eased her last garment away, his fingers caressing her legs. Lifting her left leg, he kissed her ankle, stroking his tongue across the sensitive skin beneath her medial malleolus. Up her leg that sinful mouth travelled, until he was at her knee. Then he turned his attention to her other leg, repeating every enticing action.

Suddenly Sara realized her feet were on his shoulders, her previously most private flesh fully open to his view.

Even if she were inclined to feel self-conscious, Farhan's avid expression would have swept the emotion away.

"I want to taste you."

It was statement and question rolled into one, and Sara replied by spreading her thighs a little wider, placing her hand on her belly, inviting him to take whatever he wanted.

He swooped down, and Sara cried out at the intensity of feelings bombarding her system, the unbelievable sensory overload. Her body shook, strung tight with lust from just the first touch of his tongue, his lips. Farhan held her hips, slowing his tender assault, taking her higher and higher, easing her toward an indefinable golden moment she could sense nearing. Her thighs tightened around his head, as she strained to reach that final glorious treasure.

"Easy," he murmured, not lifting his head, so that the word itself pulled her a little closer. "Relax, beautiful. Let it happen."

She wanted it, the orgasm tempting her beyond reason, but, lost in a maze of previously unknown physical delight, something held her back. Fear, carnal excess, inexperience, she didn't know which, but whatever it was, it was driving her slowly crazy.

"Farhan, please. Help me."

He growled, a low sound of need as great as her own, and his hands tightened fractionally.

"Do you trust me, Sara?"

How could he ask such a thing at a time like this? But she was compelled to whimper, "Yes."

"Then let me love you, beautiful. Let me make this good for you."

Opening her eyes, she looked down at him, his handsome face bracketed by her thighs, and the sight made her gasp. It was so intimate, reflecting a physical closeness she'd never shared with anyone before, and somehow it both increased her arousal and loosened her muscles.

Because it was Farhan. The only man she'd ever wanted this way. The only one she'd trust with her body, and knew she'd never regret doing so.

"Good," he growled and then, as she watched, he flicked her with the tip of his tongue.

And she exploded into ecstasy.

Sara's sweet cries of release echoed through Farhan's blood, pushing his own almost painful desire even higher.

Her gorgeous body twisted as he kept her orgasm going, not stopping until she pushed his head away.

Then he covered her trembling flesh with his hand, gentling her until her breathing settled slightly, and her muscles started to relax.

But he didn't want her completely satiated, not if she'd meant it when she'd said she wanted to make love with him.

No. He wanted her as ravenous for him as he was for her.

He quickly divested himself of his remaining garments, and moved up to hold her. Yet, even in the tender moment, he let his hands keep touching her, finding the places that had made her gasp with desire before, slowly rousing her back to a state of need.

He craved her kisses, took her mouth over and over. Then he moved to her sensitive neck, kissing, nibbling, licking, until those sweet little gasps and moans rang out again.

He didn't want to hurt her. That was his one worry. Her inexperience was there, hovering in the back of his mind, even as his carnal self fought for supremacy, urging him to take her hard and fast.

Sara may be the true virgin, but in a way he felt like one as well, having never *had* a virgin in his bed. It filled him with a kind of masculine pride he'd never have credited himself with being in possession of, but also weighed him down with a sense of responsibility too.

Sensing it was time, and even after rolling on the condom, Farhan still hesitated. Eventually it was Sara who pulled him close, wrapping her strong legs around him and rolling so he lay atop her, perfectly positioned.

"Wait," he growled, his body tense with the drive to thrust into her. "I want to be sure—"

"I'm sure," she replied, her voice strained, passion-drunk. "I can't wait anymore. Please."

He tried to go slowly, every muscle locked, tenderness his touchstone. But the sublime encounter was also an irrevocable one, and they both knew it. Her eyes were open, looking up into his, and although he wanted to close his in rising ecstasy, he kept his gaze locked on hers, searching for any hint of pain or uncertainty.

There was none.

She welcomed him into her body, accepted him, just as his heart had welcomed and accepted her advent into his life.

The knowledge fired through him, rendering the moment sweeter, hotter, with an edge of incipient pain he didn't know how to process.

Holding still to allow her body time to accept his, he watched her eyes flutter closed, even as her hips shifted restlessly beneath his. Still he didn't move, caught in the transcendent intimacy. Sara's gorgeous neck was arched, her face was flushed and damp, her lips slightly parted, the breath rushing between them.

She was perfect. Perfect for him. And the urge to declare her his, to put his stamp on her for all to see, was almost overwhelming. Nothing he'd ever experienced before had prepared him for this.

For making love to a woman, instead of merely seeking sexual release.

"Farhan…"

He loved how she said his name, both question and demand, her voice gravelly with desire; acceded to the demand and answered the question with long, slow thrusts. Her short nails dug into his back, and she shuddered again and again.

"Yes," she whimpered. "Oh, yes."

Her responsiveness was almost his undoing, and he had to pause to regain some semblance of control.

"Don't stop," she moaned. "Oh, Farhan, don't stop."

He was losing his grip, ready to spiral into orgasm, and he didn't want to go alone. Heaving to his knees, he pulled Sara closer, seating himself fully inside her. She gasped, her legs locking around his waist, her fingers gripping the sheet on either side of her hips.

Then he reached down, found her clitoris with his thumb, as he began to thrust again.

She came apart, crying out his name, and it was all he needed to follow her into bliss.

CHAPTER FOURTEEN

THE DAYS THAT followed were the best of Sara's life.

While in public Farhan's behavior toward her didn't change, at night he was the lover she hadn't known she'd wanted, but now realized she'd always dreamt of.

Tender, attentive to her needs, fiercely arousing her and making sure satisfaction was achieved, for them both. In her case, multiple times.

It was like being caught up in an erotic fantasy, and whenever he said, "Come here, beautiful," she knew the dream was about to come true, again.

The only incident that could have marred her happiness came the day after they'd made love for the first time, and she'd screwed up the courage to say, "If we're going to continue sleeping together, you're going to keep needing to use protection, always. Or at least until I can get back to the hospital and go on the Pill."

Farhan's face was expressionless as he surveyed her for a couple of long seconds, but his chin tipped up in that habitual, arrogant look he had. Then it seemed as though he would speak, but stayed silent.

When he didn't answer, Sara continued, "Farhan, you don't want a child, and neither do I under these circumstances."

His lips firmed into a thin line, then he replied, "Of course."

Then he changed the subject, speaking about the rest of their tour.

The switch to something so impersonal made Sara's stomach dip, and she'd wondered if she'd ruined the sexual closeness they'd only just found. But she shouldn't have worried. That night Farhan had come to her room, lightly knocking on the connecting door, not entering until she'd called out for him to do so.

"Would you welcome my company?" he'd asked, solemn-faced, his eyes watchful.

And, of course, she'd said yes.

She wanted all she could get of Farhan while she still could.

Seated at the vanity, she'd been brushing out her hair when he'd entered, and Farhan had come to stand behind her, his gaze intent on her reflection.

"I like it when your hair is down," he'd said quietly, as he'd taken the brush from her hand. "Why don't you leave it down more often?"

"It's very hard to handle, and the humidity here tends to make it go a little nuts. Even Mara has trouble getting it to behave."

He stroked the brush through so gently, she felt tears sting the backs of her eyes, and was glad he was concentrating on what he was doing, rather than on her face. It was a surreal, fairy-tale type of moment, and for once she felt she belonged in such a situation. Something about Kalyana had changed her, made her more confident, able to deal with whatever came her way.

"May I sleep in here with you tonight?" he asked quietly, still not looking at her face.

"I hoped you would," she replied.

And when their gazes met then in the mirror, a wave of need and happiness made her smile up at him.

Leaving Villa Frangipani felt like being torn away from Paradise, but it was time to return to reality, and the job at hand, at least during the day. Joined by Kavan, Mara, and Seth, they started there in Agung.

While their main mission was to survey the women on the various islands regarding their medical needs, there were also a lot of official functions they were expected to attend. It became an exhausting excursion, but at night all her fantasies continued to come true and that made it bearable.

She'd hoped taking their relationship to a physical level would somehow cool her ardor but, instead, Sara's attraction to Farhan grew more intense each day. She found herself watching his hands, his face, noticing the way he walked, hoarding the memory of each smile.

To take her mind off her obsession with Farhan, at least some of the time, she threw herself into interacting with the women, finding it incredibly informative and interesting.

"In truth, I don't think we need a women's clinic," one lady told Sara, when she visited a local hospital on one of the north central islands. "Rather, it would be better if we simply had more female doctors available at the hospital and rural clinics."

That seemed to be the general consensus among most of the women she spoke to. Some said that while dedicated women's clinics would be nice, recruiting more female practitioners would be just as effective.

By the time they were halfway through their tour, Sara felt she had a good handle on how the women felt, and reported their concerns to Farhan. He listened to her and then nodded.

"There is a disproportionate number of male doctors recruited to work here, and I'm not sure why that is. It's something worth looking into."

She knew there was no medical school in Kalyana, and many of their medical practitioners were recruited from other countries. "Are there grants, programs to encourage young women to study medicine abroad and then come back here to practice? That would be the best option, since they'd be returning to their own land, already knowing the culture, rather than bringing in strangers. And if grants are too expensive, set it up in such a way that they can work off their med school fees over time. Then they'd have a real incentive to come back."

They were sitting outside after dinner at another of the royal family's residences, this one a miniature fortress in the hills on one of the central islands. The Governor had explained that when the British had used the main town as a transshipment point, there had been periodic outbreaks of malaria because of the swampy land surrounding the port. With there being fewer mosquitos at higher elevations, they'd built the fortress to retire to, a place where they could feel secure even when in poor health. It had become a royal residence once the British had left.

It still retained the aura of its colonial past, with dark heavy furniture and overstuffed chintz-covered chairs and sofas, nothing like any of the other residences Sara had seen. Yet it also had a timeless quality she liked, harkening back to the past, untouched by the often seen need to ruthlessly drag everything into modernity. Sitting on a comfortable love seat, Farhan beside her, holding her hand and playing with her fingers, Sara was enjoying the cool, fragrant mountain air.

"Again, something to look into. I know there are a handful of scholarships handed out each year, but perhaps setting one up that's strictly for young women would be useful."

"And ensure girls are encouraged to study sciences in schools. I know Kalyana is fairly progressive and egalitarian when it comes to women's rights, but even in North America there are still ingrained biases against it. Maybe you should also think about what it would take to set up a university, so young people don't have to leave the country to study in the first place."

If she had been going to remain in Kalyana, that would be a cause she'd get involved with. But she wasn't, as she had to keep reminding herself. For once she felt as though she was where she belonged, and just the thought of leaving opened a hole in her chest.

It had nothing to do with Farhan, she told herself stoutly. While his lovemaking was amazing, catapulting her into the sexual stratosphere, there was no place in their relationship for emotion. She wouldn't allow herself to care for him, knowing it would be completely one-sided. Part of what made the intimacy between them work was both of them knowing it was safe, and neither would make things difficult.

She was on a journey of discovery, learning new things about herself, her desires and ambitions. And what she found was truly eye-opening.

Far from being the passive mouse she'd always assumed herself to be, she'd realized hidden strengths, especially in bed with Farhan. She wasn't content to let him always take the lead, set the pace. Learning his body, what turned him on and made him wild, became a mission of sorts, one she embraced with gusto.

His ears were particularly sensitive, and his back was one big erogenous zone, which she put to good use. Even on occasion in public, which, as she surreptitiously ran a finger down it, earned her some stern looks from him, making her hard pressed to contain giggles.

He'd acceded to her wishes, and they always used condoms. And when one night she'd taken the little packet from his hand and offered to put it on for him, the way his face tightened told her volumes.

After that it became a part of their play, an island of quiet in the storm of their lovemaking, although no less arousing for the tenderness of it.

"You make me lose myself," he said to her one night, as she carefully smoothed on the prophylactic, and coming from the contained, controlled Farhan, it filled her with joy.

Their tour was coming to an end, and Sara wasn't sure if she were happy about it or not. They'd been somewhat freer while traveling than they'd been in Huban, Farhan more relaxed. Yet their stint in the capital had been before they'd gotten this close. Perhaps, hopefully, their newfound intimacy would continue once they were back in the palace, despite the additional pressure Farhan would be under.

He was needed back in Huban, and their schedule would have to be accelerated.

"The surgeon who was missing the day we arrived has left the islands to return to his home, and the hospital is short-staffed. I think they may have fired him for his unreliability. The director is requesting that I do some elective surgeries to allow them to catch up.

They've already hired a replacement, but he won't be arriving for a while."

They'd spent the day traveling around the largest of the southern islands, visiting a variety of rural clinics as well as the main hospital. Here, where there seemed to be a preponderance of women from mostly conservative families, the idea of a women's clinic was more popular. But even they agreed, barring that, an increase in female doctors might work just as well.

"Women understand women better," a councilwoman said to Sara. "It's more than just not wanting a strange man touching me. It's also trying to explain to a male doctor something he has only read about in books but has never experienced for himself or has any chance of experiencing."

It was enlightening to see the difference between the attitudes in the northern islands in comparison to those in the south. They were all a part of Kalyana, but although the country itself was small, there was a lot of diversity in the way people lived and thought.

When she mentioned that, Farhan said, "That's one of the facts the monarchy ignored here for a long time. Queen Nargis treated all her subjects as though they were homogeneous, and everyone suffered for it. My father has his faults, can be stubborn and old-fashioned, but both he and my grandfather at least acknowledged the necessity of understanding the people and their various needs."

"And you're working to expand that understanding." It gave her a little rush of emotion, but she tamped it down. "It bodes well for the country's future."

His expression was pensive, and he lifted her hand to kiss the inside of her wrist, making her shiver, before he replied.

"Honestly, I feel ill prepared to rule. While I don't regret my years away, sometimes I wonder if I shouldn't have ignored my father and stayed after Ali died. Even now, my father seems reluctant to instruct me in various ways. I'm constantly feeling as though I'm winging it."

Squeezing his fingers, she said, "I can't speak to your father's state of mind, but I have no doubt you'll be a wonderful king when the time comes. You're smart, compassionate, and thoughtful." She hesitated for a moment, then continued, "Perhaps you're better off forging your own path anyway, rather than following the one set by your father and grandfather. After all, times have changed, and even the monarchy has to change with it."

He nodded, but didn't reply. The silence between them grew, but Farhan was slowly rubbing his palm up and down her arm now, and gooseflesh popped up across her back.

And when he said, "Ready for bed, beautiful?" she eagerly went with him.

How could he be so happy and in so much pain at the same time? Farhan wondered, as he watched Sara stoop down to speak to an elderly lady who couldn't get up.

They were in the village of Manan, the southernmost habitation on the southernmost island, on the final day of their tour. When Sara had heard that the oldest living inhabitant of Kalyana lived at a nursing home in the village, she'd insisted on going there to visit her. It was just another indication of Sara's heart, and Farhan really didn't need the reminder.

At all.

In truth, he resented how much joy he felt around her. Emotion wasn't a part of the plan, yet here he was, having the shell he'd so carefully built up around his heart cracked, with the danger of it falling away altogether, letting her in.

Now he felt the danger of the situation he'd created acutely.

It had seemed the perfect plan: a marriage of convenience with no chance of it lasting.

No chance of rejection.

But all that had changed. Sara had changed him, fundamentally, at a soul-deep level. She'd made him look at things differently, somehow calming the storm he'd felt himself to be in the center of. He could face the future with the kind of equanimity he'd never thought he'd achieve. Yet somehow he doubted it would be the same without her at his side.

This wasn't how it was supposed to be. He wasn't supposed to crave her—her attention, smiles, time, body—the way he did.

Every night he told himself it would be the last time he went to her, but the next he was pulled right back, following a golden bond he now felt tightening around his chest. The only good thing was that she clearly had no urge to stay in Kalyana, although her love for the country, and the people, was patently clear. She still spoke often about getting back to her family, who were still calling on her as though she was the only one who could solve all their problems. About opening a clinic in Northern Ontario. Calling Trinka to check on Coconut, the dog she wanted to take back with her.

The dog he'd secretly, stupidly, sent a plane for, so it would be waiting for her when she got back to the palace.

Wanting to please her, like a besotted fool.

They still had months to go on their agreement. Would this drive to have her keep growing, until he wanted nothing more than to make her stay? Everything inside him rebelled at the potential agony such a situation would engender, yet there was a part of him that already hated the notion of her leaving at all.

It was untenable, but he'd got himself into the situation, and couldn't see a way out.

Do you even want one?

Only pride stopped him from growling aloud at the thought, and it took all his concentration to adopt a neutral expression so no one would guess his inner turmoil.

Sara finished talking and laughing with the elderly lady, who was approximately one hundred and four, according to the records, and came back over to join him and the rest of the official party. Her face was glowing, the love and joy she imparted to everyone around her almost visible to the naked eye. His chest ached just from looking at her, seeing the luminous beauty on display for all to see.

One of the nursing home attendants came by to whisper to the director and, as Sara rejoined the group, the director said, "I know you're on a tight schedule, but there is another patient of ours who would like to see you. He once was an aide to the Governor, and says he met you many years ago, Your Highness. If you have a few moments, I know he would appreciate it very much."

"Of course," Farhan replied.

As they walked down a corridor toward the room, the director said, "Mr. Raj has no family coming to visit him, and although he's not bedridden he's had a gastric upset, and we've kept him quarantined. He's no longer contagious, just a bit weak, and we didn't know you were coming, or we would have got him up. It will be real treat for him."

She opened a door, and ushered them into the small, neat room, where the patient lay. While his body was clearly thin and frail, making hardly a bump beneath the sheets, his eyes were bright.

Then Mr. Raj looked at Sara, and his eyes filled with tears, which overflowed down his cheeks.

Sara was at his bedside in an instant, leaning down to take his outstretched hand, bending to hear what he whispered to her.

She jerked upright, her face pale, her gaze swinging to find Farhan, as he stood at the foot of the bed.

He didn't know what the old man had said to her but her expression had him stepping closer, reaching to pull her away, but she avoided his hand.

"I-it's okay," she stuttered, but she looked past him at the other people in the doorway, and he saw the confused, almost frantic gleam in her eyes. "C-could we have a few minutes alone with Mr. Raj, please?"

CHAPTER FIFTEEN

FARHAN DIDN'T NEED to ask why, just moved toward the door, shepherding everyone in the room out in front of him, making polite noises as he went. Curiosity overwhelmed him as he firmly shut the door and turned back to the bed.

Sara was still pale, looked as though she were about to cry too.

"T-Tell him what you said to me," she said, reaching out and pulling Farhan closer.

"You are my granddaughter." It wasn't a question but a firm, convincing statement. "When I saw you on TV, saw you had married Prince Farhan, I knew."

A rush of mixed emotions fired through Farhan's blood, and he had to tamp them down, keep his voice level, as he said, "Are you sure, Mr. Raj? Princess Sara was adopted as a baby. Her roots are uncertain."

The look the old man gave him was just shy of scathing.

"She is Prince Bhaskar's daughter, and child of my daughter, Yolande. I know this to be true."

As though her legs wouldn't keep her upright anymore, Sara sank down onto the edge of the bed. Farhan noticed she hadn't relinquished Mr. Raj's hand.

"How…? What…?" She cleared her throat, and tried

again. "Why didn't you say anything when everyone was searching for Bhaskar?"

Mr. Raj shook his head, sorrow making his already wrinkled face even more lined.

"My Yolande was just fifteen when I took her to Huban, where I was stationed as part of my duties to the then Governor. I don't know how or when she met Bhaskar but, just after we returned to the south, she disappeared. No one was very interested in finding out what happened to her, not when just after that Prince Bhaskar disappeared as well, and I never thought the two things were in any way related."

"How did you find out that they were, sir?" Farhan's heart was pounding. The air in the room felt close, arid, and it took all of his control not to react to what he was hearing.

"Many years later, my daughter contacted me by letter. She told me she was living in Canada, in a place called Fort McMurray, and confessed to what she'd done. Bhaskar had convinced her to go away with him, had arranged it all through a friend in England. They were happy, she said, and I knew revealing their whereabouts might endanger Yolande.

"I didn't dare tell anyone what had happened. The Queen was almost crazed in her grief, and I, perhaps cravenly, wished most of all for my daughter's happiness. If Queen Nargis had found out what had really happened, I have no doubt she would have sent soldiers to bring them back, whether they willed it or not."

"Do...do you know what happened to them?"

Mr. Raj shifted fitfully, and Sara rose to help him lean forward, rearranging the pillows behind his back.

"Thank you," he murmured, his gaze never leaving her face.

"You're welcome," she said, but she didn't smile. Her face looked pinched, suddenly exhausted, and Farhan wanted to take her away, leave the rest of the story untold, but knew he couldn't.

No matter how painful the end might be.

"Yolande kept in contact with me after that. They had taken new names, of course, and settled in a place where there were no Kalyanese immigrants. She was lonely, and homesick, but the greatest unhappiness in her life was that she was unable to conceive. She was in her late forties when she finally told me she was expecting. I was worried, for her, for the baby, and I was right to worry."

His voice broke, and a tear trickled down his cheek.

"Yolande wrote to tell me Bhaskar had died unexpectedly and she had decided to arrange for her baby to be adopted should anything happen to her. I wrote to tell her she could arrange to send the child to me instead, but I never heard back from her, and my inquiries into her well-being were too late. I eventually found out she had died in childbirth, and no one would tell me where her baby had gone."

Farhan felt the silence like a weight. He had his hand on Sara's shoulder, felt her trembling. There was one way to make sure the story was true, but it was the effect hearing this all was having on Sara that concerned him the most. He smoothed his hand down her back, and she leaned into the caress.

"Do you remember the names they used in Canada, sir?" Farhan asked.

"Of course. Brian and Yasmine Haskell. Do you want to see a picture of your mother?" The last addressed to Sara.

"Yes, please."

"There's a box in the wardrobe. Bring it to me."

"Stay," Farhan said. "I'll get it."

When he put the small cedar casket in the other man's hands, Farhan found himself under scrutiny.

"I did meet you, many years ago, Your Highness, when you were just a small child. I hope you don't mind my telling the nurses about it, so as to see my granddaughter."

"Of course not, sir."

That earned him a small smile, before Mr. Raj turned his attention to the box. The picture was almost at the very bottom, and when he held it out to Sara, Farhan's breath caught in his throat. The resemblance between mother and daughter was obvious, their smiles identical, although Sara had inherited much from her father too. He'd seen her staring at Bhaskar's portrait in the palace, her gaze pensive, perhaps searching for the connection she couldn't feel.

Sara took it almost reverently, stared at it for a long, silent time. Tears streamed down her cheeks, but she seemed unaware of them until Farhan shoved his handkerchief into her hand.

Seeing her like that almost undid him.

His heart ached, feeling her sorrow and overwhelming joy as if they were his own.

He'd never been an emotional person. He'd pushed emotions away until they were like background noise in his life, not things that drove or spurred him on. Now he felt he was all emotion, driven by the need to protect and keep her safe.

But this encounter with Mr. Raj had made an already

complicated situation even more complex, and Farhan wasn't sure how to deal with the fallout.

Sara was wrung out.

They'd stayed with her grandfather for hours, listening to his stories of her mother as a child, reading the letters Yolande had sent her father. The last one had made her cry. Her mother's anguish at the loss of her husband had seemed to pour off the page.

She'd promised to come back and see her grandfather the following day, although they were supposed to go back to Huban that evening. Having just found him, she didn't want to simply disappear.

Farhan had questioned the nursing home staff about his condition. Anupam Raj was in fairly good health, although his stomach bug had laid him low for a little while. He was in the nursing home, they said, because he had no family still alive.

Her heart had ached when they'd said that, knowing the loneliness he'd experienced over the years while his daughter had been gone, hiding so as not to be torn away from the man she'd loved.

"Perhaps if my wife were alive, she would have realized what was happening between Yolande and Bhaskar, but she died when Yolande was just eleven, and I was raising her on my own. I was consumed by my work, trying to make sure I could give her a good life, send her to university, give her whatever she needed. I wasn't paying attention to the signs."

So much heartbreak in his life. Sara wanted to ensure his last years were happier.

But just finding him had changed everything.

She'd heard Farhan quietly ask her grandfather to

hold onto the secret of her father's identity a while longer, and the old man's promise to do so. Now she had to try to figure out what that question meant, both for her and her future in Kalyana.

The agreement between herself and Farhan hadn't truly taken into consideration what would happen should someone come forward to name her the daughter of Bhaskar. He'd been so sure no one would that he'd said a year would be long enough for them to remain married. She'd been so eager for adventure she'd said yes, never contemplating how the journey would change her life.

How being Farhan's wife, his lover, would change everything.

More and more she felt the chains binding her to Kalyana tightening.

It all felt surreal. She'd thought the story of her birth would remain a mystery. Oh, she'd believed Farhan when he'd said Bhaskar was her father, had even looked at his portrait in the palace gallery, but she'd felt nothing. He'd been a handsome face on the wall. But seeing her mother's photograph, hearing their story had brought such a welter of emotions she wasn't sure how to deal with it.

Kalyana had truly changed her forever.

And now her time here, already limited, seemed set to be cut short.

How could she leave so soon, just when things between her and Farhan were so good? When her heart wasn't ready for the separation?

"Are you all right?"

They were in the back of the official vehicle that had driven them around all day. Outside the windows it was dark, shadows of trees flashing by against an only slightly less dark sky. They'd stayed way past when they were supposed to get back to the plane, and she suspected, while she'd been caught up in the moment, Farhan had made all the necessary arrangements for them to stay the night.

She appreciated it, but couldn't muster any energy to think about anything else but her grandfather's story and wondering what would happen next.

"I'm fine," she replied, but reached blindly across the seat for his hand, desperately in need of human contact.

In need of him.

He took it, his thumb rubbing over her knuckles in gentle, soothing circles. And it did soothe her.

When had he become so important to her emotional well-being?

The question caused an icy shiver up her spine, and she pushed the thought away, too drained to deal with it just then.

"I have to return to Huban tomorrow morning."

"Yes," she replied. He had surgery scheduled for the afternoon. They were counting on him to help with the backlog. Was it terribly selfish to want him to stay, even knowing the hospital needed him?

"I'll send the plane back for you, unless you want to remain longer."

"No." She was in a fog but, even to her, her monosyllabic responses sounded rude. "No, I'll visit Grandfather in the morning and come back to Huban in the afternoon. That way I can get started making arrangements for him to come too." Having just found him, she wanted him close by.

"Leave that to me," he said, in his usual no-nonsense way. "I can handle it for you."

It made her, stupidly, want to cry again, but she quashed the urge. His poor handkerchief was already a damp, wrinkled mess from before, and she'd run out of tissues.

"I'm sorry," she said instead. "For disrupting everything."

"There's nothing to apologize for," he replied, squeezing her fingers. "You didn't plan any of this, neither was it of your making."

He was so understanding, her heart ached. Why did he have to be so perfect? She turned her hand to squeeze his fingers in return, thankful to have him on her side.

And later, when he came to her room as usual, he said, "I thought you could use some company. Not sex, just company."

That's when she knew there would never be another man for her. She was resigned to leaving, because she wanted all of Farhan, not just sexual attention, dribs and drabs of affection.

All of him; heart, body, and soul, if that were even possible. Just as she'd given him.

Nothing less would do for her.

And no other man would do either.

He held her, and she contemplated the lonely years ahead. Not unfulfilling, she decided, just not the home and family life she'd always thought she'd eventually have.

Not this feeling of safety she had lying in Farhan's arms.

Or the soul-shaking rush of emotion whenever they made love.

All the feelings of the day whirred together in her head, keeping her awake, restless.

So she rolled over, trapping him under her body.

"What is it, beautiful? Are you okay?"

She didn't want to talk. Instead, she wanted to somehow transcribe her inner emotions into the physical. Leaning down, she kissed him, taking the lead, their tongues tangling together deliciously.

He groaned, putting up no resistance, letting her love him as much as she wanted. As she slid down his body to kneel between his thighs, she could see his eyes gleaming in the weak moonlight coming through a crack in the drapes.

Over the last days she'd gotten bolder, but had never been this assertive.

"Lift," she said, tugging at the waistband of his silk pajama pants, and he did as bidden without a word.

But as she tugged them off, he said quietly, carefully, "We don't have to do this, beautiful."

She took his erection in her hand and said honestly, "I've never felt I *have* to do anything with or for you, Farhan. I want to. I need this tonight."

Taking him to the brink with her hands and mouth gave her such intense satisfaction it was as though he was touching her in return.

"Beautiful, please," he whispered, his body tense, bowing in ecstasy.

It was a plea, whether for her to stop or for the release building in him she didn't know. Giving him pleasure took her outside herself, to a place where all she thought about was him, all she felt was the love inside, now acknowledged, growing stronger each minute.

When he lunged up to take her by the shoulders and drag her body up over his, she laughed, making him growl in response.

"Are you trying to make me go insane?" he asked against her lips.

"Maybe I am," she replied, sliding back, taking him deep in one quick motion, her heart singing when she heard his rushed exhalation, blown out as though forced from his lungs.

Then she slowed, suddenly not wanting to hurry, taking her time as she rose and fell, savoring each heart-stopping sensation, feeling his body coiling and moving beneath hers. The tension built within, but she was no longer afraid of it, just let it take her to where that golden moment of bliss waited.

Farhan's hands on her breasts, her belly, pushed her arousal even higher, until she couldn't maintain her leisurely pace anymore.

"Yes. Oh, yes," she whimpered, as Farhan reached between them, stimulating her with exquisite finesse, taking her to the edge.

Tonight he lost control first, and she reveled in hearing his orgasm, knowing she'd taken him there. Then the pressure of his thumb increased, and she was flying too.

As, still draped across his body, she came down from her high, two thoughts struck her in quick succession.

She'd never been more confused.

And they'd forgotten to use a condom.

CHAPTER SIXTEEN

SARA HADN'T EXPECTED Farhan to be at the airport when she arrived back in Huban, and he wasn't. He'd slipped out of bed while she was still asleep to go to the airport, and waking up without him beside her had left her feeling lonely and afraid.

She'd hoped to talk to him about what they were going to do next. Yet, in the light of day, her fears regarding Farhan's reaction had waned, seemed unwarranted. Yes, the revelations of the day before had come as a shock, but did they truly sound the death knell to their marriage? Did they have to?

Even the thought of her grandfather's story getting out didn't frighten her the way it perhaps should. Yes, she was the only one in love, but they'd grown so close, was it unreasonable to hope one day he might love her in return?

He himself had said arranged marriages were traditional in his family, and that was what they had. Couldn't they, somehow, make it work? Even his assertion that he didn't want children didn't deter her from her optimism. If, in time, he changed his mind, or even if he never did, Sara knew Farhan was the one man for her. The night before she had been resigned to leaving him. Today all she wanted was to stay, forever.

If that made her contrary, so be it.

"Crown Prince Farhan is still in theatre, Your Highness," Kavan said, as he ushered her to the black SUV he usually drove. "He's asked me to take you back to the palace, and inform you he might not be home in time for dinner."

"Thank you, Kavan," she said, wondering why Farhan hadn't texted as much.

"And King Uttam has requested you meet with him at four o'clock, in his office."

That was new, and she doubted Farhan knew about it, since he *definitely* would have texted.

"I'll be there," she told Kavan, who informed her he would advise the King's aide-de-camp Joseph Malliot.

No doubt King Uttam wanted to discuss her finding her grandfather, and she only just stopped herself from nibbling on the side of her fingernail, as she wondered what he would have to say.

It was obvious that while Anupam Raj had been a respectable man, he was definitely not royalty. Perhaps Uttam would resent mingling her blood with the royal line, now that they knew for sure who her mother was.

When she got back to the palace and was greeted by a wriggling ball of brown fur, she knew her hopes for a future with Farhan weren't misplaced. For him to have had Coconut brought to Huban for her spoke volumes about his character and, she thought, how much he cared about her happiness.

Later that afternoon, when Joseph ushered her into King Uttam's office, she found it empty, a red macaw in a cage the only occupant. As the bird seemed to try to attract her attention, Sara noticed the French doors opening into a private garden were ajar, and she walked over to look through them.

There was her father-in-law, seated on a bench, smoking a thin cigar. He saw her in the doorway, and waved her over.

"Please don't lecture me," he said, his stern lips twitching at the corners. "I used to smoke these things all day, every day, but have cut down to one a week."

He patted the bench beside him, and Sara dutifully sat, turning slightly so she was facing him.

"With that amount of restraint, couldn't you find it in yourself to quit entirely?" she asked, although she wanted to smile, seeing Uttam so relaxed.

"I didn't want to," he replied, then took a puff. "Life is short and should, whenever possible, be enjoyed. I know my family worries about me after my health scare, but carrying the burden of rule makes me testy. I think I deserve a little treat every now and then."

"Well, kudos to you for cutting back that much and not just starting up again. Most people couldn't do it."

His chin tipped up and, in that instant, Sara saw once more the resemblance between father and son.

That definitely was where Farhan got his arrogant look but, with Farhan anyway, she knew it wasn't really arrogance that made him look down that nose of his. He did it when he was in any way unsure, or perhaps embarrassed, and trying to hide it.

"A royal must have a strong will, and do what is right, no matter how difficult that may be. Farhan has learned this, as I think you have already also."

He sounded so snooty Sara was at first taken aback and then had to suppress a giggle. Luckily, the King was studying the end of his cigar, not looking at her, and didn't notice.

Uttam fussed with his cigar for a moment, relighting it when it looked as though it might have gone out, and then, wreathed in fragrant smoke, said, "I heard about your discovery while in the south."

"Yes," she replied cautiously.

"I remember Anupam Raj well. He was still in government service when we came here in the nineteen-sixties. A respectable man, who must have mourned as much for his daughter as Queen Nargis did when Bhaskar disappeared."

"Yes," she said again, not knowing exactly where the conversation was going.

"Farhan has informed me that Anupam will be coming to live here, in the palace, to be close to you, as his last living relative."

That she hadn't known. She'd thought perhaps Farhan would find a nearby nursing home, where she could go and visit him whenever she wanted, but her heart lifted to know he'd be even closer.

"I would appreciate you allowing that, Your Majesty," she said, trying to be as formal as she could, hoping Uttam wasn't going to refuse.

He gave her a stern, sideways glance.

"Of course I will allow it. Neither you nor he had anything to do with your parents' decisions, and shouldn't suffer for them."

"Thank you."

He inclined his head slightly, before continuing, "Your parents, your father in particular, did a great wrong to my family, but now you have the chance to make it right."

A bubble of resentment rose in Sara, and she was forced to bite the inside of her lip not to answer back. He'd just said neither her grandfather nor she were responsible for what had happened, but now it was on her shoulders to fix it? How unfair could you be?

Luckily, before she lost control and responded, Uttam went on.

"The important thing now is that you give me a grandchild. Only then will it be safe to tell the people who you truly are, and they will know Bhaskar's line continues, to one day rule the country again."

Again she had to bite back a retort, annoyed by the arrogant way he demanded she bear a child, as though it were no more than telling her to cross the grass and pick him a flower. Did he not know how Farhan felt about having children? The urge to tell him, to lay it at his feet in spite, was almost overpowering.

Unaware of her resentful thoughts, Uttam said, "I was not always the best of fathers. Believe me, I'm fully aware of that fact, and now, in my old age, regret time not spent with my sons."

He gazed out over the gardens, his face as stern as ever, but Sara heard the undertone of sorrow in his voice and her anger faded, as he continued, "You know the saying? *There are three things in life you cannot recover: the word after it is spoken, the moment after it is missed, and the time after it is gone.* It is indeed true."

In that moment Uttam wasn't a king, just a man searching his soul for answers, haunted by the past and all its attendant pain.

"Yes," she replied. "It's very true. But there are still time and moments to come, words yet to be spoken."

In the silence that fell between them, broken only by birdsong, her own ghosts stirred, and she wondered if Uttam's did too.

The King seemed to shake off his momentary melancholy, reaching over to pat her hand.

"My consolation is I know Farhan will do much better as a father, and as a king."

Cautious, but resolved, she replied, "Perhaps, Your Majesty, those are words you might say to him. Ones neither of you would regret?"

He turned his stern gaze on her and she saw the pain in his eyes fade to something softer, more contemplative.

"Perhaps you're right, Sara, although old habits die hard."

"That's true too, sir, but sometimes we have to forge new ones, for the benefit of ourselves and others."

Uttam smiled, and Sara was amazed. Farhan really was the spitting image of his father, right down to the gorgeous smile.

And how stingy they were with them.

"My son is lucky to have you at his side. You'll make a good queen one day, and bear me strong grandchildren. That's imperative. With my health not being the best, I'd like to see my future heir before I die."

Taking that as dismissal, she rose. "I hope that day is a long way away, sir."

To her surprise, Uttam rose too, and bent to kiss her on one cheek then the other.

"No doubt Farhan feels the same way too," he said, in a jovial manner, turning her toward the French doors inside. "All he really wants to do is be a doctor. I hoped to let him do it as long as possible, away from the royal responsibilities we all find so onerous, but my health cut his time away short. He has much to learn, though, so it's a good thing he came back when he did, and didn't wait until he had to take the throne himself."

Did Farhan know that was why his father had let him return to Australia? Somehow she doubted it. When Farhan spoke about his father telling him to go back after Ali died, she'd heard deep pain in his voice, a diminishing of the proud self-confidence she associated with him. Hopefully, hearing the real reason, and that his father was truly proud of him, would take away the last vestiges of hurt and constraint between father and son, or at least help to bring them a little closer.

Although, dealing with two such proud men, it might not.

Uttam strode around his desk and pulled out his chair as Sara reached for the office door handle, and she had her back to the King when he said, "I was happy to hear that you refused to consider my offer of financial compensation for giving Farhan an heir. It showed good character."

She froze, not sure she'd heard the King correctly, and said without turning around, "Excuse me, sir?"

Uttam went on, as if he hadn't heard her question, "I would have been willing to pay twice as much to secure peace in our country, but it is better that you do it out of duty rather than financial gain."

"Yes, sir," she murmured, suddenly cold inside.

It reminded her forcefully of why she was there, how Farhan had viewed her when he'd found out about her. How he'd been sure that giving her money would be the way to get her to agree to his deal. He hadn't known the money, while welcome, had been only a small part of the reason she'd said yes.

But maybe he had, when he'd said she should consider the lump sum her inheritance from Bhaskar. In doing that, he'd made her feel she wasn't selling herself to him but, in fact, would be entering into a mutually beneficial arrangement.

Besides, it was different now, wasn't it? Now that he knew her? Surely he could see the money wasn't that important to her? Sure, she'd paid off her student loan, arranged to buy her parents a house and cover the up-keep, but the only other expense she'd taken on had been paying for Nonni's nurse.

Yet as she made her way back to their apartments, telling herself Farhan must, by now, know her better than to think she was in it only for the money didn't really help. Uttam's final words had dimmed the bright flame of confidence only just lit that morning.

Farhan didn't get back to the palace until late that evening, but he found Sara waiting up for him. He'd texted earlier to say there was a patient he wanted to monitor a bit longer than usual, a woman who'd undergone a bilateral salpingectomy, but who also had a history of dangerously high blood pressure that didn't respond as expected to medication.

"You didn't have to wait up for me," he said, holding himself in tight control, refusing to give in to the temptation to go over and kiss her, the way he'd gotten into the habit of doing.

"I couldn't sleep anyway," she replied. "Too much excitement over the last couple of days, perhaps. And I wanted to talk to you."

She looked tousled, as though she'd lain down and got back up again, cozy in her plush robe, her legs tucked up under her, Coconut lying across her lap. Farhan's heart contracted, his stomach ached, and he knew his decision to let her go was the right one.

He'd always planned to. Even on the days when he'd seemed to think almost exclusively about her, he'd reminded himself she wasn't meant to stay. That she'd be leaving sooner rather than later.

Meeting Mr. Raj had simply accelerated the timeline. If she didn't leave soon, his father would want to tell the people about her origins, and then she'd be trapped. Or, at least, her leaving would be more difficult.

He hadn't planned to discuss it with her tonight, had convinced himself to put it off for a while longer, but now, seeing her, wanting her so badly, he knew it had to be soon.

As Farhan lowered himself into an easy chair, he asked, "Is something wrong?"

She shook her head.

"On the contrary. I wanted to thank you for Coconut, and for arranging for my grandfather to come and live at the palace."

"How did you hear about that?"

"It was your father who told me."

Surprised at the mention of Uttam, he frowned. "You went to see my father?"

"He invited me and, of course, I went. It was an interesting talk. Do you know he let you stay in Australia as long as he did because he knew all you wanted was to practice medicine? He knew once you came home, you'd get bogged down by your position as Crown Prince and all the royal duties you'd have to take on."

Now it was shock making his eyebrows rise, even as he struggled to maintain a neutral expression. How was she able to get his father, who never spoke of personal matters, to open up that way?

Then her words struck home, and he only just stopped himself from gasping as his breath caught in his throat. Could that really be the truth? It was almost unfathomable, unbelievable. Yet he knew his father never said anything he didn't mean, so...

Desperate to change the subject, unable to discuss it further, he pulled himself together and said, "But I'm sure he didn't summon you to talk about my time in Australia. What else did he have to say?"

"He wanted to make it plain he expected me to quickly produce an heir, so he could tell the people about who my father was."

Another blow to his composure, which was becoming increasingly difficult to hold onto. Rising restlessly, he strode across to the sideboard and poured himself a finger of Scotch.

Now, more than ever, he was aware of the need to let Sara go, before it was too late.

If it wasn't already.

Memories of the night before rose, unbidden, into his head. The rush of emotion when she'd turned to him, wanting his comfort; the immediate arousal, as she'd made her delicious intentions known. Her shadowy form above him, the sensation of being enveloped by her sweet, hot body.

His desire for her didn't rise slowly, like smoke, to fill him. It was, instead, as though a hidden volcano released all its lava at once to rush through veins and sinews, burning all thoughts but those of her from his head.

He couldn't be trusted to do the right thing, to stay away, to keep his distance. It all had to end.

Taking a swallow of Scotch, he found the strength to turn and face her before he said, "Well, if my father is getting involved, perhaps it's time to put an end to this game, and have you return home."

CHAPTER SEVENTEEN

SHOCK TURNED SARA's insides to ice, and all she could do was stare at his stoic, noncommittal expression in disbelief. The flame of hope, kindled by the connection she felt to him, his actions toward her, waned to a flicker in the face of his words. "What?"

"I believe it's the logical thing to do at this juncture. What started as a simple business contract has become something far more complicated, and I think it should end, before we find ourselves in a situation neither of us wants."

The little flicker of hope died, leaving Sara cold. So cold she had to clench her teeth to make sure they didn't chatter.

When she didn't reply, Farhan continued, in the same matter-of-fact voice as before, "It's not as though we ever intended our arrangement to last very long. It's just been cut shorter by circumstances, and I'll consider your side of the agreement fulfilled."

Rising, she set Coco on the floor and turned her back on Farhan. The little dog whined, coming to lean on her leg, as Sara clenched her fingers together across her stomach. The brief respite from being under Farhan's unemotional gaze steadied her, allowed her to control the thoughts whirring in her brain.

When she unclasped her fingers before turning to face him, the blood rushing into her abused digits gave her additional strength.

"And what if our slip last night has unwanted consequences?"

An unreadable expression flashed across his face and then, just as swiftly, was gone, leaving Sara to wonder if it had even really existed.

"We'll wait to make a final decision until we know whether that is the case or not."

Carefully bracing herself so her trembling legs wouldn't betray her, Sara tried to maintain an air of cool reasonableness, even though inside she was dying slowly, bit by bit.

Pride wouldn't let her argue. Especially not in the face of his emotionless, arrogant stance.

Yet hadn't she already discovered he was often at his most emotional, his most vulnerable when he cloaked himself in haughtiness? When his chin tipped up and he looked down his nose?

She glanced at his hands, saw the white knuckles where he gripped the rock crystal glass, the bulge of the other hand fisted in his pocket.

What was he really feeling? Worried she'd make a scene? Upset his plan had fallen apart? Or was there something else?

There was no way for her to know, so all she said was, "If that's what you want."

Again there was a flash of emotion, in his eyes this time. Then he looked down at his glass as it rose once more to his lips, and it was lost to her.

There was nothing more to say, was there?

She'd turned toward her bedroom, Coco at her heels,

when he said, "In case you're wondering, I'll compensate you as though you were here for the year."

Something snapped inside her. Perhaps it had always been there, this resentment, needing only this final nudge to be released.

Did no one want her just for herself? For the person she was inside?

The King saw her as a means to reclaiming his family honor and giving Kalyana an heir.

Her sisters saw her as a means for them to keep drifting through life.

Even her parents, who she knew loved her, saw her as an emotional, and sometimes financial, prop.

And now Farhan couldn't see past her usefulness to the woman who loved him, would do anything for him, if he could only love her in return. Had the nerve to speak to her as though she were nothing but a hireling.

She deserved better than that, from all of them, and as rage built inside her, determination to get her due rose with it.

Spinning around, she glared at him.

"Don't you dare speak to me about money right now. It's bad enough knowing your father wanted to pay me to carry your baby, without you getting into the act. If you want the damn money back, I'll work the rest of my life to make sure you get it, even what you deemed my 'inheritance.' I don't need anything from you. Ever again."

He paled, took a step toward her, but she backed away from his outstretched hand. Her chest was tight with anger, pain like a band around her heart.

"No, I don't want it back, Sara. I'll not accept it. Please, hear me out—"

"No! I could forgive your father for thinking throwing money at me would be effective before he met me, but I'll never forgive you for degrading my time here, as though money was all I was in it for. I guess it just goes to show I'm better off leaving, since you clearly don't know me at all."

She heard him call her name as she spun around, but ignored him, controlling her steps so as not to run, keeping her head straight, so he couldn't see her tears.

The best days of her life had just turned into the worst, and there wasn't anything she could do about it.

Yet, despite her pain and anger, Sara sat on the edge of her bed a week after the confrontation with Farhan and cried, as she realized her period had come.

There would be no baby from her last night of bliss with him.

In the days leading up to this moment, she'd come to the realization that if she were pregnant, staying in Kalyana would be the right thing to do. She'd seen carrying his child as an out, of sorts; a way to do what she really wanted to do anyway, but without taking responsibility for the decision.

A cowardly way of dealing with the problem, which had now been taken away.

And she'd spent no time planning for her departure, ignoring the coming eventuality as though to do so would make it go away. Now she had to consider how to get not only herself but her grandfather and Coconut back to Canada too.

She'd have to ask Farhan, but he'd retreated into the stern, stoic man she'd first met; unfailingly polite but cool and distant, and Sara tried to be the same.

It was the hardest, most heartbreaking situation she'd ever been in, but she knew leaving was really for the best.

She didn't want Farhan's friendship, his companionship, or protection alone. She wanted his love as well. And nothing less would do.

Throwing herself into work at the hospital was an outlet for the nervous energy inside, and it became life-saving, allowing her to focus on something other than her dumpster fire of a life.

Just went to prove that being royalty, and rich, didn't make life all rosy.

Additional pressure from her sisters didn't help.

Mariah called to ask whether Sara was sending extra money home.

"It's the least you can do, to help Mom and Dad," she said.

But Sara wasn't falling for that. The time to stand firm with everyone in her life had come, finally.

"I've made arrangements to buy Mom and Dad a house, and I'll be taking care of the house expenses, but beyond that, I'm not taking responsibility for all of you anymore."

Even if it meant working herself to the bone to make sure they were secure, while also paying Farhan back. Despite his saying he wouldn't take her money, she was still determined to do it.

When Mariah spluttered and started trying to guilt Sara into more, she put her foot down.

"Listen," she told her sister. "You need to get your life together, and I'm willing to help you do it, but I'm not indiscriminately throwing money your way. You and Cyndi need to grow up and start taking responsibility for yourselves. You deserve more than you're allowing yourself to achieve."

That was the furthest she was willing to go, and she was drawing a line in the sand.

She couldn't bring herself to be as firm with her parents, but she'd noticed there were fewer calls and texts since Nonni had accepted the nurse and things had settled down for Aunt Jackie. Sara knew their dependence on her had been her own fault and she was resigned to continuing as she'd started, but maybe because of the distance they were finding their own way.

When she went back, it wouldn't be to London anyway. It was time to use her new-found assurance to advance in her career.

Now, drying her silly tears, she went to wash their tracks off her face, to make sure Farhan wouldn't know they had ever been there. Their breakfasts together were sporadic. She'd gotten into the habit of checking his schedule to get an idea of what time he'd be departing for the hospital in the morning. That way, sometimes she left earlier than he did, or vice versa, neither wanting to spend more time with the other than necessary. This morning, however, she planned to let him know there was no chance of them having conceived, glad it would mean her time with him, here, was up.

Staying in Kalyana was breaking her heart. It was as though love was all around her, yet just out of her reach. Her feelings for Farhan hadn't changed, even knowing Farhan didn't even care enough about her to truly get to know her, the way she felt she knew him.

Yet, did she really know him? She could have sworn there was more between them than just sex, or even friendship, but, then, what did she know? Thirty-one years old or not, in the end she'd turned out to be a silly virgin, falling for the first man who'd shown her any attention.

The thought was dismal, made her doubt some of the very attributes she prided herself on, like the ability to read people, to get a true sense of who they were. Damn him for not only breaking her heart but for making her doubt herself too.

Then she shook her head, knowing she'd done those things to herself, when she'd let herself fall in love with him.

Bracing herself, she left her room about the time she thought he'd be finishing breakfast.

Walking into the dining room, she saw him in his place at the table, reading a newspaper, and her heart stumbled over itself.

He was so handsome, even with slight bags under his eyes, and weary lines, which hadn't been there before, bracketing his mouth. He'd taken on a heavy surgical load, and the stress of doing that, along with his royal duties, showed.

Perhaps her news might lighten his load a little. It would be one less thing to worry about.

Taking a steadying breath, she walked to her chair. Hearing her footsteps, Farhan raised his head, and then stood.

"Good morning," he said, in his cool, measured way.

"Good morning," she replied, taking her seat. The attendant brought her tea, and she thanked him, then told him she would serve herself from the array of food on the sideboard. He melted away, knowing he would be summoned if needed thereafter.

"Will you still be going to the airport today?"

Farhan was looking back down at his newspaper as he asked, as though he couldn't even be bothered to meet her gaze while they spoke. It made her unbearably sad.

"Of course," she replied. "Is the flight still scheduled to arrive at ten?" Her grandfather was due to arrive from the south; arrangements Farhan had informed her of by text the day before. It was one more thing to worry about. How was she going to explain to Grandfather that, just as he'd come to live with her, she would be leaving?

"Yes."

"Good."

"Kavan will take you there. Will you be here, or at the hospital?"

The thought of mooching about the palace for three hours didn't appeal.

"At the hospital."

"I'll inform him."

"Thank you."

She turned her attention to her tea, depression settling like a cloak on her shoulders. Even in the beginning, when they'd hardly known each other, there'd been more ease between them. Now she felt as though Farhan had excised her cleanly, surgically, from his life in every important way there was.

Suddenly she was fiercely glad it would soon be over. To spend the rest of her life trapped in a marriage to a man she loved but who treated her with cool disdain would be intolerable.

Sara took a deep breath, knowing she should tell him but suddenly not wanting to, anxiety chewing at her insides at the thought of his no doubt cold reaction.

"I thought you should know, I'm not pregnant."

His head came up, and an expression she couldn't interpret crossed his face. His eyes flashed, as he stared at her, and then the stoic, controlled mask was firmly back in place.

"Thank you for telling me," was all he said, before looking back at the paper, leaving her breathless and bereft.

Farhan stared at the newspaper, the print dancing in front of his eyes, making no sense.

If he was honest, once Sara had entered the room he'd been unable to concentrate, reading the same lines over and over, the words having no meaning to his muddled brain.

Disappointment twisted in his belly, and he clenched one hand into a fist on his lap. She'd stated it so simply, without inflection, leaving him at a loss, unable to tell how she felt about the issue, left adrift on his own acidic sea of pain.

And for all his plans never to be a father, his surety he would turn out unfit for the task, regret ate at him now, and her words, when she'd accused him of never knowing her at all, still haunted him.

Locking it all away, the way he always did, had become almost impossible. She was on his mind almost every single waking moment. And now he faced the fact there was no reason for her to remain in Kalyana.

They should discuss her departure, all the plans that needed to be put in place for it to happen.

Instead he folded the paper and stood, leaving his half-eaten breakfast on the table.

"I'll let you know if there is any delay in Mr. Raj's flight."

By the time she said, "Thank you," he was already going out the door.

His cellphone rang as he was crossing the living room and, although he didn't feel like talking to anyone, he answered.

"Yes, Maazin?"

"I thought you should know, Cyclone Blandine has strengthened, and the meteorologists are beginning to think it will come this way."

Farhan stopped, forcing his full concentration on what his brother was saying. Kalyana was usually outside the path of storms in the Indian Ocean, but this one had formed further south than usual, and they'd been keeping an eye on it for the last couple of days.

"Do they have a prediction of when it might hit?"

"They're still not completely sure it will. There's some debate about whether wind shear will slow it down and eventually change the path, but I think we should continue making preparations."

"Yes," Farhan replied. They'd already put the emergency plan into action, but there was so much else that needed to be done. "By the time they know for sure whether the islands will get hit or not, it would be too late to get everything done otherwise."

"I'm putting together a further action plan right now, and I'll email it to you. Are you operating over the next few days, or will you be available to help?"

"All my scheduled surgeries are elective, so I'll cancel them. Better to not take the chance of having a patient with unexpected complications swell the ranks of the hospitalized. I'll get started on checking with the other hospitals, and making sure they're following emergency procedures."

"Good." Maazin was in full commander mode, his armed forces training kicking in. "Go over the emergency management plan, so you're fully briefed by the time you get the further action plan."

As he hung up the phone, Farhan was already thinking two steps ahead, although he was relatively sure

Cyclone Blandine wouldn't come anywhere near them. Every few years there was a scare like this, but the prevailing winds usually kept the brunt of the storms offshore, with little or no landfall. And even when Kalyana was affected, it was just outer bands bringing rain and moderately high winds.

But it was better to take all the precautions and not need to than to be caught flat-footed.

"Farhan."

He turned to find Sara standing in the doorway from the dining room. Her face looked pale, and he could see how she gripped the doorjamb, as though to hold herself up.

He was about to ask if she was okay when she said, "Please make arrangements for me to leave, and for my grandfather to follow, if he wants to. As soon as possible."

Then, before he could reply, she walked away, her back straight, head high, leaving him suddenly unable to catch his breath.

CHAPTER EIGHTEEN

FARHAN STOOD IN the air traffic control tower at Huban International, and watched the smaller of the two royal jets taxi to the end of the runway. As it turned its nose into the wind, preparing for takeoff, his stomach twisted, his chest aching with a sensation he didn't want to name.

Sara was onboard, leaving. Going back to where she belonged, he told himself for the millionth time.

For expediency's sake, they'd told everyone she had a family emergency, which necessitated her returning to Canada.

"It'll be easier right now, what with all the preparations you're all doing in case the cyclone comes close," she said, her voice distant, as though she was already gone. "Once I'm settled, you can arrange for Grandfather and Coconut to join me."

Mr. Raj was the one person she'd been honest with. At least, Farhan assumed she'd been honest with her grandfather, since he'd agreed to go to Canada, but he hadn't been privy to the conversation. All he knew was Mr. Raj, while still as polite as before, had given him what could only be described as sorrowful looks the last time they'd met. But he hadn't expressed an opinion, or offered any advice, for which Farhan was immensely grateful.

His phone vibrated in his pocket, but Farhan ignored it, all his attention on the jet. He distantly heard the pilot ask for clearance, the familiar call sign making him clench his teeth with the effort not to tell the controller to deny them the right to take off.

Letting her go was the right thing to do. Why, then, did it feel so wrong?

Then, before it seemed he even had time to blink, the jet was airborne, banking, turning northwest.

He watched it until it was out of sight, frozen inside, thankfully numb.

As he finally forced his feet to move his phone buzzed again, and this time he answered.

"Yes, Maazin?"

"Father wants to see us both in his office. Have you left the airport yet?"

"On my way out now. I'll be there in twenty minutes."

"Did Sara get off okay?"

Just hearing her name threatened to break him, but he simply said, "Yes. See you at the palace."

They'd all been working flat out, trying to make sure everything in the emergency management plan was implemented, while Blandine waltzed back and forth in the Indian Ocean like a deadly flirt. Each time they thought they were clear, she sashayed south again, and they were back on alert. No doubt Uttam wanted an update on their preparedness, but Farhan wasn't in a position to add much to any discussions.

Oh, he'd done his part. Flying to Agung to take supplies and make sure the hospital there was following protocols, as well as overseeing the plan to evacuate people from some of the outlying clinics if necessary. But it had all been done on autopilot, his entire brain taken up with thoughts of Sara leaving.

Now, settling back in the car, he tried to get up to speed on what had been happening elsewhere, but couldn't concentrate on the emails Maazin and others had sent. Instead, his mind insisted on taking him back through every moment of the time with Sara, from the jolt of attraction he'd felt that first night on her doorstep, to the moment she'd said goodbye.

"Be well, Farhan. Be happy." He'd wanted to answer, but his throat wouldn't work. It had been the expression in her eyes that had rendered him mute. One he recognized, but, even after all they'd shared, still didn't want to name.

He started as Kavan shut off the SUV, realizing they were already at the palace, although he couldn't remember a moment of the drive.

Get yourself together.

He needed to be on his toes to deal with his father right now.

The meeting went fairly quickly, with Maazin, thankfully, carrying most of the load, but when they rose at the end, Uttam said, "Farhan, a word."

Suppressing a sigh, he sank back down into the chair, was surprised when his father dismissed his aide, who usually stayed at his side in all meetings. Uttam fussed with some papers on his desk for a moment, leaving Farhan to wonder what, exactly, was going on.

When the door closed behind the others, his father finally turned his attention to Farhan.

"When is Sara coming back?"

He should have known it would be what was on his father's mind. It was the first time Farhan was glad his father's vision was so poor, so he couldn't see how the question caused his son to flinch.

"When she's settled things in Canada, sir."

"It was a bad time for her to leave, right in the middle of the preparations for the cyclone."

Farhan felt his hackles rise, but he kept his voice level, as he replied, "Sara did her part before she left. She ended up taking charge of the patient audit, and did a great job of it."

Uttam waved a hand. "I know." Then he shifted in his chair, as though uncomfortable, before continuing, "I would feel better knowing she was here to keep an eye on you, if the storm comes."

The words rocked Farhan back in his chair, literally. Then he understood. His father worried about losing another heir.

"Don't worry, sir. I'll be careful."

Uttam shook his head. "It doesn't matter if you are, Farhan. It won't stop me worrying about you, and your brother. Both of you have the drive to serve others, and would put yourselves in danger to do it, no matter the cost. It is a good attribute, and one of the many reasons I'm proud of you, so I suppose I shouldn't complain."

Too shocked to reply, Farhan stared across at his father, who had his chin tipped up and was looking down his nose, clearly uncomfortable with his unaccustomed display of emotion.

"Sara reminded me that just because I missed opportunities to speak or offer praise before, it doesn't mean new opportunities wouldn't arise. I felt this was one I shouldn't let pass. I grew up in a different era, Farhan. One where men didn't express how they felt, and were expected to keep everything locked inside. It became habitual for me, but I'm glad to know you don't have to follow suit. It will make you a better husband and father than I have been."

It was like looking in a mirror, but seeing his own reflection clearly for the first time, hearing a truth only his father, his mirror image, could tell.

Emotion wasn't the enemy. Locking it away was.

Sara too had tried to tell him that he didn't have to follow his father's lead, but he hadn't listened, too intent on holding onto past hurts, so as not to experience them again. And, in the process, he'd lost the best gift life could have given him.

Sara.

He rose, then hesitated. Found the words, then said them. "Thank you, Father. This means more to me than you could know."

Sara had the private lounge in Dubai International Airport to herself, and was glad of it. A steward fussed over her, until she told him, kindly but firmly, that she had all she needed.

What a lie.

What she needed was to get home to Canada, and get on with rebuilding her life. The delay—something about the plane needing a small repair—wasn't helping at all.

They were supposed to have flown straight on to London, where she would overnight, and then continue the journey the following day. The unexpected stop would be frustrating if she weren't so numb.

Even now, five hours into the trip, she couldn't believe she'd actually left Farhan, forever. Yet it was the right thing to do, for both of them. Hopefully one day he would wake up and realize he was so much more, so much better than he gave himself credit for. That he had more to offer than just being a surgeon, or a prince, or even a king, and it was within his capabilities to do all of them well, as well as being a wonderful husband and father.

As for her? She'd survive, but she was leaving love behind. Not because it was too painful, but because there would never be anyone like Farhan in her life again. He was one of a kind, and all she wanted. No one else would ever compare.

She closed her eyes, leaning her head back, ineffably weary, homesick for the place she'd just left her heart in.

"Is this seat taken?"

Eyes flying open, she spun in her seat, unable to believe what her ears were telling her.

But it was true. Farhan Alaoui, Crown Prince of Kalyana, was lowering himself into the seat beside her.

"What are you doing here?"

He hesitated before answering, and then his chin tipped up, and he said, "I came to Dubai to tell my wife that I have been the biggest fool that ever was. That I love her with all my heart, and I'm hoping she'll come home with me, so I can prove to her, every day and every night, that I understand now."

"U-understand? Understand what, Farhan?"

"That running from my emotions, or locking them away, doesn't mean I don't have them. That fleeing from pain doesn't mean it won't catch up. That loving you isn't something to fear, but something to embrace, and be grateful and thankful for.

"And I understand, too, how I hurt you when I treated our relationship as though it were still a business deal, despite knowing it was far more. But I didn't want you to suffer, financially, for my own cowardice."

He reached for her hand, curved his fingers around hers, the touch like a balm to her battered, sorrowful soul, as he continued, "And I am grateful, and thankful for you, Sara. Perhaps you don't love me, but I know without a doubt you care about me, and if that's all you want to give, I will gladly take it."

Amazed, she shook her head.

"But you must know I love you, Farhan. That I didn't argue when you said I should leave because I couldn't settle for the crumbs of your affection, no matter how nicely you treated me or how good we were together in bed."

His fingers tightened on hers almost painfully, and his eyes flashed with that dark fire she loved so much. "Crumbs? You have my whole heart, beautiful. My soul. You're my everything. I should have told you how devastated I was when I heard you weren't pregnant; how much I'd hoped and prayed you were, so you would have to stay with me. If I have the honor of being father to your children, no one in the world would be happier than I."

Heart pounding, she stared at him, trying to decide whether he meant it or not.

But it was there, in his eyes, the tense set of his gorgeous mouth, even that arrogant tilt of his chin, letting her know it was real.

"Oh, Farhan."

And he must have heard the answer in her voice, as he reached over the arms of their club chairs to pull her close.

"Tell me you love me again, beautiful," he whispered into her ear. "I need to hear it again."

So she told him, and, when pressed, promised to tell him every day for the rest of their lives.

For an instant time seemed to slow, allowing her to commit the moment to memory, like a snapshot. And in that single frame, safe once more in Farhan's arms, life truly was perfect.

"My Princess," he murmured. "My love, forever."

And Sara knew, like everything Farhan said, it was the truth.

The Surgeon Prince was hers, for always.

* * * * *

ROYAL DOC'S SECRET HEIR

AMY RUTTAN

MILLS & BOON

For my Prince Charming,
who swept me off my feet twenty years ago
when we first met and who continues to do so.

CHAPTER ONE

IT HAD BEEN a long time since she'd been home. Jeena's heart beat triple time as the relief plane that was carrying medical supplies and her team of doctors and nurses approached the island kingdom of Kalyana.

She took a deep calming breath as the cloud cover evaporated and the jewel of an island set against the Indian Ocean came into view.

Her home.

Only Kalyana hadn't been her home. Not for a long time. Not since that night ten years ago when her father had woken her up and told her they were leaving Kalyana.

They were *all* leaving because they were in danger.

She hadn't wanted to go and didn't know where they were going, but her parents needed her and she needed them. So she'd left Kalyana for Canada.

She hadn't regretted it. It had been for the best. Still, she'd never thought she'd see Kalyana again.

She glanced down at her Canadian passport gripped tightly in her hand and *hoped* she'd be allowed in.

Her father had made it clear they couldn't go back. They should never go back. They hadn't been banished, but her father had said they weren't welcome in

Kalyana. Because of her indiscretion, they would be judged. Harshly.

Jeena still found that hard to believe in this day in age, but her father had been adamant. He wanted to protect her and her unborn child.

The Canadian consulate had assured her that the visa had been cleared. That there shouldn't be any issues.

There shouldn't be a risk of someone waiting to pounce on her to ask her about her son and pry into her private life. She knew deep down there was nothing to fear. She hadn't done anything wrong.

All she'd done was become pregnant and decide to have her child. A lot of women were single mothers so there was no reason she would have to watch her back, but still those old anxieties were creeping into the back of her mind. The night her father had insisted they leave. He'd been so scared. He'd thought they were in danger and Jeena knew that someone had made him think that.

And it was all because of who her son's father was. If it had been someone else, they probably wouldn't have left…

"Why do we have to leave?" she asked.

"Lady Meleena said that the King will take your child!" her father said. *"We have to go to keep our family together. Your child would be looked down upon. Do you really want that?"*

"No." She shook her head. *"But we can't afford to leave."*

"Lady Meleena will help us. She just asks that we never come back. That we never contact anyone and keep your pregnancy secret. I promised her that for your safety."

"How does Lady Meleena know?" Jeena asked,

confused. "No one but Mother and you know. Did you tell someone?"

"Of course not!" her father exclaimed. "Someone at the clinic told her."

"Why would someone at the clinic tell her?"

"Because people know about who you were seen with and it wasn't long before Lady Meleena put two and two together. Meleena's father invests in my plantation. There would be scandal for all of us, and Lady Meleena wanted to take care of us."

"I'm pregnant. I didn't commit a crime!"

Her father hugged her. "Of course you didn't, but Lady Meleena knows first-hand how an illegitimate child with a parent in the aristocracy can be treated. Look at her half-brother Kamal. He was treated so poorly by his peers and then he died in that terrible accident."

"But—"

"No buts!" her father snapped. "We're leaving. It's the best thing for you and the baby. It will protect our family's name and avert scandal for all concerned."

Guilt coursed through her. "Yes, Father. You're right."

Jeena shook the memory away and clenched her Canadian passport tighter in her fist.

The consulate might say that she was cleared to return and work in Kalyana, but was Lady Meleena, soon-to-be royal bride, okay with it?

They'd left ten years ago to save face and her father was indebted to Lady Meleena for her assistance, but then three years ago Lady Meleena had become engaged to the father of Jeena's unborn baby and a little part of Jeena couldn't help but wonder if Meleena had had her eyes set on a certain prize right from the start.

It had bothered her for years that Lady Meleena had taken such an interest in her.

Does it matter? He wouldn't have married you anyway. He couldn't. His family would have chosen his bride, and they wouldn't have chosen a farmer's daughter.

Her stomach twisted and she tried to relax on the last little bit of the long trip from Canada to Kalyana, only she knew she wouldn't feel at ease until they landed and she was cleared by customs. She was breaking her father's promise to Lady Meleena about never returning.

You didn't promise.

Jeena relaxed then. She was different now. She wasn't such a pushover.

This had been her home, whether Lady Meleena liked it or not. She was going to do her job here. She had no wish to interfere in Meleena or Maazin's life.

Even then, she wasn't sure she could relax, visa or not. She glanced out the window again and a lump formed in her throat, tears stinging her eyes as she saw the island get closer.

Home.

This was where her family had lived and thrived on the same vanilla plantation for generations and it was all her fault that it no longer belonged to her family. All because she'd got involved with and fallen in love with the wrong person.

"You okay?"

Jeena glanced at Teresa, one of the other doctors who had come to help with the relief efforts.

"Yeah, fine." Jeena forced herself to smile brightly. "Just missing my son."

Which wasn't a complete lie. She did miss her son.

She'd never really been apart from him for this long and with this much of a distance between them.

He was safe in Canada with her parents. His competitive junior hockey team was in the finals and they were playing at Scotiabank Saddledome, which was a huge deal. He'd gone on and on about it for months. As had her father.

Syman was the reason her parents had taken Lady Meleena's aid and come to Canada, and why she needed them. She couldn't have raised him alone in Kalyana or Canada. She couldn't have become a surgeon without their help, and becoming a surgeon had been hard even with their help.

Still, there were things Syman would never know about Kalyana. Things she'd experienced that he'd never get to, like playing on the sand of a pearl-pink beach or swimming in a turquoise sea. Running through her father's vanilla fields or climbing a palm tree to stare out over the Indian Ocean.

Canada had been a good home for them and Syman loved his life there, even with the ice and snow that Jeena had never gotten used to. That she didn't miss.

If you'd stayed in Kalyana, Syman wouldn't even be interested in hockey.

Kalyana was near the Seychelles and was very traditional. Hockey wasn't one of the sports played in Kalyana. If she had raised Syman here, he would probably be into cricket.

Or polo?

Jeena shook that thought away. She didn't want to think about Syman's father and how she had met him during a divot stomp at a match she should've never been at. She had only gone because her friend had dragged her along and during the divot stomp she'd lost her footing and been rescued by the man of her dreams.

Well, she hadn't been completely sure when she'd first met him. Maazin had been a known playboy and she'd known she should keep away, but when he had been with her, he hadn't been the bad boy that everyone had said he was. He had been different.

So kind and caring.

And the more time they'd spent together, the more she'd truly believed he'd loved her.

Her heart skipped a beat just thinking about him. She'd been a fool. Young and naive.

Don't think about him.

Only it was hard not to. He was never really far from her thoughts. The older Syman got, the more he looked like his father, the more she saw the only man she had ever loved. Syman was all the good parts of his father. He was kind and caring. Also driven and stubborn.

Her heart may have been broken, but she loved Syman and she was grateful that her time with Maazin had given her her son.

"You'll see Syman soon. And I'm sure his team will win the tourney," Teresa said brightly, interrupting her thoughts of Syman's father.

Jeena chuckled. "They'd better or he'll be lamenting it until next hockey season."

Teresa laughed and went back to her book.

Jeena glanced at the reading material she'd brought for the long flight from Dubai, which was just one of the flights she'd been on since they departed from Vancouver. She really didn't know which way was up and given that there was a significant time zone difference, she couldn't help but wonder if Syman had actually won his tournament. Maybe he'd already played?

I should be there.

Only this was her job and her father had taught her and given her a work ethic she stood by. Kalyana needed her and her new country, Canada, needed her to represent them in the best possible light. She understood the customs. She knew the terrain and the people.

Even if it meant facing something that she wasn't sure that she was ready to face.

And when she closed her eyes she could still feel Maazin's arms around her, but then she was reminded of the pain when he'd turned his back on her, when Lady Meleena had told her he'd chosen his duty over her. When Lady Meleena had told her father that Syman would be an outcast. That Jeena would be an outcast because he would not marry her, even though he knew she was pregnant.

Then, a few years later, it had been announced that Prince Maazin had chosen his bride. None other than Jeena's supposed savior, Lady Meleena.

She shouldn't care, but it made her angry. Jeena knew her family had been manipulated.

Don't worry about it. Maazin isn't part of your life.

And she had to keep remembering that.

He hadn't been there for her when she'd had Syman. Neither had he been there when she'd scrimped and saved, worked odd jobs while attending medical school. That had been all her. She didn't need him. She was better off without him.

Syman was better off without him.

Are you sure?

"We're making our final descent into Huban. Please buckle up. It's a bit windy and there has been some damage to the airstrip from the cyclone so it might be a rough landing," the pilot said over the speaker.

"Here we go," Teresa said, setting down her book and buckling up her seatbelt.

Jeena nodded and pulled her seatbelt tighter. She kept her eyes focused on Kalyana as it got closer and closer. She could see the damage. Trees ripped from their roots, buildings along the coast destroyed, but there on the main terminal still flew the blue, green and gold flag of Kalyana. Untouched and fluttering in the strong winds in a clear blue sky. A sight she'd thought she'd never see again.

It helped tame the erratic beat of her heart.

She was home.

Maazin waited on the edge of the tarmac in a van to help transport medical supplies to the makeshift hospital that he and Farhan had set up between Huban and the southeast district, which had been the hardest hit when Cyclone Blandine had ripped through Kalyana.

Kavan, the bodyguard who also acted as chauffer-pilot, had seemed keen to accompany Maazin, but he'd eventually agreed it was best he stay with Farhan, Maazin's older brother, Sara, and her grandfather, Mr. Raj. Ever since the cyclone had hit, Farhan had been jumpy, fussing and fuming over his new bride.

Not that Maazin could blame him.

If he had someone he loved...

Maybe if he still had the one woman he'd once loved he would've felt the same way that Farhan did, but he didn't have anyone.

He didn't deserve anyone. Not even the arranged marriage his father had set up three years ago. Not that he'd really cared for Lady Meleena. It had just been expected and since Maazin had lost the only woman he'd loved when she'd left in the middle of the night, he had settled for the bride his father had chosen. Or eventually settled. After everything that had happened when Jeena had left, he'd spent some time doing what good he could.

He'd served in the Royal Guard and earned his doctorate as a surgeon in the guard. It gave his life meaning, after all his past actions had caused so much pain. His service was the least he could do.

Which was why he'd agreed to marry Meleena. His father had guilted him into it and he had been tired of the nagging to find a wife. He'd had no interest in Meleena, so had had very little to do with her.

Of course, Meleena hadn't liked it too much when he'd devoted his life to healing others, to serving his country, and had ignored her. She'd left him, but no one knew about that yet and that's the way his father wanted it. There were diplomatic policies and contracts at play and his father wanted to wait until it could be properly addressed after Kalyana recovered from the devastation of Blandine.

So he had no one.

No one to worry about. No one to care.

Which was what he deserved.

It was best that he handle this. He was just as capable a doctor as Farhan and Sara were. This was what he lived for. This was all that had mattered since Jeena had left and his brother Ali had died trying to help him. The last thing he wanted to do was put Farhan or Sara in danger.

His mother had already suffered enough because of him. He wasn't going to put Farhan in harm's way when he had military training and could manage this kind of disaster situation with ease. Not that they were in much danger now. The cyclone was over. It was just a matter of picking up the pieces. Cyclone Blandine had done severe damage to the islands.

He couldn't remember such a storm ever hitting Kalyana.

His father King Uttam was all for Maazin helping with relief efforts. He should be a part of it. Farhan was an excellent doctor, but he didn't have the training Maazin had.

However, his mother Queen Aruna was a little more reluctant to hear a prince of Kalyana was out there helping with relief efforts and getting his hands dirty. She thought it was unsafe.

Of course, even if she didn't show it, Maazin worried his mother had never been happy with anything he'd done since Ali had died.

But Maazin wanted to help.

He *needed* to help.

Still, his mother had made her reservations clear...

"You're a prince!"

"So? What else should a trained surgeon be doing, Mother?"

"You're only a surgeon because of your time in the Royal Guard."

"So what would you have me do?" Maazin asked.

"You should stay in the safety of the palace."

"And tend to royalty? To aristocrats?"

"Perhaps. And perhaps if you had done more of your royal duties and spent time with your betrothed, Lady Meleena wouldn't have left!"

"I don't care that she left, Mother. I don't love her. I couldn't stand be around her."

"Ali did his duty!"

"I'm sorry that I'm not Ali."

His mother's had a faraway look as she murmured, "You're right. You're not..."

Maazin winced. He hadn't wanted an arranged marriage. Especially with someone his father had chosen only for the betterment of the country.

Your father chose for Ali and he'd been happy. Your father chose for Farhan and he's happy with Sara.

He ignored that niggling little thought.

Right now Kalyana needed him. When Ali had been alive, he'd always been out there lending a hand, and that was the least Maazin could do since he was responsible for Ali's death.

You're not.

Only he felt he was. And he was sure his mother felt that he was responsible for Ali's death. Ever since then his mother had been cold and distant. With him especially.

And he hated it that he was the cause of her grief, that he was just a living reminder of her pain. And he couldn't help but wonder if she wished it was him who'd died instead of Ali.

He pushed that thought aside and watched as the Canadian plane landed with much-needed supplies. Cyclone Blandine had done so much damage and they hadn't been very prepared. Storms had come and gone, but there had never been a cyclone like this. It had formed out of nowhere and so quickly and it had struck so hard.

There was no way they could prepare for quite how extreme it was and they were lucky that it hadn't done even more damage.

The plane from Canada that he'd been waiting for made its landing. Maazin had made sure that the airport runway in Huban had been cleared of debris so that they could receive assistance from other countries, like Canada, and he had his sister-in-law Sara to thank for that assistance.

The plane circled as the winds were high.

Maazin waited with bated breath as the plane came around again then touched down. He didn't know why he was so nervous about this plane landing, but something about this was eating away at him.

He hadn't felt like this in so long.

The last time he'd felt like this…well, he didn't want to think about her.

This was not the time to think about it. It was not time to think about Jeena. Of course, she was never far from his mind. He was always thinking of her, whether he liked it or not. Always wondering why she'd left him. It drove him mad.

"They're ready for us, Your Highness," his driver, Kariff, said.

Maazin nodded. "Let's go and fill this van with supplies and their doctors. The southeast region is in dire need of supplies and medical help."

Kariff nodded and drove the van toward the large plane that had dropped its rear door to make a ramp, ready to start unloading its precious cargo of medical supplies and doctors to aid them.

Kariff parked close and Maazin got out of the van. He opened the side doors and the back so that Kariff and a couple of the other men he'd brought with him could start loading up.

"Who should we be reporting to?" a female voice asked, which sent a shiver of recollection down his spine. He knew that voice. He knew it well because it was burned into every single neuron in his brain. Just the mere sound of her voice fired them off, bringing every bitter-sweet memory to the surface.

Maazin turned around and came face to face with someone he'd never thought he would see again.

His blood froze and everything around him stopped. He couldn't quite believe his eyes and he wondered if he was dreaming. It was like she had walked right out of his dreams, like nothing had changed, like time had stood still. She hadn't changed one bit. Her rich, dark brown hair was tied back in a braid, just like the first day he'd met her. Her skin was still a warm, rich tawny color.

Her deep brown eyes widened and her red lips, lips he remembered so well the taste of, dropped open for a moment and a subtle pop of coral colored her cheeks. She was just as shocked as he was.

Jeena.

In an instant he remembered when he'd first seen her. She'd looked so out of place and uncomfortable on the polo pitch.

She'd worn a long emerald dress and high heels as she'd teetered on the grass, trying to flip over a divot.

He'd been so entranced by her and had wondered who she was...

"You'll fall over, trying to flip those divots in those heels."

She looked up, embarrassed. "Pardon?"

Maazin knelt down and took her foot in his hands. "May I?"

She pursed her lips and nodded. He removed her shoe and pried off the large chunk of turf that had been impaled on the end of her stiletto heel. He replaced the shoe and then stood, steadying her in his arms, catching a scent of her perfume.

Jasmine and vanilla. It was intoxicating and he was instantly drawn to her.

"Thank you... Your Highness."

"Ah, so you know who I am."

"Everyone knows who you are," she whispered, and wouldn't look at him.

"Well, I am at a loss. I don't know who you are. I have never seen you at one of these events before."

She smiled. "My name is Jeena. I am here with my friend as her guest."

"And who is your friend?"

"Aishraya Raj." Jeena nodded in the direction of her friend. "Her husband is a diplomat, but I've known Aishraya for a long time."

Maazin smiled and bowed at the waist. "Well, allow me to welcome you to our little match..."

Maazin tried to calm the pulse that was now thundering in his ears. She had been the only one to truly *see* him.

The world thought he was this playboy and he let everyone believe that. The tabloids, his parents all believed it and it had got him off the hook of so many responsibilities, but Jeena had seen past that.

He had been so in love with her. He'd wanted to marry her, even though he had always been afraid and not interested in marriage because he'd felt it would tie him down, just like his royal duty.

And he hadn't wanted to drag Jeena into a life of protocol.

She had been free. Which was why he'd wanted her.

Jeena had left him. Left him without a word, and it was because of her leaving that he'd gone to that party to drown his sorrows and then called his brother Ali to get him.

And that had cost Ali his life, because after she'd left, Maazin had decided to take the bad boy road everyone thought he traveled. Ali came to sweep his indiscretions under the rug and died trying to cover up his mistakes.

It had destroyed him when Jeena had left. It was his own fault, though, because he knew he'd driven her away. He didn't deserve her and he certainly didn't deserve anything now. He knew that.

"Maa... Your Highness." And she curtseyed.

He was angry that she had almost addressed him with familiarity, like he wanted, but had then changed it to a formal address and curtseyed in deference to his station, which he hated.

Were they such strangers?

Yes. They were now. She'd left. He'd never left Kalyana. He'd never left in the dead of night, not telling anyone where he was going. And when he'd tried to find her there'd been no trace of her. It was as if her whole life in Kalyana had been erased.

She'd cost him so much.

You were the selfish one. She cost you nothing.

"I'm surprised that you've returned to the country you abandoned with such ease," he snapped.

Her expression hardened. "My apologies, Your Highness. I'm the lead surgeon on this relief mission. I'm representing Canada and I'm here to deliver your supplies and lend my services to *your* country." She turned on her heel and walked away.

She was a doctor?

Maazin was shocked, but as she stormed away he couldn't help but smile to himself. She still had that spirit he'd admired in her.

That fire.

That had been hidden under the surface, something

she'd tried so hard to control, but he'd known what a strong woman had been under that demure exterior.

It's what he'd loved so much about her then.

Now, to see her standing her ground, it surprised him, but pleasantly so.

It woke up a piece of him he'd thought was long gone and as he watched her walk away, giving out orders, he knew that working with her would be a challenge.

One he hadn't expected.

CHAPTER TWO

JEENA DIDN'T KNOW what she had been expecting. She knew one thing, she hadn't planned on seeing him. Actually, she hadn't expected to see him at all. What was a prince of Kalyana doing at the airport, collecting medical supplies?

Not your concern.

And she had to keep telling herself that.

She was stronger now. She could handle seeing Maazin.

Can you?

She'd changed, but had she really expected a bad boy rebel prince to have changed in the last ten years?

No. Well, maybe? One could hope. Other than his engagement to Lady Meleena, Maazin hadn't really been in the papers. Perhaps he had changed? She'd always wondered if that image he'd projected before she'd met him had been an act. She knew one thing was for sure, his appearance hadn't changed at all.

It was like time hadn't even touched him at all.

When she'd seen him there, she couldn't believe her eyes. It was like all those years ago when he had knelt down in front of her on the polo field and stopped her from embarrassing herself in front of a social class that she had not been comfortable being around at all.

His ebony hair was shorter than it had been. Gone were the long curls that had framed his face when they'd first met and he was now clean shaven. He'd lost the neatly trimmed beard she'd loved so much. His skin was deep, lustrous gold and warmed by the heat and sun from Kalyana. And he'd lost some of that baby fat that came with youth, but those green-gray eyes were still the same as they'd bored deep into hers, totally riveting her to the spot.

Making her quiver with desire. Even after all these years apart her body still reacted to him. She remembered the feeling of those strong hands on her, the taste of his lips as he'd brushed kisses lightly on hers.

How safe he'd made her feel when his arms had been wrapped around her.

He turned his back on you and Syman, remember...?

"He knows," Meleena said in a scathing tone.

"He knows?" Jeena asked, stunned.

"Yes."

"How do you know that he knows?"

Meleena rolled her eyes. "My father is very close to the royal family. That's how I know. Prince Maazin can't commit to you."

"I don't believe that."

Meleena fished out a check and held it out to her. "Here. Compensation for your...situation."

It was like a slap in the face and her heart clenched as she stared at it.

This was all she was worth?

The fact he knew about her pregnancy and had turned his back on her made her firm her resolve. She wouldn't be duped again by anyone.

She was no longer that foolish innocent who could be swept off her feet by a dashing Prince Charming.

He hadn't been there when her family had sold off everything to start a new life in Canada.

Neither had he been there when Syman was born.

Syman, who had those same eyes as his father.

Syman.

Her heart sank. He always was curious about his father and as he got older she knew it was something she would not be able to keep from him. Not when he could go online and look Maazin up.

He'd learn his father was a prince and a playboy. How his father had turned his back on her. His father's whole private romantic life had been splashed across tabloids around the world. The only romance not there and not known was hers. Lady Meleena's parents had paid people off to keep that secret.

"Dr. Harrak!"

She turned and saw Maazin coming toward her and her heart skipped a beat again.

Stand firm.

She crossed her arms and narrowed her resolve. How many people had tried to push her around when she'd been a resident and learning to become a surgeon because she was short at only five feet four? Too many and Jeena had had to rise above all of that and make sure that her voice had been heard above the others in a competitive medical program.

And on top of all of that she'd raised Syman.

She was stronger than some spoiled and pampered prince who was coddled by parents who gave him everything and ruled a country.

She could handle him. She wasn't going to let a prince sweep her off her feet again. She didn't need saving or a knight in shining armor.

And she wasn't going to be sent back to Canada because he and his fiancée were uncomfortable with her presence in Kalyana.

"I have every right to be here," she snapped when Maazin caught up with her.

"What?" he asked, frowning.

"I have a visa and clearance from the consulate to represent Canada and assist in this humanitarian and relief aid effort. Kalyana may not be my home any longer…"

"I'm aware of that," he answered stiffly. "What I came over to say was sorry. I'm sorry for embarrassing you like that."

Jeena was shocked, but she didn't let him know that. That was different. The Maazin she remembered had been a bit arrogant with people he'd felt deserved it, but he had always been kind and gentle to her. She'd often wondered why he hadn't shown that side of himself to the public.

Of course he'd turned his back on her. She wasn't going to be fooled again.

It had been a painful lesson to learn that she didn't need a prince to come and save her and that she was more than capable of saving herself.

"No apology needed, Your Highness. I forgot myself for a moment, you are absolutely right, I left Kalyana for another country, because it was right for me. Now I'm here on behalf of Canada. I'm home now and I'm here to help." She curtseyed again.

"Jeena, stop that." He was annoyed. She remembered how much he hated protocol. She knew she was getting to him.

Good.

"Stop what, Your Highness?"

"Curtseying and calling me Your Highness. Jeena, we know each other intimately."

"That's Dr. Harrak to you, Your Highness." She crossed her arms and leaned forward. "Perhaps we knew each other once, but a lot has changed. I prefer the formality, Your Highness."

His eyes narrowed. "Fine."

She nodded and felt a bit of satisfaction knowing that she had won that battle. It felt good.

Did it?

"Well, Dr. Harrak," he said, exaggerating her name. "My driver Kariff and I are to take you to the southeastern region, which was hardest hit by the cyclone. Our doctors have been working non-stop since the cyclone hit four days ago and they could use a break."

Jeena smiled. "Of course, Your Highness."

He stood there. "Well?"

"Well, what?" she asked.

"We have to leave."

"I'm waiting for you to lead the way, Your Highness. It's only proper."

He rolled his eyes and turned around and started marching stiffly toward the van, the tail of his blue kurta billowing out behind him.

If she really wanted to bite back at him, now would be the time to tell him that he reminded her of his father, which had always used to annoy him as well.

She chuckled softly and kept that to herself.

Right now, there were patients waiting for help and that was all that mattered to her, but it was nice to have a little victory over the man who'd broken her heart.

A man who had ruined her for all others.

A man who still had a piece of her heart, whether she liked it or not.

* * *

The ride in the van was uncomfortable and tense. Maazin sat in the front next to Kariff while she and her team were crammed in beside medical equipment and gear. There would be another van coming soon to take the rest of the supplies and gear into Huban, but right now they were transporting what was most needed to the hardest hit region. That had been her plan. Get to work, help out and keep out of sight.

She might not really care about her father's promise to Lady Meleena but she didn't want the drama that would come with it.

The press didn't know about Syman or her romance with Maazin and she preferred it that way.

The only reason she was here was to save lives.

As the van navigated the damaged streets of Huban, Jeena's heart sank to see the destruction. The little wooden shacks of the poorest hadn't fared as well as the colonial buildings that had been built by the British over a century ago.

There were downed power lines, crumbled stone and debris everywhere.

"Hold on," Maazin said over his shoulder. "This part of Huban was flooded quite badly. The water has receded enough to allow passage, but it will be a bumpy ride."

Jeena bit her lip. Her head began to spin and her pulse thundered in her ears. A panic attack was coming on and she needed to center herself. She needed to gain control, but it was hard. She didn't like water too much. She was fine if she was on a large boat or had her feet firmly planted on the ground, but in a van going over a washed-out road, this she didn't like.

And she closed her eyes and tried to not think about

that time when she had been a young girl and she'd wandered too far from her parents' home and down to the small creek that ran adjacent to the plantation.

She'd been playing in the water when it had begun to rain, but since there had been no lightning and it had been so hot and dry, Jeena had just stayed where she was and enjoyed not being hot for once.

It was then that a flash flood had ripped down the mountainside. She would have been swept away if she hadn't gripped that low-growing palm. She'd held onto the trunk of that tree for what had felt like an eternity as the water had rushed past her, trying to snatch her away and wash her out to sea.

And she remembered the terror of it all.

The water that had rushed over her while she'd clung to life, while she'd tried to breathe and not take water into her lungs. The weariness of trying to stay afloat had begun to set in.

And then she remembered the strong arms of her father reaching down to pluck her from the swollen creek and into the safety of his arms.

She'd gotten into trouble, but not too much as her father had felt that she'd learned her lesson about doing dangerous things and not listening to them, but really she hadn't learned her lesson. Not really.

And how had she repaid her parents?

She'd become involved with a prince of Kalyana, even though it was forbidden because he'd been destined to marry someone of his father's choosing.

Her parents had got her out of the country to protect her. Lady Meleena had helped before'd she got engaged to Maazin a few years later. Her parents had lost everything.

They love Syman, though.

Still, she should've learned to curb her reckless ways that day she'd almost drowned and maybe then her parents would still be in Kalyana and she could've been here with the cyclone had hit and she could've been helping right from the start.

But you wouldn't have Syman.

No. She wouldn't have had Syman and for that she couldn't regret her past mistakes. Even though she regretted everything about falling in love with a prince, there had been one bright spot to the whole thing and that was her son. And that thought made her feel guilty for wishing her mistakes away.

He was her world and she missed him. Especially at this moment when she could do with a smile and a hug. She really missed her son.

The van rocked, jolting thoughts of Syman out of her head. She gripped her seat as the van made its way through another washed-out section of the road. The rushing water caused the van to sway, but it wasn't deep.

It was deep enough for Jeena's pulse to thunder even more loudly in her ears and for beads of sweat to break across her brow. Her hands felt clammy as she dug her fingers into the upholstery of the seat.

She looked up and saw that Maazin was watching her in the rearview mirror. He looked concerned and she tried to shake it all off. The last thing she wanted was for Maazin to feel bad for her.

Or, worse, think that she couldn't handle this, because she could.

Jeena looked away and the van carefully made its way through the water and back onto dry road as they made their way out of the capital city of Huban. Jeena took a deep breath of relief and glanced out of the window. She could see the palace rising in the distance.

It had sustained some damage, but it still stood there, like a rock, reminding all the people of Kalyana that the country was still strong.

And a blowhard loud-mouthed king ruling them.

Well, not really. King Uttam might not be her favorite person in the world, but he wasn't a terrible king. He was a fair ruler.

And she saw a lot of his stubbornness in Syman. When Syman set his mind to something, there was no convincing him otherwise. It made her laugh from time to time. At least Syman was strong.

He had a strong personality. One she hadn't had until she'd had him and had worked her way through medical school.

"We're nearly at the hospital," Maazin announced.

Jeena didn't respond. She just looked out the window toward the Indian Ocean, remembering precious days gone by and how it was all her fault that her son couldn't enjoy this with her.

Maazin watched Jeena as she and her team had a quick meeting and then started to move around the makeshift hospital that was set up in an old shanty town, or what was left of a shanty town now that it had been leveled.

Something had bothered Jeena in the van when they'd crossed through that water and he couldn't help but wonder what.

It's not your concern.

And it wasn't. She wasn't his and could never be his.

Still, he was drawn to her and he was worried that something had happened to her and he felt responsible.

"You all right?"

Maazin turned to see Farhan standing beside him. Farhan looked exhausted and Maazin couldn't blame him. He and Sara had been working hard to help since the storm had started. Farhan hadn't been here when Maazin and Jeena had had their torrid and short love affair.

So there was no need to explain it all now.

It was over.

And it wasn't Farhan's business.

It was Maazin's pain to bear.

"Nothing, just..." Maazin scrubbed a hand across his face. "Tired and relieved that help is here."

Farhan nodded. "So am I. Sara has been working herself to the bone and she needs her rest."

"Take her back to Huban and get rest. I'm going to stay and help the Canadians and help Kariff unload the medical supplies."

"You should rest too," Farhan suggested. "You've been working non-stop since even before the cyclone hit."

"What for? I have no wife and I like to keep busy."

"You're going to work yourself into an early grave, brother." Farhan turned and left and Maazin let out a breath that he hadn't even known that he was holding.

He glanced back over his shoulder to see Jeena sitting next to a patient's bed and talking with the elderly woman, who seemed to recognize her.

Why had Jeena left?

"She's left," his mother said with finality.

"What?" Maazin asked, stunned.

"Your paramour. She is gone. Now you can do the duty we all must, and marry someone of the lineage to be your bride."

"I don't believe you," Maazin said hotly. *"Jeena would never do that."*

His mother walked calmly over to her desk and

pulled out a letter, handing it to him. It looked like Jeena's handwriting.

His mother held it out to him between two fingers. "Read it."

Maazin snatched the letter from his mother and quickly read the letter. It didn't sound like Jeena, but it was her writing.

"Where did you get this?"

"Meleena found it."

"Why would Meleena find it?" he asked.

"Her father has invested in the Harrak plantation and she's trying to prevent a scandal for a family her father supports."

Maazin read the letter again and couldn't believe it.

It stated that she was leaving him because she couldn't stand being linked to a prince who had a check-ered past full of women and gambling. Even though she knew those things weren't true...even though he had never been unfaithful to her. He'd wanted to marry her.

Maazin crumpled up the paper. "She would never leave her parents. I'm going to find her."

He turned to leave but his mother cleared his throat and Maazin turned back.

"Her parents are gone too. They left Kalyana with her. This morning, in fact. They should already be in Dubai."

"Where are they going?"

His mother shrugged. "Who knows? They didn't tell me. Kalyanese people are free to come and go out of their country as they please."

Maazin had gone to her parents' vanilla plantation, which was on the westerly side of the main island. And his mother had been right. They had left and their plan-tation had been for sale. It had made no sense.

And he'd felt betrayed.

So he couldn't help but wonder why they'd left and why she was now back. She'd fled in the middle of the night like she'd been afraid. So why had she come back?

At least now he knew where she had gone and what she had done with her life these past ten years. She'd become a surgeon!

He hadn't expected that.

Why not? You became one too.

"You okay?"

Maazin turned around to see Jeena standing next to him.

"Perfectly," he said.

She cocked an eyebrow. "You sure?"

"Yes," he snapped, and then he sighed. "Sorry. I'm tired. It's been non-stop since we set up this hospital."

"I can see," she said gently, and then tilted her head to the side. "I thought the Royal Guard set up this hospital?"

"They did. I'm part of the Royal Guard."

Her mouth dropped open and then snapped shut. "You're a member of the guard? Since when?"

He wanted to tell her since she'd left and he'd had that drunken night, the night his brother Ali and his wife Chandni had died.

After the funeral he'd joined the guard to give back and try to appease the pain and guilt he'd felt for surviving when they hadn't.

And when he'd served his first year he'd decided to become a surgeon, to save even more lives.

It won't bring Ali back.

He cleared his throat. "I've been a member of the Royal Guard for almost ten years."

"That seems so unlike you."

His spine stiffened and he wanted to ask her who she thought he was. He hadn't been the one to leave. He'd stayed and made the most of the heartache she'd caused.

"Help!"

Maazin spun around as a man came in carrying a lifeless boy. He ran toward the man, who looked exhausted and sick. He scooped the boy up in his arms.

"Your Highness, please...my son."

"What's wrong?" Jeena asked, coming up beside Maazin and looking at the boy.

"He's burning up," Maazin stated, touching the boy's face.

"He started complaining of abdominal pain two days ago and there was blood..." The boy's father looked pale.

Maazin's stomach dropped and he felt sure he knew what it was.

The boy's father was probably a farmer who got water from the river. After the cyclone the water source had probably become contaminated.

"We need to isolate the boy and his father. I think it's dysentery," Maazin said to Jeena under his breath so as not to alarm the others in the hospital.

Jeena nodded and Maazin took the boy to the back of the hospital. There was a small building that they had the use of with a few rooms for cases such as this. Jeena led the boy's father to one of the rooms as well.

They had to get the two of them away from the other patients as bacillary dysentery was highly contagious, and since Maazin had picked the boy up without gloves he was going to have to go on a course of antibiotics as well and burn his clothes.

At least Jeena had on a surgical gown and gloves, as well as a mask. She was prepared and Maazin had been too busy thinking about the past and letting Jeena's presence unnerve him, so that he hadn't thought about dysentery being a problem after a cyclone. He hadn't changed into scrubs. He hadn't set up to deal with such a contagious disease, and he was kicking himself for not doing it sooner.

He was a fool, but right now he was going to try and save this young boy's life.

The boy winced and moaned in pain, but had a high fever and was completely out of it. Maazin set him on a bed and then got about setting up an IV with a bolus of fluids, electrolytes and antibiotics.

Jeena got the boy's father into the room beside him and through the small window that separated these two rooms he could see that she was doing the same and instructing a nurse, who had put on a hazmat suit, how to set up the quarantine.

Jeena then slipped out of the room and came to him. She looked at the boy and Maazin thought he saw a pained expression on her face.

"You're going to need to get out of those clothes and go on antibiotics in the other room."

"I know," Maazin said. "And you'll have to as well."

She nodded. "I know. I've changed and disposed of the gown, gloves and mask. I'll have the decontamination shower just to be sure, and then get the course of antibiotics."

"I want to make sure my patient's fever comes down." Maazin glanced down at the boy. So small and so sick. He hated seeing his people suffer.

"Your patient? I didn't realize you were a doctor." And he could hear the surprise in her voice.

"Yes. I'm a surgeon, a surgeon in the Royal Guard.

My brother Farhan and I have been working here since the cyclone hit. I do my duty to my people!"

"Wow, I'm surprised," she said.

"What? That I'm a doctor or that I'm competent?" he snapped.

Jeena's cheeks flushed in embarrassment. "I'm sorry."

"Thank you," he said. He appreciated her apology.

"Either way, you need to take precautions. Princes are susceptible to dysentery too."

"I'm not leaving my patient!"

"I can take care of that, Your Highness." A Canadian doctor he was not familiar with came into the room in a hazmat suit. "I think you best go and clean up so we can keep the infection from spreading."

Maazin sighed. "Fine. You're right."

He followed Jeena to where the showers were. She slipped into one of the stalls and Maazin made his way to the other stall. As he passed by, he glanced down at her phone, which was buzzing, and was shocked to see a picture of a little boy on her phone. At first glance it reminded him of his late brother, but there were no pictures of Ali in a hockey jersey. And then it hit him.

The picture was of a little boy with gray-green eyes like his, looking back at him.

And suddenly he felt a bit dizzy.

CHAPTER THREE

JEENA WATCHED THE bolus of antibiotics dripping down and into her arm. It was unlikely that she had dysentery, but given the extremely infectious nature of it, she didn't want to take any chances.

People who weren't treated died.

And it was a painful way to die.

Maazin was in the bed next to her, he was wearing scrubs instead of the kurta that he'd greeted her in and he looked angry as he was hooked up to an antibiotic drip. He was brooding. This seemed to be more like the Maazin she remembered.

Of course she couldn't blame him. She'd be annoyed too if someone questioned her like she'd questioned him.

It just took her completely by surprise that he had served in the royal guard and become a surgeon too. He had never really talked about what he wanted to do because there was no expectation for him to do anything. He was a prince.

And she was impressed that he'd done something with his life.

I wonder what Lady Meleena thinks of his work?

Jeena was annoyed that she let that thought slip in

and she was angry at herself for questioning him. She'd apologized, but she knew he was still angry with her.

"We should find out if anyone else is in that farmer's home," Jeena said. "They'll all have to be treated."

"It's just the man and his son. I'm told the boy's mother died last year in a farming accident," he said.

"Oh, I'm sorry to hear that."

Maazin wouldn't look at her. The bolus of antibiotics was apparently far more interesting.

Of course, she couldn't really blame him. Their first meeting a couple of hours ago hadn't been the warmest.

She sighed and closed her eyes, trying to make the best of a tense situation.

"Who is that boy?" he finally asked, breaking the silence.

Her stomach twisted in a knot. "What boy? The farmer's boy?"

He turned and looked at her and then she knew. She glanced down at her phone on the bed beside her. She'd noticed that she'd missed a call from Syman when she'd gone into the shower and she was also very aware that when Syman called his picture showed up on her phone.

And she was also aware of Syman's striking resemblance to certain members of the Kalyanese Royal Family, but she was annoyed that he was asking her who he was.

Had he expected her to use that money to get rid of her pregnancy?

If he had and wanted the money back, she could pay him. The money was still sitting in an account. She hadn't spent a dime of his pity check.

"Who is the boy?" he asked again, his voice calm, but there was a hint of anger in there and that sent a shiver of dread through her.

"My son," she stated. "Obviously."

"Your son? How old is he?"

"Nine. Again obvious."

Maazin's eyes narrowed and then he looked away. There was no sense in hiding the fact that Syman was his. She guessed by his expression, his tone and the fact that Syman was nine that he knew. And there was really no denying it. Syman had the same dark, long curls as Maazin had once had and the same stunning eyes.

He didn't say anything else to her, but she wasn't surprised as the nurses returned to check on them, which was good because emotionally, right now, Jeena didn't want to talk about it. She was afraid if she did she was going to break down and cry.

That was when her phone rang and Syman's face popped back up on the screen. Maazin's gaze locked on that picture.

Not now.

She had to answer it.

"Hi, Syman," she said, answering the phone and feeling Maazin's gaze boring into the back of her skull.

"Hi, Mom!" Syman's voice came from the other end. "We won!"

"You won. That's wonderful."

"Yeah, I'm so excited to get to play at the Saddledome. Grandpa said he's going to take me out for pizza."

"That's wonderful."

"You okay, Mom? You sound a bit weird."

"I'm okay. I'm here in Kalyana and you can tell your grandparents I'm okay."

"Actually, Grandpa wants to talk to you."

"No—" she began, but it was too late as Syman handed the phone over to her father.

"Jeena, are you okay?" her father asked.

She could hear the worry in her father's voice. She remembered how troubled he'd been when he'd found out she was carrying Maazin's baby. Her father had been so terrified Syman would be taken away or that they'd become outcasts.

"I'm okay, Dad. I'm fine."

"You're sure?"

"Yes. I'm working now, though." What she wanted to tell him was that Maazin was here and that he knew about Syman, but now was not the time.

"How bad is the damage?" her father asked. "Have you seen…? How much have you seen?"

Her father was asking about their plantation and whether she'd seen it. Even though her parents had left to protect her and even though her father insisted he didn't care for his old plantation, she knew he did. She knew her father missed his home country.

"I'm outside Huban, in the southeastern district that was hit the worst. I really have to go, but I'll talk to you later, okay?"

"Okay, Jeena. Be safe and avoid… Be safe."

"I will, Dad."

Her father had trailed off. She knew he'd been going to say avoid Lady Meleena and Maazin, but he hadn't.

Jeena ended the call. She felt like she was going to throw up. This was not how she'd planned this trip to go. All she wanted was to do her job and then head back to Alberta to be with Syman and her parents.

She wanted to lie low.

The last thing she'd wanted to do was run into Maazin but, of course, karma had had other plans. The nurses finished with Maazin and they were left alone again. He wouldn't look at her. He just stared ahead.

"Is he mine?" he finally asked, breaking the silence that had fallen between them again.

"What do you mean, is he yours? Of course he is." She swallowed the lump in her throat, one that had formed because of the tears she'd been holding back for so long. He acted like he didn't know about Syman. Maybe he'd forgotten and that wouldn't surprise her.

She and her unborn baby had been so insignificant to him, why would he give them a second thought?

"How can I be certain?"

"He's nine years old and you were my first." Jeena wanted to tell him that he was her only lover. That his betrayal of her, his abandonment when she'd needed him most had broken her so completely that she didn't trust anyone else with her heart.

And she had her son to look after. There was no time for romance. All she had was school, Syman and her parents.

The people who mattered most.

"Why didn't you tell me that I had a son?" Maazin asked.

Jeena snickered. "Really?"

"What do you mean, really? You obviously didn't want me to know or you would've told me."

Jeena rolled her eyes. How could she have been in love with someone so stubborn was beyond her. "Don't be so precious. You knew. You've just forgotten."

He opened his mouth to say more but the nurses came back and they removed her IV as she had finished her dose of antibiotics. After she was cleared to go, she slipped off the cot and left the isolation area. She wouldn't be allowed to work on patients until she'd been clear for twenty-four hours and she was annoyed about that, but it came with the territory in emergency medicine. She walked out of the medical tent and made her way down to the beach.

The heat of the sun felt good on her skin. It was way better than the bitter cold Canadian winter that her mother still hadn't gotten used to.

She sat down on the beach and closed her eyes, drinking in the Vitamin D and listening to the sound of the waves lapping gently on the pearl-pink sand. Her mind drifted back to the last time she'd sat on a pearl-pink sand beach like this.

"Jeena, you are so beautiful," Maazin whispered against her ear.

A shiver of delight traveled down her spine and she couldn't quite believe that he'd taken her out on his yacht to Patang Island for a private dinner.

There were no guards here.

It was just the two of them on the sandbar, under the moonlight, with the ocean wind caressing their skin.

She knew that he had a bit of a reputation, but he hadn't been unfaithful to her. They'd been inseparable and she was so in love with him.

He kissed her again, cupping her face and making her melt into his arms. She was so in love with him that she couldn't remember a moment of what life had been like without him.

Life had been so dull and colorless until she'd met him.

"Be with me tonight," he whispered.

She nodded, and he scooped her up in his arms and took her to the private bower he'd built on the sandbar. Their own private retreat, where they were alone, with just the light from the moon reflecting on the ocean accompanying them...

"Jeena."

She opened her eyes and shook the erotic memory from her mind.

She knew it was Maazin.

"I know you have a lot of questions, but since I can no longer work on patients for the next twenty-four hours I have to figure out a way back to where we're being billeted and try to get some sleep."

What she really wanted to tell him was that she didn't have to time to play these games.

"I can take you there. I have my Jeep around back and maybe then we can have a meal together and we can talk about this in private."

She stood up. "Of course, because you wouldn't want a scandal."

"No. It's not that. It's for your protection and for his. Besides, we're the only two potentially exposed to the dysentery. We can't afford others to be exposed. We need all the help in the hospitals tending to the injured."

He was right.

And she felt silly. He was trying to offer her an olive branch and she was being cranky. She was better than this.

"Fine. I'd appreciate a ride."

Maazin nodded. "My car is over this way."

She followed behind. She knew it was for the best they talk this through, but she didn't want to. What was in the past was in the past.

Or at least she thought it was.

Maazin wasn't going to take her to the hotel where the relief workers were staying. Instead he was going to take her to his home. It was better that they didn't expose anyone else to possible infectious dysentery.

He'd sent Kariff out to warn the other farmers and

plantation owners in that area who used that water source to avoid using water from the creek and he ensured the palace was made aware of the dire situation and that bottled, safe water would be provided to all who needed it.

He didn't say anything to Jeena as he drove back to Huban.

Thankfully he had also had a house that was not part of the palace. Maazin felt it was easier on his mother not to be under the same roof. So he'd chosen a colonial-built home just outside the city. He liked the privacy it afforded and what the two of them needed was privacy.

He was still in shock over the fact he had a son and he was going to find out who had kept this information from him and why. Maazin knew the mail and any correspondence to the royal family was monitored for their own safety, but he was so angry that someone could have done this.

His son.

His nine-year-old son. One that reminded him so much of his beloved brother Ali. Except the eyes. The eyes on that boy were his.

A son he didn't deserve.

Ali's family had been taken from him and it was a cruel twist of fate that he, the one responsible for Ali's death, had a son.

"Where are we going? I thought the hotel was near the hospital?" Jeena asked, her voice rising in panic.

"It is, but I don't think it's safe that we stay close to the field hospital for the next twenty-four hours, so I'm taking you back to my place."

Her eyes widened. "Oh, I don't think so! I'm not going to the palace. You need to stop this vehicle right now."

"What is wrong?"

"I'm not going to the palace."

"I never said we were." And he couldn't help but wonder why she was so worried about going to the palace.

"You said we were going to your home."

"I don't live in the palace."

She looked at him in disbelief. "Right."

"No, really I don't. I bought a colonial home just outside the city. It was the old British consulate. It's walled and gated, so pretty secure. My father thought maybe letting me have my own place would curb some of my less desirable behavior."

"Did it?" she asked.

"No, not right away…" It wasn't the house that had given him a taste of being a responsible adult, it was the unbearable heartbreak Jeena had caused him by leaving him without any explanation and Ali's death.

Maazin had blood on his hands as far as he was concerned. And since Ali had died, he'd been trying so hard to right all his wrongs.

He hadn't had a drop to drink for ten years, but right now he felt like getting drunk.

Jeena seemed to calm down again once he assured her that they weren't headed to the palace. He turned off the main promenade that led to the palace and headed down the road toward the beach.

His home had sustained a bit of damage, but Maazin had made sure everything had been made secure when he'd known that the cyclone would definitely hit. He'd moved out all his staff and this was the first time he'd been back after Blandine. He'd been so busy with helping his people that he hadn't even thought about his home.

He parked the Jeep and then hopped out.

"Where are you going?" Jeena asked.

"The power to the gate has been cut. All power is being diverted to essential services only. Luxury items like powered gates are not essential." He unlocked the gate and then pushed on it to open it.

Once it was open he climbed back into the Jeep and drove it inside, then parked and repeated the process to close the gates.

He was relieved to see that only a few boards had been taken off and just one of the shutters was broken.

There were some fallen trees, but the larger ones still stood and no branches or trees had fallen on his house.

Jeena climbed out of the vehicle and looked at his home. "It's nice. I like the cerulean blue. It reminds me of the ocean."

He nodded. Pleased that she liked it. "It's what I was going for. This place is peaceful and it's nice to come here and not be a prince."

"I'm sure it's so very taxing." She walked past him, her arms crossed as she looked all around his garden. He wasn't sure if she was commiserating with him or being sarcastic, but had a feeling it might be a mix of the two.

And he didn't care. He was going to make her a simple meal out of the supplies he had in the house and then he was going to find out more information about his son.

He climbed up the steps onto the covered deck and prised off the wooden boards and then unlocked the door.

"Right this way, Dr. Harrak."

Jeena followed him into the hallway and he flicked on the light, glad he'd had back-up generators installed last year.

There was a bit of water pooling on the marble floor,

but for the most part everything looked to be in the same place as before the cyclone had hit.

"Wow, so this was the British Consulate?"

"It was moved to downtown Huban, but this is where the British had a seat for many years. Colonialism at its finest. Why don't you make yourself comfortable in the sitting room and I'll see what I have to eat."

Jeena nodded and found her way to the front sitting room. It was a cool room that he liked to use in the heat of the summer as it got breezes from the ocean and didn't have the direct sun.

In the kitchen there were bananas, which had gone bad, on the counter, so he tossed them and cleaned up the marble counter top so as not to attract insects or vermin, and then he looked in the fridge, which was still running.

He had absolutely no idea what to make.

He might like his independence, but he had staff who cooked and cleaned for him. When he'd been in England for medical school, his father had made sure that he'd been well taken care of and had wanted for nothing.

Even when he'd been serving in Kalyana's military and continuing his medical training to be an army surgeon, he'd had servants.

He knew how to make a few things, but he really didn't want to make toast for Jeena.

"Is everything okay?" she asked, peeking into the kitchen.

"No. I… Fine," he said, throwing up his hands. "I'm a pampered, coddled prince and I don't know how to make you anything that might be slightly edible. I can make toast and a pot of tea. Would you like that?"

Jeena bit her bottom lip, trying not smile. He'd

always found that endearing, but right now he was slightly annoyed.

"Let's see what you have." She padded over to the fridge. "You have enough to make a nice Greek salad. Tomatoes, feta and olives. Would you like that?"

"That sounds wonderful." Now he was smiling and couldn't help but chuckle. "Would you show me?"

"How to make a salad?"

He nodded. "Yes."

"Sure." She pulled tomatoes, cucumber, feta and olives from the fridge and then wandered over to the pantry and pulled out olive oil, vinegar and oregano. He hadn't realized that he'd had all these things.

"Don't you need lettuce?" he asked. "It is a salad."

"If you want a traditional Greek salad then you don't have lettuce. You wouldn't happen to have any lemons, would you?"

"Yes, here you go." He handed her a couple. "Can we add lettuce too?"

"Why?" she asked.

"I like it and I think it might go bad soon."

Jeena wrinkled her nose. "Okay, let's see what we can salvage of it, but you know now it's not a true Greek salad."

"I'm sure I'll survive," he teased, pulling out the head of lettuce.

Jeena got to work and was washing the salad ingredients with bottled water. "Perhaps you should boil some water. If you're under a boiled water advisory, it would be safe."

"I have a lot of bottled water. I'm prepared for emergency situations. They wouldn't let a prince living on his own be without the essentials."

"Oh, good." Jeena finished what she was doing and

then pulled out a cutting board and knife. "Do you have a big bowl?"

"Probably," Maazin said lightly. He went hunting through the cupboards until he found a large bowl. "Will this do?"

Her eyes widened. "That's massive, I'm sure it'll do."

"Too big?" he asked, glancing at it.

"For the two of us, yes, unless you have someone else coming over?"

He noticed there was a hint of apprehension in her voice and he wanted to ask her what she was so afraid of. First she'd been afraid of going to the palace and now she was worried about who else could be coming.

Did she know about the arranged marriage?

Of course she does. Who in the world doesn't?

The only thing people didn't know about was how the engagement was off and he couldn't tell anyone yet. He'd promised his father that. The people had loved Lady Meleena, or at least the idea of a fairy-tale wedding, not knowing that she was a spoiled and self-centered woman. Her father was from the Kalyanese dynasty, but they no longer lived in Kalyana and had made their home in Dubai. The last time Maazin had seen Meelena had been over a year ago. She'd been fed up that he'd chosen duty over her. But he'd never fancied Meleena. They'd been first introduced at that same polo match where he'd met Jeena, but the moment he'd seen Jeena all other women had paled in comparison...

"Your Highness," Meelena said.

She was very beautiful, but he could tell she was less than impressed to meet him. There was no spark or zest for life in her eyes and she seemed bored. Like every other debutante in his social circle.

Maazin bowed. "Excuse my dishabille."

She looked him up and down with no interest. "You're playing a match. I would expect nothing less."

Maazin tried to think of something else to say, but he couldn't. She turned and sipped her champagne and made it clear that she didn't really want anything to do with him.

Did his father really expect him to marry Meelena? She was not his choice and never would be.

His eyes then fell on a beautiful woman in the most stunning emerald dress and ridiculous heels on the polo field.

Meleena followed his gaze. "What a fool," she snorted derisively.

"Excuse me," Maazin said quickly, and strode across the pitch to help her.

"So making a salad is extremely complicated, Your Highness," she teased, interrupting his thoughts.

"Oh?" he asked, crossing his arms.

"Yes." She smiled brightly at him and any tension that was between the two of them melted away. It was so easy with Jeena.

Why did she have to leave?

"You chop the lettuce like this."

He rolled his eyes and stifled a laugh. "Can I try?"

She handed him the knife and he cut the lettuce.

"You've done this before," she teased again.

"I'm not completely helpless," he said dryly.

"Just a moment ago you said the opposite, Your Highness."

"Call me Maazin."

A blush tinged her high cheeks. "I can't do that."

"Why?" he asked.

"It's not right. It's not proper."

"Well, we're alone."

"So?" she asked, nervously.

"You can call me Maazin. Please. I prefer it."

She glanced at him. "Fine, but only because we're alone."

He chuckled softly and finished chopping the lettuce and dumped it into the bowl. "Now what?"

"Let's chop the tomatoes." She handed him one.

He tried to chop it up correctly but ended up butchering it, spreading seeds and juice everywhere. Jeena chuckled and took the knife back.

"How about you go change and I'll finish here?"

Maazin nodded. "It's probably for the best."

As he left the kitchen there was a knock at his front door. Maazin cursed under his breath and went to answer the door.

"Yes?" he said, not thinking and opening the door. Thankfully it was just Joseph Malliot, his father's aide-de-camp, standing on the doorstep. He looked worried.

"I'm sorry for disturbing you, Your Highness. I went to the makeshift hospital and was told that you and another doctor had left."

"Yes, we were potentially exposed to dysentery. We have to be isolated for the next twenty-four hours, it's highly contagious."

Joseph worried his bottom lip and then stepped forward. "Your father got wind that it's a female physician staying with you and he's concerned about your upcoming marriage to Lady Meleena. Or rather..."

"That the doctor will find out and let it slip to the press that I'm no longer engaged to Lady Meleena."

Joseph nodded. "Yes, Your Highness."

"That's why he sent you to the camp?"

"Well, no. He wanted you back at the palace. Your

mother is still a little concerned that you're working out there alone and without any kind of protection."

Maazin sighed. "I'm glad she's worried about my safety, but I can assure you that there is nothing untoward between myself and the other doctor. You can tell them I'm safe at my home and once I'm sure I'm not contagious then I will come and see them and assure them of these things myself."

Maazin shut the door on Joseph. He didn't meant to be rude, but he didn't want Joseph to get ill. His father would be lost without Joseph at his beck and call.

And if Joseph got sick because of him, it would just be one more thing his mother could blame him for.

"If it wasn't for your reckless ways then Farhan wouldn't have had to come back and step up as the next in line. I had been training Ali to be King since his birth. He was ready to be a great king. But because of your foolish ways he's dead."

Maazin swallowed the lump in his throat and his stomach twisted, he felt like he was going to be sick.

He was a failure.

He had killed his brother. The woman he loved had left and his son didn't even know he existed. It was too much to deal with and his eyes drifted to the locked bar, which he knew was stocked, but he turned his back on it. He wasn't going back down that path.

Not again.

CHAPTER FOUR

Jeena had finished making the salad, but there was no sign of Maazin returning and she was worried. What if he'd passed out?

What if something had happened to him?

She crept out of the kitchen and made her way into the hall.

The large colonial house was eerily quiet.

And then she heard faint grunts coming from the far side of the house. She found another hall off the dining room, past the library and into what looked like a home gym.

Maazin had stripped off the scrubs and was in shorts and sneakers. He wasn't wearing a shirt and Jeena was taken aback. She knew that he was in good shape, but she wasn't prepared to see him standing there and doing a deadlift. The sweat dripped down his back and all of his muscles bulged as he arched his back and lifted what looked like a lot of weight.

His eyes focused on her standing in the doorway in the mirror he was facing. He finished his lift and then dropped the weights with a large clang on the mat.

"Jeena?" he said, surprised to see her there.

"You didn't come back," she said. "I was worried that maybe you fainted or were in distress."

"No, sorry. I was just... I needed to blow off some steam." He grabbed a towel and wiped his face.

And she couldn't blame him for blowing off some steam. She could do with some of that. She hadn't even been in Kalyana twenty-four hours and already her world was being turned upside down.

"There's some salad in the kitchen for you. I'm hoping you have a room for me and maybe I could have a quick shower? I feel pretty gross after that flight from Canada to Dubai and then here, then having to deal with dysentery."

"Of course. I'll take you to the guest room and I'll make sure you have a change of clothes."

"You keep women's clothing around?" And then she realized that was a stupid thing to say. Everyone knew that he was engaged to Lady Meleena. It had been announced to the world. Why they still weren't married was a mystery. Three years was a long engagement.

How would you know?

The Crown Prince Ali's death and Maazin's military service probably had something to do with it. But whatever the reason, it should not concern her. She would do well to remember that. Maazin had chosen Lady Meleena over her. He hadn't loved her at all and had made his feelings pretty clear when he hadn't come for her or fight for their love, even though he'd known she'd been pregnant. She was probably the only one who'd been in love in the first place.

"No, I don't have women's clothing on hand, but I can lend you one of my kurtas while your clothes are washed."

"I would appreciate that. Thank you."

Maazin nodded and led the way out of his gym and

back out into the main foyer and up the stairs. He led her to a room that was above the gym and opened the door.

"This is the guest room and there's a private bath. It's the nicest guest room as it's under a shade tree and faces the pool out back. Though, until we're cleared of any infection, I wouldn't advise a dip in the pool. In the closet you'll find some plain kurtas that will fit you."

She nodded. "Thank you, Your Highness."

His expression softened. "Just Maazin. Please."

And it was sincere and gentle.

She nodded. "Maazin. Thank you."

He nodded and then left the room, closing the door behind him. Jeena let out a sigh of relief that she hadn't known she'd been holding. She walked over to the window and peered outside. The sun was beginning to set, the brilliant orange-gold light reflecting off the infinity pool that seemed to melt into the cerulean-blue ocean horizon.

Jeena sighed again.

She pulled out her phone and saw that she had an attachment of pictures. She opened it, not caring about the roaming charges at the moment, and smiled when she saw pictures her father had taken of Syman's hockey game.

Some were blurry, but there were a few good ones.

And there was a sweet one of Syman and her father after the game, enjoying a slice of pizza. Then there was a picture of Syman and her mother. Her mother was tucking Syman into bed and there was a caption that said they all missed her and loved her. Tears welled in her eyes.

She missed them too.

And she knew that her mother and father were very worried for her sake. Jeena couldn't help but wonder what would have become of her parents had they still been on the plantation. How would they have fared?

Would they have gotten sick like that boy and his father?

Would her mother have died from a farming accident?

Why was that family still getting their water from the creek?

Maybe it was good that her family gone to Canada. Canada had been good to them. Her father had learned how to farm in Alberta and had a small ranch of his own. Instead of vanilla, he'd built greenhouses and cultivated flowers.

Her mother would do flower arrangements and Jeena was a surgeon. Syman may not be able to experience the same childhood she'd had, but he still had so many opportunities.

And he was living on a farm, just a different one from the one she'd grown up on, and the best thing of all was that he was free to choose who he loved.

Who he married.

There was no protocol that decided his life for him. *Until now.*

Jeena worried her bottom lip. Maazin knew about Syman and she couldn't help but wonder what he'd do with that information. There was no more denying it. Would Syman be harassed by the tabloids? He was illegitimate, but he was Maazin's son nonetheless.

Prince Ali hadn't produced any children with his late wife. Farhan didn't have any children, not yet anyway. Maazin had a son.

Syman was an heir, even if he had been born out of wedlock.

Yeah, but Maazin doesn't seem too interested in knowing about his son now, does he?

And Maazin was due to wed Lady Meleena. She had no doubt that Meleena would do her duty and produce a legitimate heir.

Until that time, though, Jeena was going to hold her breath and hope that Maazin didn't tell King Uttam about Syman's existence.

She couldn't lose Syman to Kalyana.

Jeena cursed under her breath.

She hoped that neither of them got sick, because she wanted to put as much distance between her and Maazin as possible, return to Canada and forget that she'd ever came back to the home that had turned its back on her.

Maazin paced and he was feeling a bit nervous, waiting for Jeena to come downstairs. He'd thought about this moment so many times. What he would say to her, but now that she was actually here, he didn't know what to say.

And they had a child together.

He felt deprived of that. It angered him.

Why did she hide it from me?

And he couldn't help but think it was because he was such a bad influence. He was the black sheep of the family. The rogue. The troublemaker.

Before Ali's death, he hadn't partied as hard as his family had always believed, he'd just wanted them to think that at the time so they wouldn't rely on him. So that he could be himself, so he could trick himself into believing that he was free.

He had, after all, been the third son at the time.

There hadn't been much expectation on him to settle down and produce an heir. And that had been fine by him. Then he'd met Jeena and had started to think about settling down. Until she'd left him, and he'd decided to actually live like everyone believed he'd lived. That's why Jeena had left him, so he'd indulged, just a hundred times worse than he should have.

Then Ali had died.

And Maazin had understood the errors of his ways, but it had obviously been too late. Ali was dead and he'd driven Jeena off, with their child.

He had to show her that he'd learned from his mistakes.

That he could be responsible, and maybe she would let him see the boy. To get to know him.

Do you really deserve that?

It was clear by Jeena's actions that she had no intention of returning to Kalyana permanently and Maazin had to help his country. They had to rebuild Kalyana and then break the news that he wasn't marrying Lady Meleena.

He turned around and saw that Jeena was standing uncertainly in the doorway, wearing one of his white linen kurtas. Her long dark hair was braided over her shoulder and he swore he had never seen a more beautiful sight.

Even though she'd broken his heart by leaving him all those years ago, he still thought she was the most breathtaking woman he'd ever seen.

The years hadn't changed that.

His heart may have hardened and he may have accepted his fate as a servant to Kalyana, but that didn't change the fact that he was still enraptured by her refined beauty. He was drawn to her spirit. She was a like a breath of fresh air. Still, after all this time.

"Won't you have a seat?" Maazin said, motioning toward one of the chintz couches was in the formal sitting room. The formal sitting room still had that old-world feel of the British colonies to it.

It wasn't furnished to his taste, but he only used this sitting room for visiting dignitaries. If he had his way, he would go with minimalistic.

Jeena took a wary step into the room. "This room doesn't seem to belong to you."

The corner of his mouth quirked up. She knew him so well. "You're right, but my father wanted me to leave it alone as it's part of our history. Winston Churchill came here when it was still the British Consulate. Would you like some tea?"

She nodded. "I would like that."

Maazin slipped out of the room and into the kitchen to grab the tray where he'd already prepared the tea, adding some sliced lemon. He brought it out to her.

"I'm impressed," she said as he set the tray on the table between the two overstuffed chintz sofas that were across from each other.

"With what?" he asked, handing her a cup and saucer.

"You're not completely helpless in the kitchen. You know how to put together a formal tea service."

He chuckled. "Well, teatime is still a thing here in Kalyana. I know it's not something that's done in Canada."

"We have tea."

"Do you have teatime? As in a meal?"

"No. Well, my parents do. They did continue with some of their old customs." She took a careful sip of her tea. "This is good."

"I know." He leaned back. "Your parents live in Canada now too?"

A strange expression crossed her face. "They do."

"They had a prosperous plantation."

"I know, but now they own a prosperous set of green-houses just outside Calgary." Her eyes went wide and he could tell that she was annoyed that she'd let it slip. Let her location slip. He was relieved. Canada was a big country. You could get lost in a country that big.

"That's in Alberta, isn't it?" he asked.

"Yes," she said carefully, and set down her teacup. "Why?"

"I always wondered where you had disappeared to." He wanted to add, "when you left me all those years ago," but couldn't quite bring out the words to say it.

"Well, now you know. Just outside Calgary, but just outside Calgary is a large area."

"But given the agricultural industry of the Canadian prairies and indeed Alberta itself, how many large greenhouse operations are there in that area and how many grow and sell tropical flowers? Which I also find interesting, because I wouldn't think there was a big market for tropical flowers in Alberta."

Her dark eyes narrowed and he could tell that he was treading on dangerous ground.

"Poinsettias are tropical and need heat, but are much loved at Christmas, which is bitterly cold in Alberta."

"It's impressive they found such a niche market, but that's not surprising given that they left their home country with basically nothing."

Her lips pursed. "What does it matter? People leave all the time."

"Your family left behind their prosperous vanilla plantation. I know they sold that plantation for peanuts. Way under value. They took a significant hit financially and I know that your father is a savvy businessman."

"So?"

"So? That I did not understand. I did not understand why he would sell for next to nothing a plantation that had been in his family for generations."

Jeena stood to her feet. "My father had to sell our beloved family home. There was no choice. I was pregnant by a prince who couldn't care less. What choice did I have?"

He was floored by her anger. He hadn't known she was pregnant, but she was acting like he had known. "What do you mean, I couldn't care less? I didn't even know!"

She crossed her arms. "Your fiancée is the one who helped my family leave. She said that you knew and she gave me a check to take care of my costs."

Maazin saw red. "Meleena knew?"

Tears filled Jeena's eyes and she worried her bottom lip, nodding. "She did."

"I wasn't engaged to Meleena then," he said, but he was angry.

He knew that Meleena was manipulative, but he hadn't known this. It made sense now why she'd supposedly found the letter that Jeena had left.

"I'm aware of that and I always wondered if she was trying to get me out of the way so she could have you. I guess she won."

"She didn't win," Maazin said, shaking her head.

"You're engaged to her."

"No. No, I'm not."

Jeena's eyes widened. "What do you mean?"

"She's ended it and my father has kept it secret. There are some things to work out, but Lady Meleena ended it and I was quite relieved."

Jeena sat down slowly, looking a little pale.

Frankly, he was feeling a bit ill. Meleena had manipulated them both.

Still, that didn't bring back Ali or his wife. They were gone and Maazin still blamed himself for it all.

"So you really didn't know?" she whispered.

"No. I didn't. If I'd have known…" He trailed off, because he didn't know what to say. What if he had known? He would have gone after her? Of course he would have. He wished he had, not only for Jeena's sake but also for Ali and Chandni. But even if he hadn't gone out to that party, and Ali and Chandni hadn't died, he knew that the future for him, Jeena and their unborn child would still have been fraught with uncertainty. Would his family have accepted her? Would she have wanted this life? Would he have wanted his son to have the same life he'd had?

He wasn't sure.

But none of it mattered anyway. Ali and Chandni were dead, and he had to live with the guilt. Jeena and Syman had built a life in Canada that did not include him. And he had to accept that too.

It was too much to process and he felt awful. He hung his head.

"I think I need to rest," Jeena said quietly, her voice breaking slightly as if she was grappling with the same amount of emotion he was. "It's been a lot today."

He nodded. "I know."

She got up and left.

He didn't follow.

Maazin tossed and turned all night. It was all he could do not to go and see Jeena. He wanted to make things right, but he wasn't sure that he knew how.

It was early morning when finally he gave up any

pretense of trying to fall asleep and got up, showered and dressed. When he got downstairs he found Jeena waiting calmly in the hall. She was dressed as well, in her now clean clothes. Her hair was braided back and she looked like she was ready to flee.

Again.

"Jeena?" he asked in surprise. "What are you doing up so early?"

"I need to get back to work. My team has been working all night and I've been lounging about here."

"You were hardly lounging about on purpose. We had to wait to make sure that neither one of us was infected."

"And we're not. We would've had symptoms by now, so I need to go back to work. My phone is dead, though, my charger is in my gear back with my team and your phone line is dead so I couldn't call a taxi to come and take me back to the makeshift hospital."

"The phone lines on this side of Huban are still out of order, but you wouldn't have been able to order any cab to come here and take you to the southeast district. No cab driver is equipped to handle that road. Only medical personnel and the army have permission to even try to traverse the roads."

Jeena sighed in resignation. "Will you take me, then?"

She didn't seem to want to rely on him. Not that he could blame her, he'd been hardly reliable in the past, but that was the past. This was different.

The only thing that wasn't different was that Ali was dead and he was responsible. That was his burden to bear.

The past is the past.

He nodded. "I'll drive you, of course."

"Thank you."

Maazin came down the rest of the stairs and grabbed his keys. He opened the door for Jeena while he finished locking up his home. He wasn't sure when he would get back here again and until the roads were open outside the city he wasn't sure when his small staff would make it back here.

They drove away from his home and back toward the southeastern district in near silence. He didn't know what to say. She'd had his child and he hadn't been there. He hadn't known about it.

Unless Syman isn't yours?

No. Syman was his. He knew that without a doubt.

It was one of the things he'd adored about Jeena when they'd first met. She had been so different from all the women in his social circle. She had been honest and good.

Or at least he'd thought she was until she'd left him.

One thing he did know, he had to get to the bottom of this. After he'd made sure that Jeena got back to the makeshift hospital and was reunited with her team, he was going to head straight to the palace and demand some answers from his parents.

"Have you heard from…?" He trailed off because it was hard for him to even think about the fact that he had a son. A son he knew nothing about.

There was so much he wanted to know about him but, then, there was so much he was afraid to know, and then there was a part of him that felt that maybe it would be better that Syman didn't know him or anything about this life.

Syman was currently free and he envied the boy that. Still, he was Syman's father and he wanted to know him.

You don't deserve to know him. You cost Ali his life. You don't deserve to have a child.

And he had to keep reminding himself of that.

"Syman?" she asked.

"Yes."

"I haven't heard from him since my phone died and I'm sure he's worried that he hasn't heard from me. I know my parents will worry."

Maazin nodded. "Well, they'll certainly be relieved when you tell them that you didn't contract dysentery."

She smiled. "Of course."

He hated that there was this awkwardness between the two of them, but he was the one to blame for that. He'd foolishly believed that she'd written that letter. It was clear now she hadn't. He hated that the both of them had been manipulated by Meleena.

At least Jeena hadn't destroyed anyone's life. She started a new life in Canada and prospered. He'd wallowed in self-pity and had caused his brother's death.

"So, why did you agree to marry Meleena?" she asked.

He almost lost control of the car. "What?"

"Maazin, clearly you loathe her or rather loathed her. Why did you agree to marry her?"

He sighed. "I didn't loathe her. I didn't particularly care for her but 'loathe' is a strong word."

She cocked her head to one side, studying him. "Fine. So why? Why get engaged to her and then let the engagement go on for so long?"

Because I couldn't get over you.

"It's my duty to marry and…" He had been going to say "produce an heir," but in reality he'd already done that. Illegitimacy aside, Syman was his heir.

Jeena's cheeks flushed with crimson. "I get it. You

need a legitimate heir and, believe me, that's not why I wanted you to know about Syman. I don't need anything from you, Maazin. I haven't needed you."

That cut him to the quick.

I haven't needed you.

And he deserved it. He truly did.

No one really needed him.

Only his patients, which was one thing he never took for granted. His patients needed him, his people needed him and he would keep that promise he'd made all those years ago when Jeena had left and Ali had died, his promise to dedicate his life to his work and making sure everyone in Kalyana was taken care of.

Properly.

"Well, it doesn't matter now. It's done. The past is in the past," he said quickly.

He was done talking about this.

There was no point to discussing it further. The truth was out and even though Meleena had ruined a life with his son, it had been his own actions that had killed his brother and sister-in-law. Jeena was right. She didn't need him in her life, and he truly deserved it.

That was karma for you.

CHAPTER FIVE

I WISH I had never said that to him.

It had been a couple of days since Jeena had last seen Maazin and had said those hurtful words that she was now regretting, even if they had been the truth.

She hadn't needed him in Canada. There were times she thought she did but, no, she didn't really need him. She was raising Syman to be a capable man.

And she'd learned that from the moment she'd walked through the doors of that first hospital in her intern year. A single mother in a foreign country. She'd had to rely on herself. Jeena had learned to rely only on herself.

Still, it wasn't his fault. He didn't know she had been pregnant. They had both been manipulated, but he didn't say whether he would've come to her aid. He'd trailed off, which made her believe he didn't want the responsibility.

Or that he was afraid of it.

And they weren't married. A prince had to produce a legitimate heir.

Still, she shouldn't have said that to him and she was regretting her words. She'd forgotten herself. When she'd been studying to be a doctor there'd been so many times that she'd had to really fight for her education.

To be heard. Especially because she was a woman and she was a woman of color and an immigrant to Canada to boot. She'd had to become tough and fight for what she wanted and sometimes she was more brusque than she needed to be.

And that had been one of those times.

Maazin hadn't said much to her. He'd dropped her off so she could get checked out by her team and rejoin them in their relief work and then disappeared.

She would catch glimpses of him, but he was busy doing his work and wouldn't even look in her direction. He was acting like she wasn't even there.

It's for the best and what you wanted. He knows about Syman. You've done your part.

Which was true. From the moment she'd known she'd be returning to Kalyana, she'd been terrified about running into him again, but now that it hadn't been as bad as she'd thought it was going to be, she liked being around him.

She'd forgotten how charming he could be.

His charm is why you got into trouble in the first place.

And as she watched him across the hospital, checking on his people and being so tender and gentle with the sickest and poorest of the Kalyanese people, it warmed her heart. This was a different man from the playboy who'd swept her off her feet.

He seemed at ease and he was putting the poorest of the poor above himself.

He cared about something. He seemed passionate about something, instead of just coasting, like he had before.

Maybe he had changed?

How much could a member of the Kalyanese royal

family change, though? They were bound by protocol and restrictions. They had everything, yet they weren't free. Maazin had told her that many times when they'd been together.

He was bound by duty and Jeena was very aware of the security personnel that surrounded the hospital. She didn't want this kind of life for Syman.

"So, you're the other Canadian Kalyanese doctor I've been told about."

Jeena startled and turned to see the bright smile of a beautiful woman, one who she recognized from photographs that had been plastered everywhere when Crown Prince Farhan Aaloui had wed his Canadian bride, Dr. Sara Greer.

"Your Highness." Jeena gave a small curtsey in deference to Sara.

A blush stained Sara's cheeks. "You don't need to do that."

"I do. I may be Canadian now, but I am Kalyanese and you are the Crown Princess. You will be my Queen one day."

"I'm really not used to all this bowing and scraping," Sara admitted. "I would like it if you just called me Sara."

Jeena nodded and smiled. "I would like that."

"Good," Sara said, relieved. "I was hoping that I was going to have a chance to run into you."

"Oh?" Jeena asked.

Sara motioned for them to head over to a quiet area, out of earshot of any patients, and now Jeena wondered if she knew about Syman too.

"I was wondering how long your team was planning on staying here? I asked, but couldn't get any definitive answers from anyone."

Jeena relaxed. "Oh, well...our work visas have been cleared for us to remain for at least two weeks minimum, but given the state that Kalyana is in after this cyclone it could be longer."

"That's what I was hoping for."

Jeena raised an eyebrow. "You were hoping we'd stay longer?"

"Well, not for that reason. I have been speaking to Farhan about the need to promote women in STEM programs and encouraging Kalyanese women to pursue STEM as a career. Especially in medicine, but there's no university here so young people have to study abroad, and a lot of families can't afford to send their children off-island for education."

Sara was right. Jeena had always had an interest in science and medicine, but her parents hadn't been able to afford to send her to a school to study abroad, which had been the only option.

Even though they hadn't wanted to go to Canada at first, it had worked out and Jeena had got her education.

"How do I fit in?" Jeena asked.

"I thought we could get together and work on a proposal to support young women in studying medicine abroad and returning to practice here. I'd also like to explore the possibility of Kalyana having its own university. As someone who grew up here, I would love to pick your brains. And maybe then we could speak to young women and inspire them. Let them know there are options for them. Both of us are successful Kalyanese doctors." Sara smiled brightly. "It's all just a bunch of jumbled hazy thoughts in my head, but I would love your input."

Jeena smiled. "I think that's a great idea."

"Right?" Sara crossed her arms. "I knew that I would like you. You think like me."

"I appreciate that. I don't find many people who think like me. Of course, living in Alberta I was the only one from Kalyana."

"I understand that. Where I grew up in London, Ontario I didn't really run into people from our country either. Of course, I was adopted and for a long time didn't even know that I was Kalyanese."

"That's a shame," Jeena said, and then quickly corrected herself. "Not because you were adopted, but that you didn't know anything about Kalyana. It really is a wonderful country and I've missed it."

"Can I ask something else?"

Jeena knew what was coming and she wanted to say no, but she couldn't. "You want to know why I left?"

"Yeah, it's obvious you love it here so much."

"I do. I love my parents more and my father had an opportunity to make his dreams of becoming a tropical flower farmer a reality. There wasn't enough land to fulfill his needs in Kalyana, so he moved to Canada when the opportunity came. I'm their only child and I wanted to become a doctor. As you say, there isn't really opportunity here in Kalyana for young women to do that, so I went with them. I haven't regretted it and I'm glad to be back here and helping the country of my birth."

It was all a lie, but Sara didn't need to know the sordid details.

Sara smiled. "That's lovely."

"Your Highness?"

Sara spun around to see a security guard waiting. She bit her lip and then turned back to Jeena. "I have to go. It was wonderful to meet you, Dr. Harrak."

Jeena bowed her head. "The pleasure is all mine, Your Highness."

Sara left with the security guard and Jeena let out of a sigh of relief that she hadn't even known she was holding. She was so worried that Sara had been told about her past, that Sara knew about Syman that...well, she didn't know what.

She was just so worried that others would find out about her and Syman. No one needed to know that Maazin was Syman's father.

Jeena had the feeling that someone was staring at her and she glanced over to see that Maazin was looking at her with curiosity.

Don't think about him.

She turned back to her work. He had made it clear that he was mad at her and she'd said something she completely regretted, but maybe this was for the best.

He leaned over, his breath on her neck making a tingle run down her spine. "I see that you've met Sara."

"I thought you weren't talking to me, Your Highness?" she replied.

"Yes, well I was curious when I saw Sara come in and introduce herself."

Jeena sighed. "Look, about what I said..."

He held up his hand. "I don't want to talk about that. What did Sara want?"

"She wanted me to help with her initiative to promote the STEM programs to young women in Kalyana. I told her that I would back her on that. Help her with her ideas for her proposal. Talk to other young women interested in the sciences."

"You're not here for long, how can you?" he asked, crossing his arms. "For that matter, why did she ask you to participate in this?"

"She asked me because I am Kalyanese and even though her heritage is Kalyanese, she was born in Canada and feels that I would have a better perspective of the needs here, as I grew up here."

Maazin cocked an eyebrow. "I can see that."

"I'm glad," she replied saucily. "Was that all you wanted to discuss?"

"Actually, there's a medical emergency on a small island north of Agung and I could use your help. We can take the royal yacht, which is loaded with supplies, and go and treat the village that has been cut off since Blandine hit."

Even though she knew it wasn't a good idea to be alone with Maazin and on his yacht, no less, she couldn't turn her back on patients who needed her.

"Okay." She nodded and set down the chart she was working on. "When do you want to leave?"

"Within the hour. Gather what gear you need, in case we have to stay overnight. I'll make the other arrangements and have a car come and get you to bring you down to the harbor." He turned and left before she had a chance to protest, before she had a chance to change her mind.

This is not a smart idea.

But, really, this was part of her mission to Kalyana.

She really didn't have a choice. This was what she was here for.

Maazin did the final checks on the yacht. Soon Jeena would arrive and he would set out on the hour-long sail to the island north of Agung. He would rather take the helicopter, but there was nowhere to land safely on the small island of Petrie because Blandine had damaged it so badly.

"Sara mentioned that you were getting your yacht ready to head out to Petrie."

Maazin glanced down onto the dock and saw that Farhan was standing there. Off in the distance were the security guards, ever-present when the Crown Prince was around.

"I am." Maazin walked onto the dock. "Is there an issue with that?"

Farhan shrugged. "Mother isn't happy about it. She thinks that you should send one of our doctors who is not royal blood, or the relief workers. You know Mother and how she worries."

Do I?

It didn't seem to him his mother cared much for him. Not since Ali had died. He knew his mother blamed him. She barely acknowledged him. It cut him to the quick. He'd managed to make his peace with his father. If only he could make things right with his mother, but he doubted that would ever happen. She was too hurt, too distant, and he felt responsible.

Actually, he was responsible.

He was certain she viewed him as a disappointment.

"You quite all right?" Farhan asked, cocking his head to one side. "You look out of sorts."

"I'm fine. A bit tired. I'm sure you heard about my little exposure to dysentery the other day."

"Yes. I did and don't worry, all that is being taken care of. The farmers in that area have been supplied with clean water and proper sanitation is in place."

"I'm glad to hear that."

"I know it's been a bit of an effort and difficult, but with the help of our allies we're getting the help that we need."

Farhan was ever the diplomat and Maazin had no

doubt that he would be a great king one day. Even though it was Maazin's fault that Farhan had been put in that position in the first place.

"Did you want something else?" Maazin asked. "The other doctor will be here soon and we'll need to get going if we're to make Petrie Island before nightfall."

Maazin didn't mean to be so curt with Farhan, but he didn't want his brother around when Jeena arrived. Not that Farhan even knew who Jeena was. He hadn't told anyone about Jeena. The only ones who knew about her and the history he had with her were his mother and Lady Meleena apparently. No one else knew.

And no one needed to know about it.

Still, he didn't want Farhan meeting her and saying something to their father. And given the nature and turmoil that Kalyana was currently in, he wasn't sure how he was going to start that conversation.

"What, who, me?" Farhan asked.

"You didn't come here to see me off," Maazin said plainly.

"Fine. Mother wants you to return to the palace and Father is giving in to her." Farhan rubbed the back of his neck. "He says you don't need to be here."

Maazin could tell that Farhan felt uncomfortable telling him this.

Maybe go with Farhan and appease your mother?

Only he didn't want to. He'd promised to take Jeena to Petrie Island and this was part of his duty to his people. There were Kalyanese on Petrie Island who had lost everything and were in dire need. They needed him.

And that trumped his need to please his father.

"I can't," Maazin said quickly. "I promised those displaced people that I would take help and I will be there. Do you not think that's the right thing to do?"

Farhan sighed and nodded, rolling his shoulders. "I do."

"Thank you."

"Well, at least I tried, but…" Farhan trailed off and looked uncomfortable. "When you return I strongly urge you to return to the palace. Father is not well at the moment and it would be good if you returned. He's been asking you to come back to the palace since Blandine hit and you've been avoiding him. You need to go and see him."

"I know." Maazin knew that his father was feeling poorly. With his condition and the cyclone devastating Kalyana, it hadn't been good for their father, but he had a hard time being around his family. It was better to keep them at a distance.

It was easier that way.

"Good luck on your trip. If you need anything, please call and I will send for assistance."

Maazin shook his brother's hand. "Thank you."

Farhan turned and walked over to the dark SUV with tinted windows and Kalyana flags. A security guard held open the door for Farhan as he slipped into the back.

Maazin waved as the SUV drove away from the harbor.

Maazin knew there was security watching him, and he knew there would be an attaché of security following the yacht to Petrie, but Maazin didn't need as much of a detail as the Crown Prince did.

Of course, Ali had had just as much security and that hadn't helped him.

"You shouldn't have gone to that party. What were you thinking?" Ali lambasted him, yelling above the rain that was pouring down and the constant swish of

the wiper blades. "You left your security team behind. Do you know how foolish that was?"

"So?" Maazin asked, but he could barely keep his head up. He didn't care much about anything. Jeena was gone and his pain wouldn't end.

"Don't be so hard on him, Ali," Chandni whispered gently. "His heart is broken."

"It doesn't matter. He's a prince. He should behave better."

Maazin snorted. "I'm third in line to the throne and, unlike you, Ali, I can do whatever I want."

"Or whoever," Ali snapped back. "Honestly, Maazin, when will you grow up?"

Maazin was going to answer, but before he could there was a large bang and the world turned upside down and went black...

"Hey, you okay?"

Maazin jumped and realized that Jeena was standing beside him. He hadn't even seen her arrive. She carried a duffel bag and his security team was unloading medical supplies, as well as food and water from the back of the van that had replaced Farhan's SUV.

"Fine." Maazin scrubbed a hand over his face. "I'm okay. Sorry, I just zoned out."

"If you're sure..."

"I'm fine." Maazin turned away from her. "We'd better get loaded up and get on our way to Petrie before it gets too late."

He just had to put it all behind him.

He had to put the memory of Ali behind him, just like he had to put the memory of Jeena and how broken he'd been when she'd left behind him as well.

It was all in the past and, wish it as he might, he couldn't go back and change anything.

The past was the past and his future was tied to serving his country and that was it. Maybe, just maybe then he could forgive himself for the damage he'd done.

Maybe.

CHAPTER SIX

THE WATER MADE Jeena a little nervous, but she felt safer being on Maazin's yacht and today was a beautiful, perfect day to be on the water.

Jeena raised her head to the sky and drank in the warmth of the late afternoon sun. Back in Calgary it was a bitter minus forty degrees Celsius and nothing like the beautiful eighty-degree weather that was here.

Just another thing she'd missed about Kalyana. She'd missed the warmth and sunshine. She was not a fan of winter or darkness. The only thing she liked about winter and darkness was the northern lights. That was something she was not sure she'd ever get tired of seeing.

She gazed out over the waters of the Indian Ocean, where all the islands that made up Kalyana lay. Beyond Kalyana lay the continent of Africa, Madagascar and then there was India, Yemen, Oman and the Maldives.

She'd forgotten what it was like to take a boat out to one of the far-flung islands of Kalyana. Looking east, she could make out the pearl-pink crescent of Patang Island.

On Patang Island had been the first time she had been with Maazin. She'd given her heart and soul to him that night, with no thought to the future and what it might hold for them.

Her cheeks heated as she thought of that night.

They had been on this yacht then too.

Their first time had been on the island, but then he'd carried her back to the yacht and made love to her again in his cabin. His arms around her, his hands in her hair and his mouth on hers. She'd been completely lost.

He'd been the only one to ever make her feel that way.

She'd been a fool.

And she had been such a fool to fall for a prince. What had she been thinking? She'd been so naive. So innocent. Well, she'd learned the hard way about trusting her heart to someone. The only one she could depend on was herself.

Jeena snuck a peak at Maazin at the helm, his white linen shirt billowing, his eyes focused on the horizon, and her pulse began to beat just a bit faster.

Damn him.

She hated that he still had an effect on her. Try as she might, she was still pulled toward him like a moth to a flame and she knew, just knew that if she allowed herself to get sucked in, she would get burned again.

This time she wouldn't let her heart lead her to disaster. When her work here was done she'd just leave and head back to Canada. There would be no struggle for her family. She wouldn't be as afraid. There was a life waiting for her in Canada. A damn good one.

Syman was her world and she was going to make sure that he was protected. She didn't want him sucked into this kind of life.

But Syman needs to know his father.

And it was that little voice she couldn't quell. Maazin

deserved to know Syman and Syman deserved to know his father. She was just still afraid that Maazin would take Syman from her as Syman had royal blood. It's what her parents feared. She couldn't lose Syman, but she couldn't deny a father and son.

Maazin looked at her. "You seem lost in thought."

"Not really lost in thought." It was a lie. She didn't want to tell him what she was really feeling. "Just enjoying the warmth and the sun."

"It's not really that warm."

"For me it is. It's bitterly cold in Canada. I'd forgotten how hot and wonderful the weather is here when the dark of winter hits."

"Dark of winter?" Maazin asked, raising an eyebrow. "Surely it's not that bad."

"Yes. It's that bad." Jeena pulled out her phone and scrolled through the photos to find the picture she'd taken when her father had had the laneway to the greenhouse plowed out a month ago during a bad blast of snow.

"Look at this." She got up and walked over to him, holding up her phone to show him the picture. He looked at it, raising his eyebrows.

"Wow," he said. "That's a lot of snow."

"Right. It gets so cold and dark." She exited the photo app. "There was so much snow and Syman was so mad that hockey had to be canceled for the night."

She closed her eyes and groaned inwardly. She hadn't meant to mention Syman again, but then again Maazin hadn't really asked much about him either.

"You've mentioned that he likes hockey," Maazin said. "Does he like other sports?"

"Baseball in the summer. Soccer as well."

"Football, you mean," Maazin said with a smile.

"Yes, I suppose European football is known as soccer there. He doesn't play American football. Though he is a fan of the Saskatchewan Roughriders, which is CFL over NFL."

"What's the difference?" Maazin asked. "Or is there one?"

"Oh, there's a difference, and people get really tetchy about it if you don't know."

He smiled, his eyes twinkling. "Do you know the difference?"

"Of course."

He cocked an eyebrow. "Well?"

"Well, what?"

"What's the difference?"

"Does it matter?" she asked.

"Yes." He smiled at her, a lazy half-smile.

"Why?"

"Because," he teased. "You don't really know."

She chuckled. "Fine. I don't really know."

"So there's no difference, then?"

"Not really. I think it has something to do with field size. CFL is a bigger field size than NFL."

"Is there no cricket or polo in Canada?"

Jeena shrugged slightly. "They aren't really big in Canada."

"That's a shame. Perhaps…" He pursed his lips, as if he was going to offer to teach Syman cricket, but then thought better about it. It made her feel sad on one hand, but relieved as well. If he didn't want to be part of Syman's life or if he wasn't going to be around, she didn't want Syman to get hurt.

If he wanted out then he needed to say something.

She wasn't going to let Maazin hurt their son like he'd hurt her all those years ago.

Still, there was a part of her that wanted him to ask and know their son.

"You can ask me anything about him, you know. Anything you want," she said gently.

"I appreciate that."

She wanted to tell him that what she'd said the other day about not needing him didn't mean that she didn't want him to care about Syman. She just didn't want him to feel obligated to care for them, when he couldn't.

There was an almost palpable tension and she hated that it was so awkward around him. She remembered a time when it had been so easy between them. When they would talk for hours, laugh and make love.

Heat bloomed in her cheeks and she wandered to the starboard side of the ship to look out over the water. She leaned on the railing and sighed, trying not to think about the past, but everywhere she looked there it was. The past, calling to her.

Like a siren calling a doomed sailor to his death.

"You seem lost in thought again," Maazin said gently.

"Just…memories." She looked back at him. His expression was soft and he smiled at her, sending a thrill through her.

"I know. I was thinking the same thing. We took many a ride on this yacht."

"You liked the sea," she said.

"Don't you?" he asked.

"Yes… No. Water does frighten me. It's beautiful, but it's slightly terrifying."

"Then why did you come on yacht trips with me?" he asked.

"You liked it and I wanted to be with you."

He smiled gently at her, those gray-green eyes twinkling at her. "I thought you liked it and I wanted to please you."

"So you don't like it, then?"

"Yes and no. I like my yacht, but it wasn't because I liked cruising around on my own. I liked the privacy that it offered. Out here I can just be me. I'm not a prince. I'm no one."

She nodded. "I can understand that."

"I haven't asked much about Syman yet. I'm sorry. I'm processing it, but I want to know. I truly do."

"Look, I know I dropped this bombshell on you, but you had the right to know. I thought you did know."

"I understand. We were fooled."

She could hear the frustration in his voice.

"I am sorry."

"It's not your fault. And if I see her again...well, let's hope I don't."

"It's in the past," Jeena offered. Although she wouldn't mind taking a swift shot at Meleena.

"I am curious about one thing, though," Maazin said.

"What's that?" she asked.

"Why didn't you go to the press?" Maazin asked. "If you felt I hurt you, betrayed you, why didn't you tell the world what a vile, vicious man I was?"

"I'd never have done that. We were starting a new life away from Kalyana and didn't want to draw attention to ourselves. And I didn't want my child dragged into all of this. I didn't want him photographed or have the media follow us. There was so much going on when he was born. Your older brother Ali and his wife had died and—"

"I'm aware," Maazin said quickly, and a strange expression passed over his face. She had obviously touched a sore spot about Ali and she wondered what had happened. All she knew was that he and his wife had died in a car crash.

That was all anyone had ever been told.

"I'm sorry for your loss. I know how close you were to Ali."

Maazin nodded, but he wouldn't looked at her and she knew that whatever conversation they were having was over.

"For what it's worth, I'm not the kind of person who would ever go to the press, Maazin. I would never hurt you like that."

He nodded, but didn't look at her. "Thank you."

She sat back down and focused on the ocean. Off in the distance she could see dark clouds rolling in. It was fitting for how she felt. For how Maazin obviously felt, given the tension between them.

Or at least it felt fitting.

For the rest of the trip to Petrie Island the atmosphere was tense. Jeena didn't say anything and neither did Maazin. The dark clouds were still in the distance, but Jeena had a real sense of foreboding as she watched them.

Even Maazin seemed on edge about it. As they approached the island Jeena gasped in shock. She remembered coming to Petrie Island with her grandfather a lot. He would sell vanilla on the island every Sunday and often take her.

The little island just north of the larger Agung was always bustling on a Sunday when the market came in.

There were other smaller islands all around the main island of Kalyana and all these small communities would come together and congregate on Petrie. They would share stories and sell their wares.

She remembered a weaver living on the island who would weave beautiful saris the color of the sea shot with gold. Her mother had one still.

But as they got closer to the island and Jeena could see the devastation, her heart sank. Houses had been toppled, trees uprooted and the small harbor that housed the islands' boats had been destroyed. Boats were capsized or washed ashore and irreparably damaged.

It was like a war zone.

It was awful.

Maazin pursed his lips and frowned. "It's worse than I thought."

"No one from Kalyana has been out this way since Blandine?" Jeena asked in shock.

"No. We've been unable to get here. There were so many wounded and sick on the main islands. Then those in further outlying areas were coming to the main island to seek help. No one from Petrie came, but now I understand why, they were unable to."

Maazin docked his yacht at the main pier, where police officers and first responders who lived on the island were waiting for his arrival.

Jeena's stomach twisted in a knot as she watched Maazin greet the men and women who were waiting for him. There was a lot of deference and saluting, but Maazin was quick to shut that all down.

"I've brought medical supplies," he told the man who Jeena assumed was the chief of police. "And a surgeon. This is Dr. Harrak."

Jeena climbed down onto the dock and shook everyone's hands.

"Jeena, this the chief of police on Petrie. His name is Mustafa. Mustafa, this is Dr. Jeena Harrak. She is Kalyanese, but is from Canada."

"We're so glad you've come, Your Highness," Mustafa said. "We have so many wounded. Our first aid and first responder teams have done what they can, but we have some who require surgical intervention."

"I'm here to help. Have all your buildings been damaged by the cyclone?" Jeena asked Mustafa.

"Not all. Those closest to the water have been. The city hall is standing as it was made from cement and cinderblock. We have moved all the wounded and sick there. It's sheltered and has a generator." Mustafa looked exhausted. "We have an elderly gentleman who was brought to us last night by his daughter. He lived on one of the smaller islands. He was a weaver and one of our medics said he suspects that the man has appendicitis."

Jeena bit her lip. "That's not good."

"No, he's very ill. The medics have set him up with an IV antibiotic drip, but if it's appendicitis he really needs to get off island and have surgery."

"There might not be time to get him off island," Maazin stated.

"You're right. We'll have to check him." Jeena frowned. "I could perform an emergency surgery if I had to."

"Can you?" Mustafa asked, surprised.

"Of course. It's what I'm trained for," Jeena replied. "You said the man was a weaver?"

Mustafa nodded. "Yes, and a tailor, the only one in Petrie. He's been selling his fabrics, saris, kurtas and lenghas here for over twenty years. He's very talented."

Jeena smiled. "Yes. My mother has one of his saris. She cherishes it."

Mustafa grinned. "Harrak is your surname?"

"Yes."

"Is your grandfather Rami Harrak?" Mustafa asked.

"Yes, that was my grandfather. My father took over his plantation, until…" She trailed off, trying not to think about the night she and her family had left their home. "My parents live in Canada now."

"Good for them," Mustafa said, and Jeena was thankful he didn't ask any further questions. "I'll take you to my truck and get you over to the courthouse. My other officers will make sure all your gear and supplies get there too."

Jeena nodded and then glanced at Maazin, who was staring at her with an unreadable expression on his face. She looked away quickly.

She didn't want to share that pain with him.

One for which she had blamed him for so long when it hadn't been his fault.

The drive to the courthouse that had been converted into a makeshift hospital didn't take too long. There wasn't much flooding and any rubble from the houses near the coast of the island had been cleared away. As had the trees. There were tents and a sort of makeshift shanty village the closer they got to the center of the town where the market was.

"Thankfully our water supply wasn't disrupted as it comes from a natural spring and because of our generator we're also able to have our desalinator up and running," Mustafa mentioned offhandedly as he drove through the streets.

"I'm glad. There was a small outbreak of dysentery on the main island that we were able to control," Maazin said. "I'm glad there is nothing like that here."

Jeena was glad too. Something like dysentery or another infectious disease would wreak havoc on the close-knit community of Petrie Island.

It didn't take long for them to get to the courthouse.

"We're here and I'll take you right to our most urgent patient, Mr. Patel." Mustafa parked and Jeena grabbed her duffel bag, which carried an emergency surgery kit. Something she always carried with her when she was going off into disaster zones.

Maazin followed Mustafa and Jeena followed them.

The medics had done a great job setting up the make-shift medical center. Jeena was impressed, but right now she wanted to take a look at Mr. Patel.

"He's in here. Our paramedic is with him."

"Thank you, Mustafa," Maazin said.

"Your Highness." Mustafa bowed.

Maazin held open the door for Jeena and she walked into the room. She could tell the man was very ill.

"Your Highness," the paramedic said with a curtsey.

"Please, it's okay. Can you tell us about Mr. Patel?" Maazin asked.

The paramedic nodded. "Mr. Patel was brought in early this morning. His daughter said he was complaining of lower right quadrant abdominal pain. Upon palpation we noticed he was guarding and his temperature was one hundred and two. He has been unable to pass a bowel movement and his blood test came back with a high count of white blood cells."

"So he's fighting an infection," Jeena said. She walked over to the bed and examined the patient. Mr Patel was just as she remembered him, slightly older, but he still looked the same.

"Yes," the paramedic said. "With antibiotics we've managed to bring his temperature down a bit, but it's rising again."

"Without an ultrasound it's pretty hard to tell if it's definitely appendicitis," Jeena said. "But from the description, it's not dysentery."

"There's no blood or mucus," the paramedic said. "It was our worry too, but Mr. Patel's daughter said he's been drinking bottled water. He's not a stranger to cyclones and storms."

"You've done an excellent job here," Jeena remarked, and she continued her examination. "You wouldn't happen to have certification in anesthesia, would you?"

The paramedic's eyes widened. "No."

"I do," Maazin said.

"That's good, but I do need someone to assist me."

"I can help with that. I'm training to be a surgical nurse," the paramedic said. "It's just been hard to get to a school, it's so costly…"

Jeena understood that only too well. There was no medical school in Kalyana and going abroad was very expensive, which was why her dream of becoming a surgeon hadn't been realized until she'd been banished and had moved to Canada.

"What's your name?" Jeena asked gently.

"Ayesha."

"Well, Ayesha, if you think you have a good handling of surgical instruments I would gladly have you assist me while Prince Maazin does the anesthesia."

"Thank you, Dr. Harrak."

"Please go prep a sterile room so that we can operate on Mr. Patel immediately."

"Of course." Ayesha left the room and Jeena went straight to her duffel bag to pull out her surgical kit.

"Are you sure this is wise?" Maazin asked, and she could hear the concern in his voice.

"If we don't do it, he won't survive the trip back to the main island. We have to."

"But with a paramedic assisting you?"

"She was smart enough to set up the IV and take his

blood. You heard her, she wants to be an operating room nurse, a scrub nurse, but there's no little or no support available for her. This is what Sara was talking to me about so earnestly."

"I agree more could be done," Maazin said. "But this is a man's life."

"Exactly. I can do this, you'll be in the room and Ayesha is more than capable of assisting me."

Maazin looked uncertain. "What choice do we have? You're right. Very well, I'll be there and we can do this."

Jeena touched his arm. "Yes, we can do this."

Mr. Patel started to rouse and looked a bit surprised. "Your Highness?"

Maazin smiled at the man. "Mr. Patel, we're here to help you."

"Help me?" the patient asked, confused.

"You have appendicitis and Dr. Harrak from Canada and myself are going to take care of you."

Mr. Patel nodded and looked over at her. He smiled at her. "I recognize you."

Jeena smiled down at him. "I would say so. I saw you every weekend when I was a child."

"You are not Canadian," Mr. Patel said.

"I am now, but I'm back home to work and to help."

Mr. Patel closed his eyes. "Good. Good."

Jeena checked his pulse rate, which was racing. "We need to get him into surgery now."

If they didn't, Mr. Patel was going to get peritonitis and die.

Maazin thought that Jeena was foolish thinking about operating on Mr. Patel in a makeshift hospital on the small island of Petrie with a paramedic as her assistant and without ultrasound assistance or other specialized equipment to do the surgery.

Ayesha had done a great job in prepping a small, well-lit room. Jeena's instinct was right and Mr. Patel's appendix was on the verge of rupturing, which would have meant a bad case of peritonitis, and as he was over seventy, his chances for survival in a disaster situation like this would not have been good without surgery.

Maazin felt bad for wanting to wait to transport him to Huban. He wouldn't have made that journey.

Now, here they were in a small courtroom and they were saving a man's life. Not only that, Jeena was inspiring a young Kalyanese paramedic who had aspirations of doing so much more. Jeena was wonderful. There was no other word to describe it.

He couldn't help but smile from behind his surgical mask as he watched her.

She was so strong and she didn't even know it.

Or she hadn't known it when they'd been together. She had changed. She was fierce and it made him want her all the more.

You can't have her.

And that thought replayed over and over in his mind as he watched Jeena work and explain things to Ayesha as they removed the enflamed appendix and cleaned out the infection from Mr. Patel's abdomen.

He was also jealous of Jeena.

She had more hands-on practical knowledge than he did. Maazin had training and he'd done work in the field, but rarely. His father ruled Maazin's schedule and there wasn't much time to really practice medicine or teach it. He may have been a military surgeon, but he didn't get to practice as much as he'd like to. As much as she obviously did.

He'd moved away from medicine into politics and diplomacy, something Maazin hated more than anything.

If he'd not been born into the royal family, if he'd had the same freedom as Jeena, then she would've never left Kalyana. They would be together, married, and Syman would know who he was.

A lump formed in his throat as he thought about Syman. A boy who loved sport as much as he did. Not that he knew anything about ice hockey, but he could learn.

That's if Jeena would let him get to know Syman. He was so afraid Jeena wouldn't let him. She'd offered to talk about him, but he didn't quite believe she was actually going to tell him about Syman. She was determined to protect their son, and he understood why.

Maazin lived his life in the spotlight as a member of the royal family. Nothing of his was private. His whole life was on display.

Even if he did meet his son, he wouldn't want to burden him with this life. This horrible public life that he couldn't escape. That he was bound to forever, not only by birth but by his mistakes, which had made him second in line to throne until Farhan had an heir.

Still, he was a father. There was duty there. He'd never thought of having children, but now he had one he had to do the right thing by him.

He had to prove to Jeena that he could.

Do you deserve a second chance?

No. He didn't and that thought sobered him up.

"Now let's close up," Jeena remarked.

"This is an amazing opportunity, Dr. Harrak. Thank you," Ayesha said.

"You're very welcome and thank you for assisting me."

"Yes. Thank you, Ayesha," Maazin said, finally finding his voice.

"Thank you, Your Highness," Ayesha said nervously.

They finished closing up Mr. Patel and Ayesha promised to monitor him post-op so that Jeena and Maazin could go out and assess the rest of the Petrie Island villagers who had been hurt during the cyclone.

Jeena washed up and disposed of the scrubs and then placed the instruments in a biohazard container that was filled with antiseptic.

"That's a handy kit you had," Maazin commented as he cleaned up.

"This isn't my first time heading to a disaster area. Of course, this is my first one out of Canada."

"What have you dealt with in Canada?" Maazin asked.

"Mostly things like accidents or avalanches in the mountains. Sometimes a hiker falls down a cliff and you have to attend out in the field."

"Avalanches?" Maazin asked in amazement.

"Or mudslides. I know Kalyana has had its fair share of those." She shuddered then and shook her head as if shaking away a bad memory.

"Why are you shuddering?"

She sighed. "When I was a child, I was almost swept out to sea by a flash flood during a particularly bad rainstorm. It terrified me, but I've overcome that fear. Still, every once in a while when I think about it, the terror comes right back."

So that's why she isn't fond of water.

"I'm sure," Maazin said quietly. He knew exactly what she was talking about. There were times when that accident came back to mind, flooding back, and it sent him into a tailspin. He hated the helpless feeling that came with it.

He hated being reminded of that horrible night and its aftermath. How his parents had everything hushed up. People had been paid off and no one knew Maazin had been drunk and fighting with Ali as Ali had been driving during a rainstorm.

No one knew Maazin was the reason Ali was dead.

He was the shame of his family.

"You okay?" she asked.

"I'm fine. And I will help."

"I assumed you would," Jeena teased. "You are a doctor too, Your Highness."

"I don't have as much practice in the field as you."

"Aren't you an army surgeon?" she asked.

He nodded. "Yes, but royal duties outweighed a lot of my opportunity for really getting out there and saving lives. Though I lend a hand when I can, still it would be nice to have the freedom that you have. I would like to learn more."

"That's too bad."

"What is?" he asked.

"That you're so trapped by that royal title."

"It is. I much prefer my medical work and working with people to protocol and diplomacy."

She nodded. "Still, with your power you could advocate for change. I admire that power you have to make a real difference."

"I can do that. Yes. And I plan to."

"You do?" she asked.

He smiled at her. "I mean, with Sara's initiative to promote STEM sciences and medical sciences, in particular to women, and to bring a university to Huban.

Kalyana needs this. I think you should help her and I will too."

Jeena smiled brightly, her lovely dark eyes twinkling with that sparkle he hadn't seen in so long. "You will?"

"It's clear that something needs to be done. You did a wonderful job with Ayesha and you saved Mr. Patel's life."

"Thank you."

"Now, let's go and help some others."

"Good idea." Jeena grabbed her medical kit and they left the small courtroom where they had just operated on Mr. Patel. Maazin sighed and ran his hand through his hair.

The panic in him was rising and his shoulder twinged where it had been dislocated the night Ali had died, as it always did when he was about to have a full-on panic attack.

Right now he had to calm himself down.

He felt useless, but if he didn't get his emotions under control he would indeed be useless to everyone.

"Your Highness?"

Maazin spun around, annoyed that he'd been interrupted. Mustafa stood there and Maazin could tell that he was nervous.

"What's wrong? Tell me."

Mustafa handed him a piece of paper. "This came in. There's a storm brewing. Not a cyclone like Blandine, but it's headed straight for Petrie. I've sent my crew out to bring those who are in the tent city here, but I need more help."

Maazin nodded. "I'll come with you. Let's go."

He hurried after Mustafa. Jeena and the first responders who were here could tend to the wounded, but right now he needed to help Mustafa bring in the others. It may not be a cyclone that was headed for Petrie, but a storm hitting an already ravaged island was dangerous enough.

And it appeared that he and Jeena were spending the night here, whether she liked it or not.

They were stuck.

Jeena walked among the cots that had been salvaged, along with the other mattresses and bedding that were scattered across the floor. The displaced and uninjured survivors were put in another courtroom. The little courtroom that they'd used to operate on Mr. Patel earlier in the day had been cleaned.

The storm had struck an hour ago. It was strong and the wind howled fiercely, scaring the small children who had already been through the turmoil of Blandine.

Jeena was exhausted, but she wanted to make sure that everyone was taken care of.

There was a quiet calm, broken only by the odd cough.

All the wounded and sick were stable. Mr. Patel was doing well and Ayesha was staying with him, as was his daughter.

Where did Maazin go?

Jeena had been looking for him since she'd heard that he'd gone out to collect the villagers and bring them to the safety of the courthouse. She'd seen him briefly helping Mustafa board up the windows, but now he was gone.

He was probably hungry and she had a bowl of jasmine rice and vegetable curry that Mustafa's wife was dishing out to everyone.

Maazin had to eat.

She wandered down another hall toward more offices, and found Maazin in one of them, sitting behind the desk, brooding in the shadows.

She knocked on the door. "I've been looking for you."

"Ah, I just needed a few moments and Mustafa thought that I would be comfortable in here." He rolled his eyes. "Apparently a prince needs a giant room all to himself."

"Do you?" she asked, amused.

"No. I would be more comfortable on my yacht, but my security team, which arrived just after us, advised that this would indeed be a safer location."

"I believe they're right," she said. "I have food. Mustafa's wife is making food for everyone and it's good. Very filling."

"It smells good." Maazin reached over and flicked on a small torch. The generator had been powered down to conserve fuel until the storm was over. Jeena came into the room and set the small metal plate down in front of him, together with a fork.

"Did you eat?" Maazin asked.

"I did. I wouldn't lie and say it was good if it wasn't," she teased, and she sat down in the chair on the opposite side of the desk.

Maazin took a bite. "That is quite wonderful."

"See, I don't lie."

He smiled at her. "How is Mr. Patel doing?"

"He's doing well." That was the truth and Jeena was relieved about that. He had been so close to death. "He's our most critical case and he's stable. Everyone else is in good shape too. For being such a small island with no doctor here, they're doing remarkably well."

"Well, let's hope they do eventually get their own

doctor. My father listens to Sara and I'm sure he'll support her ideas."

Jeena snorted. "Right."

Maazin cocked an eyebrow. "My father does a lot of good."

"I know he does, but you can understand my derision, can't you?"

"No. I don't, actually."

"Kalyana is trying to be a modern country. Yet there's nowhere to teach people past high school. Your father has been King for a long time and that change hasn't happened yet."

"He has been King for a long time, but he isn't the ultimate rule-maker. There's parliament and procedures."

"So your father's ideas are not put through? Are you saying he's wanted a university?" she asked in disbelief.

Maazin sighed. "Fine. He can be stubborn and maybe not always think so progressively. He's getting better."

"You do agree with them anyway, don't you?"

Maazin sighed. "Yes."

"Like the marriage thing?" Jeena regretted asking him about it the moment the question left her lips, but she couldn't help it. She didn't understand why Maazin had agreed to marry Lady Meleena if he hadn't loved her. Maazin had always told her that he was against arranged marriage, even though his parents and Ali's arranged marriage had been successful.

He'd always told her that he wanted to marry for love and now he wasn't. It just didn't make sense.

Unless he actually had loved Lady Meleena.

"You weren't forced into it, were you?" Jeena asked, embarrassed that she was assuming that he was an unwilling participant.

"No. I agreed to it."

It stung, even though she didn't want it to sting.

It's because you still care about him. After all this time, you still care deeply for him.

"I'm sorry, then. I didn't mean..." She trailed off, not sure of what to say next, and she stood up to leave. "I'm sorry."

She tried to leave the room, before she continued to put her foot in her mouth. She really didn't know what had come over her, but as she tried to leave she felt a hand on her arm, pulling her back, and she saw Maazin standing behind her.

How had he got to her so fast?

His touch sent a shiver of delight down her spine. And suddenly all she could hear was the sound of her pulse racing in her ears and the rain hammering against the roof.

She forgot everything else as she stared up into those eyes she'd loved so much. The eyes of the man that she'd loved so much, the man who haunted her dreams.

She looked away. It was too much.

"Jeena, it's not like that. I agreed to it because it made diplomatic sense, because it's my duty. That's it. I didn't love her."

Jeena looked up stunned. "You didn't?"

"No."

"Didn't you care for her at least? I mean, you agreed to marry her."

"Because it was my duty but, no, I didn't care for her because she wasn't you," he whispered. He took a step closer to her and touched her face, like he had all those years ago on Patang Island.

Her heart skipped a beat and her body shook, craving more of his touch. And then, before she knew what was happening, his hands were in her hair and he was pulling her close, kissing her, and she let him.

She let him kiss her, very gently, and her body began to melt, powerless.

There was a knock at the door and Jeena jumped back, embarrassed by what she'd let happen.

"Jeena..." Maazin pleaded.

She shook her head. "No. I'm not falling into that trap again."

"I'm not engaged," Maazin said.

"It doesn't matter. This can't happen."

"Why?" he asked.

But before she could say anything further, before she fell into the trap of believing and trusting him again, she opened the door to find Ayesha there.

"Dr. Harrak, it's Mr. Patel. His temperature has spiked again."

"I'll be right there."

Ayesha nodded and left.

Jeena took a calming breath and looked back at Maazin. It was too late for them. Even if he was no longer engaged to Meleena, he was off limits. She couldn't be with him again, she was too afraid of being hurt, and when this was all over she was going back to Canada, back to her son, and would try to put this whole thing behind her.

CHAPTER SEVEN

THE STORM BLEW itself out overnight, although there was a storm raging inside him. He knew he shouldn't have kissed her, but he'd been unable to prevent it.

And even though no one else was supposed to know that his engagement to Lady Meleena was over, he'd wanted Jeena to know. And he was glad he'd told her. He was just angry with himself for kissing her.

What had he been thinking?

At least no one had seen them. Jeena may know his engagement was off, but the rest of the world didn't.

His parents would be furious if the announcement was made now. Hadn't he done enough damage to his family?

Still, he'd been unable to help himself. When he was around her she made him feel alive again.

Maazin tossed and turned all night, guilt eating away at him.

He was so selfish.

In the morning Maazin went out with Mustafa to survey the damage, which was minimal thankfully. The last thing Petrie Island needed was to have more of the small island torn apart.

Still it was clear to Maazin that Petrie needed more

help than he and Jeena could offer. It would take a long time to repair the damage that Blandine had done. Thankfully not many lives had been lost.

Maazin got on the satellite phone in his yacht and called Farhan for assistance, and Farhan promised he would send more manpower and supplies needed to rebuild Petrie.

It only took about five hours for shelters, food and water, to arrive, as well as a relief physician who was a young doctor from Kalyana, which mean that he and Jeena could leave.

Her time was almost up. Farhan told Maazin that Jeena had been called back to Canada now that Kalyana was getting back on its feet. She would be leaving soon.

The thought of Jeena having to leave again struck him with a sense of dread that he wasn't prepared for. The official date hadn't been given by the Canadian consulate, but Jeena's time in Kalyana was coming to an end and he didn't like it one bit.

You should be relieved.

He should be happy to have this closure. He now knew what had happened to Jeena all those years ago so he would never have to wonder about that again. It had given him the closure he needed so he could move forward.

Really?

No, he didn't really believe that, because he knew deep down that he would never be *over* Jeena and that kiss they'd shared last night just proved how much he still wanted her. Even after all this time when he'd thought she'd betrayed him and left him.

When he'd realized Jeena had left he hadn't cared about anything. And that lack of care had cost Ali his life and eventually set Maazin on the path to right his wrongs and save others by serving his country.

His dedication and passion for that had driven Meleena away and disappointed his parents yet again, but he didn't care that Meleena had left.

He'd never loved her.

He didn't even like her.

It was Jeena. Always Jeena.

He still wanted her. Wanted no other, it was just that he couldn't have her. He didn't deserve to have her.

And it was clear that Jeena no longer wanted him. She no longer wanted a life in Kalyana when Canada offered so much more for her. It was for the best.

And he wouldn't subject Jeena to this life of protocol, this shackle of being a member of the royal family.

He wouldn't do that to his son.

His son. As much as he didn't want this life for Syman, he wanted to be a part of Syman's life. Why did it have to be so complicated?

Perhaps it doesn't?

Maazin finished loading the yacht with the supplies the islanders didn't need and then saw Jeena coming toward him with her duffel bag on her back and carrying the biohazard container with her surgical instruments.

The duffel bag looked larger than her and he didn't know how she was carrying it all so easily. He met her down on the pier and held out his hand.

"What?" Jeena asked.

"Let me carry that for you."

"I can carry it. I'm used to carrying it."

"That must be heavy," Maazin remarked.

"I can deadlift over a eighty-five with ease and back-squat with the same. I think I can handle this."

He raised his eyebrows. "What?"

Jeena chuckled. "You think you're the only one who works out? I do strength training. I have to be able to manage out in the field on my own or with very little help. Who else is going to carry my gear?"

Maazin was impressed and he took the biohazard bucket. "Let me at least make sure this secure so we don't have a mess. The ocean is a bit choppy after the storm."

"Deal."

Maazin helped her on board and they secured everything and then cast off from Petrie Island, heading back south toward the main island.

Jeena sat beside him on the bridge and that tension that always seemed to be there settled in again. He hated that. Talking to her had once been so easy, but he'd been a different person then.

He'd felt more free. He hadn't necessarily been free, but he'd felt more free. Of course, that relaxed disposition had caused nothing but trouble. It had caused nothing but a world of hurt and pain that he was never going to be able to make up to anyone.

Not to his parents.

Not to Farhan.

Not to Jeena.

And not to himself.

He deserved his sentence. He deserved the unhappiness, and the best he could do was try and take care of his people.

"I want to thank you again for the work you did on Petrie," Maazin said, breaking the silence.

"You're welcome. That's why I'm here."

"Would you have come back had it not been for the cyclone?" Even though he knew the answer to that.

Jeena's expression was sad. "No. I didn't want him growing up here as an illegitimate lovechild."

Maazin flinched at her harsh words. "I am sorry. I wouldn't have let that happen."

Jeena shrugged. "I did what was best for myself and for Syman. My parents chose to give up everything to come with me. I can never repay them enough. They didn't have to come with me, but if they hadn't given up so much to support me, I wouldn't be a surgeon now."

"I am sorry. Your family shouldn't have had to give up so much just because of who I am."

Tears welled up in her eyes and she looked away. "Thank you."

"I have received word from the consulate that your orders have been changed and you will be called back to Canada in a matter of days."

Jeena brushed away her tears. "What?"

"Kalyana is getting back on its feet and Canada has called back its special services. Not to sound too clichéd, but the British are coming."

"That doesn't make sense." She checked her phone and frowned. "You're right, my orders have arrived. In five days we'll be heading back to Canada."

"You'll be able to see Syman again," Maazin said gently. He was trying to give her something to be happy about because maybe if she was happy then he would feel happy too. Right now, he didn't feel happy about it.

Though it was for the best that she leave.

"Patang Island," Maazin remarked. "It looks so peaceful now."

Jeena nodded. "I wanted to go back. I wanted to visit all my old haunts before I left again, because it would probably be the last time I saw them."

"Well, let's go, then," he offered.

"What?" Jeena asked, confused. "We can't go to Patang Island."

"Why not?" Maazin asked, turning the wheel to head his yacht around to the lee side of the island, where they would be safe and wouldn't come up on a reef. From there they could take the small dinghy out to the sandbar and he could give her a short time of peace.

Later, he would take her back to her family's old home. He owned the plantation now and kept up the vanilla production. Jeena's old family home was used as a small bed and breakfast establishment now, but was currently empty because no tourists had been allowed to come to Kalyana since Blandine had hit, and any tourists that had been in Kalyana had been evacuated.

Not that many tourists took the long trip to Kalyana. The Seychelles were much more popular, and didn't have quite the pomp and circumstance that Kalyana and his father demanded.

"Maazin, this is crazy," Jeena shouted above the wind as he sped toward the island. "Your security team will go bananas when you don't pass their certain check points in time."

"So let them. We're safe. Kalyana's waters are monitored. Let's just take this moment. You wanted to go back to Patang Island and we shall."

Jeena smiled. "Okay."

He came up on the lee side of the island and anchored in a safe spot where they wouldn't run aground from shifting tides but were safe from the waves or any surges.

"Why don't you change out of your uniform? There may be some women's clothing in the main berth. Farhan and Sara sometimes take the yacht out."

"That sounds good." Jeena disappeared below deck

and Maazin let out a sigh as he listened to the gentle waves in the shelter of the island and the large reef that surrounded it lap against the side of his boat.

What're you doing?

He didn't know. He just wanted to give this to her. He just wanted to spend this time with her. When she left this time he didn't want her to leave and think about him or this country with bad thoughts.

And when Syman asked about him, if he did, then he would know that he was always welcome in Kalyana.

"Are you okay?"

Maazin turned around and took a step back when he saw Jeena in an emerald-green sari. It was the same color as the dress she had been wearing that first time he'd seen her. It took him right back to that moment.

And his breath was literally taken away.

"You look beautiful," he murmured.

A flush of pink rose in her cheeks. "Thank you."

"You ready?" he asked.

"Yes," she said nervously. "I think I am."

He smiled and took her hand. He climbed over the side first and down the ladder into the dinghy. She followed and he helped her, slipping his hands around her waist and guiding her safely down. It made his pulse quicken and the urge to kiss her, like he'd done last night, overtook him, but he held back.

He didn't want to scare her off.

This time on the island was to give her another memory of her homeland. It was something for her to cherish before she left again, and he wanted her to have that untainted.

He didn't want to make it any more awkward than it was between them. All he wanted at this moment was to give her a good memory. It was the least he could give her, especially when he'd missed so much.

He guided the little motored dinghy to the sandbar and cut the motor when he got close. He leaped over the side into the cool water and pulled the dinghy ashore.

Jeena stood up and without thinking he just lifted her up, gripping her waist and setting her down on the shore. She gasped when he set her down and he stared into her dark, warm eyes, lost for a moment.

"Maazin," she whispered.

"Yes."

"You can let go of me."

"Right," he said quickly. "Of course."

She blushed and took his hands in hers. Her hands were so tiny, so soft. "Come on, let's enjoy this moment of peace."

"Good idea."

Only she didn't let go of his hand and he didn't pull it away. He liked holding her hand as they walked barefoot on the sand. It was windy, but he didn't care. It was beautiful out here. The ocean and whitecaps. The sun reflecting against the water and causing it to sparkle. The sand seemed to shimmer like diamonds. They walked over to the lone piece of driftwood that Maazin had hauled up out of the water ten years ago. It was a place to sit.

"I can't believe that it's still here," Jeena said wistfully.

"Well, it was quite large, but I'm surprised it hasn't rotted away to nothing."

Jeena smiled and let go of his hand to run her hand along the rough wood. "I'm glad it's still here. That night…"

"The night we conceived Syman."

A blush tinged her cheek. "Yes."

"That was a magical night for me too. I'm sorry that I missed his birth, I'm sorry that I wasn't there for it all."

She nodded and sat down on the log. "Me too."

"Does he ask about me?" It was a question he'd been avoiding and he was afraid of asking it, but he had to know. It was eating him up not to ask.

"He does," Jeena said quietly, looking at her hands.

"What have you told him about me?"

"I told him you lived in Kalyana and I told him that I had lost touch with you, but that if you knew about him, you would love him."

Maazin nodded and sat down next to her. "That is true."

He wanted to tell her that if he had known it would all have been different, but he wasn't sure about that. He knew one thing—he was sad that this life with Jeena and his son had been taken from him. That he'd never got the chance to ask her to be his. He'd never seen his son as a baby. Never held him in his arms. He'd missed so much.

And you are responsible for taking Ali's life.

That thought grounded him. He didn't deserve it. Ali had never got a chance and he didn't deserve it either. It was fitting justice for his sins.

"Tell me about his birth. Tell me about Syman's birth."

Jeena looked at him like he was crazy. "What?"

"Tell me. When was he born?"

"June twenty-sixth. It was a Friday and he was born in the morning. He came out screaming and had all this dark hair, even on his bottom." She chuckled about that. "I thought he was going to be made fun of for being so hairy, but it was just lanugo and it fell out as he got older. Then he was this chubby, happy baby who slept all night in a bassinet by my bedside. Everyone who saw him loved him."

It cut him to the quick to hear about this. He'd been denied that precious time. He hadn't had a chance to hold him in his arms, to kiss his head and sing him to sleep.

"It must've been hard on you, getting a medical degree and having an infant."

"It was. My mother and father were my lifeline. If I didn't have them, I wouldn't be a doctor. They knew how much I wanted to be a doctor when we still lived in Kalyana and before I met you they were saving up all they could to send me to England or Australia to get my education, but then I attended that polo match and met you."

Maazin touched her face. "I'm sorry that I ruined your life."

Jeena touched his hand, still cupping her face. "You didn't ruin my life, Maazin. You gave me this great gift. Syman is a wonderful boy and my life in Canada is good. Do I wish that things could have been different and that I'd chosen my life in Canada myself, instead of it being thrust on me, yes, but my parents are better off there than they were here. We have a good life. Don't feel bad."

"You are too kind. Kinder than I deserve."

"What're you talking about?"

Maazin sighed. "I am the one who killed Ali."

Her eyes widened. "What're you talking about?"

"I'm telling you the truth. I am the one who killed Ali. It was my fault."

* * *

It took Jeena a moment to let the words sink in. What did Maazin mean that he was the one responsible for killing Ali?

"I thought it was a car accident?" she asked.

Maazin stood and was pacing on the sand, rubbing the back of his neck. "It was."

"Were you driving?" she asked.

"No."

"Then I don't quite understand how you're responsible for your brother's death."

"I was drunk. I had gone to a party that I shouldn't have been at. There was drinking and some drugs. I didn't do the drugs, but I was very drunk and I couldn't call security to come and get me. I was already splashed across the tabloids and when I called the palace, drunk again, Ali took it upon himself to come and get me. His wife came with him." Maazin closed his eyes and she could tell that it was hard for him to continue.

"Go on," Jeena urged gently. "What happened?"

"Ali came, of course. He was such a good brother." Maazin took a deep breath. "He came and got me. Both of them scolded me, of course, for being blind drunk and at a party I should not have gone to. Not that I did anything, I just got drunk with my friends. The house was up in the hills and while we were driving home a rainstorm hit. It rained very hard, or so they tell me, I don't remember. What I remember is Ali yelling at me, telling me that I had to pull up my socks and behave better.

"Then there was this loud bang and screaming and we were upside down, before it went black. I woke up in agony because my shoulder was dislocated and I was under the wrecked car. Ali and Chandni were dead."

Jeena gasped and she could see the pain in Maazin's eyes as he poured out his story to her. It was obvious that it weighed heavily on him and that it had been traumatic.

"Maazin, you were not responsible for your brother's death."

"Of course I was!" he snapped. "If he hadn't been such a good brother he would've sent someone to come and get me. But he didn't. He came himself because I begged him not to tell Father. I was terrified or… I really don't know. I don't remember much about the phone call. Only that I wanted Ali to come and get me. And if I hadn't been so insistent and he hadn't been such a good brother he would still be alive. And so would Chandni.

"It wasn't just his life I ruined. I ruined my parents' lives. Ali was my father's favorite. And then I ruined my late sister-in-law's parents' lives. They lost their daughter. And then Farhan was made Crown Prince. He had to come back from Australia and give up his life there…"

Jeena stood and walked over to him, and reached up and touched his face. "It's not your fault. Ali loved you, but it's not your fault that he and his wife chose to come get you that night. You are not to be blamed."

"Lady Meleena blames me for the end of our farce of an engagement."

Jeena's heart skipped a beat. "Oh?"

It shouldn't matter to her that his engagement was over. She shouldn't care, but she did.

"When Ali died I devoted my life to saving others and my duties. They took all my attention."

"Is that why the engagement went on for so long?"

He nodded. "Partly, but mostly I didn't care about her. There was only one person I cared about."

"I cared about you too," she said softly. She truly had never stopped caring about him.

There had been no one else.

Don't fall for him again. Don't do it.

He took a step closer to her. Those gray-green eyes twinkled as he caressed her face. Her body trembled like a traitor to her own mind under his touch.

And before she knew what was happening he wrapped his arms around her and kissed her, just like before, and she was lost to him. Her body wanted more.

She hadn't been able to stop thinking about that kiss that had snuck up on them in the office on Petrie. She wanted to forget that kiss because she was leaving and nothing could happen between them, even if that pull of attraction and feelings was still there.

It was off limits.

She couldn't give everything up for a chance with him. She didn't come from his world any more. She didn't want that kind of spotlight on her or Syman.

And as much as she wanted this kiss to continue, she knew that it couldn't. She couldn't let it continue so she pushed on his chest to move him away from her.

"We can't," she whispered, trying to calm the erratic beat of her pulse and quell the fire that was in her blood. "We can't."

"Why not?" he whispered, leaning his forehead down to hers. Their foreheads were pressed together, their arms around each other.

"You need someone to be your wife and I am not that woman. I can never be that woman."

Maazin nodded. "I understand. I'm sorry for kissing you. It's just that around you, I lose myself. It feels like all those years ago."

"I know, but it's not." She tried not to let the tears stinging her eyes spill down her cheeks. She wanted to tell him that she wanted to be his and that she'd never got over him, but that was selfish. Syman had a life in Canada. He had friends and loved his school, his hockey and his home.

Her parents had given up so much so that they could go with her and help her. Now they were prosperous and she couldn't ask them to give it all up to chase a whim.

Her mother had tried to warn her all those years ago that getting involved with Maazin was a bad idea, but she had been young and foolish then…

"You shouldn't get involved with the Prince," her mother said quietly. *"Nothing good can come from that."*

"What do you mean? He loves me. I know he does."

Her mother took her hands. *"I have no doubt. Who could not love you? You are beautiful. But you are just a farmer's daughter and he is a prince."*

"But Kalyana is a free country and he's the third son."

"Jeena, please be careful. I don't want you to get hurt…"

She should've listened to her mother back then. If she had she wouldn't have fallen in love with a man who was off limits. A man who had ruined her for all others. But she had been young and so foolish.

She wasn't going to make that mistake again. When she'd been sent to Kalyana, she'd promised herself that she wouldn't let herself be sucked in again.

She had to remind herself of that.

"We should go," she said, stepping away from him. It was safer to put some distance between the two of them.

Maazin nodded.

Jeena turned and walked back to the dinghy. There was a cool wind and it caused a shiver to run through her. The sun disappeared behind a cloud and suddenly things didn't seem so rosy and lovely on Patang Island.

It had lost its sparkle and magic.

It just reminded her of a life with a person she loved that she could never have. The best thing she could do now was walk away and try to just forget about Kalyana and Maazin's kisses, even if she knew that was going to be a hard, hard thing to do.

An impossible thing to do, but it was for the best.

CHAPTER EIGHT

THE MOMENT THAT Maazin docked in the harbor, there were several limousines waiting, as well as his brother's personnel. He had a bad feeling about what he was seeing.

He glanced over at Jeena, who had changed back into her medical uniform. She bit her lip, worrying about it, and he could see the fear in her eyes.

"Don't worry," he said. "They're here for me."

"Don't be so sure. We did take a detour and I am not Lady Meleena. Remember the world thinks you're still engaged to her."

"That I am aware of," he said quickly. "No one else knows about you, Jeena, and no one else knows about my broken engagement. You are a doctor, a Canadian doctor. It's all proper."

"If you say so." She didn't sound too convinced. She tried to walk past him, but he held her back.

"I won't let anyone hurt you," he said, and he meant it.

"Thanks," she whispered.

The moment Maazin's yacht was tied up and he helped Jeena down onto the pier, Farhan, flanked by two bodyguards, came quickly toward them. He was frowning and there were dark circles under his eyes.

A shiver ran down his spine.

Oh, God.

"Farhan?" Maazin asked, barely getting the words out.

"Maazin, it's Father. He took a spell this morning and we've been waiting for your return." Farhan glanced over at Jeena. "Are you Dr. Harrak?"

"Yes," she said nervously.

"Oh, good. We were looking for you. Your team said that you were able to perform a catheterization under less than ideal circumstances and that you were the best."

"I… I am, but…" Jeena was stumbling over her words and Maazin knew it was because of who his father was. His father was the King. She was terrified of operating on the King.

He knew what she was thinking. She thought she already had a bad reputation with the Kalyanese people.

"Jeena, nothing bad will happen to you at the palace, not while you are under my care."

Jeena looked at him and nodded. "Of course. Of course I can help His Majesty."

Farhan cocked an eyebrow. He was confused, but he wasn't about to argue about reasons now out on the public pier at the harbor. "Well, the royal motorcade will take you both to the palace."

Maazin put his hand on the small of Jeena's back and urged her to take a step forward. A bodyguard stepped forward and took her duffel bag from her.

Another took her surgical kit. Maazin stuck by her side as they were ushered into a limo where Farhan was already seated. Jeena chewed on her lip again and began to wring her hands.

Maazin wanted to reach out and comfort her, but Farhan was watching her with interest.

"Dr. Harrak, are you quite all right?" Farhan asked.

"Fine. It's just, I've never operated on royalty before. Never done a cardiac cath procedure on a king!"

Farhan smiled. "It'll be okay, I assure you. We have everything you need. I would do it myself, but I can't, as you know, being his son. So even Sara is unable to operate. It's driving her a bit mad, because she wants to help."

Jeena chuckled, but Maazin could still hear the nervousness in her voice.

"It'll be quite all right. You are a capable surgeon. You did an appendectomy in a courthouse and Mr. Patel is going to make a full recovery because of it, and you taught a first responder the ins and outs of being a scrub nurse. You are capable of this. Do not think about who he is, just think of him as any other patient."

Maazin's words were meant to calm her.

"Think of him as any other patient."

Which was easier said than done, but she was going to try. She had to try. They approached the palace and passed through Huban's gate and up to the palace. It sat on top of a hill and reflected the rich history of Kalyana's Eastern influence. It was like a fortress, but surrounded with lush, green vegetation. Or at least it had been, but when cyclone Blandine had blown through, the leaves had been stripped away and trees toppled. As they came closer to the palace she could see gardeners trying to clean up the mess that Blandine had left in her wake. The drive was littered with brightly colored petals that had been trampled down and crushed into the road.

It was sad.

The palace with its warm-hued stone walls and arched windows had been the center of Huban. It had been the heart of Kalyana and now it looked the worse for wear. As if Kalyana's heart had been broken.

At least her spirit hadn't been broken. Of that Jeena was sure.

The limo pulled up in front of two, large ornately carved doors that were immediately opened. Farhan slid out and Maazin followed, but Jeena felt frozen.

"Jeena?" Maazin asked. "Are you coming?"

"Yes."

She could do this. She'd sworn an oath as a doctor to do no harm and she was going to stick to that oath. She was not going to put her medical career in jeopardy because she was worried about operating on the Kalyanese King. And she wasn't going to embarrass her new country by being the Canadian doctor who couldn't save the life of the Kalyanese King.

Forget that!

She was going to save his life. For as much as she was nervous about operating on King Uttam, she loved Maazin and she knew that Maazin cared about his father. Even if he seemed to blame himself for Ali's death.

Maazin held out his hand, which was breaking protocol, and she smiled at him. She reached out and took his hand as he helped her out of the limousine. His hand was strong and he believed in her. She was going to do this for him.

Once she was out of the limo, he let go of her hand and she took another deep breath, calming her nerves.

Here we go. You've got this.

She straightened her shoulders and held her head high as she followed Farhan and Maazin through the large double doors into an entranceway of white marble and creamy stone walls that gleamed brightly.

"Maazin, so you've finally decided to grace us with your presence."

Jeena glanced up to see Queen Aruna standing there, regal and poised. She didn't smile and she didn't seem to look worried or have any kind of emotion as she looked at her sons.

Maazin walked over to his mother and took her hand in his, bowing over it.

"I'm sorry, Mother," Maazin apologized. "I was only doing my duty to my people."

"Yes. That's all very well and good, but we had to send Farhan out to fetch you. Your yacht was late getting in."

Jeena could sense the tension, the coldness and the detachment between Queen Aruna and Maazin. It was like they were strangers rather than mother and son. Perhaps Aruna did blame Maazin for Ali's death. There was a huge rift between them.

It was sad.

She was so close to Syman. She could never treat Syman with such aloofness.

"I'm sorry, Mother." Maazin stepped back and the Queen's hardened gaze fell on her.

Jeena curtseyed. "Your Majesty."

"Dr. Harrak, I am so glad you've come and I understand from my daughter-in-law that you're also Kalyanese."

Queen Aruna addressed her very politely, but Jeena could hear the undercurrent of displeasure and Jeena realized then Queen Aruna knew *exactly* who she was.

"Yes, Your Majesty." Jeena straightened. "How can I be of assistance?"

"Farhan, you're a doctor—please explain it to our dear doctor and then take her to your father to perform the procedure. Please excuse me, but I haven't slept in the last twenty-four hours." Queen Aruna excused herself. She turned back up the stairs and disappeared out of sight.

Farhan turned to her. "Dr. Harrak, my father has a pulmonary embolus and he needs catheterization to remove it before it does further damage. My father has had a stroke in the past and he suffers from macular degeneration as well as atrial fibrillation."

"And none of your surgeons can perform it?" Jeena asked.

"Not under these conditions. In a hospital, yes, but we were told by your team that you were able to do it and you had done it successfully before." Farhan looked over at Maazin. "Again, none of us in the royal family can assist you, but there are some of the finest royal physicians in attendance. He is prepped and waiting for the procedure. He's had a sedative and is groggy."

Jeena nodded. "Take me to him."

Farhan bowed his head and gestured to show her the way. She was led down a hallway to a small antechamber and a room that was used a formal sitting room for visiting dignitaries. Only now it had been transformed into a procedure room.

Jeena glanced through the window and saw that King Uttam was laid out and prepped. They were just waiting for her.

You've got this. This is just another patient. He's not a king. He's a human being who needs your help. He's not your King right now. He's a patient. Just an ordinary, normal patient.

"There are scrubs in this room here and a place to scrub in," Farhan offered. "I'll leave you to it. Maazin, if you'll follow me."

"Just one moment," Maazin said. He took a step toward her and his presence was reassuring. She wished that he could stay with her. She wanted him to stay, she needed him there while she did this procedure on the King of her homeland.

She didn't want to be known as the doctor who killed the King of Kalyana.

"You can do this," Maazin whispered.

"I'm frightened," she whispered back. "This is your father…the King."

"He's just a patient. This is like any other patient you'd work on and try to save. You can do this." He took a step back and turned away with his brother.

Jeena took another deep breath and then went to get changed. She quickly changed into the scrubs that had been left for her, cleaned herself up and then headed into the makeshift procedure room.

Another doctor was there.

"Dr. Harrak, I'm Dr. Imran Patel, and I'll be your assist."

Jeena nodded. "It's a pleasure to meet you."

Jeena walked over to the King and looked down at him. He was mostly out of it, but not completely under. The King's gaze locked on to her and he smiled, as if she was an old friend and not some commoner who'd had his secret illegitimate grandchild. He probably didn't even know about Syman. Which was for the best.

"You look familiar," the King whispered.

"My name is Dr. Harrak. Jeena Harrak. I'm from Canada, previously from Kalyana."

The King's eyes widened. "I've heard of you. You have a son, don't you? A son who plays hockey."

Jeena's heart dropped to the soles of her feet and

she felt faint. How did he know about Syman? How did he know that Syman played hockey? And then she realized that Kalyana had been keeping tabs on her for some time, even from as far away as Canada. She had been a fool to think otherwise.

It rattled her completely.

She wanted to turn and run. She wanted to run back to Canada and hide Syman, but she couldn't do that. She couldn't turn her back on a patient who needed her services, even if she felt like that patient posed a threat to her family.

She would save King Uttam's life and if he came for Syman, she would remind him how she'd saved his life and perhaps he would feel he owed her a debt and that debt would protect her son from this life of protocol and pomp.

Maazin was worried about Jeena. She looked so nervous, doing the procedure on his father, and he couldn't blame her one bit. If the situation had been reversed he would feel the same way. He couldn't stop pacing as he waited with Farhan in their father's office.

Maazin knew that his constant pacing was antagonizing his father's macaw Sophie, because she would squawk every so often when he got close to her perch.

"You're driving that bird crazy with your incessant pacing," Farhan remarked calmly. "Truth be told, you're driving me crazy too."

"I can't help it. I'm worried about her." And then he pinched the bridge of his nose and cursed inwardly for the slip.

"Are you having an affair with the Canadian doctor?"

"What're you talking about?" Maazin asked, trying to keep calm.

Farhan rolled his eyes. "I see the way you look at her. Be careful. The public thinks you are still with Lady Meleena."

"I'm not!" Maazin snapped. He was annoyed with his brother's questions.

"Having an affair?"

"I am not with Lady Meleena and not having an affair with Dr. Harrak. At least..."

"At least what?" Farhan asked cautiously. "You're not having an affair with Dr. Harrak, are you? Please tell me you're not."

"No, but... I did."

"When?" Farhan asked, confused. "You've been nothing but faithful to Lady Meleena. Even when you two were apart for so long."

"And look where that got me. She had her own countless affairs."

"I'm sorry she hurt you," Farhan said.

Maazin ran his hand through his hair. "Meleena did hurt me. But I couldn't care less about her and the men she saw. It was something else."

"Really?" Farhan asked.

"I never wanted to marry Lady Meleena."

Farhan rolled his eyes as if to say, *I know that.* "You promised Father."

"So?"

"I married who Father told me to marry."

"And I'm glad it worked out for you and I'm glad it worked out for Ali too and our parents. I'm glad for every arranged marriage that works out, but..." He scrubbed his hands over his face. "Ten years ago, before Ali died, I was in love with someone else and that's Jeena. I adored her, worshipped her and I wanted only her. Then she vanished. Mother told me she'd left and there was a letter Meleena found. I was distraught and hurt. Little did I know that Jeena left because she was pregnant and she was afraid of having the illegitimate child of a prince."

Farhan's eyes widened. "She was pregnant and Meleena knew? It all seems very odd."

"I know."

"Should we let Jeena be operating on Father, then?" Farhan asked with a frown, getting to his feet. "She's the mother of your child."

"She won't harm him. She takes her oath seriously. She came to Kalyana because of her love and respect for Canada and Kalyana. She is the last person to do him harm."

"How did you find out about…your child?"

Maazin nodded. "Syman. I have a son. A son I've never met and his name is Syman. He's nine."

"Why didn't she tell you about him? Even if she left for Canada with her parents she could've called or mailed a letter, even gone to the tabloids."

"She wanted to protect her son and Meleena told her that I didn't want our child. That I didn't want her."

"And clearly you did."

"Yes."

Farhan ran his hand through his hair. "And yet Father arranged for you to marry Meleena, who manipulated all this? If Father had known about his grandchild, he would have insisted you marry Jeena. Father loves his children."

"He loved Ali," Maazin said bitterly, and then his shoulders slumped. He hated bringing Ali up.

"When are you going to stop blaming yourself for that?" Farhan asked.

Maazin didn't answer him. Instead he looked back at the portrait of their father that hung on the wall. Next to it was a portrait of Ali.

Ali had been his parents' favorite.

And Maazin had destroyed that. His mother had made that all too clear to him.

I'm sorry, Ali. So sorry.

"Well, that explains her nervousness," Farhan said, breaking the silence that had descended between the two of them. "I thought it just had something to do with operating on the King."

"Well, I'm sure that's part of it," Maazin said.

"What're you going to do about your son?"

"I promised Jeena that I wouldn't hurt her and it would hurt her if I tried to claim him and bring him into this life. I don't want to do that to him."

"He has a right to know who his father is," Farhan stated. "He has a right to know where he comes from."

Maazin sighed. "I know, but..."

Do I really want him to know? Do I deserve to have him in my life?

He left Farhan standing there and walked out onto the terrace. He didn't want to talk about it any more. He didn't want to dwell on the things he couldn't have. He'd hurt Jeena just as deeply as she'd hurt him.

There was no going back. Even if he desperately wanted to.

She'd made it clear that there was no going back for her.

* * *

Jeena pulled off her surgical mask and then walked out of the room. The King had tolerated the procedure well and she'd removed the clot. He was being moved to his own bed to recover.

Jeena slid down the wall and tried to take a few calming breaths.

She'd saved King Uttam's life, but he knew about her son.

He hadn't actually acknowledged that Syman was Maazin's but he knew about her son. How did he know about him?

She wanted to call her parents about it and ask their advice, but she didn't want to send them into a tizzy.

Jeena closed her eyes and tried to find her center, a place that had always calmed her. That place was standing out on her bedroom balcony overlooking the green lush hills, the fields of vanilla, and beyond all that she was tall enough to see the ocean.

How she wished she could go back there.

Even for a moment.

"How did it go?"

Jeena opened her eyes to see Maazin standing in the shadows.

"Are you supposed to be here?"

"Father's been moved. I'm allowed to be here." He smiled. "Are you all right?"

"No. That was… It was hard and I feel dizzy. I wish I could reach out to my parents and talk to them about it, but I don't want to worry them. That's the last thing I want to do, so I was trying to find my happy place."

"And where is that?" Maazin asked.

"My old home. The plantation."

"Then let's go," he offered.

"Shouldn't you be here or with your father?"

"It won't matter I'm gone. He won't care."

Jeena tilted her head to the side. She could see the pain in his eyes, the blame he bore. "Are you so sure?"

"Do you want to go or not?" he asked.

"I do, but my family doesn't own it any longer."

"I know," Maazin stated. "I went there after you left. I thought maybe your parents would be there and I could ask them where you'd gone. I saw that they had left too and the plantation was for sale, so I bought it."

Jeena's eyes widened and she couldn't believe what she was hearing. "You bought it?"

"Yes. I own it. It's still a plantation and during tourist season I rent it out as a little cottage. It's empty at the moment. There are no tourists in Kalyana. We can go there."

Even though she knew she shouldn't go with him, she wanted to go back home. Just for a moment, even if it was with him.

A man who made her lose all control.

A man she couldn't have but still cared for. A man who still owned her heart, even if she didn't want him to.

"Yes! Please."

Maazin nodded. "Go and change and we'll sneak out of the palace and head over there."

Jeena nodded and got up. She hurried off to get changed. She was shocked that Maazin had bought it. It had been his money that had allowed her parents to start a new life in Canada and she'd had no idea.

Why would he buy it?

She shook that thought out of her head, because all

she cared about right now was that she got to go home. Even for a brief moment.

She was going home.

CHAPTER NINE

THE CLOSER THEY go to her home, the more excited and emotional Jeena got. She recognized the road they turned down, although it was a better quality road than she remembered. She closed her eyes and thought about all the times she had come down this road on her way home.

There had been some changes, but the scent of the fields and the sight of the orchids that she knew so well hit her, and a tear slid down her face.

Her father had liked to grow his vanilla orchids on wooden poles, as originally orchid vines had grown up trees and her father had always believed that the wood added to the productivity of the fruit.

And he had spent hours and hours checking on the flowers.

He had loved his plantation. He had known everything about it and he'd given it all up for her. She was still in shock that Maazin had bought the plantation. Why had he done that?

As they rounded a bend she cried out as she saw the fields. The vines were still growing on wooden poles. Some were old still and there were also fresh ones, but the fields were neat and tidy, just like she remembered.

She wiped away the tears as she drank in the sight.

"Can you stop the car?" she asked Maazin.

"Of course." Maazin pulled over to the side of the road and Jeena slipped out. She walked up to the fence and climbed up. Teetering precariously, she took a picture for her father. He was sleeping now, so she would send it to him later so it would be the first thing he saw when he woke up.

"We tried to keep it the same," Maazin said, coming up behind her. "Your father knew his stuff and he was admired around these parts. So I made sure that the man who farms this land now does it the way your family has always done it."

Jeena nodded, fighting back tears. "I still can't believe you bought it. Why did you buy it?"

Maazin shrugged. "I didn't want to see it ruined. You loved this place and I didn't understand why your family left. I know why now, but at the time I thought that maybe you would come back and I wanted it here, waiting for you."

"Thank you." She brushed away tears again. "Let's see the house. Please."

"Of course."

They climbed back into the Jeep. Jeena was swallowing back all the emotion that was welling up inside her. She drank in the sights. This was her happy place. This was the place she always came back to in her mind when she was scared, when she was hurt and when she was uncertain.

This was home.

And it was her fault that her family was no longer here.

Maazin pulled into the driveway.

And Jeena cried silent tears as she looked up at the house. The vines still grew on the outside. They weren't vanilla orchids, just plain orchids that her mother loved. The stone path was the same and there was the swing on the big old banyan tree that was said to have grown up through an original post of the first home that had been built when her ancestors had first come here from India in the seventeenth century.

It was all the same. Untouched.

Except it really wasn't the same. Her family wasn't here. It was her home, but the heart of it was gone. It seemed so lonely. So cold.

"Shall we go inside?" Maazin asked softly.

"Yes."

Maazin unlocked the door and stood back, letting her go in first. There were some changes, mostly modernizing to accommodate tourists, but the layout was still the same. Jeena closed her eyes and swore that she could hear her father singing as he came home from a long day in the fields.

She could smell her mother's cooking on the stove. The aroma of her saffron rice wafting in the air. And then the memory of her family frantically packing all their belongings, their sadness as they'd left this house for the very last time.

Jeena climbed the stairs to the room at the top that had been hers. It was no longer her childhood room, but had been converted into a loft space with a gorgeous balcony. A romantic getaway for lovers overlooking the vanilla fields. She opened the balcony doors and walked outside. The sun was setting in the west.

Shades of red and orange reflected off the blue water that lay beyond the rolling green hills filled with flowering vanilla. She could see the path to the creek where she'd almost drowned. And then she saw it, the palace in the distance. She'd forgotten that she would be able to see it from up here. When she'd been a child she'd dreamed of being a princess and wondering what it was like to live in such a palace.

Now she knew and she didn't want that.

Don't you? If you had it you could have Maazin.

It was all too surreal. She wrapped her arms around herself, hugging herself because she was overwhelmed. She'd never thought that she would be back here, that she would be able to see her childhood home again.

"I did make this change to your room. I'm sorry," Maazin said from the door, interrupting her thoughts.

"It's okay," she said, glancing back at him. "You've done a beautiful job and I'm thankful you kept so much the same."

He stood behind her. "I didn't want to change anything too much. I so wanted you to come back."

She looked up at him and her heart began to beat faster. "I wanted to come back too."

He touched her cheek, brushing his thumb across her skin. "I cared for you, Jeena. I still do."

"Maazin, don't say that."

"I can't help it, Jeena."

"Maazin, I... I cared for you too." A tear slid down her cheek. And it was true. She did.

I still love you.

Only she didn't say it out loud. She was terrified how quickly she'd let him back in.

"Jeena," he whispered.

"I know that you can't make a commitment to me and I have to leave again." And even though she knew she shouldn't, she just wanted this one night with him. This one last night to lay the ghosts to rest. To have the closure she needed, so that she could return to Canada and know that her life here was over. And there would be no pull, nothing to lure her back.

"I want you, Maazin. Please."

He pulled her into his arms and kissed her, very intensely.

His touch felt so good. She'd forgotten how wonderful it felt to be wrapped up in Maazin's strong arms. How safe he made her feel. How he made her body sing with pleasure. When she was with him everything else melted away. There was only the two of them.

Jeena wanted to forget all the pain, the loneliness, the anger she'd felt these last ten years. For once she wanted to feel like her old self again. She wanted to feel like that girl who had been swept off her feet by her Prince Charming.

She wanted to taste passion again. Hot, heady, sweet passion.

She wanted Maazin. He was all she'd ever wanted and if she couldn't have him forever then she wanted this one night.

Jeena melted into that kiss, pressing her body against him.

"Jeena," Maazin whispered huskily. "Are you certain?"

"Yes." She ran her hands down his chest, feeling his heart beating under her palm. It was racing, just like hers. "Please just be with me. Be with me tonight for one last time."

Maazin gave in with a moan and took her in his arms, scooping her up as he'd done ten years ago on Patang Island. He carried her from the balcony into the room toward the bed.

Jeena's pulse was racing with anticipation over what

was going to happen. She had missed this. She'd missed this intimacy, this connection that she had with him.

They sank onto the mattress together, kissing. His hands were in her hair. She wanted to just feel him pressed against her.

No words were needed because she knew that at this moment they both wanted the same thing.

Each other.

The kiss ended only so they could both undress each other, slowly, kissing in between because Jeena didn't want to break the connection between them. She didn't want to miss any stolen moment together.

"Jeena, I wanted you the moment I met you," Maazin whispered against her ear. "I still want you."

"I wanted you too." She was terrified of opening herself up to him. To be vulnerable to him again.

It was different this time, though.

Are you certain of that?

Jeena shook that thought from her head and let herself melt into the moment.

She wanted this.

They lay next to each other, both exposed and naked. She couldn't get enough of touching him, feeling his muscles ripple under her fingertips, running her hands over his skin and through his hair, but the most heady feeling was having his strong hands on her again.

Caressing her and making her body heat like it had been touched by electricity.

Maazin kissed her again, his lips urgent as he pulled her body flush with his.

This was it.

This was the moment. He pressed her against the mattress. His hands entwined with hers, his body so large over her she felt safe wrapped up in his arms.

Maazin gave her a kiss that seared her very soul. The warmth spread through her veins and then his lips moved from her mouth down her neck, following the erratic pulse points under her skin.

She let out a mewl of pleasure.

She wanted him inside her. Badly.

He stroked her cheek and kissed her gently again, his lips nipped softly at hers, one hand on her breast and the other stroking her between her legs. Desire coursed through her. It was overwhelming to let herself go with him.

Letting these wild emotions that she'd bottled up for so long come loose again.

He kissed her deeply as he entered her. She cried out as he slowly filled her, wanting more of him.

She couldn't get enough of him.

She wrapped her legs around him, urging him to go even deeper, to take all of her. To completely possess her.

Everything else, all her worries, her pain, her heartache melted away in that moment that the two of them connected again. It felt so right to be with him, yet it was wrong, but she didn't care right now.

It was just the two of them moving together in complete bliss.

It wasn't long before both of them came, close together in shared pleasure. A tear slid down her cheek as it ended.

Maazin wiped it away. "Did I hurt you?"

"No, no it's just... I don't want it to end."

He kissed her. "Neither do I."

He held her close and when he rolled over on his back, he brought her against him. His arm around her, holding her tight as if he was afraid to let her go. Jeena didn't mind. She clung to him just as tightly and she was just as terrified that he would let her go as well.

It frightened her that he still had this hold on her.

The Prince she could never have.

Beautiful.

She was so beautiful. Maazin couldn't believe that it had happened again. He couldn't believe that he was here, lying in Jeena's arms again. It was what he'd dreamed about time and time again, but had never thought would be a reality.

And he was so glad that it had happened, but he was worried about what this meant.

He wasn't sure that Jeena even wanted him in her life.

Or would want him to live in Canada. If he gave up his place in the line of succession he was pretty sure it would kill his father. And then he couldn't help his people.

Also, the winter and the cold did not sound appealing in the least bit.

It would be worth it to be with her, wouldn't it?

It would be, but he couldn't leave Kalyana. He couldn't do that to his father, his mother or his brother. He'd promised Sara too that he would help with her education plans.

And why did he deserve happiness? He didn't.

Yes, you do.

And he wasn't even sure that Jeena wanted him. She'd wanted him this night, but she'd told him it was just for this one night.

He was torn.

Maazin slowly moved and got out of the bed. He pulled on his trousers and headed out on the balcony to enjoy the night breeze. The sky was clear and full of stars. He could see the distant glow of Huban and the palace all lit up.

Usually, he didn't mind looking at Huban lit up at night, but tonight he resented that he had been born to this life. He felt so trapped.

And he was selfish for thinking that way. Ali had never thought that way. Ali had been such a good brother and good son to their parents. He would've made a great king, but they would never know that now, thanks to him.

When will you stop blaming yourself for that?

Maazin turned his back on the palace and looked at Jeena, sleeping so soundly in the bed. There had been times in the ten years they'd been apart and his heart had been broken over losing her that he'd wished that he'd never met her. And he had no doubt that she'd felt the same way too.

But now he was glad that she did. Even if he couldn't have her forever, he was glad to be with her here at this moment.

He checked his phone and there were a few messages from Farhan.

Father is stable. Where are you? Where is Dr. Harrak?

Maazin didn't even bother responding. He'd told the security guards that he was taking a Jeep and going out to the plantation and that was all anyone needed to know. He was glad his father was stable, and that he was asking about the doctor who had performed the surgery.

All very good signs. Unless…unless his father found out he was romantically involved with Jeena and he was worried that Maazin would blow the secrecy about his engagement to Meleena being over. Perhaps Farhan had told their father about Syman.

If Jeena learned that his father knew about Syman she might flee again, and then he would never know his son.

Do you want to know him? Does he want to know you?

He knew deep down that his people would love Jeena, just as they loved Sara. And they'd be thrilled about Syman.

It was all just a dream, though. A fantasy he couldn't have, that he was afraid to have.

The sound of a phone vibrating on silent caught his attention and he noticed that Jeena had dropped her purse on the balcony floor. He picked it up and found her phone. When he touched it, it unlocked and a little boy's face looked up at him.

Oh, God. What have I done?

"You're not my mom," Syman said, confused.

"No. I'm not. Your mother is sleeping and… I heard her phone ringing."

The boy cocked his head to look at him better. "Who are you?"

"I am…" Maazin trailed off. He wanted to tell Syman that he was his father, but he couldn't. It wasn't his place. "I am Prince Maazin of Kalyana and you must be Jeena's son, Syman."

"Wow. A real prince? For real?"

"Yes," Maazin said, smiling. "Your mother has been helping out in her home country."

"I know."

Maazin could not stop staring at the boy. He saw himself in that face, but there were pieces of Ali and Farhan too.

"Well, I just wanted to speak to Mom, but if she's sleeping…" Syman trailed off as someone in the background called him. "Just talking to a prince, Grandpa. It's okay. Mom is sleeping."

There was some rushed talking in the background and Syman looked confused.

"Oh, Prince Maazin, my grandpa wants to talk to you, is that okay?"

Maazin's heart skipped a beat. "Very much okay. I will tell your mother you called."

"Okay. Here's my grandpa."

Syman's face was replaced by Mr. Harrak's and he was stunned to see Maazin.

"Your Highness," he said sternly. "Where is my daughter?"

"Sleeping. She worked very hard today on my father. The King."

Mr. Harrak's eyes widened. "What?"

"My father almost died today, Mr. Harrak, and your daughter performed a medical procedure on him at the palace. She's tired."

"She should not have been at the palace," he said worriedly. "I am sure you know why."

"I do now and I aim to find out what truly happened."

Mr. Harrak didn't look convinced. "My daughter has a tender heart. Please, Your Highness. Don't hurt her again."

"I don't want to do that, Mr. Harrak."

"We all know you are to marry Lady Meleena."

Maazin sighed. "I will not hurt her and I want to show you something." He turned the phone around. "Do you see it?"

"It's pretty dark…" Mr. Harrak said. "Is that vanilla? Is that…?"

"It's your plantation." Maazin turned the phone back again. "I own it and I will return it to your family."

"You don't need to do that, Your Highness."

"I think I do."

Mr. Harrak said nothing at first. "Thank you."

"Goodbye, Mr. Harrak."

"Your Highness."

Maazin ended the call and hadn't realized how much he'd been shaking. How sweaty his palms had become and how he'd crossed a line he hadn't intended to.

"Who were you talking to?"

Maazin spun around and saw that Jeena had got dressed again and was standing in the balcony doorway, her arms crossed, and she didn't look too pleased.

"Your father." Maazin held out the phone.

Jeena took it from him. "You weren't talking only to my father. You were talking to Syman. This is his number. You were talking to our son? Why did you answer my phone? You had no right to do that."

"He's my son too," Maazin stated. "I went to get the phone to hand it to you, it unlocked and I accidentally answered it. I did not tell Syman that I am his father. Though I think he should know."

"He should, but are you going to be there for him?"

It was a valid question and he was stunned. Also, he was afraid. He didn't know the answer, he didn't have an answer for her.

Jeena looked unconvinced and she went through her messages. She frowned. "My flight home leaves in six hours."

"Six hours?" Maazin asked, his heart sinking. "I thought you had a few more days."

"The flight was bumped up. No doubt your father has regained his full faculties."

"Why do you think my father had a hand in this?" Maazin asked, confused.

"He knows about Syman! He knows about my son."

"Our son," Maazin corrected her.

Her eyes narrowed. "Would you want to keep around the former lover who bore your playboy son's illegitimate child? No, you'd ship her off so she didn't further endanger the reputation of the monarchy. You'd send her away and not have the scandal. Especially when the world thinks that son is still engaged to another woman!"

"You make my father sound like a despot. He's not. A bit of a stickler for tradition, but not a despot." It was a bad attempt at trying to lighten the mood and it only annoyed her further.

"Don't make light of this."

"I'm not. I'm telling you he had nothing to do with your orders being rescinded."

"Okay. Fine, but I'm still a threat to this secret." Jeena sighed, she shook her head. "I have to get back to my team. We have to pack to leave. You need to take me back to Huban."

"Jeena, we need to talk about this."

"What is there to talk about? I'm endangering the secret. I have to leave."

Maazin was stunned. "What're you talking about? I still don't understand how he'd know you or Syman. I didn't tell him."

"He knew me."

"He'd had sedation. People handle sedation in a very peculiar manner."

She shook her head. "He said my name and asked about my son that plays ice hockey. He knows about my son. How?"

"That I don't know."

Jeena sighed. "It's for the best I leave."

"Are you sure?" he asked.

"Can you promise me anything?"

"You said we didn't need to promise each other anything."

"Why do you push everyone away?"

"You're doing the same thing," he snapped.

"I'm protecting my son."

"Our son."

Jeena sighed sadly. "You think you don't deserve happiness, but you do."

"I don't! It's my fault Ali is dead. I don't deserve happiness. My family can't bear to be around me. They look at me and are reminded of it all. I'm the shame of the royal family. I have to do what they want, I took away too much."

"You didn't. You say you have to do what they say, but you don't always."

"What do you mean?"

"You became a doctor, you joined the royal guard. You're freer than you think."

"How would you know? You weren't here and you're the reason why I became reckless. Losing you destroyed me!"

"And you don't think it hurt me?" she asked, her voice trembling.

"No one died because of you. I killed my brother and his wife. You were free. You had a family who loved you. I have no one."

A tear slid down her cheek. "That's right. You have no one. Take me back to my team in Huban, Maazin."

He nodded. "Of course."

There was no point in arguing any further about this. She had her orders and she had to obey them.

She had a duty to her new country, just as he had a duty to Kalyana.

They collected up their things in silent tension. There was no convincing Jeena to understand his point, and she had to leave Kalyana anyway. She had to go back to Canada and he was going to get to the bottom of this. He found it very odd that his father knew who she was and that he knew about Syman.

As they headed outside there was a flash of light, several flashes that blinded him, and Jeena screamed as Maazin realized that it was paparazzi.

She turned towards him and he held her close, shielding her from the photographers. He didn't know how they had found them here.

Maazin got Jeena safely into the Jeep and pulled away as their vehicle was swarmed by photographers.

He sped away, leaving them far behind in the dust.

"What the heck was that?" Jeena asked, breathlessly.

"The popular press and the tabloids," he said in an undertone.

"How did they find us?"

"I don't know, but I do know one thing. If this reaches Canada, everyone will know that Syman is my son."

"This is why I shouldn't have come. This is why I should've just kept my distance from you and not told you about Syman! This is not what I want for him."

"You think I want this for him?" Maazin asked. "I don't want this life for him, but sometimes we have no choice."

"Yes. I understand that too well." Her voice shook

and she didn't say more. He didn't know what to say to make it right either.

You know what to say.

He drove up to the Canadian consulate and thankfully there was no paparazzi there.

Jeena looked at him. "Please don't come to see me off tomorrow."

"Why?"

"This is going to spread everywhere and I just want to leave without drawing attention to my team. Or at least any more attention than is already being drawn. I want to leave Kalyana with my head held high."

"You can come back to Kalyana. I promised to give your father his plantation back."

"Come back to Kalyana and do what, Maazin? Have my son marked as an illegitimate son of a prince? Have the press hound me and Syman?"

"Jeena, please. I need you."

"You don't need me and you can't have my heart. Not until you stop blaming yourself for your brother's death. Not until you realize that it's your life to live. You may be a prince, but Kalyana doesn't own you as much as you think it does."

"I'm a prince. Of course Kalyana owns me and I owe my country everything," he snapped. "You don't understand what I give up for this country."

"You're right I don't fully understand, but I do understand what you're giving up. I won't put my heart in jeopardy. I did once before and it nearly destroyed me. I'm not the same person I was all those years ago."

"Jeena—"

"No. No. Goodbye, Maazin."

She slipped out of the Jeep and up the steps of the Canadian consulate, leaving him heartbroken.

Alone.

She was right. Even if her family got back their plantation there was nothing really here for her or for Syman except shame and pain. Even though Jeena hadn't broken up the engagement the world would soon think she did.

He wouldn't be able to have Syman in his life.

Unless you tell your father you're done.

And that was what Maazin was going to do. He was going to drive back to the palace and tell his father. He wanted Jeena and it didn't matter if that meant his own banishment. He wanted his son and a family with Jeena. Only Jeena. Like he always had.

He wanted her by his side. Always and forever.

CHAPTER TEN

"THIS IS OUTRAGEOUS!"

Maazin could hear his father raging from the other side of his bedchamber door. And he knew exactly what it was about. He knew that the press and the photographs of he and Jeena had come out.

Maazin knew this because he'd seen the headlines himself.

Seen the pictures of he and Jeena on the balcony, kissing and embracing. There were also photos that he hadn't been aware they'd taken, their stolen moment on Patang and when she'd stayed over at his place when they'd suspected they might have contracted dysentery.

Maazin didn't even knock when he opened the door to see his father propped up in bed and holding one of the trashy tabloid magazines in his hand.

"Father, you really shouldn't be over-exerting yourself."

His father dropped the magazine and glared at him. "What is the meaning of this?"

Maazin approached the bed and glanced at the magazine. It wasn't the only one that carried the story. Maazin and Jeena's faces had been plastered all over the national papers as well.

The headline was something along the lines of him betraying Lady Meleena. Still, they'd promised Lady Meleena that they wouldn't announce that the engagement was off for another month.

He'd broken that promise, but he was tired of taking on other people's problems. He was tired of keeping all these ridiculous secrets to avoid scandal. He was tired of blaming himself and of doing what made others happy.

Jeena was right, he had to stop blaming himself for Ali's death. He'd been so consumed these last ten years over losing her and then Ali dying that he was living in this perpetual hell of his own making.

He had to live his own life.

Ali was not coming back.

"I think you understand the meaning, Father," Maazin said calmly. "I'm sorry that the world knows I'm not marrying Lady Meleena before everything could be smoothed over."

His father waved his hand dismissively. "I don't care. That was her father's request. So we lose some trade deals. I have more important things to worry about. What I don't want is you returning to your old foolish ways."

"What foolish ways?"

"Sleeping around. Not taking care of yourself."

Maazin smiled. "I'm not, Father."

"Aren't you?" His father pointed to the photo in the tabloid. "This is my surgeon! The Canadian surgeon, yes?"

Maazin nodded. "I love Jeena Harrak. And I have for some time."

"What do you mean, you love Dr. Harrak?" Uttam asked, confused. "You've only just met her."

"Father, don't be obtuse. You know exactly who Jeena is."

His father frowned. "I know that she was the Kalyanese Canadian who performed my procedure and that she had a son who likes hockey."

"How do you know about her son?" Maazin asked curiously.

His father waved his hand in annoyance. "I always ask for the dossiers on my physicians. It's part of their security clearance. I was intrigued by the notion of ice hockey and I was pleased that someone from Kalyana had returned to help. I was making polite conversation."

"Father, do you know why Jeena Harrak left Kalyana."

"No."

Maazin scrubbed a hand over his face. "Jeena and I were involved in a romantic attachment ten years ago, before Ali died."

Uttam looked completely lost. "What?"

"She is the daughter of a vanilla plantation owner and we were in a romantic relationship for months. Then she left and I never knew why, until she came back to Kalyana. She left because she was pregnant with my child and believed Lady Meleena when Meleena told her I didn't want her, that we'd take away her child as he or she would be illegitimate."

"She had your child?" Uttam asked, shocked.

"Yes. I have a son. My son the ice hockey player!"

Uttam leaned back against the pillows, shaking his head in disbelief. "I have a grandchild? I would never have forced Meleena on you had I known Jeena was pregnant or that you were with Jeena. I would have allowed you to marry."

Maazin nodded. "That is good to know, Father, but

too little too late. Her parents sold the plantation and took her to Canada, where she gave birth to my son, Syman. My son, who I didn't get to know. My son, the ice hockey player."

"I can't believe you have a son," Uttam said quietly.

"I do. One who was stolen from me because of Meleena's meddling. Do you ever wonder why I started drinking so heavily during that time? It was because Jeena had left me and I had no idea why. Maybe if she hadn't left we'd be together and I wouldn't be blaming myself for Ali's death. Maybe Mother wouldn't hate me so much for killing her favorite son!"

Maazin heard a gasp and turned to see his mother standing behind him. He had no doubt that she'd heard every word he'd said, but he didn't care. It was the truth.

It's how he felt.

It's how she'd made him feel for the last ten years and he was tired of letting her make him feel this way.

Maazin turned on his heel and left his father mulling all that over.

Right now he had to get to the airport and stop Jeena from getting on that flight to Canada. He had to tell her that he chose her and that he'd finally stood up for her. That he wasn't going to abandon her again. That he wanted her.

Farhan was pacing in the entranceway when Maazin came down the stairs.

"What was going on up there?" Farhan asked. "I heard all this loud talking and thought it best not to go in."

"It was for the best," Maazin said quickly. "I told Father about Jeena. And I also told him about Syman, my son with Dr. Harrak."

Farhan's eyes widened. "Wow. I'm sure he took that well."

"Well, it certainly shocked him. I have to get to the airport. I have to stop her and tell her how I feel. I can't let her out of my life again."

"And if she doesn't want this life, this life of protocol?"

Maazin sighed. "I'll give it up for her. I'll live in Canada. I'll just disappear like Bhaskar did."

Farhan groaned. "That won't help anyone."

"I know and least of all you. I never told you that I'm sorry that you're in this position. That it was my fault you are now next in line to the throne."

Farhan took his arm. "I don't blame you. Even though you've been blaming yourself for ten years, I don't blame you for what happened to Ali. He made the choice to go and get you. It was a terrible accident. You have to stop blaming yourself for his death. You have to live your life."

Maazin clapped his brother on the back. "This is what I'm trying to do. I have to stop her from going back to Canada."

"You're too late," Farhan said. "I just saw the flight off. She was on it."

Maazin's heart sunk. "Well, then I need to clear this whole thing up and then I'm going to Canada to get her back."

Jeena knew that her team had seen the tabloids and the newspapers. They were friendly enough with her, but they were keeping their distance on the long flight home and that was fine by her. Even though Maazin and Meleena's engagement had ended some time ago, the world didn't know that.

In the world's eyes she was the other woman.

She was nursing her heart, which had been wounded again.

When she'd gone back to Kalyana, the last thing she'd wanted to do had been to let her heart be hurt again by Maazin, but of course that's exactly what she'd done.

She'd been a fool and the worst part of her being humiliated was that the press had caught wind of it all and it was everywhere.

When she'd talked to her father when they'd landed in Abu Dhabi to refuel, she'd found out that the press had located her parents' place and that they had been photographing Syman. Now Syman was afraid and confused.

He didn't know what was going on.

Her heart didn't matter, but Syman's heart did. This was not what she wanted for him. Her parents were disappointed and she was disappointed in herself too.

She craned her neck and could see Calgary airport coming into view. Her stomach clenched and she hoped that there wouldn't be any press there, but she didn't have high hopes of that. They would be around.

She just hoped her father wasn't being followed or harassed.

The plane landed and she closed her eyes, hoping and praying that she could just get home and be with her son.

Jeena hurried to get off the plane. She could see that there were people staring at her as she made her way across the airport and she could see from the corners of her eyes that her face was plastered everywhere.

Oh, God.

She went to the baggage claim and tried to ignore all the pointed stares. She picked up her gear bag and then spotted her father.

He gave her a sad, worried half-smile and then took one of her bags as he leaned over and kissed her.

"Father," she whispered. "I'm so sorry."

"None of that. Let's get out of here. There is press waiting so your mother is doing circuits and is coming up again to pick us up."

"And what about Syman?"

"He's staying with his friend Thomas for the night. Thomas's mother will bring him back tomorrow morning. Early, to avoid anyone seeing him."

Jeena's stomach did a flip-flop and she tried not to be sick. She hated this.

She followed her father out into the bitter cold. Jeena kept her head down as photographers snapped pictures and she realized that this was the first time she'd had to keep her head lowered in her new country.

For the first time since she'd come to Canada this was the first time she couldn't hold her head up high and she hated that. She was the other woman here too.

She climbed into the car and tried to hold back the tears that were threatening to spill. This was the worst.

Her mother drove away and for a few moments they didn't say anything.

"Tell us what happened, Jeena," her mother said. "The press is saying a lot of things, but I want to hear it from you."

Her parents exchanged a worried look in the rearview mirror as Jeena tried to explain what had happened between Maazin and herself, and how Lady Meleena had lied to them all.

"You are in love with him," her mother said. "It's understandable. The heart is forgiving when it's in love."

Jeena nodded. "I didn't want to forgive him. I didn't want anything to do with him, but we kept getting thrown together and it happened. The King knows about Syman."

"I had no doubt that he did," her father remarked. "Especially after the Bhaskar disappearances years before. The King keeps tabs on things. At least with Princess Sara that Bhaskar mystery was solved. It was a worry in Kalyana for so long and it did, eventually, have a happy ending."

"Well, I won't be going back to Kalyana. Maazin made it very clear that duty comes before the heart."

What she didn't say was that Maazin blamed himself. He thought he didn't deserve anything. Maybe he didn't want it and he was using his guilt as an excuse.

She didn't know and she didn't care. She was tired of caring.

Her father nodded but didn't say anything, and that was for the best. She was exhausted, both physically and emotionally. She'd thought she'd found her Prince Charming, but she hadn't. There was no happy ending for her after all.

There was no prince waiting to sweep her off her feet.

There was nothing but a heart that had healed and been broken all over again, and she had no one to blame but herself for that.

All she wanted was to see her son, but she was glad he was safe with Thomas's family.

That gave her some time to figure out what she was going to tell him about his father, the Prince.

CHAPTER ELEVEN

"WHAT DO YOU MEAN, you told everyone your engagement to Lady Meleena has been off for some time?"

Maazin winced as he heard his mother snap that across the room.

"It's simple, Mother. I told you that it's time to come clean so Jeena's name can be cleared. She's not the reason the engagement ended."

Queen Aruna took a deep breath. "I do understand that, but do you realize the embarrassment that you've caused us? They think you've gone back to your playboy ways! We paid off a lot of people when Ali—"

"I know, to cover up my indiscretions."

"No!" Uttam said. "To protect you from those papers. To protect Ali and Chandni's memories, but now they're saying all these awful things about you, Maazin."

"Yes. I've seen the tabloids."

His mother frowned. "The world should know it was Meleena who had the affairs. It was Meleena who drove off Jeena. All these years. We were all fooled."

Maazin was stunned. "Sorry, what did you say? Are you saying that you're angry with me because I did throw Meleena under the bus, as it were?"

His mother sighed. "I believed Meleena when she told me Jeena wasn't really pregnant by you."

"Wait, you knew she was pregnant?"

Queen Aruna nodded. "I did, but Meleena convinced me it was a hoax. Meleena told me that Jeena was going to blackmail us. You already had a bad reputation, so I was grateful to Meleena, and she said she would help take care of the problem. She would take care of the rumor…another one of your indiscretions. I thought Meleena was doing right by you in getting Jeena to leave, by paying her off and sticking by you."

"I still don't understand. How did you know Jeena was pregnant?"

"The doctor informed me. I knew you were in love with Jeena. I was happy, but then Meleena convinced me it was a lie and that Jeena was using you. I wanted to protect you."

"Meleena hurt us all," Maazin said bitterly.

"She may not have loved you but she wanted to marry you, Maazin, so she lied to all of us."

"I remember," Maazin said. "Now I remember that."

Uttam nodded. "She found out about Dr. Harrak's pregnancy and took it on herself to ruin your life. Meleena knew that you were going to choose Jeena and not her."

Seeing his son's furious expression, he reached out and placed his hand on Maazin's arm. "She's gone, Maazin. She's not worth your time. She's someone else's problem now."

"That's not good enough! She cost me ten years with the woman I love. She cost me time with my son!"

"I am sorry." Aruna motioned for Maazin to sit on the edge of the bed, where she was sitting next to Uttam. It looked like his mother was about to cry. "No one should lose precious time with their child. I have wasted time with you, Maazin. I was scared your reckless lifestyle would cost me you as well, but I want you to know I don't blame you for Ali's death."

"You don't?" Maazin asked, stunned.

"No. I thank God every day you survived. Oh, at first I was angry that you had gone and done something foolish. That you were reckless again, but Ali did not have to go and get you, and it was an accident."

"That's what Farhan said," Maazin said quietly.

Uttam nodded. "He will make a fine king. One day. Not soon!"

Aruna smiled. "Stop blaming yourself, Maazin. You deserve to be happy. Ali would want that."

Maazin took his mother's hands. "And he would want you to be happy too."

Aruna's smile wobbled. "I will try. I am sorry if you've blamed yourself all this time. I don't blame you. I love you."

Maazin hugged his mother while she cried, and he felt a huge weight lift from his shoulders.

Maazin smiled at his parents. "So what do I do?"

"You go and you marry Dr. Harrak. You marry her and make things right. You may have lost those years with your son, but he's still young and you have time with him. Cherish that time with him and bring him to Kalyana." Uttam's chest puffed out. "Illegitimate or not, he is my grandson and I want him here with me. Life is too short."

"What do you think, Mother?"

Aruna brushed away a tear. "I want to know my grandson too. I want to know Syman and I want to apologize to Jeena. It's my fault as well. I am sorry my grief over the loss of Ali has made you feel that way,

but when Uttam told me we have a grandchild, well..."
More tears gathered in her eyes. "I want to meet him."

"I do too." Maazin stood up and kissed his mother on the cheek. "I'll have to take the private jet, then, to Canada. And we'll have to call the prime minster and get clearance to enter Canada."

"You leave that to me," Uttam said, and then he saw the stern look from his wife, which basically told him that he was treading on dangerous ground. "Or perhaps Farhan can arrange it?"

"Thank you, Father." Maazin bowed quickly and turned to leave.

"Maazin, wait!" his mother called out.

Maazin turned around and his mother held out a ring. "It was Queen Narubi's ring. Please give it to Dr. Harrak. Please let her know that we welcome her here. Explain to her it was not our doing. We were led to believe the wrong thing. Had we known the truth... she wouldn't have had to leave. She is welcome here and she would make a good wife for you. I'm sorry."

"That's right," Uttam shouted from the bed. "If I'd known that you were in love with her and that she was pregnant with our grandchild, I would've insisted you marry her straight away."

"Thank you." Maazin kissed his mother on the cheek again. "I will make this right. I promise."

And if Jeena didn't want to marry him and come to Kalyana, he would let her be, but he was hoping that in her heart she still loved him, just as much as he loved her.

He wanted her to know that she would be safe and protected. That she wouldn't be trapped. Things were changing and they were changing for the better. Perhaps this was a life he would want for his son.

Perhaps it wasn't so bad after all.

Maybe together he and Farhan could change the face of the Kalyanese monarchy.

And if Jeena did agree to come and be his wife, he would have to go about building some kind of indoor ice rink so that his son could keep up with hockey. Just the thought of that brought a smile to his face.

The whole future lay ahead, bright and full of sunshine.

If only Jeena would say yes.

Farhan had worked with the Canadian government to make sure that no one got wind of Maazin's arrival in Calgary. He didn't want Jeena to know that he was coming. Or the media. He didn't want her to flee.

He wanted to let her know that she would've been accepted.

One petty person whose pride had been hurt had ruined their lives for the last ten years and Maazin only hoped that it wasn't too late. He only hoped that he hadn't ruined his chance with her.

Kavan, Farhan's bodyguard, had accompanied Maazin to Canada and was going to make sure that the press kept their distance, as well as drive him to Jeena's home. Farhan had insisted on it because Kavan had been with him when he'd gone to Canada to track down Sara, and he was familiar with the country and driving conditions there in snowy and icy conditions.

As the plane approached the runway at Calgary International Airport Maazin let out a shudder when he saw white on the ground. In the distance he could see the city and smoke rising from the buildings into the clear blue sky.

The large Calgary Tower stuck out in the skyline.

"It's very cold down there, Your Highness," Kavan commented.

"I agree," Maazin said. "Jeena told me it was cold."

"I think this is colder than those ski trips that you and your brothers took in Kitzbühel."

"I believe you're right." Maazin shuddered. "You made sure that customs has already cleared us and that the Canadian government is on board with our hushed operation?"

"I have the assurances from the prime minister himself. He's quite a charismatic man."

Maazin smiled. "I'm glad to hear he's so accommodating."

The plane landed smoothly and was directed to a private runway on the far side of the airport, reserved for foreign dignitaries, royalty and the prime minister.

There was a small fleet of cars waiting, which would accommodate Maazin's small staff and security. As requested, the Kalyanese consulate hadn't added the flags to the cars as it was a private visit and Maazin didn't want to catch any one's attention as they made their way north out of Calgary to a small ranch between Calgary and Airdrie.

It would be easy to locate the Harraks' ranch, because it was the only property in the vicinity that had a large number of greenhouses, and the Harraks were known for growing and selling poinsettias.

As Maazin stepped off the plane it felt like his skin was being cut by sharp knives. It was bitterly cold and he didn't like it one bit, but for Jeena he would brave anything. Even freezing cold temperatures and biting, nasty wind.

The Kalyanese ambassador to Canada was waiting and he was wearing a parka.

"Your Highness, I have a parka for you."

Maazin nodded and gladly allowed the ambassador to slip it on his shoulders. "This is awful!"

"Nothing like beautiful Kalyana weather." The ambassador smiled. "Everything is ready for all your people."

"Thank you."

The ambassador stepped back, the door to the SUV with tinted windows was opened and he slipped inside. Kavan took his place in the driver's seat. Maazin adjusted the temperature settings in the back and then slipped off the parka.

"Are you ready, Your Highness?" Kavan asked from the front.

"Yes. Let's go." Maazin touched the breast pocket of his designer suit to make sure Queen Narubi's ring was still there. His pulse was racing as Kavan punched in the co-ordinates on the GPS and then slowly drove away from the private jet. The rest of Maazin's people were going to the embassy in Calgary.

There would be a car following them for security, at his father's insistence. If Maazin had his way, he wouldn't, but then again, with the media pestering Jeena and her family and his son, he didn't want to take any chances.

He sat back and looked out at the scenery, which was very different from Kalyana's. They drove north on a large highway with cars everywhere. He noticed a lot of the vehicles on the highway were trucks and they were all white.

"Why do you suppose so many of the vehicles are white, Kavan?"

"Something to do with the oil fields, Your Highness, but I'm not certain."

"Oil fields?" Maazin really didn't know much about Canada, but one thing was for certain, the endless stretch of open plains without trees or sea to break the horizon was slightly unsettling. But if this was where Jeena was happy, if this was where she wanted Syman to stay, he would get used to it.

He would stay and do whatever she wanted.

He wasn't leaving without her. He wasn't walking away from her again, even though he didn't know that he had done that in the first place. He didn't know that she had been sent away. All these years he'd thought she left him.

And for all these years she'd thought he'd walked away from her.

Now it was time to make everything right.

It was time for him to claim his family, like he should've done ten years ago.

It felt like it took an eternity to drive forty minutes to the outskirts of Calgary and then on a side road off the highway that turned into a gravel road that had a sign pointing to the Harraks' greenhouses.

Maazin couldn't believe the large stretch of land that Mr. Harrak possessed. It put his small vanilla plantation to shame. Before they even reached the main house Maazin could see the greenhouses and through the fogged windows he could see the red of the poinsettias.

Kavan made another turn and they approached a raised ranch-style house. Kavan drove as close as he could. Maazin's pulse was thundering in his ears. To the side of the ranch house there was a small ice rink and there were kids out on it now, skating. He couldn't help but wonder which of those boys was Syman.

He was finally going to meet his son.

"Hey, Mom! There's a strange car parked in front of the house!" Syman shouted as he skated by her, gesturing wildly.

Oh, no.

Jeena turned around and was worried that the press was ignoring her father's restraining order and they were coming to get a glimpse of Syman again. Her phone was in the house because it was so cold out that the battery would die within minutes.

She hoped that her father had seen the cars approach and had the good sense to call the Royal Canadian Mounted Police about the restraining order violation. The RCMP had promised to protect her after a particularly intrepid paparazzo had gotten into one of the greenhouses and done substantial damage as he'd tried to get information about her parents.

Not to mention one photographer who had scared Syman senseless when he'd got off the school bus.

Since she'd got back three days ago there had been endless harassment.

And she was getting sick and tired of it.

She started marching in the direction of the SUV when she saw who had got out of the back. She froze in her tracks and her heart skipped a beat.

Maazin?

He was completely inappropriately dressed for this crazy cold snap that they were currently having.

"Maazin?" she called out.

He spun around and then started walking toward her.

"Jeena, thank goodness…"

"What're you doing?"

"I've come to see you."

"I get that. I mean, you're going to freeze to death standing out here without a coat on." She glanced behind her. "Why don't you have a coat?"

"I do. I left it in the car."

"Let's get inside and tell Kavan to come in as well. It's too cold to leave the car running."

"Well, if it's too cold, why are there children out there, playing on the ice?" Maazin asked.

"They're dressed for it and they'll be heading inside soon. They had to get their practice in. My father can manage the boys. He'll take them into the greenhouse staff lunch room for hot chocolate. Let's go into the main house."

Maazin nodded and motioned to Kavan, who was shivering as well.

Jeena opened the door and ushered them both inside.

"Mother!" Jeena called out. "We have guests."

"Oh, no. Not the press again!" Her mother came around the corner and then froze in her tracks when she saw Maazin. She instantly curtseyed. "Your Highness."

"Please. There is no need to do that, Mrs. Harrak."

Her mother stood up slowly and then looked at Jeena for an explanation. Jeena shrugged and took off her bulky winter gear. "Mom, will you take Kavan into the kitchen and give him a nice hot cup of coffee?"

Her mother nodded. "Of course. Follow me, Kavan."

Kavan waited until Maazin nodded and then followed her mother into the kitchen. She finished taking off her winter gear and then stood in front of Maazin, completely shocked that he was here in Canada and standing in her parents' front hall. It was surreal. Of all the scenarios she'd pictured in her mind of Maazin coming to get her, this had not been one of them. A royal prince of Kalyana, wearing an expensive suit and standing in a tiny front hall that was littered with twenty pairs of wet snow boots, not to mention a bunch of knapsacks.

"It smells a lot like feet here," he teased, obviously trying to break the tension.

"You're standing by the shoe rack and there are a lot of sweaty boots there."

Maazin glanced down. "So I see."

"What're you doing here?" she asked, still feeling stunned.

"I came to see you."

"Why?" she asked.

"Is there a place with more privacy where we can talk?" he asked.

"Sure. Follow me." Jeena didn't want to talk with him in the house because Syman might come bursting in after all his friends had been picked up. Attached to the house was her father's first greenhouse and it was a place where he still grew a small batch of vanilla orchids. It was quiet and warm in there.

She led him into the greenhouse and shut the door behind them.

Maazin looked around. "Your father grows vanilla here as well?"

"Just a small batch. He sells it on the weekends at a local organic market." She crossed her arms. Her heart was still hammering in her chest and she couldn't quite believe that Maazin was here, in Canada.

"So, will you finally tell me what you're doing here?" she asked.

"I came for you."

She blinked a couple of times. "Pardon me?"

"Jeena, you know I'm not marrying Lady Meleena. The moment I dropped you off at the Canadian embassy in Huban I went straight to the palace to have it out with my parents. I told them I was tired of hiding the fact I'm not marrying Meleena and I was going to marry you."

"I thought you couldn't promise me anything? I thought you didn't deserve happiness?"

"I was wrong."

She tried not to let her mouth drop open in shock. Her pulse was thundering in her ears and it was very hard to breathe. "How did your parents react to your news?"

"Not well at first."

"Of course. I'm the last person they'd want you to marry."

"No, you need to stop that. It's because my father didn't know Syman was mine. Meleena had them all believing you were going to blackmail us. They believed Meleena paid you off and saved the royal family from another one of my scandals. Meleena wanted to marry me, so she hurt us both. She lied to us both."

Jeena swallowed the hard lump that was forming her throat. "What?"

"My father wants you to know that he would never have forced me to marry Meleena had he known I wanted you. He would've been thrilled had he known you were pregnant with my child. My mother is thrilled too, but Meleena had convinced her you weren't pregnant. In fact, they're both very happy to have a grandson. They both want to meet him."

The room began to spin and Jeena didn't know how to take this information. She sat down on a bench and took a couple of deep breaths.

"I don't… I don't know what to say. We have a life here in Canada…"

"I know and if that is what you choose, then I choose it too."

"You choose it too?" she asked, confused.

Maazin dropped to his knees in front of her and took her hands in his strong ones. "You're trembling."

"I'm scared," she whispered.

"I am too, but if Canada is where you need to be then I will live here. What I can't do is live without you in my life. I can't live without Syman in my life. I've spent too many years thinking that I didn't deserve happiness or love because of my actions, but I was wrong. I was wrong about so many things. You were right, but I was scared. Scared to lose you again."

Jeena didn't know what to say. Tears stung her eyes, because he was saying all the right things. It was everything she'd wanted to hear ten years ago. It was everything she'd wanted to hear four days ago.

"How can you live in Canada? Your duty is to Kalyana. You're a prince."

"I can live wherever I want and return to Kalyana if I'm needed, but if you choose to come to Kalyana with Syman, you can continue your work there. My father has already passed the decrees and legislation to start the ball rolling on a university. A university that promotes the STEM program to women. Sara still wants your input."

"Are you serious?"

"Yes. The University of Kalyana will happen and it will happen in the next year."

"I'm glad to hear that." She was still shocked. "The world thinks I'm the other woman."

"No. My father straightened it all out and will make

a formal speech soon. After the whole Bhaskar thing, the people don't want heirs running off. They don't want scandal for Kalyana. Everyone is thrilled we have a child."

"Oh." Jeena still couldn't seem to think straight. It was everything she'd wanted to hear ten years ago. She couldn't quite believe it.

Maazin reached into his pocket and pulled out a ring. One that she had seen on the hand of Queen Aruna. "Marry me, Jeena. Marry me like you were supposed to have done ten years ago."

Her pulse raced and she felt like she was going to faint.

"Yes," she whispered.

"Yes?"

She nodded. "Yes."

He slipped the ring on her finger and kissed her, and she couldn't stop the flow of tears. Tears that she had been holding back for so long they came pouring out of her. Maazin kissed away those tears and held her.

"I'm so sorry, Jeena. So sorry for it all."

"It's not your fault. I should've trusted you. I was terrified to be pregnant and alone in a country so far away from the one I knew. I blamed myself too. I blamed myself for letting you take my heart when I felt like I didn't deserve you."

"You deserve me, but I don't deserve you," Maazin said.

"Yes, you do."

They kissed again.

"And I would like to go back to Kalyana," she whispered.

"What about Syman and his life here?" Maazin asked.

"We can always come back and visit. My parents

will stay here. I know that. They have found happiness here. And I wouldn't leave them behind unless I knew that there was a private jet to come and get them whenever they wanted to come home." She was teasing him.

He smiled at her. "Of course. Whenever they want to do that and whenever Syman wants to return to Canada, we will get him here. He'll just have to get used to bodyguards and security."

"Mom? Where are you?"

Jeena took a deep breath and stood up. Maazin followed her and she could tell that he was nervous.

"It'll be okay, Maazin. I've told him. He knows."

"He does?"

Jeena nodded. "It's okay. He wants to know you. You deserve to be in his life."

Maazin nodded. "Yes. Good. I want to be his father. I want him in my life."

"And he will be. It might take some time, but he wants to know you."

Syman came running into the greenhouse. "Mom, you won't believe—"

Syman stopped and stared up at Maazin. "It's you! The Prince I talked to over the phone."

"Yes. It's a pleasure to finally meet you." Maazin held out his hand and Syman shook it.

"What're you doing here?" Syman asked.

"I've come to ask your mother to marry me," Maazin said.

Syman looked at her. "Mom?"

"Syman, Prince Maazin is your father. You remember me talking about those newspaper men and other people following you around?"

"You mean that I'm a prince?"

"Yes," Maazin said. "I'm afraid so."

Syman nodded. "Cool."

Maazin knelt down to look Syman in the eyes. "I'm sorry I've been away for a long time."

"Mom said you didn't know about me."

"I didn't, and it's no one's fault, but know this, if I had known about you I would've come sooner. Do you forgive me?"

"Yes." Syman nodded. "You're here now for good?"

"I'm staying for as long as you need to, before I return to Kalyana."

Syman frowned. "Mom?"

"The thing is, we have to move to Kalyana for a while," Jeena said. "Are you okay with that?"

Syman worried his bottom lip. "Do they have hockey there?"

"No," Maazin said. "Not yet, but your grandfather the King promised that a hockey arena would be built and maybe you could show the other children there how to play."

Syman cocked his head to one side. "I like that, but what about Grandma and Grandpa? Would we ever see them again?"

"Of course, whenever we wanted," Jeena said. "And they can come back to Kalyana and see you. For now, for a little while, we have to go back to Kalyana. You have to meet your other grandparents and your uncle and his wife."

Syman nodded. "So we get to go on a plane trip?"

Maazin chuckled. "Yes. A private jet, in fact."

"Cool. Okay, I'm okay with this. Can I go ask Grandma for a cookie?"

Jeena laughed. "Sure."

"Thanks!" Syman ran off.

"That was relatively easy," Maazin remarked.

"It'll take some time for him to process it," Jeena admitted dryly. "Then there will be a lot of questions."

"It'll take some time for him to get to know me. I understand that. I'm willing to wait." Maazin wrapped his arms around her. "I'm just not willing to wait ten years again to make you my wife."

"Neither am I. I love you, Maazin. I always have. There has never been any one else. I've only loved you. I've only ever wanted you."

Maazin tipped her chin. "I've only loved you and from that first moment that I saw you out on the polo field, you're all I've ever wanted as well. You're all I'll ever want. I was a fool to think otherwise."

Jeena laughed and kissed him gently. "Yes. Yes, you were."

Maazin ended up spending two weeks in Canada. There was a lot to do to prepare for the journey back to Kalyana.

Instead of staying at the embassy, though, he stayed at the Harraks' home, so that he could get to know Syman better. And though it took some time, Syman accepted Maazin as his father and was soon showing him the affection he so desperately wanted from his son. Affection he'd never thought he deserved.

Maazin reveled in those moments when he was able to tuck Syman in for the night and have the boy wrap his arms around him and call him Dad. That meant so much to him. The more that he got to know his son, the more of Ali and even his father he saw in him.

There was a stubborn, defiant streak in Syman that reminded Maazin very much of his father. And Ali too. And Maazin knew that deep down Syman and Uttam were like two peas in a pod.

Jeena, with the help of higher up government officials in Canada and Kalyana, was honorably discharged from her services to the Canadian armed forces. It was hard for Jeena to let go of her team, but she had plans to work closely with Sara and promote that program about women in the STEM program in the new university.

That gave her something to be passionate about and something to do beyond a life of protocol and charity events.

Maazin, Jeena, Syman and the Harraks had all watched King Uttam's speech to the media about Jeena and Syman. It was clear from the public's feedback that no one held any animosity toward Jeena. No one thought she was the other woman any more and Kalyana was excited to have another royal heir.

And although Maazin offered them their vanilla plantation back, Jeena's parents were much happier in Canada.

They hated being so far away from Jeena, but they were glad that they could return to their homeland with their heads held high and that their daughter was soon to be a princess.

Or rather she *was* a princess because before they left Canada Jeena and Maazin married in a civil ceremony at the Kalyana embassy and Syman was legitimized.

The line of succession would soon change yet again as Sara, Farhan's wife, was expecting a baby.

And that was fine by Maazin.

When they boarded the private jet at Calgary International Airport there was a lot of media waiting to get a glimpse of the new royal family of Kalyana, but Kavan and his team of security managed to keep the media at a distance.

It excited Syman that the prime minister of Canada

had come out to see them off and that he was going on his first ever plane ride.

Of course, the novelty of a long flight soon wore off on Syman, but Maazin enjoyed having him on the plane and keeping him entertained by playing games with him and reading with him. Syman had a hard time sleeping but finally drifted off on the last leg of the trip from Abu Dhabi to Huban.

Maazin made sure he was secured on the couch portion of the private jet and covered him with a blanket, and he slept there for the last few hours.

"I hope we can wake him in enough time to see the welcome ceremony when we land," Jeena remarked. "I also hope he's not too grumpy for your father. He's a bit of a grumpy bear when you wake him up too soon."

Maazin smiled. "The same with my father. They're so alike."

"I hope that it goes smoothly." She was worrying her bottom lip again.

"It will. Trust me. My parents are thrilled."

"It's hard to do that. Even though I really should, because it wasn't your fault and it wasn't my fault. I'm glad that whole thing is behind us and I'm glad Meleena is no longer in Kalyana."

"Yes. She's safer away from Kalyana too, because if I ever see her again I'm going to— She's better off far away. She cost me too much." Maazin glanced back at Syman, who was rousing as the plane began to descend as they got closer to Huban.

"Well, we can't maim her we're both doctors and we've promised to do no harm." Jeena winked.

"That remains to be seen," Maazin teased.

Jeena started rubbing her hands together. She was wearing her mother's treasured sari, the one she'd managed to save, the one she'd bought on Petrie Island that the weaver, Mr. Patel, had made.

"That color suits you," Maazin said. "Your mother has good taste."

"I think so too. It's always been one of my favorites and I wanted to show my support for the people."

"Smart." Maazin took her hand and kissed it. "You will make an excellent princess."

The plane made its final descent into Huban and Jeena managed to wake Syman up. He was grumpy for a few moments, but when he realized they were landing and that soon he'd meet the rest of his family, he perked up.

The plane landed and Maazin could already hear the crowds cheering. As the plane taxied around he could see a sea of blue, green and gold flags waving and the red carpet, with the royal motorcade waiting at the end.

This was it.

The plane's engines stopped and Maazin took her hand, giving it a squeeze. Then he took Syman's hand and the door opened.

Maazin stepped out of the plane with Syman by his side. The cheers were deafening and Syman trembled.

"It's okay. They're happy you're here. Just wave."

Syman worried his bottom lip like his mother and then waved.

Jeena came behind them and they walked down the steps together. When they reached the red carpet King Uttam and Queen Aruna, followed by Farhan and Sara, came to meet them.

Maazin could see that his father was having a hard time hiding his emotions as he looked at the little boy who was so obviously his grandson.

And Uttam broke protocol to get down on one knee and hold out a Kalyanese flag to his little grandson.

"Welcome to Kalyana, Syman."

Syman smiled at him and took the flag and then did what Maazin had not expected and threw his arms around Uttam's neck.

Uttam was shocked, but then wrapped his arms around the boy and lifted him up in his arms, beaming with pride.

Jeena was fighting back tears.

Uttam turned to her. "Welcome home, Dr. Harrak. Or should I say Princess Jeena?"

"Your Majesty." Jeena curtseyed and Maazin bowed.

"Let's get out of here, shall we?" Uttam set Syman down and took his hand in his.

Maazin took Jeena's hand and both of them turned to the cheering crowds and waved.

"I'm a bit scared," Jeena whispered.

"Don't be scared. I shall protect you. I shall always protect you and I will never let anyone hurt you again. I love you."

"I love you too, Your Highness."

EPILOGUE

One year later

"Now!" BELLOWED UTTAM from across the cricket pitch. "Isn't this much better than ice hockey?"

Syman lowered the cricket bat. "No, but it's fun. I like it, Grandpapa."

Uttam laughed. "Good!"

"Good!" Sophie squawked from her outside perch, making Syman laugh, which in turn made Uttam laugh and then Aruna laughed from where she was sitting under an awning with her newest grandchild, Farhan and Sara's little boy, Ali, in her arms.

Jeena was wandering away from the cricket and the tent. She was hot and uncomfortable and still had a couple months left of her pregnancy.

Her parents were coming for a visit soon and she couldn't wait to see them again. They video-called most nights with Syman, and Maazin had taken Syman and her back once to visit them, but once Jeena had found out she was pregnant, with twins no less, she couldn't go anywhere and she was feeling a bit cooped up.

Maazin had been busy with the university plans and helping to get Kalyana back on its feet. New homes were being built. Homes and businesses on Petrie Island, and many of the other islands, were almost all rebuilt now and things were going smoothly.

Kalyana was thriving again and would be more than ready if another cyclone like Blandine hit. Jeena loved being back in her home country, though she did miss Canada, but she loved being with her people again and being with Maazin. If only she could get back to work.

She really hated not being able to work out in the field, but Maazin was being way too overprotective.

"Where do you think you're going?"

Jeena turned around to see Maazin strolling towards her, carrying a glass of iced tea. He handed her the glass and she gladly took a sip.

"I was uncomfortable. The canopy your mother had set up might keep the sun off everything, but it doesn't keep out the heat."

Maazin reached out and touched her belly. "You really should be sitting down. With twins you could be early. You're a doctor, you should know better."

"Haven't you ever heard that doctors make the worst patients?"

Maazin cocked an eyebrow. "No. I haven't heard that."

"Well, they do." Jeena sighed. "I promise I'll go and sit down again. I just wanted a little walk to see if I could catch a breeze."

Maazin kissed the top of her head. "Remember the cool breezes on Patang Island?"

"Yes. I do." She closed her eyes. "Are you offering to take me there?"

"No. Not in your condition, but tonight when we go home we can go for a swim in the pool. Just the two of us."

"What about Syman?"

"He wants to spend the night with Grandpapa."

They both looked back to see their son finally catch a cricket ball on the end of his bat. The ball rolled over to Uttam who fell back, acting like he'd been hit, but really was hoping to catch Syman unawares to get a hug from him.

"They really are alike, aren't they?" Jeena asked.

"It's uncanny." And it was. She had always sort of suspected that Syman's stubborn streak and athletic side came from Maazin's side of the family. She'd just had no idea how well Syman would take to Uttam. Syman also loved Farhan and Sara. And since Sara was Canadian as well, she understood what it meant when he used words like "tuque" and "pop" to her.

And Syman doted on his newest cousin. Almost like a big brother would.

Syman fit in so seamlessly with his newfound family it did her heart good.

"So, what do you think? Do you want to go for a swim later with me?" her husband asked huskily, interrupting her thoughts.

Jeena stood on tiptoe. "How about we go back now? No one will notice if we leave."

"They'll notice if we leave. Father has this big meal planned with some dignitaries and… You don't look too impressed."

"I'm exhausted and I think if we told your father that I was he'd let us leave now. Do you really feel like having a dinner with all these stuffy people and talk politics in this heat?"

Maazin wrinkled his nose. "No. You're right. Not particularly."

"I think he'll understand if we slip away." She wrapped her arms around him. "We can go home and swim now. We can also swim later and then just spend the rest of the evening in bed."

"I think that plan is what got you into this condition in the first place," Maazin teased.

Jeena laughed. "What do you say, Your Highness?"

Maazin chuckled and kissed her. "That sounds like a good plan, my love. That sounds like a good plan indeed."

"Good." She kissed him. "Have I told you today that I love you?"

"No, but why don't you tell me now?" he said archly as he kissed her again.

"I love you. I didn't believe in all those old fairy-tales, the ones where a prince came and swept a girl off her feet, but now I'm a believer."

Maazin caressed her cheek. "I just wish my sweeping you off your feet had gone a bit more smoothly and in a more timely fashion."

"That only happens in movies. Real life is a lot messier and I wouldn't have it any other way."

Maazin kissed her again before taking her hand as they walked off together.

Happy that their happily-ever-after had come at last.

* * * * *

COMING SOON!

MILLS & BOON

Coming next month

HEALING THE SINGLE DAD'S HEART
Scarlet Wilson

None of this had been planned. When Lien had appeared at the door it had seemed only natural to call her over to say hello to his parents. He'd half-hoped it might give them some reassurance that he and his son had actually settled in.

Instead, it had opened a whole new can of worms.

He felt his phone buzz and pulled it from his pocket. A text from his mother. Three words. 'We love her.' Nothing else.

Guilt swamped him. What was he doing? As soon as Lien had sat down she'd fallen into the family conversation with no problems and been an instant hit with his parents.

He couldn't pretend that hadn't pleased him. He'd liked the way they'd exchanged glances of approval and joked and laughed with her.

But it also – in a completely strange way – didn't please him.

Part of him still belonged to Esther. Always had. Always would.

He'd found love once. He'd been lucky. Some people would never have what he and Esther had.

How dare he even contemplate looking again?

His mother had pushed him here to start living again. Not to find a replacement for his wife.

The thought made his legs crumple and he slid down the wall, his hands going to his hair. For a few seconds he just breathed.

He was pulling himself one way and another. Guilt hung over him like a heavy cloud.

He knew why he was here. He knew he'd been living life back in Scotland in a protective bubble. It was time to get out there. That was why he'd accepted the tickets and climbed on that plane.

But what he hated most of all was that he did feel ready to move on. He was tired. He was tired of being Joe, the widower. It had started to feel like a placard above his head.

But part of him hated the fact he wanted to move forward. He was tired of being alone. He was tired of feeling like there would never by anyone else in his, and his son's life. He was tired of being tired. Of course, he had no idea about the kind of person he was interested in. The truth was, the few little moments that Lien had caused sparks in his brain had bothered him.

It had been so long and he couldn't quite work out how he felt about everything yet. Of course he'd want someone who recognised that he and his son were a package deal. He'd want someone who could understand his usual passion for this work. These last few weeks had mirrored how he'd been a few years before. Every day there was something new to learn. Someone new to help. It was what had always driven him, and he knew that, for a while, he'd lost that. But Vietnam was reawakening parts of him that had been sleeping for a while.

Continue reading
HEALING THE SINGLE DAD'S HEART
Scarlet Wilson

Available next month
www.millsandboon.co.uk

MILLS & BOON
MEDICAL
Pulse-Racing Passion

Set your pulse racing with dedicated, delectable doctors in the high-pressure world of medicine, where emotions run high and passion, comfort and love are the best medicine.

MILLS & BOON

THE HEART OF ROMANCE

A ROMANCE FOR EVERY KIND OF READER

MODERN

Prepare to be swept off your feet by sophisticated, sexy and seductive heroes, in some of the world's most glamourous and romantic locations, where power and passion collide.
8 stories per month.

HISTORICAL

Escape with historical heroes from time gone by. Whether your passion is for wicked Regency Rakes, muscled Vikings or rugged Highlanders, awaken the romance of the past.
6 stories per month.

MEDICAL

Set your pulse racing with dedicated, delectable doctors in the high-pressure world of medicine, where emotions run high and passion, comfort and love are the best medicine.
6 stories per month.

True Love

Celebrate true love with tender stories of heartfelt romance, from the rush of falling in love to the joy a new baby can bring, and a focus on the emotional heart of a relationship.
8 stories per month.

Desire

Indulge in secrets and scandal, intense drama and plenty of sizzling hot action with powerful and passionate heroes who have it all: wealth, status, good looks…everything but the right woman.
6 stories per month.

HEROES

Experience all the excitement of a gripping thriller, with an intense romance at its heart. Resourceful, true-to-life women and strong, fearless men face danger and desire - a killer combination!
8 stories per month.

DARE

Sensual love stories featuring smart, sassy heroines you'd want as a best friend, and compelling intense heroes who are worthy of them.
4 stories per month.

To see which titles are coming soon, please visit

millsandboon.co.uk/nextmonth

LET'S TALK

Romance

For exclusive extracts, competitions
and special offers, find us online:

 facebook.com/millsandboon

 @MillsandBoon

 @MillsandBoonUK

Get in touch on 01413 063232